BOOTPRINTS

An angry Father. A hurting son. A healing only God can bring.

Deborah Beachy   Sharon Beachy

First Printing	May 2013	5M
Second Printing	July 2013	5M
Third Printing	December 2013	7.5M
Fourth Printing	August 2014	5M

© Copyright 2013 Shady Acres

All rights reserved. No part of this publication may be reproduced, stored in a retrieval system or transmitted, in any form, or by any means, electronic, mechanical, photocopying, recording, or otherwise, without the prior permission of the publishers.

ISBN: 978-0-615-81222-9

For additional copies, contact your local bookstore or:

Call: **Mervin & Sharon Beachy**
270-265-9221

Write to: **James & Deborah Beachy**
430 Elkton-Trenton Road
Guthrie, Kentucky 42234

Design & Layout Rosetta Mullet

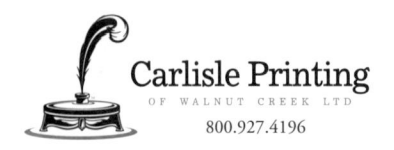

Carlisle Printing
OF WALNUT CREEK LTD
800.927.4196

DEDICATION

To all sons everywhere, and their fathers.

Bootprints

FOREWORD

Although some of the incidents in this book are true, it has not been written to copy, demonstrate or reveal only one person's life, rather to glorify our Savior Jesus Christ, and explain how there is hope for any person who finds himself in a similar situation.

ACKNOWLEDGMENTS

The writing of this story has by far not been a solitary effort on our part. We would like to give special recognition and thanks to the following:

Wilmer Beachy, who first had the vision for this story and believed we could write it.

Our dear husbands, James & Mervin, for sharing the vision and supporting us throughout the consuming months of writing. Your encouragement kept us going when we might otherwise have given up.

Our review board, Wilmer Beachy, Daniel Beachy & Melvin Troyer, for the hours you spent reviewing each chapter. Your suggestions and advice were valuable in keeping us on track.

Janice Etter, for your excellent job in editing. Your keen perception and insights have made this book better.

Our friends, for your prayer support and continued interest and enthusiasm. You buoyed us on.

The team at Carlisle, for your helpfulness and patience, and for the great job you did with the design and printing.

Bootprints

CONTENTS

CHAPTER ONE	1
CHAPTER TWO	9
CHAPTER THREE	17
CHAPTER FOUR	27
CHAPTER FIVE	35
CHAPTER SIX	45
CHAPTER SEVEN	55
CHAPTER EIGHT	67
CHAPTER NINE	77
CHAPTER TEN	87
CHAPTER ELEVEN	99
CHAPTER TWELVE	111
CHAPTER THIRTEEN	121
CHAPTER FOURTEEN	131
CHAPTER FIFTEEN	141
CHAPTER SIXTEEN	153
CHAPTER SEVENTEEN	163
CHAPTER EIGHTEEN	173
CHAPTER NINETEEN	183
CHAPTER TWENTY	193
CHAPTER TWENTY-ONE	203
CHAPTER TWENTY-TWO	213
CHAPTER TWENTY-THREE	223
CHAPTER TWENTY-FOUR	237
CHAPTER TWENTY-FIVE	247
CHAPTER TWENTY-SIX	261
CHAPTER TWENTY-SEVEN	271
CHAPTER TWENTY-EIGHT	281
CHAPTER TWENTY-NINE	291
CHAPTER THIRTY	303
CHAPTER THIRTY-ONE	315
CHAPTER THIRTY-TWO	327
CHAPTER THIRTY-THREE	337

CHAPTER ONE

JASON CROUCHED BEHIND the feed barrels and listened to Barabbas. Barabbas was the big black bull Daddy had brought home from Thad Thompson's sale. Jason didn't like Barabbas. He was always crashing around in his stall, always mad.

Barabbas' stall was only ten feet away from the feed barrels. Jason watched chunks of dirt and straw churn out from between the bars. He listened to the monster's bellows roll thundering down the alleyway.

Jason licked his lips. Were his legs shaking or was the floor shaking beneath Barabbas' hooves? He felt something prickle his neck. A round, fuzzy spider. Jason flung it away. There were lots of spiders behind the feed barrels. Mice too. It was not a good place to hide, but Jason was too afraid to risk finding a better one.

Barabbas' shaggy head thumped against the bars of his stall. Fierce red eyes glared in Jason's direction. Jason cowered down out of sight. He was afraid of Barabbas, but he was even more afraid of Daddy.

Anytime now Daddy would discover the broken window and come

looking for him. Jason trembled. He knew his daddy. He would be very upset. If only he could stay hidden until suppertime, then he could sneak into the house. He'd be safer near Mom.

Jason thought about what had happened. He and eight-year-old Matthew had seen some starlings on the milk house roof. Starlings were pests. They were always invading martin houses, and sometimes they killed baby martins. Cold-blooded thieves, Daddy called them.

Jason had watched the starlings strutting across the roof. He had an idea. "Let's throw some big old rocks at those starlings!" he said. "We can pretend they are Goliath and we are David." Only this morning Mom had read them that story out of the Bible storybook. "Starlings are so bad that I bet God will send the rocks straight to their heads, just like He did for that old Goliath."

Matthew was enthused. "I get to throw first because I'm the oldest." He shook a finger at the starlings as he pried a prime looking rock out of the mud. "Your time is here!" he shouted.

Jason watched as Matthew fired the rock. He waited to see the starling fall dead. But the rock didn't go in the direction it was supposed to. It was heading for the milk house. Jason watched in horror as it shot straight through the window and disappeared inside. Showers of glass flew everywhere.

Matthew's face turned white. "Quick!" he hissed. "Daddy's in there!" The boys dashed for the barn, swung open the heavy door, and burst panting into the dim alleyway.

Matthew snatched a pitchfork and hustled into a calf pen. Maybe if Daddy came to look for him, he would think he had been bedding down the calves all the while.

But a pitchfork was too hard for Jason to use. His brown eyes darted around for a hiding place. The feed barrels. Surely Daddy wouldn't think to look for him there. He flew down the alleyway, past the calf pens, and the pony harness, and Barabbas rumbling in his stall. He ducked behind the feed barrels and waited.

Barabbas was having a fit. But even above the racket, Jason could hear Daddy's loud voice calling for Luke and Danny. Luke and Danny were the little boys and they were always throwing stuff around, seeing who could throw the farthest. No doubt Daddy thought it was them who had broken the window.

Luke's high-pitched voice shrilled in protest. "But Daddy, it wasn't us! We were in the house helping Mom bake cookies and we just came out! See, we brought you a cookie."

PETER KAUFFMAN IGNORED the still-warm cookie and strode for the barn. If it wasn't the little boys, that left the other two. He ground his teeth in frustration. It was ridiculous, the way his boys were always wrecking and losing things. Last week they'd broken the handle on the scoop shovel. This week they'd lost his best hammer. And now this window. This was the last straw! How was a man to get ahead in life if his boys were always making such expensive mistakes? Peter's chest heaved as he thrust open the barn door.

Matthew was working furiously in the calf pen. When he glimpsed his father behind him, he fought down panic. He couldn't act scared if his plan was going to succeed.

Peter's words were clipped and to the point. "I'd like to know whose idea that broken window was."

Matthew forked some straw into a corner. Whew. This was going to be easier than he'd hoped. Daddy was not asking **who** had done it, he was asking whose **idea** it was. And the idea was definitely not his.

"The window?" Matthew tried to sound casual. Careless even. "Oh, that was something Jason hatched up. He's hiding down there somewhere." Matthew pointed down the alleyway.

Jason peeked between the feed barrels and saw the boots approaching. Daddy's boots were very big and very tall, and they clomped. They clomped past the calf pens and the pony harness and Barabbas' stall. They started to clomp past the feed barrels, but then they turned around and came back. Jason heard them kick loudly against the barrels.

Jason knew he had been discovered. His whole body shook. A rough

Bootprints {3}

hand clamped down on his shoulder and jerked him to his feet.

Daddy's voice was loud. "Looks like you're the guilty one all right, hiding like this. Well, hiding won't lighten your punishment any." Daddy dragged him out.

Jason tried to wriggle free from Daddy's grasp. "B-but Daddy, it wasn't"…

Peter silenced his son with a glare. "Don't go fishing for excuses now." He searched along the wall and found a small board.

IN THE CALF pen, Matthew cringed as he listened to the dull thuds of Jason's punishment. Maybe he should've just owned up and taken the punishment himself, like he deserved. But no, he knew how much Daddy's spankings hurt, especially if he was upset. Matthew took a deep breath. He was glad it wasn't him.

JASON STUMBLED OUT of the barn, furiously wiping his eyes on his shirt sleeve. Daddy had told him to stop yammering and get the chickens fed. When Daddy said something he meant it. Jason tried to choke back his sobs, but his heart hurt worse than his back, and that hurt badly.

Jason rounded the corner of the milk house. He saw the hole in the window and the shards lying on the gravel. Jason stood still. He had to stop crying. "I didn't do it," he whispered. "I didn't."

Should he pick up the glass? Glass was dangerous. He had gotten a piece in his foot once and it had made a deep cut. He didn't want that to happen again. He bent to pick up a piece, but then he heard footsteps. Footsteps that clomped.

Jason dropped the glass and fled to the chicken house. He didn't want to see Daddy again, not yet. Daddy could find someone else to pick up the glass.

For a while Jason watched the chickens pecking at their cracked corn. Then he trudged to the house. He met his sister, Heidi, at the door.

Bootprints

"What's wrong Jason?"

Jason tried to dodge her. "Nothing."

"Yes, there is. You were crying. What happened?"

Heidi could be nosy. Jason pushed past her into the wash house.

Heidi yelled into the kitchen, "Mom! MOM! Something bad happened to Jason!"

Mom hurried to the wash house. She looked at Jason's tear stained face. "Go set the table, Heidi."

Reluctantly, with an anxious glance over her shoulder, Heidi obeyed.

"What happened, Jason?" Mom asked. "Did you hurt yourself?"

Jason blinked hard. "No."

Mom knelt beside him and put her arm around his shoulder. "Can you tell me what's wrong?"

Jason leaned against Mom. She smelled good, like supper. He looked at Mom and she looked at him. "Daddy spanked me," he whispered. "He-he said I broke the window, but I didn't. I-it was Matthew."

"How did he break it?"

"We were throwing rocks at some starlings on the roof. Matthew hit a window."

"Why didn't you tell Daddy, Jason?"

"I-I couldn't."

"Oh, son." Sarah Kauffman's heart ached for her boy. How she wished Peter would take more time to listen to the facts before he punished his children. She looked out the window and saw her husband striding up the walks, Luke and Danny scurrying behind him.

Sarah gave Jason a tight hug, then stood up quickly. "Wash your face," she said, "and go sit at the table. "Tonight I'll explain to Daddy."

When Peter walked into the kitchen a few minutes later, his wife was ladling soup into a serving bowl. Jason sat at the table, staring dejectedly at his plate. Peter glanced sharply at Sarah, but she avoided his eyes. Had she been babying Jason? The thought irritated him and added to his disgruntled feelings about the window.

Bootprints {5}

JASON THOUGHT SUPPER would never end. Not once did he look at Daddy. Not once did he look at anyone else. He crumbled crackers into his soup and ate it, but he didn't really want it. He didn't even enjoy the peanut butter cookies.

After supper, Jason went into the living room. He felt like slipping upstairs to bed, but he knew better. No one was allowed to go to bed before Daddy read the evening prayer.

Jason sat on the far end of the couch. One by one the rest of the family trickled in to take their places. Daddy reached for the little black prayer book, and then they knelt. Jason thought Daddy's prayer lasted awfully long. There were a lot of words he couldn't understand. Could God understand? Probably. Mom said God knew everything.

Jason thought about the broken window. Likely God knew about that too, by now. He felt a little bit afraid of God. But he did not know why. Mom said God was good. Jason thought God was hard to figure out.

SARAH WAITED UNTIL all the children were in bed, except for Amy, before she talked to Peter. She picked up Amy and sat on the rocking chair. She rocked, trying to muster her courage.

Peter was reading the *Farm Journal*. If he heard his wife clearing her throat, trying to get his attention, he gave no heed.

Sarah's hands trembled against Amy's blanket. Should she push this or not? She didn't want to. Then she remembered Jason's stricken face. She heard herself say his name.

"Peter?"

Peter finished reading his paragraph then looked up, annoyed. "Well?"

"About the window…"

Peter's face darkened.

Sarah shifted nervously. "J-Jason said he didn't break it. He said it was Matthew."

Peter waved the *Farm Journal*. "How do you know he wasn't lying?

Matthew said it was Jason's idea."

"Maybe it was his idea, but did he break the window?"

"Listen Sarah, it doesn't matter who broke it. The main thing is that it's going to cost a lot to fix it. Windows are expensive."

Sarah felt desperate. Peter wasn't getting the point. She tried to steady her voice. "Peter. If Jason didn't break the window, he shouldn't have been punished. Don't you think so?"

Peter tossed the magazine aside and stood up. "You're a good wife, Sarah, but you pity the children too much. I think Jason lied to you. Come, it's time for bed."

Sarah followed Peter to bed. In the room above them their five-year-old son had just cried himself to sleep.

Bootprints

CHAPTER TWO

"JASON, TIME TO get up!" Matthew aimed a brisk poke at the snoring lump beneath the covers.

Jason huffed, rolled over, and finally cracked an eyelid. Matthew was hurrying into his shirt as if his life depended on it. That was Matthew. Asleep one minute and in high gear the next.

Jason tried to clear the fog from his head. "Did Daddy call us?"

"Uh-huh." Matthew struggled with his stockings. "Come on! It's Sunday so we have to hurry for sure."

Jason dragged himself upright and yawned. He wasn't used to getting up so early. But he was six now and Daddy said he was old enough to help with the chores in the morning.

THE MORNING WAS not going well for Peter Kauffman. He had overslept a few minutes and that was a minor crime. To oversleep on a Sunday morning was unthinkable. On top of that a heifer had freshened and it had taken him thirty minutes to get her to the barn. It was fine that

Bootprints {9}

she had twin calves, but what mattered was that they were about to be late for church.

Peter squinted at the clock on the milk house wall. The boys should have been out here ten minutes ago. Had they no sense of duty? He grabbed the milker and headed for the nearest cow. In his haste he did not notice that it was Annabelle. Annabelle was their worst kicker.

As Peter held up the milker the door rattled open behind him. He jerked his head around. "Where have you—"

Peter was stopped short by a colossal blow to his left arm. He dropped the milker and leaped away. He felt his face grow hot. A glimpse of his sons' eyes angered him further. He snatched a rubber strap from the railing and cracked it across Annabelle's leg. She danced and strained in the stanchion. Three more blows followed and Annabelle bawled. The other cows stopped eating and began shifting nervously.

Peter threw down the strap. "That'll teach you!" He rubbed his arm and bent to pick up the milker.

Matthew and Jason cowered against the door. Daddy was angry again. This would not be a good day.

"Get busy!" Peter roared.

Matthew yanked Jason's hand and scooted out the door. They had to get out of the way.

Peter thought the morning could not possibly get worse. But it did. When he had finally prodded his family through the chores, through breakfast, and through devotions, he ran to the barn to hitch up. He was not in the habit of running – no doubt he looked like a clown with his coat tails flapping and his hat jouncing precariously – but they were twenty minutes behind schedule, and reason called for action.

Peter rushed into the barn and unsnapped Ranger's tie rope. He jerked on the bridle, but the horse balked. Peter jerked again, then again. That was strange. Ranger was always eager to get out and run. Peter peered at Ranger's legs and then he saw it. The right front knee was swollen and hot.

There was no way they could use Ranger like that. But what would

Bootprints

they do? Stay home? No, not going at all would be worse than arriving late. Or would it? Peter wasn't sure.

The rest of the family was on the porch, waiting on the surrey. Peter's eyes fell on Jane. If they went, it would have to be with her.

But take Jane to church? Jane was steady and dependable, but slow. And huge. She dwarfed the surrey.

Peter did not relish the thought. It would be humiliating to clomp into the church yard with Jane. Peter stood for a moment. Then he swiped the brush over Jane's broad back and threw on the harness. He had made up his mind.

They were quiet on the way to church. Baby Amy prattled in her mother's arms. Luke and Danny discussed the difference in size between Jane's hooves and Ranger's, until Daddy told them to be quiet.

Jane's enormous hindquarters bobbled tediously. She lifted one foot – clup. Then another–clop. Peter leaned out the storm front and jiggled the reins. Jane swished her tail indignantly and lunged into a lumbering gallop. Peter writhed in his seat. He had cows that were more graceful than this. He pulled on the reins and Jane reverted, relieved, to her usual pace. Clup. Clop.

JASON THOUGHT THEY would never arrive, but finally their destination inched into sight. Jason craned out the window. A long line of white-shirted men was winding into the shop. "Daddy, hurry!" he exclaimed. "The men are going in already!"

Peter silenced his son with a stare. He herded Jane into the driveway and searched for a discreet parking space. Never, in all his married life, had he been late for church. He was always one of the first to arrive after the ministers. In fact, he often arrived before Deacon Henry's. But then Henry had a habit of being late.

Peter tugged Jane to the hitching rack. He felt sick.

AFTER CHURCH, JASON sought out his friends, Allen and Philip. They stood under a shade tree and talked until it was time to go home.

Bootprints {11}

"I can hardly wait until Friday," said Philip.

The boys smiled at each other.

"Me neither."

"Me neither."

Friday would be the first day of school. It would be a new venture for the three friends.

"Yesterday I went to town with Mom," Allen said, "and we got all my school stuff. Pencils, erasers, tablets, crayons, just everything."

"My daddy got me a new pencil box," Philip said. "It's light brown and has horses on it. Three of them. I already put my pencils and stuff in it."

Jason wished he had a pencil box like that. Maybe Daddy would get him one, when he went to town this week. But Daddy was always grumbling about spending too much money. What would a pencil box cost?

Deacon Henry walked up. He was Philip's daddy. He smiled at the boys and shook their hands. "So you are school boys now," he boomed. "That's a pretty big step in growing up! Why, you're getting to be little men!"

The boys grinned at each other and stood up straight.

Henry put his hand on Philip's shoulder. "Ready to go home, son?"

Jason watched Philip walk hand in hand across the yard with his father. *Philip's daddy must really love him,* Jason thought. *Does Daddy love me?*

JASON DIDN'T LIKE Sunday afternoons. They had to be quiet and take naps. Jason thought a nap in the middle of the day was a waste of time. He liked Sunday evenings better. Mom made popcorn then, and Jason loved popcorn. It was almost as good as chocolate pie, which was Jason's favorite food of all.

While Jason ate his popcorn, he thought about school. He thought about Philip's new pencil box. He imagined how nice it would be to open his desk and see the pencil box his own daddy had gotten for him. And how fun it would be to lift the cover and choose just the right pencil.

Jason took a sip of cider. A pencil box would be a handy thing to have. It would help him keep his desk neat. Matthew had told him that Teacher Margaret was particular about neat desks.

Jason scooted off his chair and went into the living room. He tried to keep his voice from shaking. "Daddy?"

Daddy's bushy eyebrows pushed over the top of the *Budget* and creased at Jason.

Jason cleared his throat. "Uh, Philip said – he said his daddy got him a nice pencil box to put his things in when he goes to school. It has horses on it." Jason swallowed hard. "I – I just wondered if you could get me one too."

Daddy stared at Jason for a long moment, making him wish he had never asked. "We'll see," he said finally. Then the eyebrows slid back down behind the *Budget*.

Jason shuffled back to the table. He picked at his popcorn and thought about Daddy. Daddy didn't love him. He knew it now, for sure.

IT WAS WEDNESDAY morning before Peter made it to town. He parked behind the post office, then pushed open the swinging doors of Brent's Merchandise. He pulled his list from his pocket and picked up a basket. He collected a box of screws and a bag of hinges. He went to the household selection and got a few items for Sarah. He glanced at the list. That was it.

But no, not quite. There was something else Peter hadn't put on the list. He wished he hadn't remembered. The pencil boxes.

It was bad stewardship to waste money on unnecessary things. But Henry had bought one for Philip. It sounded like something Henry would do, catering to the whims of his children. It wasn't any wonder the man wasn't getting ahead.

But to have Henry's children ahead of his own? Peter tapped his work shoe against the tiled floor. It would be embarrassing. He turned around and began searching for school supplies. He finally found some paper and pencils, but no pencil boxes.

Peter walked to the checkout counter. "You have any more school supplies?" he asked the teenaged cashier.

"No, sir, we don't," she said as she bagged Peter's purchases. "But you could try *Family Dollar* across the street. They usually carry school supplies this time of the year."

"Thank you." Peter paid his bill and went outside to stand on the sidewalk. Should he or should he not? He took out his wallet and counted his remaining cash. It should be plenty, but he felt foolish to go into the store for nothing except a couple of silly pencil boxes.

An image of pleading brown eyes pricked Peter's conscience. He shifted restlessly, then strode across the street.

Family Dollar did have pencil boxes, eight different kinds. Peter looked helplessly at the selection and scratched his head. How was a man supposed to know what kind of pencil boxes his children preferred?

His eyes landed on a pink one with cream colored flowers. Peter picked it up. Heidi liked flowers, so she would like this one. But for the boys? He remembered Jason said something about one with horses. Peter looked at each box. No horses. But here was one with deer on it. Maybe he would like that one. And Matthew? Peter decided to get one with deer for him too. Relieved, he carried the boxes to the counter.

On the way home Peter berated himself for being a fool. Pencil boxes indeed! His father would scoff at the notion. Peter could picture him, six-foot-one and shaking a fist. Tersely pointing out what the money *should* have bought. Necessities, like flour or salt. Definitely not pencil boxes.

Peter pulled Ranger to a stop at a cross roads. His son's eyes swam before him again. He had been weak. His dad would not have done that. Peter felt ashamed and foolish.

When he got home, Peter took his purchases inside and plunked them on the kitchen table. "There's your things," he told Sarah as she appeared in the doorway.

Bootprints

The children heard their father's voice and came running. It was always fun going through the groceries.

Peter glanced at the clock. It was almost chore time. He slipped into the entrance and began pulling on his boots. Through the crack in the door, he saw Sarah trying to unpack the bags amidst the swarm of wiggles and chatter around her. When would she find the pencil boxes?

"Jason," said Sarah, "here's some toothpaste. Maybe you could put that away. Heidi, put the cheese into the refrigerator. What's this?" Sarah's voice took on a strange note.

Peter edged closer to the outside door and felt for the latch. He strained his ears.

"Why, look children, Daddy got pencil boxes for you!"

Exclamations of delight followed. Quickly Peter stepped out the door. Maybe pencil boxes weren't a bad idea after all. With a sheepish grin, he headed for the barn.

Jason held his new pencil box reverently. He stroked the smooth green sides and admired the deer on top. He hugged it to his chest and ran upstairs with it. Daddy loved him after all! But he wasn't going to cry. Daddy had gotten him a beautiful pencil box. Jason tucked the precious gift beneath his pillow.

"Make sure you thank Daddy for your gifts," Mom told the boys before they went out to chore.

After supper Jason sidled up to the brown recliner. He wasn't afraid, not much. "Daddy?"

Peter lifted an eye from his magazine. "Yes?"

"Um, thank you for the pencil box."

"So you like it?" Peter had to know.

"Oh, yes! I think I like deer better than horses even."

"Good." Peter gave Jason a rare smile. "Take good care of it now."

"Oh, don't worry, Daddy, I will!"

That night Jason slept with one hand on the pencil box his daddy had given him.

Bootprints

CHAPTER THREE

JASON LIKED SCHOOL. He liked Teacher Margaret too. She was kind like his Mom and she liked his new pencil box.

Every morning after devotions, Jason opened his pencil box and took out a pencil, his large pink eraser, and the school bus pencil sharpener that Allen had given him for his birthday. Then he slowly closed the lid with its smooth silver clasps, and looked at the graceful deer on the front. Daddy had given him that pencil box.

The first few weeks, Jason did his best. He printed his vowels and numbers slowly and carefully. He kept his colors from zooming out of the lines. He made his scissors cut just right.

Then one day Teacher Margaret told the first graders to do an extra page in math. Jason stared at it and frowned. So many numbers!

"If you keep at it you should be able to finish before lunch time," Teacher Margaret encouraged. "Remember to do your best."

Jason had just been ready to make a paper chain for Luke and Danny. He wanted to take it home tonight as a surprise. Now he had to do this dumb math page! He had already done two pages in the first period! Jason glared at Teacher Margaret's back. She was not fair.

He picked up his pencil and began to make a row of ones. Ones were boring – nothing except straight little lines. He decided to draw hats on top of his ones to make them more interesting. He drew big hats and little hats and middle-sized hats. Then he drew a sun in the corner, so Teacher Margaret would know why his ones needed shade.

It took Jason a long time to finish the row of ones. It took him even longer to finish the twos. Twos were a pain. Jason would rather do almost anything else right now than make twos. Like wash the dishes even. Or take out the slop. At least taking out the slop didn't take as long as this endless page of math.

"Jason," said Teacher Margaret in a no-nonsense voice, "are you keeping busy?"

Teacher Margaret didn't understand. Jason sighed. He scratched down several numbers. Then he noticed the tip of his pencil. It was a little bit dull. Carefully, Jason sharpened his pencil. He blew off the dust and sharpened it some more. He pressed the tip of his pencil against his arm to test its sharpness. He wanted to get it just right.

By lunch time all the first graders were done with their math except Jason, who was only half finished. Teacher Margaret looked at Jason sadly. "You did not stay busy," she said. "You will have to stay in at recess to finish your page."

"Oh, but I can't!" Jason exclaimed. "We're going to play kickball and it's my turn to pitch!"

Teacher Margaret slipped on her sweater. "I will pitch until you're done," she said. " If you hurry, you will still have plenty of time to come out and play."

Jason was frantic. He tore into his remaining math. He did not draw any more hats and he did not sharpen his pencil. He wrote as fast as he could.

In five minutes, Jason was done. He pitched his math book on Teacher Margaret's desk and hustled out the door.

WHEN JASON ARRIVED at school the next morning, Teacher Margaret called him to her desk. Jason's heart sank when he saw his math book in her hands.

"Good morning, Jason," she said. "Did you have a nice walk?"

Jason nodded and eyed his math book.

"Jason," said Teacher Margaret, "I was disappointed when I saw your page." She pointed her red pen toward the row of hatted ones. "Can you explain what this is about?"

Jason hastily showed her the sun. "They needed hats to keep the sun out of their eyes."

Teacher Margaret did not look amused. "Drawing is for art class or for your spare time, Jason. When you do it while you should be working, you are wasting your time." She pointed to another row of numbers. "Can you tell me what these are?"

Jason peered at the page. "Oh, those are sixes. Or no... no, those are eights."

"Did you do your best, Jason?"

Jason studied the floor. He had done his best with the hats, but Teacher Margaret was not interested in the hats. She was interested in the numbers, and he had not done his best with the numbers. He had scribbled because he had not felt like doing that page. And at recess, when he had hurried to get done, he had scribbled even worse.

Suddenly Jason remembered something. "You *told* me to hurry," he reminded her.

Teacher Margaret frowned. "Maybe I did," she said. "But listen, Jason, you must never hurry so much that you don't make your numbers correctly. You must still do your best, okay?"

Jason nodded and watched as Teacher Margaret picked up her eraser. She rubbed it back and forth across the page until all the big hats and the little hats and the middle-sized hats were gone. And all the sloppy numbers. Then she handed the book to Jason. "Take this to your desk and do it over," she said. "Work neatly this time. And –" she smiled a tiny smile – "no more hats!"

Bootprints

Jason got busy. He had known Teacher Margaret was particular about neat desks, and now he knew she was particular about neat work. From now on he would try to please her. Skipping recess was no fun, and doing his math over was even worse.

JASON DID TRY for awhile, but before long he started to get careless again. Teacher Margaret talked to him. "You must do this page over, Jason. It is too sloppy." She looked sad. "You are not doing your best."

Jason was tired of doing his best. His workbooks were no longer shiny and new. They were smudged and dull and even a little wrinkled. The lessons were longer too. It took too much time to do them neatly.

Teacher Margaret told Jason that someone who is sloppy and careless when he is young, will grow up to be like that too. She said if he wanted to be a man that people would like and depend on, he must start developing good habits right now.

Jason didn't think school work had anything to do with being a man. Sometimes Teacher Margaret had some strange ideas.

One day Teacher Margaret told Jason to stay in at recess – again. Jason sighed and watched the other children race to the playground for a game of Prisoner's Base. He already knew what his teacher wanted. He had scribbled his English lesson as fast as he could, so he could get back to his library book. He had guessed for some of his answers and even skipped several. Now, judging by the grim expression on Teacher Margaret's face, he'd have to do the whole thing over. Jason's sigh came all the way from his toes.

Teacher Margaret laid Jason's English book on his desk. Today she did not talk about becoming a man.

"Your sloppiness is becoming a bad habit," she told him. "I think it's time we let your parents know about this problem. I wrote a note for them." She handed Jason a blue paper. "Put it in your lunch box and give it to your mom or dad when you get home."

Jason's fingers trembled as he stuffed the note into his lunch box. Daddy would be mad. Jason would get a whipping. He picked up his pencil and tried to write. Terror swelled his throat and blurred his vision. Why hadn't he done his best?

MARGARET SAW JASON'S shaking hands. Later, she kept an eye on him from her desk. She saw his tears and his trembling chin. *Was I too harsh?* she wondered. But no, her talks and mild punishments had done no good. Contacting his parents was the next step. Proper communication between teacher and parents was important.

Margaret was a stranger in the community and didn't know the people well. She wondered about Jason's parents. She had met his mother in church and liked her. Margaret couldn't picture his father.

MARGARET DIDN'T KNOW Peter and Sarah Kauffman, but Peter knew who Margaret was. At least he knew her dad. They had grown up in the same community, Peter and Simon had. Simon had eventually relocated to Ridgeville, but Peter had kept up with him enough to know he had become a highly successful business man. Peter admired Simon – he had a head on his shoulders. And Margaret? Well, she was his daughter, wasn't she?

Now this. Peter scowled at the blue slip in his hand. He had been sorting mail and had spied it in the trash can. Why hadn't Sarah shown this to him? Or at least told him about it?

Peter banged down the top of his desk. "Sarah!"

Sarah appeared in the doorway, holding a broom. Peter waved the offending paper in front of her face. "What's this all about?"

"Oh." Sarah twisted the broom in her hands. "Jason brought it home. Yesterday. I – I didn't have a chance to tell you yet." She looked nervously at her husband. "But… I was going to."

Peter leaped to his feet. "This needs to be dealt with! There's no reason for my son to be doing poor work in school! What will his teacher think?" Peter clapped his hat on his head and strode out the door.

Sarah's mother-heart propelled her after him. "Please, Peter, don't

Bootprints

be too hard on Jason. I already talked to him." She wanted to tell Peter she had gotten Jason to apologize to Margaret, but Peter had gone, slamming the door behind him.

Sarah heard the dishes clattering in the cupboards and cringed. Why was Peter always so angry? What would he do to their children?

JASON HEARD HIS daddy coming. He heard the clomping of his boots even before the chicken house door crashed open. He clutched the feed pail with whitened knuckles. He stared at Daddy's knotted eyebrows and red face, and knew. Daddy had found the note.

"Come out, Jason!"

Jason came out. Tripped over the narrow step, stumbled, stood back up.

"Set that pail down and look at me!"

Jason set down the pail and looked at Daddy. Eyes dilated with fright.

Peter was holding the note by a corner. He dangled it in the air. "I'm not going to stand for my son making problems in school!" Peter was shouting. *What if Margaret carried home tales about Peter Kauffman's slothful children?* Peter clenched Jason's arm in his fist. "Come with me. We're going to make sure this doesn't happen again."

Jason stumbled after his father. They entered the milk house, the two of them alone. Daddy grabbed a rubber strap.

It was *the* strap. The strap Daddy used on Anabelle when she kicked. "No!" Jason pulled back. Surely Daddy wouldn't use it on him!

But Daddy did. When he was finished, he tossed the strap to the floor. He said, "That will help you to remember! Now you tell your teacher you're sorry. Tell her tomorrow morning."

Jason was sobbing too hard to tell Daddy that he had already apologized to Teacher Margaret today. He staggered out the door. Daddy wouldn't believe him anyway.

Jason climbed the ladder to the hayloft and found refuge between

Bootprints

two bales of prickly alfalfa hay and cried. *Daddy doesn't love me. Daddy doesn't love me. Daddy doesn't love...* On and on it went, a chant of torment.

THE NEXT MORNING Jason opened his pencil box. He took out a pencil, his large pink eraser, and his sharpener shaped like a school bus. Then he pushed the pencil box underneath some books. He did not spend any time looking at it. It hurt him, his pencil box.

Jason tried not to sniffle as he wrote his numbers. He thought about Daddy. He didn't want to think about him, but Daddy had told him to apologize to Teacher Margaret. He didn't know what to do.

Jason knew his daddy. Daddy expected to be obeyed. But Jason had already apologized once, and he was afraid of what Teacher Margaret would think if he did again. He thought about it until his head throbbed. Finally he decided not to. Maybe Daddy would forget.

But forgetting was not one of Peter Kauffman's faults. He snagged his son that evening as he was heading for bed. "Did you apologize!" he demanded in a voice that meant *you better had!*

Jason quaked. "Y-yes."

"Did you really? What did she say?"

Jason's mind raced. What had Teacher Margaret said yesterday? "She said – she said that she forgives me."

Daddy nodded and turned back to his magazine. He seemed satisfied. Jason zipped up the stairs.

MARGARET WAS AMAZED at the difference in Jason's work. It improved overnight. "I did the right thing in letting his parents know," she decided. "They must be very supportive."

JASON WAS SURE he wouldn't slack off again, ever. He was not about to risk another spanking, if he could help it. Sometimes he got spanked when he had no idea why, but he would never do something on purpose that would make Daddy mad. Jason's hand went down to the welts on his legs, and he shuddered. He would be the best boy in school after this, see if he wouldn't.

For several months Jason did his best. He labored over every letter and every number. He erased and tried again, until his large pink eraser was worn to a nub, and he had to ask his mother for new one.

MARGARET SHOOK HER head as she graded his flawless pages. His parents made no effort to come and talk with her, but they obviously did their homework well. She had never seen a child improve so rapidly and so much.

Margaret visited her parents over Christmas. "I try to work peacefully with all my school parents," she told them, "but I wish more of them would be like Jason's."

Simon sat on the wood box and unlaced his shoes. "Now I don't want to say anything against anybody," he grunted. "Maybe Peter Kauffman has changed since I last saw him. All I'm saying is, keep your eyes open. Things aren't always what they seem."

Puzzled, Margaret turned back to the stove to flip the pancakes.

ONE MORNING IN February Teacher Margaret had a surprise for the class. She held up a colorful box with two puppies on the front. "I got this puzzle for you in town yesterday. I'm going to put it right here on this table and you may work on it in your spare time." She set the puzzle down. "But remember, you still must do your best. I don't want you to rush through your lessons just so you can work on the puzzle."

Jason looked at Philip. Philip looked back. Then both boys bent over their math books. They liked Teacher Margaret and they liked her surprises.

Jason didn't mean to be careless. But in his eagerness to work on the puzzle, he was. He forgot about how much Daddy's spankings hurt. He forgot that he wasn't going to slack off again, ever. All he could think of was the puzzle on the table. He loved puzzles, especially this one. The puppies looked so real he thought they might start wiggling any minute.

Jason left his school bus pencil sharpener and pink eraser in his pencil box. He rushed through his lessons, then rushed to the table. He sorted out the pieces of the brown puppy's face and fitted them together. He grinned at the bright little eyes and the drooping tongue. He did not see Teacher Margaret's distressed look as she graded his books.

At last recess, Teacher Margaret asked Jason to stay in. Jason watched her come down the aisle with his reading book, and he knew what was coming.

Teacher Margaret laid the book in front of him. "I am sorry to see you are falling back into your old habit."

Jason stared at the letters wobbling across the page, and panic gripped him. Would Teacher Margaret make him take another note home? He couldn't keep from crying. Somehow he must make her understand!

"I – I forgot," he sobbed. "But I'm s-sorry. I'll do it over now."

"That's a good idea," Margaret agreed. Jason's reaction dazed her. Why, he was literally trembling!

Jason looked fearfully at his teacher and gulped. His words came out in a rush. "Y-you won't tell my Daddy? Please don't! I *will* remember after this. I promise!" He gripped his pencil and waited for her answer.

"No, I wasn't planning to tell him this time," Teacher Margaret said slowly. "But because you hurried so you could work on the puzzle, we will still need something to help you remember. You will not be allowed to work on the puzzle tomorrow."

Jason sighed with relief. He didn't care about the puzzle, not as long as Teacher Margaret didn't tell Daddy.

MARGARET WENT BACK to her desk and tried to work. She watched Jason out of the corner of her eye. Never had she seen a child so

Bootprints {25}

terrified. The odd thing about it was that the second she told him she wouldn't tell his daddy, he had calmed down. Something wasn't right. Margaret thought about her father's words. *All I'm saying is, keep your eyes open. Things are not always what they seem.* Did her father know something about Peter Kauffman that she didn't? What had triggered Jason's intense reaction? Obviously something more than needing to redo his work.

Margaret sat at her desk and wondered.

CHAPTER FOUR

"It's warm enough to go barefoot." Jason Kauffman slung his coat over his shoulder and wiggled his toes. They felt hot inside his shoes.

"Better don't," said Heidi. "Mom says we have to wait until we see three bumblebees, at least."

The three eldest Kauffman children were walking home from school. Matthew bounced his lunch box. "I'm glad it's Friday. Only two more weeks of school after this. I can't wait."

"Me either," agreed Heidi. "Jason, what are you doing now?"

Jason had stopped walking and was peering at the stubby growth alongside the road. "I'm looking for bumblebees, that's what."

"Forget about the bumblebees and hurry up," Matthew ordered. "You know what Daddy does if we get home late."

"Hey," said Heidi, "do you think Daddy will come to the end-of-the-year program?"

Matthew shrugged. "Who knows? Sometimes he does and sometimes he doesn't."

Bootprints

Jason abandoned his search and trotted after his siblings. "He has to come this year," he puffed. "Because us first graders' poem is about fathers. Teacher Margaret said we all have to look at our fathers when we say it, because it's a trick-boot for them."

"A *what*? Oh, you mean a *tribute*." Heidi laughed. "Well, don't set your hopes too high, Jason Kauffman. Sometimes Daddy has things to do that are more important than us. You know that."

Jason's shoe scuffed against the pavement. Yes, he knew. But this was an exception. His poem was for Daddy. So Daddy must come.

It was that simple.

"THERE'S A BIG chance for rain tomorrow." Peter Kauffman spread grape jelly over his toast. "So I'll have to get the rest of the corn planted today."

Silence plunged over the breakfast table. Jason's spoonful of granola halted halfway to his mouth. He stared at his daddy, brown eyes filling.

"But Peter." Sarah's voice was weak. "Today is the school program."

"I know." Peter was eating busily. "I planned on going until I heard the forecast. Then I decided I better do what's important." He frowned at the expressions around the table. "Look, there's no need for the rest of you to get so unstrung. I'll hitch up Ranger and you can still go."

Jason determined that he wouldn't cry. But his chin wobbled and his throat burned, and before he knew it, something wet plopped into his cereal. "Please, Daddy." Quiet pathos laced his voice. "My poem is for you. Don't you want to hear it?"

Peter's nose twitched. He looked at Jason, then looked away. "Uh, it's not that I don't want to." Peter's voice was gruff. "Maybe-"

Maybe he should go, after all. He couldn't bear the look on Jason's face. Or on the faces of the rest of the family. Maybe it wouldn't hurt too much to leave the corn. He could still get it planted by the first of next week, unless there was some huge downpour.

Sarah and the children waited breathlessly. "Maybe-". Maybe Daddy was changing his mind?

Peter cleared his throat. He opened his mouth to say yes, he would go. But than an image blitzed through his brain. His father. Tall and stern. "What!" Peter could almost hear the sneering words. "You mean you're going to some silly program when there's corn to be planted? You call that managing your business? Huh? Well, don't come crying on *my* shoulders if you don't get ahead in life."

Peter blinked. "Maybe-". The word dangled in the air. "Maybe, uh, maybe I can come next year."

Around the table, everyone resumed breakfast. But the silence lingered. Jason was not the only one with something wet dripping into his cereal bowl.

JASON HOPED HIS trembling legs would keep him upright. He looked out over the huge crowd of people. Faces, faces, and more faces, none of them Daddy's. Surely Daddy was the only one who wasn't here. Jason choked back a tiny sob. How could he say his tribute to Daddy, when Daddy was home planting corn?

It was Philip's turn to recite. He started in a loud, clear voice, and didn't seem nervous at all, he was that busy smiling at his daddy.

Deacon Henry sat in the front row, and he smiled back at Philip. He listened carefully and nodded his head.

Jason hung his head as he stepped forward to take his turn. "My father-" he said softly. He looked down. "My father-" he said again, but his throat was choked and his mouth pasty. He couldn't do it. Daddy wasn't here. Daddy cared more about his corn than he did about Jason. A tear stood in his eye as he faced the crowd.

Deacon Henry had seen Sarah Kauffman arrive without her husband. Now as he looked at the dejected little boy in front of him, his heart ached. He caught Jason's eye and smiled.

Jason felt a tiny bit better. "My father," he said for the third time. This time he did not stop. He said his verse all the way through, and he looked at Philip's daddy for every word.

Philip's daddy nodded and smiled. When Jason was finished,

Bootprints

Deacon Henry did something he hadn't done for Philip's poem. He pulled out his handkerchief and blew his nose.

THE SCHOOL PROGRAM was over. It was summer time. Jason loved summer. He ran and laughed and shouted and played. Of course, he worked. Mostly he worked, because Peter Kauffman believed that hard work was the only cure for mischief.

All too soon it was August, and time to head back to school. Jason packed his things into a Wal Mart grocery bag, and put his pencil box on the very top. The pencil box was a little bit scratched now, but it was as dear to Jason's heart as ever.

Teacher Margaret welcomed her students back. Jason gave her a shy smile as he arranged his books in his desk. Then he ran to the ball diamond with Allen and Philip. School again. He was ready for it.

JASON LEANED OVER his math book. Second grade math was tougher than first grade, but Jason liked it. He liked to figure things out.

Jason's desk was the last one in the third row, nearest the door. He heard scuffling on the gravel outside. Were they getting visitors? Jason watched the door. He hoped so. Sometimes he got bored, but not when there were visitors to watch.

The latch wobbled, and then the door swung open. Jason watched wide-eyed as a stout, red-faced woman puffed inside. She jiggled a baby with one arm and towed a skinny little boy along with the other.

Teacher Margaret bustled up the aisle. "Come right on in!" she invited. "My, what a nice surprise! The visitor's bench is right over there, under the bulletin board."

The woman lowered herself onto the bench and untied her bonnet strings. Teacher Margaret introduced her to the class. "This is my cousin, Sophia," she said. "And this is Sophia's little boy, Sammy."

Teacher Margaret's cousin. That made Sophia an important guest, Jason knew. He watched as Sophia thunked her bonnet on the bench and jostled the baby, who was squeaking inside its blankets. Jason

Bootprints

thought Sophia looked like a very interesting cousin.

"Ruthie, why don't you go to the library and get a few books for Sammy," Teacher Margaret directed. "And Naomi, you can give the guest book to Sophia."

Jason turned back to his math book. It was hard to keep his attention on it, now that there were visitors in the room. He peeked at them while pretending to tie his shoe. He noticed a big fat fly buzzing around Sophia's face.

Jason felt sorry for Sophia. He knew how annoying a fly like that was. It kept you from enjoying anything else. What if Sophia didn't enjoy her visit all because of the fly? Jason watched anxiously as Sophia waved at the fly with the baby's burp cloth. Maybe she would go home and tell her family that she wished she hadn't come. Jason took a deep breath. Wouldn't that be dreadful, Teacher Margaret's cousin feeling like that?

Teacher Margaret looked around the room. She didn't see the fly buzzing around Sophia's face, but she saw something else. "Jason," she said crisply, "why aren't you working?"

Jason's neck grew hot. Hastily he bent over his math book and began filling in the answers for a row of addition.

Nine plus four. Jason scratched his head. Did that make eleven? No…fourteen. Jason wrote down a one and a four. But that didn't look right either, somehow. He thought it over carefully. If he had nine pencils in his pencil box, and someone gave him four more, how many did that make? Jason squeezed his eyes shut and debated. Thirteen! Yes, that was it.

Jason reached for his large pink eraser and erased the fourteen. He also erased the answer next to it, accidentally. Jason scowled at the eraser. It was too large. It didn't fit comfortably in his hand, and it always erased more than it was supposed to. It was not a practical eraser like the small round one that Philip had.

Jason looked at his eraser, and then he looked at the visitors. Sophia's plump hand was still batting at the fly. Jason had an idea. He opened

Bootprints {31}

his pencil box and took out his scissors. He snipped off several chunks of eraser. He would help Sophia, and kill the fly.

Jason put a piece of eraser against his suspenders and pulled back. Then he checked to make sure that Teacher Margaret was still discussing earthworms with her fourth grade science class.

It wasn't that he was doing anything wrong, Jason told himself. It was just that Teacher Margaret might not understand how annoying it would be to have a fly zooming around your face.

Jason leaned slightly to the right and popped his suspender. The chunk of eraser went flying, but it didn't hit the fly. It hit Sammy in the middle of his forehead.

Sammy gave a little leap on the bench, and his freckles stood out in shock. He looked around.

Jason was upset. He had missed the fly! He grabbed another chunk of eraser from the pile. He tried to aim more carefully this time, but it vanished into the deep, dark depths of Sophia's bonnet. The fly buzzed and buzzed.

Sammy looked all around. He spotted Jason, busily preparing for his third shot. Sammy was interested. He smiled at Jason. Every time Jason popped another chunk, he smiled some more.

Jason forgot about the fly. He was entertaining Sammy now. Soon all his chunks were used up. Jason studied his eraser. He picked it up and held it in his hand. It was still pretty big. He snipped off a few more pieces.

Jason knew he should be doing his math, but he was giving Sammy a good time, and that was important. Teacher Margaret always said they should do everything they could to make their visitors' stay enjoyable. Anyone could see that Sammy was enjoying himself. Sophia was watching the science class. She did not notice what was happening. At least not until a piece of eraser came out of nowhere and hit her right on the nose.

Sophia lurched on the bench and gave a little cry. Teacher Margaret came up the aisle. "Is something wrong?" she whispered.

Bootprints

Sophia rubbed her nose. She pointed at the floor, which was littered with bits of… well, whatever it was.

Jason's ears burned as he crouched over his math. Sophia had no sense of humor. And, oh no, Sammy was pointing in his direction. The little tattletale!

Sophia labored to her feet. No, she told Teacher Margaret, she wasn't staying any longer. She reached for her bonnet, and a chunk of eraser fell out and bounced to the floor. Sophia stared at it. Clutching her baby as if to shield it, she puffed out the door.

The classroom was silent as Teacher Margaret picked up bits of eraser and dropped them in the trash can. "It's recess time," she said. "Jason, please remain seated. The rest of you are dismissed."

Jason's eyes darted to the drawer where Teacher Margaret kept her wooden paddle. Jason had never gotten spanked in school before, but Teacher Margaret's face was so grim that Jason didn't doubt he would get spanked now. His heart pounded. What could he say?

Jason was afraid. He thought about Daddy, towering over him in his mud-caked boots, hitting and hitting him. Jason squirmed. He couldn't stand getting spanked like that by Teacher Margaret. He must talk her out of this somehow. Could he do it? He wasn't sure.

He had to try. He gathered himself together and smiled his nicest smile. "I wasn't trying to hit Sophia." Jason tried to smile again. "There was a huge fly back there. It was pestering Sophia. She couldn't even listen to your class, it was bothering her so." Jason sneaked a look at Teacher Margaret and noticed her expression had changed. He rushed on. "I wanted Sophia to have a good time, that's why I tried to kill the fly for her. I almost did too, one time."

Margaret stood helplessly beside Jason's desk. She had been aghast, humiliated, at his blatant disrespect to the visitors. Yet here he was, making it out to be some noble deed.

"Sophia didn't know you were trying to hit the fly. She thought you were trying to hit her." Teacher Margaret fingered the butchered eraser. "And you know our rule about creating disturbances. This was a serious disturbance, and you wasted your eraser. See, it was almost new, and now there's hardly anything left."

"But Teacher, I'm not sloppy anymore. I don't need such a big eraser." Jason studied Teacher Margaret. She looked a little softened, but he was still worried about the spanking.

What else could he do? Jason blinked rapidly. Rubbed his hands over his eyes. "I-I'm sorry," he said in a sad voice. "I shouldn't have. I just didn't think." Jason tried with all his might and squeezed out a tear. "I'm sorry I did that. Will you please forgive me?"

Teacher Margaret looked at the teary eyes begging her. "Of course I'll forgive you, Jason, but…"

Margaret felt at a loss. Spanking had indeed been her intention. What other punishment would have been strong enough? But she dreaded using the paddle and Jason looked so sweet and innocent. Those puddly eyes. Margaret felt her resistance crumbling. "But I want you to write a note of apology to Sophia."

Forget about the spanking. It was too great a thing, for someone so profoundly repentant. Margaret handed Jason a tissue. She had begun her session by feeling terribly upset, but now all she wanted to do was reach out and comfort the dear little boy in front of her.

Jason reached into his desk for a pen and a piece of paper. *Dear Sophia*, he wrote. He couldn't believe this measly note was the extent of his punishment. He snuffled into the tissue, pretending to be sorry. Inside though, he felt pretty good.

Jason was only in second grade, but he could do something he bet lots of big boys couldn't do. He could fool the teacher. He could get by with things. There were other ways to keep from being punished than always being good.

{34}   *Bootprints*

CHAPTER FIVE

JASON KAUFFMAN WAS not a big boy, but he already knew a lot. He knew that life wasn't fair. Life was a fight where you had to look out for yourself. If you didn't, you were going to be stomped under. You had to be tough, if you wanted to make it.

Jason was no longer little. He was big enough to figure things out. He knew his daddy was not like Philip's daddy. Or Allan's daddy. Their daddies liked their sons. They talked to them, and answered their questions. They did things together. They were friends.

Jason's daddy was not his friend. He did not talk to Jason, unless it was to order him around. Or to point out his mistakes. He often thrashed him. Sometimes Jason wondered if Daddy would care if he died. Wouldn't he just be relieved? Jason guessed he would. He was such a useless son.

Jason had hurts stacked inside of him, way up high. He was afraid of his daddy. That fear was always in the back of his mind.

Over the next several years, his teacher noticed a change in Jason.

His eyes were masked and defiant. Margaret wept more than once as little by little they shut her out. Jason did not let her see into his heart anymore, and Margaret did not know what was wrong. She did not know why Jason seemed to set himself against her. She did not know she was dealing with someone who was struggling with all his might just to survive.

Jason simply would not do what he was told. Both his parents and his teacher noticed this. They thought it was rebellion and punished accordingly. Peter beat his son. If there was one thing he wasn't going to tolerate, it was rebellion. Rebellion must be squashed, and if it took drastic measures to accomplish that, then so be it.

Nobody knew that authority spelled PAIN to Jason. Nobody knew that behind the increasingly bold exterior was a numbness. Jason dealt with the pain in the only way he knew how – fighting its source.

In the second grade, Jason found that he could manipulate authority. He became quite good at it in the ensuing years. It was a way to stay in control of a battering world.

Jason often got in trouble at school. Sometimes he dragged Allen and Philip into trouble with him. Margaret could deal with Allen and Philip. She could feel good about their responses and her decisions. But Jason frustrated her.

If Margaret approached Jason about his actions, he turned things around so that she ended up feeling like the guilty one. He convinced her that he was helpless, mistreated, to the extent that she often withheld his punishment.

Margaret didn't know that Jason deliberately worked on her emotions in order to protect himself from discipline. All she knew was that when she stopped teaching at the end of Jason's sixth year, she felt a huge relief at turning this difficult child over to somebody else. She also felt a deep sadness at having tried her best, but having failed in the end.

JASON KAUFFMAN STARED at the blank white sheet in front of him. He made a little dot in the center and scowled at it. He glanced around the classroom. Everyone else was engrossed in the freehand art project that Teacher Lucy had assigned them.

Jason glowered at Teacher Lucy's back. Why did she have to think up such a stupid idea? Freehand art indeed! Jason was a whiz in math and reading. He could do vocabulary and science alright too. He could even make a passing grade in English. But he could not draw.

He had tried three different pictures already. Mountains. A dog. A boat on a pond. But it was useless. He might as well walk a tight-rope as draw.

Jason raised his hand. Teacher Lucy didn't notice. He shuffled his feet and cleared his throat.

Finally Teacher Lucy came to stand beside him. "Yes, Jason?"

"Do we *have* to do this?"

"Why yes, I want everybody to draw a picture."

"But I can't draw!" Jason slumped down in his seat.

"Just do your best." Teacher Lucy smiled. "That's all I ask for." She turned and walked away.

Jason's cheeks got hot. He banged his desk lid as he searched for his sharpener. He exhaled – as loudly as he dared. Teacher Lucy didn't seem to notice.

Jason looked across the aisle at Philip. Philip smiled in sympathy, than turned back to his own picture. A simple one, to be sure. A barn with a tree beside it, and fields in the background. Not bad, though.

He looked at Allen. Allen was just putting the finishing touches on a horse. A horse that was rearing skyward, with his left foreleg pawing the air. The head and muscled chest looked startlingly lifelike.

Allen caught Jason's admiring look. He winked and grinned. Then he finished the curly mane flowing back from the arched neck.

Jason dragged his eyes back to his own sheet. Empty, except for some gray smudges and the little dot in the center. He picked up his eraser and rubbed it back and forth. The dot disappeared. Jason huffed the bits of eraser to the floor and stared at his paper.

"Recess time," announced Teacher Lucy. "Put your books away."

Gratefully, Jason stuffed the sheet into his desk. He snatched his ball glove and darted out the door, into the crisp, autumn sunshine. "A good ball game is a hundred and one times better than freehand art!" he yelled at Allen. "No, it's a thousand and one times better!"

Allen grinned. "Come on, man, it wasn't that bad."

"I would think so too, if I could draw as well as you can. How did you get that horse so perfect anyhow?"

Allen glanced around and lowered his voice. "I'll tell you. I just laid a paper on top of a coloring book picture and made a few dots around the outline. Then all I had to do was connect the dots and fill in the details." He laughed.

Jason pitched the softball into the air and caught it neatly as it came down. "Teacher Lucy said we may not trace."

"It wasn't tracing, Jason. Dots aren't the whole picture, you know." Allen spied Teacher Lucy coming out of the schoolhouse. "Come on, team!" he yelled. "We're in first!" He started to sprint away, then spun around and slapped Jason's back. "Try it, man. It's easy."

IT WAS EASY. Jason borrowed Allen's coloring book and paged through it until he found a picture he liked. A beaver sitting on a log he had just felled across a creek.

Before he placed the paper on top of the coloring book, Jason scanned the room. Teacher Lucy was writing on the blackboard, and no one else seemed to be watching him either. Except Allen, who dropped his eyelid in a sly wink.

Jason returned the wink and began making dots. He liked the feeling this gave him. The surge of adrenaline, of doing something risky without getting caught. Proving that rules could not contain him.

The picture turned out well. When Jason handed it in the next day, Teacher Lucy was surprised. "Why, Jason Kauffman," she said, "this picture is excellent! I can't see why you claimed you can't draw!"

Jason flashed an easy smile and returned to his seat. He brushed away a twinge of guilt, and concentrated instead on the pleasure of having outwitted Teacher Lucy.

TO JASON'S DISGUST, Teacher Lucy decided to have freehand art every six weeks. As she passed out sheets for their second assignment, she said, "You all did a good job last time. We've got some real artists in here." Her eyes rested momentarily on her seventh grade boys. She smiled.

Jason kept his eyes on his desk. He felt guilty, but he fought that down. It wasn't tracing! It was the best he could do, under the circumstances.

He borrowed Allen's coloring book while Teacher Lucy searched for some flashcards in her bottom desk drawer. He decided on a picture of a deer. A magnificent ten-point buck.

It took longer to make the dots. The deer's rack required lots of dots. He was almost finished when -

"Jason!" Teacher Lucy was standing beside him.

Jason jumped violently, causing his pencil to screech a jagged line across his carefully made dots.

"What are you doing, Jason?"

Jason struggled for words, but with every eye in the classroom staring at him, he felt blank.

Teacher Lucy held out her hand. "Give it to me. I'll see you at recess, you understand."

Jason's cheeks burned as he watched Teacher Lucy slide the sheet into her planner. He tossed the coloring book into his desk and tried to read. The words blurred together in dark, undulating waves. He closed the book. Hunched his shoulders. Worried.

How had Teacher Lucy managed to sneak up on him like that? He'd been a fool, not keeping a better eye out. Now she was up there, probably trying to think up some huge punishment. Would she tattle to his parents? Jason took small, fast breaths. He stared at Teacher Lucy, and suddenly he was angry.

It was Teacher Lucy's fault, this thing. If she hadn't made him draw in the first place, it would never have come to this! And Allen. He was to blame too. Jason cast a dark look at his friend. Allen had dreamed up the dot system. He had told Jason about it, and same as dared him to try it. It was his fault that Jason was now in trouble.

By recess time, Jason had his defense plotted out. He waited restlessly while Teacher Lucy muddled through some papers on her desk. He wished she would hurry up and get to the point.

Lucy was nervous. Something about Jason Kauffman made her quail. He was so tall. Almost a head taller than she was. And…crafty. Yes, *crafty* was the word. She did not look forward to dealing with this case. This slippery, aloof boy.

Jason watched Teacher Lucy approach his desk. He swallowed a surge of relief. Teacher Lucy did not look confident. It would be easier than he had thought, pulling the wool over her eyes.

Lucy laid the paper in front of him. "This is cheating, Jason." She struggled to make her voice sound firm, but instead it sounded quivery. Irresolute. She clutched the side of his desk.

"I'm sorry." Jason knew that apologizes held great sway. So did tears. Tears made any female melt in her tracks. He dropped his head into his hands. He was too old to cry for real, but he could look sad.

He explained how it was all Allen's idea. How he would never in a hundred years have thought of something like that himself. How he had questioned it at first, but finally given in and done it, since Allen insisted it wasn't cheating…

Lucy's knees trembled with relief. She had expected a scene from Jason. Or at least a ruse of some sort, to try and get the best of her. But here he was, a drooping bundle of remorse. When he was hardly to blame.

Teacher Lucy pointed at the paper. "I'll let you off, Jason, this time. But I want you to erase the dots and start over." She paused. "I'm sorry Allen got you into this. Would you please tell him I want to talk with him?"

{40} *Bootprints*

Jason uncoiled his frame from the desk. "Sure, Teacher." He walked outside, and a smug grin lit his face. He was a man victorious! Let life do what it will, it couldn't best him, as long as he stayed one step ahead. Just like this.

THWACK! JASON SWUNG his hoe viciously and another thistle toppled over. He picked it up gingerly and dropped it into the wheelbarrow. He hated this job. Especially on such a scorching day. He took out his handkerchief and wiped the sweat from his face. Summer vacation wasn't even something he looked forward to, he thought, for it was only an unending circle of work, work, work. How would it be after next term, when he would be out of school?

The wheelbarrow was almost full. Jason grasped the handles and trudged toward the burn barrel behind the barn. It was almost a relief to dump them, better than hoeing.

Daddy stepped out of the barn as Jason came puffing past behind his load. "Soon's you've dumped those," he said, "I want you to catch Dynamite and shine him up. A horse dealer will be stopping in before long to look at him." He gave his son a hard look. "Remember, I can get more from him if he's spruced up decent. I expect a good job."

Jason sighed as he pushed the wheelbarrow. He never had any time to rest. Or do any of the fun things that other boys did. Like making birdhouses with scraps of wood. Or swimming. Or fishing. Only last Sunday Philip had told Jason how his daddy had taken the whole family to a nearby lake to fish. They had caught lots of fish.

Jason had never gone fishing. He wanted to so very much. He had asked Daddy that evening if they could go sometime.

Daddy's answer had been swift and ruthless. Even now, as Jason dumped the thistles, the memory prickled. "Nope," Daddy had said. "Fishing's a waste of time. Only lazy people have time to fish."

Jason forgot about fishing as he walked to the pasture to get Dynamite. Dynamite was a horse Daddy had bought at the Clifty horse sale, two months before. He was supposed to be a fill in for

Bootprints {41}

Ranger, who was getting older and didn't have the stamina for long distances anymore.

Dynamite lifted his magnificent head when Jason whistled. He let Jason walk right up to him and snap the rope around his neck. Jason would be sorry to let him go. He loved this horse. He was so beautiful, and swift. Jason didn't mind that Dynamite balked sometimes. The horse was a dream in every other way.

They had tried to talk Daddy out of selling him, but Daddy was firm. "I will not put up with a balker. We cannot risk being late for church. We must have a dependable horse."

Jason led Dynamite to the hitching rack and began brushing his silky black sides. Balking was a bad habit of course, and arriving late for church was embarrassing. But still, this was a superb horse, and it rankled in Jason's heart to give him up again, so soon.

Jason had just finished polishing Dynamite's hooves when the prospective buyer arrived. He parked his fancy rig at the edge of the yard and came over to Jason. He pushed back his hat. "Your father around?"

"I'm right here." Peter had started across the lawn at the first sound of the diesel motor. He stepped around Dynamite's left side and shook hands with the man. "This is the horse, sir. Nice, isn't he?"

The man agreed cautiously and Peter rushed on. "We've never had such a gentle horse before. My wife can drive him and my children can catch him anytime. Why, I sent my son here to bring him in and brush him just now, and he did. I didn't do a thing. Plus, he's fast, he's traffic-safe and sound. And like I said, he's mighty good looking. You and I both know that's a bonus."

"So why are you selling him, if you like him so well?" the man asked. Jason was listening. Now Daddy would have to say that the horse balked. He wondered what the man would say. Maybe he wouldn't like a horse that balked either. He looked at Daddy.

Daddy cleared his throat. "Well," he said, "I decided he's just too small for my surrey. I need a bigger horse." He scratched his head.

Bootprints

"Wish we could keep this one though. He can sure put on the miles. And he's never shied at anything."

The man walked around Dynamite and inspected him closely. He opened the horse's mouth and looked at his teeth. He picked up the feet. Finally he asked, "How much do you want for him?"

Peter glanced at the gleaming, top-of-the-line outfit at the edge of the yard. "Well, I was hoping to get thirty-five hundred for him." He saw a slight frown cross the man's face and hurried on. "But since it's a smaller horse and you have a trailer along to haul him anyway, I'll let you have him for three thousand, how's that?"

Jason was astounded. Hadn't he heard Daddy tell Mom that he had bought the horse for two thousand? Why was he asking for so much more?

But the man was shaking Daddy's hand again. "It's a deal," he said. A few minutes later, Dynamite was going out the lane in the shiny silver trailer, and Daddy, with a pleased smile on his face, was stuffing the check into his wallet.

THE NEXT MORNING Daddy read Acts five for devotions. Jason was paying attention. Ananias and Sapphira had died because they were dishonest. Dishonesty was a serious sin in God's eyes.

Daddy closed the Bible and looked at his children. "You heard what happened to Ananias and Sapphira because they lied," he said. "Remember that. Lying is sin!"

Jason looked at Daddy and thought about the horse he'd sold last night. Daddy had not told the man that Dynamite balked. That was dishonest too, wasn't it? Jason had a funny feeling. Suppose Daddy would die because he had not told the truth?

After devotions, Jason edged up to the desk where Daddy was balancing his checkbook. He was afraid to ask, but he had to know. "Uh, Daddy?"

Daddy scrawled down another figure, than glanced at Jason out of the corner of his eye. He waited.

"I, uh, I just wondered how come you didn't tell that man that Dynamite balks?"

Peter glanced at his son. "I didn't tell him because he didn't ask. Everything I said was the truth, wasn't it?"

"I-I guess."

"Well then. What he doesn't know, won't hurt him." Peter turned back to his checkbook. "I'd appreciate it if you'd go mind your own business now."

Jason slipped out the door. He felt confused. Somehow, Daddy's dealings didn't seem honest to him. But Daddy said it was alright. Maybe it was.

A memory from last school term jogged through his mind. Teacher Lucy had called his dot idea cheating. But how could that be cheating any more than what Daddy had just done? It was the same principle, wasn't it? What the buyer didn't know, wouldn't hurt him, until he found out. What the Teacher didn't know… Well, anyway, Jason had learned something.

He was growing up.

CHAPTER SIX

JASON JERKED OPEN the door at the far end of the parlor to let out another batch of cows. "Hurry up!" He tapped them with the broom handle, trying to speed them up.

Cows, he thought, were of all farm animals the most cumbersome and poky. He brought down the broom handle, harder this time. It rattled against Annabelle's ancient hipbones and bonged against Carmen's skull. Carmen stopped to look at him with surprised, hurt eyes.

"Get going!" snapped Jason. His eyes shot to the clock on the parlor wall. Quarter till six and twelve cows to go. He rushed around, prodding the next batch into place. Would he be finished before Daddy and Matthew came in from the fields? He snatched a handful of paper towels. He had to be done because Daddy expected it.

Jason moved swiftly among the cows. Hurrying. But carefully. Daddy would come in here later tonight to make sure everything was done right. He always checked up on Jason.

Jason might have enjoyed milking, if milking was all there was to it. But the pressure of doing a perfect job, and still getting done on time, made it hard. He scurried around the parlor with fear of failure snarling at his heels. In his nervousness, he did not remember until he was almost done. *The water tank.*

"Now you be sure and have it filled before we come in with the teams tonight." Daddy's eyes had bored into Jason's. "Don't forget it either. The horses will be thirsty."

But Daddy had so many instructions. *Fill the water tank. Measure out feed for the horses. Give the sick cow an injection. Finish the milking on time. Do this, do that.*

And don't forget, not even the tiniest detail!

If he did, he would be in trouble.

Jason had mentally reviewed the list, all the while he was milking. But it was so long. And his mind was muddled with anxiety. He had forgotten the water tank, and now he might not get it filled on time.

Jason left the cows and dashed to the horse barn. In the semi-darkness of the interior, he stumbled against the stack of feed bags. Three of them pancaked off the side and collapsed to the floor. Jason leaped over them and plunged the hose into the nearly empty tank. "It'll take at least ten minutes for it to fill," he thought. "I can't wait that long."

He strode to the calf hutches, where Luke and Danny were just finishing up. "Hey, boys." His voice was commanding. "I want you to go to the horse barn and keep an eye on the water tank. As soon as it's full, shut off the hydrant."

Luke and Danny looked at each other. Frowned, and looked at Jason.

"That's your job!" Luke knew better than to argue with Daddy, but Jason wasn't Daddy. He had no right to give them orders. "I heard Daddy tell you to do it."

"And you heard *me* tell *you* to do it, Luke Kauffman!"

Luke glared at Jason. "We were just ready to go to the orchard to look for bird nests!"

{46} *Bootprints*

"Forget the bird nests!" Jason headed for the milk house. "You're too old to be playing around like that. Now go and do as I said."

"You're nothing except a big old boss!" Luke yelled after him.

"Bossy, Bossy, Bossy!" chanted Danny.

Jason slammed into the milking parlor. Why couldn't the little boys respect him like they should? They were so bratty. He attached the milkers to another round of cows. The steady pulsing throbbed in his ears.

It was like a lullaby, almost. Jason could relax now. Everything was under control.

It was six-thirty by the time the last cow had lumbered out of the parlor. Jason went to the fly-speckled window and gazed at the plodding teams outlined against the flaming June sunset. Daddy and Matthew were working late tonight.

Jason felt some of the urgency loosen in its chokehold on his neck. He breathed deeply and looked out the window. What he wouldn't give, to be out there in Matthew's place. Riding along behind the horses and feeling the tug of horsepower through the lines. Listening to the clink of the harness and the scratch and rustle of the young corn. Watching the soil spread out in moist black ribbons behind him.

Jason sighed and turned away from the window. There was no use asking for the privilege. Or even reminding Daddy that Philip had been working in the fields for two years already.

"My boys," declared Daddy, "will not drive a team until they are old enough to plow a straight furrow and handle the horses. And that's not until they are fourteen and out of school!"

A sense of injustice rankled in Jason's heart. He was just as strong as Matthew was, and a whole lot better with horses. Yet Daddy clung to his unreasonable opinion, and instead of allowing Jason to take turns with Matthew, he left him to do the chores.

Jason didn't mind the chores, but he minded that Daddy didn't trust him. He didn't believe in him, was always checking his work for mistakes.

Jason thought about Deacon Henry. Henry had confidence in his son. He and Philip were a team, doing everything together. If Philip made a mistake, Henry was right there to help him correct it, but he never shouted or called him useless.

Jason's daddy called him useless. Jason hated that ugly word. But it was the truth – he *was* a useless person. It didn't matter how hard or fast he worked, in the end he was still the same. Useless Jason Kauffman. If he wasn't, Daddy wouldn't say so. Daddy might be mean, but he never lied that Jason knew of.

Jason began the tedious job of hosing down the parlor. Every extra minute that Daddy and Matthew spent in the fields was an extra minute for him to concentrate on doing a good job.

Would Daddy notice if he took extra pains tonight? Jason hoped he would. He imagined the things Daddy might say on his round to see if everything was done right. Like, *Good job, son. You're a real worker already.* Or, *Glad I can depend on you when I'm not here. You're on the way to becoming a real fine man.*

Jason's life revolved around his father. He was always striving and struggling to win Daddy's approval. Every time he did something, he tried to do his best. Maybe Daddy would praise him. Put a hand on his shoulder and say how glad he was to have a son like him.

But Daddy never praised. Daddy checked and scolded and found fault. Jason didn't give up. He longed to be loved and accepted by his father.

When Daddy hammered him down and said *you are so useless,* Jason worked through the hurt and tried again the next time. *Maybe,* he'd think, *maybe if I try just a little bit harder, it will be different.*

But he would never be good enough. It was like a merry-go-round that spun in endless circles. Try. Fail. Try. Fail. The search for approval from his daddy.

Jason remembered the things he'd done wrong last night… The little bit of scum remaining on the edge of a milk can. The dusty corner of the alleyway that his broom had missed. The scoop shovel on the floor, instead of propped against the wall.

Bootprints

Tonight Jason made sure those things were taken care of. He double-checked everything, trying to look at his work the way Daddy would look at it later. He dared to hope. Maybe tonight would be the night when Daddy wouldn't find anything wrong. Maybe, even if he wouldn't say the words, he would nod his head. Jason thought what it would mean, just a little nod of Daddy's head.

Jason walked around, looking at the clean parlor, the cows eating their hay, and the calves lying peacefully in their hutches. It was all in order. Everything was the way it should be. He felt elation pushing back his weariness. He was always tired, under the weight of responsibility. But tonight everything was perfect. Such a good feeling.

Jason started past the horse barn on his way to the house. That's when he heard it. A trickle. Like running water. For a split second he was confused, and then it hit him, in a bone-chilling wave.

The water tank!

Jason raced into the horse barn. His horrified eyes strained through the murky dimness at the water pouring over the sides of the tank, sullenly flooding the entire lower end of the horse barn.

Jason reeled. He splashed through the flood and turned off the hydrant. Silence settled over the barn, broken only by the sound of water as it sloshed across the floor.

Jason looked around in a daze. The feed bags he'd carelessly knocked over were soggy heaps in the water. Besides those three, the two bottom ones on the stack were also soaked. Organic feed at that. The priciest kind on the market.

Jason picked the plastic feed scoop out of the water. *What would Daddy say?* It was the question that leaped from the disaster, and it terrified Jason. His mind shifted into overdrive. There was no doubting it – someone would get a beating. Jason's hands clenched into fists. He had tried so hard tonight. He just couldn't bear it, to have it end by being beaten. He would tell Daddy how it was. How he'd told the little boys to shut it off, and they hadn't. He'd put the blame on them.

He heard the thud of hooves and the creaking of harness outside.

Bootprints {49}

He took a fast, deep breath and squared his shoulders. Daddy was back.

Jason knew he didn't have a chance if Daddy came in and discovered him in the mess. It would be better to go outside and meet him, tell him the story before he discovered it himself. He sloshed through the water and burst out the door.

"Daddy!" He made his voice angry. "You won't believe what Luke and Danny did! I turned on the water to fill the tank, ages ago. The boys were already done with their chores, so I told them to shut it off. I told them three times, but just now I discovered it was still running! You won't believe the mess!"

Daddy sailed from the seat of the cultivator. "Unhitch the team." He strode for the horse barn, the fresh mud on his boots making them thud even louder than usual.

Jason began unhooking the tugs. He heard the clomps slow down, pause, then pick up speed as they retraced their path. Jason peeked over Chester's tall back and saw Daddy come boiling out of the barn. "The boys!" He was panting. "Where are they?"

"They're goofing off in the orchard." Jason hid his fear on scorn. "Looking for bird nests or something."

Daddy stalked to the corner of the barn. "Luke! Danny!" he bellowed. "Get up here right now!"

Jason saw two little forms drop from the apple trees and race toward the barn. A sliver of sympathy pricked his heart as he thought of what his brothers faced. He slipped the bridle from Belle's head, and remembered a little boy from years ago, crouched behind cobwebby feed barrels. The little boy's teeth had chattered with dread, and not because of the huge black bull in the pen beside him. Because of his father.

Jason's vision blurred as he remembered how he'd felt, being dragged from his hiding place by calloused, unloving hands. He remembered the board that Daddy had used to whip him. Heard the whistle of it as it cut through the air and collided with his backside. The pain had been terrible, more in his heart than in his body.

Jason tried to shake off the memory. He saw Daddy snatch Luke

{50} *Bootprints*

and Danny by the collars and push them along in front of him. "Why didn't you turn off the water?!" he roared. "Now just come see what a mess you made! Feed all soaked! What a waste!"

Terror pinched the boys' faces as they were propelled past Jason in high gear. Jason averted his eyes. He couldn't help thinking how similar this situation was to the one from long ago. Both times the idea had been his, and both times the idea had gone sadly awry, not because of him, but because of his brothers.

Jason tied the horses to the hitching rack. He thought of the slick way Matthew had palmed off the punishment on him the first time. This time – Jason felt a surge of adrenaline – he had set himself free. He had learned this from Matthew, and he was good at it. So what if it was at the cost of somebody else?

Jason heard sharp cracks and screaming wails emanate from the barn. He knew what it was like to be in that place. He felt sorry, but he swept that aside. He had to be tough and hard if he wanted to make it. There was not room for caring about somebody else. If somebody got bulldozed in order for him to protect himself, then that's just the way it was. A man had to look out for himself in a world like this. Any kind of softness was punished. Softness was a crack in the armor, a chance for people to get at him. If he was hard, nothing could hurt him.

Jason walked away from the horse barn and the cries of his brothers. It was a relief to have escaped the whip this time. Daddy's whip cut more than skin.

JASON REACHED FOR his hat and strode for the door, then paused at the sound of his name. "First thing this morning," said Peter Kauffman from his desk, "I want you to fix the granary door. Ever since the storm the other night it's hanging crooked. Looks sloppy, and we can't have that." He bent over his bookwork again, then spoke over his shoulder, "Use that new cordless drill and put the hinges on tight. But be careful – the thing was expensive."

"I know how to be careful," muttered Jason to himself, "to not be

Bootprints

told it a hundred times a day." He found the drill in the shop and fitted the right bit into the slot. Then picking up a few screws, he walked to the granary.

Jason fixed the door. He had learned to fix things years ago, and he felt pretty good about his abilities. He made sure the door was straight and latched properly, and then he took the drill back to the shop.

Jason never knew quite how it happened, but as he reached up to put the drill into the cabinet, it caught the edge of the steel workbench and snapped the bit clean off.

Jason heard the sound and watched in horror as the broken bit rolled across the concrete. He reached down and picked it up. What should he do? Daddy would be furious.

Jason rolled the broken pieces between his fingers and thought hard. He opened the bit box and thought some more. Slowly he laid the bit in its proper place. Then he laid the other piece against it. By turning it carefully, you couldn't even tell it was broken.

Jason closed the box and slid it onto the shelf beside the drill. Daddy would discover the broken bit someday, but maybe by then he would have forgotten that Jason had used it.

However, just two weeks later, Daddy decided to make a new barn door. "The old one is starting to rot and needs to be replaced. Luke, go get me the drill and the box of bits beside it."

Jason heard and trembled. Thankfully, he remembered he was to spray Round-up along the fence rows. That would take him out of Daddy's sight for the forenoon at least. And maybe, just maybe, Daddy wouldn't use that particular bit.

WHEN PETER KAUFFMAN picked up the bit he wanted, he was startled to have it fall into pieces in his hand. His mouth twitched in anger. Which one of his careless sons had broken this thing? Bits were expensive!

"Luke!"

Luke jumped, and almost let the board drop that he was holding in place.

Bootprints

"Did you drop this box?"

"No, Daddy."

Did you bump it against anything when you brought it out here?"

"No, Daddy, I was real careful."

Peter paced back and forth. Who had used the drill last? Jason! Yes, Jason must be the culprit. He would tackle him the minute he came back from spraying.

Peter was washing up for dinner when Jason came inside. He stopped right in the middle of sudsing his arms and stared at Jason. "Didn't you use the drill the other week?"

Jason kept his back turned. "Yes."

"Did you use the sixteenth inch drill bit?"

Blink. "Yes."

"Well, it's broken in half and I'd like to know why!"

Jason had had all forenoon to prepare his answer. "Why, it worked just fine when I used it." He managed to sound surprised. "It wasn't broken then."

"Hmmph!" Peter splashed water over his arms and wiped them on the towel. He looked at the rest of the family, seated around the table. "Someone had to do it! Matthew?"

Matthew scowled. "I've never used that drill."

Danny shook his head vehemently when questioned, and Heidi was indignant that Daddy had the nerve to question her. What did she know about drills?

It was a mystery. Nobody knew what had happened. Peter forked chunks of meatloaf into his mouth. Was it possible that he himself had broken it? Maybe bumped it against something? But no, he was almost certain he hadn't.

Peter never did figure out what happened to his bit. He just knew that *someone* had broken it. Perhaps he suspected that *someone* had outwitted him in his own game.

Bootprints

Bootprints

CHAPTER SEVEN

JASON KAUFFMAN TWISTED open the faucet and grasped the green rubber hose. It lurched and kicked, belched and sputtered. It acted the way Jason wanted to act. Like kicking out at life. At Daddy specifically.

The hose shuddered and water began spraying over the concrete. Jason hauled the hose to the far end of the milking parlor to begin washing up.

He replayed the scene in his mind. He had just chased the last batch of cows from the parlor when he heard the coarse rattle of wheels on the driveway. He had hurried to the window. Rubbed away the dust and peered out into the late summer sunshine.

An open hack was parked beside the barn. Jason's pulse quickened as he recognized the occupants. Allen and his father.

Allen's father was a shop worker, because, Jason had heard Peter say more than once, he didn't have enough backbone to stick to farming. He was gentle and easy-going, a trait that most people appreciated. Not Peter. "A weakling, that's what he is," he'd told Sarah scornfully.

"If he'd dig in and be a little more aggressive, he'd have his place paid off already, instead of going around and wheedling loans off of hard working people like us."

Peter hadn't loaned Allen's dad the money, Jason knew. He'd sent him away with the admonition to apply himself to life and earn his own way.

Now Allen's dad was back and Allen was with him. Were they going to try again? Jason hurried for the door. Maybe if he talked to them, he could get them to leave before Daddy discovered they were here. Daddy didn't have much respect for Allen's dad, and he didn't do a good job of hiding it.

But as Jason hurried through the door, he discovered he was too late. Daddy was already coming from the barn. Jason groaned and stepped back inside. He left the door open, so he could peep around the corner and listen to the conversation. After all, if Allen could be in on this, he could too.

Allen's dad sat on the seat, a genial grin on his face. If he had been shamed by Peter's previous rebuff, he did not show any traces of it now. "Hello, neighbor!" he greeted jovially. "A nice evening, not?"

"I suppose." Peter squinted at the man on the hack. "You here on business?"

Allen's dad chuckled. "You might call it that. Allen and I are on our way to do some squirrel hunting over in Jake Sweeney's woods. Since we were coming right past your place anyway, Allen convinced me to stop and see of Jason can come with us."

Allen leaned forward. "My mom packed us a picnic supper and I counted the sandwiches. There's plenty for three, and for dessert–" he grinned at Peter "–we have chocolate pie. If there's anybody who likes chocolate pie, it's Jason. Can't he come?"

Jason waited breathlessly. *Squirrel hunting! And chocolate pie!* He rarely got the chance to do anything with his friends. They were too busy, Daddy always said, to waste time on nonsense.

But squirrel hunting wasn't nonsense. They could eat the meat and save on several packs of hamburger. Daddy was always looking for ways to save. Jason stared at Daddy, willing him to say yes.

But Daddy didn't hesitate. "We've got chores to do," he said. Then he turned and walked away, his big boots scratching the gravel.

Jason smashed his fist against the wall. "That's just an excuse!" he snarled through clenched teeth. "Daddy was in here five minutes ago and saw for himself that I'm almost done! He just doesn't want me to have any fun! Does he think having fun is some sort of sin?"

Jason heard the hack jolting out the lane. Rage and disappointment choked him. He could hardly breathe. Blindly he began hosing down the parlor, his last job for tonight.

There were times when Jason thought he hated his father, and now was one of those times.

Strained silence cloaked the supper table. Sarah had gone to extra efforts to prepare a special supper – stuffed pork chops and lemon meringue pie – but no one felt like eating with the sullen anger hanging between Peter and Jason.

Jason hurried upstairs the minute he dared. He was glad Matthew was choring at Mark Weavers and wouldn't be home tonight. He could have the bedroom to himself.

Jason sat beside the window. He saw Daddy stomping through the dusk, going to check on a sick cow. "I wish you wouldn't be my daddy," Jason whispered. "I don't like you, not one little bit."

Jason couldn't argue with Daddy to his face. Nobody knew how it felt to be yelled at and punished every day of his life. To be denied the privileges and good times that other boys had all the time. He couldn't tell Daddy these things to his face, but he could tell him up here in his bedroom, where no one could see or hear.

Jason sat beside the window and let his anger tower within him. He attacked his daddy. He told him how mean he was, to not let him go hunting with Allen. He told him he was warped and stingy, and all the other ugly things he could think of. This was his only way of getting even. He was fighting back for the things Daddy did to him.

Gradually the angry monster spent itself and slunk away. Jason was drained and dejected. "Why was I ever born?" he wondered. "I'm no good, nothing except a stupid, useless hunk of flesh."

The twilight deepened. Jason's thoughts rolled in his mind, around and around and around. *I must be a mistake. If I wasn't, Daddy would love me. He would be nice to me. He wouldn't call me useless or dumb, if there was anything in me to love.*

Jason wallowed in his misery. *Nobody could love someone like me,* he thought. But he wanted – how he wanted – for his father to love him.

Opposing forces clashed in his chest. One cried out for love. The other snarled he wasn't worthy. He twisted and turned in his chair in front of the window. He wished he could go outside and run. Run through the wind and the dark, away from his pain. But he had tried it already, and he knew. Pain couldn't be outrun. It was like his shadow. The faster he ran, the faster the shadow ran.

Jason moaned. His father wasn't there to reject him, but he knew enough to reject himself. It was hopeless. He'd never amount to anything. He wasn't even out of school yet, and he was already tired of living. What good did it do to live, if it brought only condemnation and ridicule? He had read a story recently of a boy who had died from cancer. Jason didn't usually like to think of dying. But tonight, up here in his room, it didn't seem that bad.

Dying would be an escape. Daddy couldn't get him anymore, if he was dead. Neither could his pain. What would it be like, to be forever removed from Daddy and pain?

Jason turned from the window and looked distractedly around the room. His eyes fixed on a piece of paneling, in the corner, that had come partially loose from the wall. A corner of something peeked out of the crack.

Mystified, Jason walked over and pried back the paneling. Must be Matthew had hidden something behind there. He carefully drew out a magazine.

Jason stared at the cover and knew he shouldn't be looking at such a magazine. But it gripped him, with a strange, transfixing power.

Jason turned the pages. His pulse pounded. His eyes riveted on the images. His senses whirled. It was late when he finally eased the magazine back into its hiding place.

He had found his escape. It was easier than running. Better than dying.

In the following weeks, Jason returned to the magazine again and again, whenever his struggles threatened to overwhelm him. The magazine made him forget, momentarily. It gave him pleasure, when nothing else in the world did.

JASON PLOPPED A notebook into the bottom of the Wal-Mart bag, then added his ruler, crayons, and pencil box. He dreaded the school term.

"Because," he told Heidi, " what boy my age likes to be trapped in a stifling old school house?"

But there was more to it than that. Jason knotted the bag and parked it beside his lunch box. He wasn't about to admit it to Heidi, but he was scared.

Teacher Lucy had resigned last spring. All summer Jason had wondered who the new teacher would be. He had considered various possibilities, but he hadn't ever considered Josiah Gingerich.

When Sarah announced the news one evening at the supper table, Jason was appalled. A man teacher! He tried to imagine Josiah's husky frame striding around the classroom, and his deep voice rumbling out orders.

Allen and Philip were enthused. They thought it would be fun. But Jason couldn't shake his fears. He had learned the only way to keep people from controlling him was to control them. Last year Teacher Lucy had been easy prey. All he had needed to do was tower over her with a silent, unflinching stare, and she had begun to unravel.

But Josiah was a man. A man was not gullible like a woman. Trying to manipulate a man would be as difficult as pulling a plow all by yourself.

It unnerved Jason to think that his ploys might not work with Josiah. If Josiah got the best of him, he would be stripped of his armor. He would be exposed to pain, shame, and ridicule. He had felt those arrows many times in his life. His heart was pocked with holes.

Nobody cared about his heart. Nobody cared that they were grinding it into hamburger. So Jason had built walls around it. He had tried to protect it by outwitting authority. He had learned to be quick and smart because authority was always lurking in the shadows, ready to ambush with their deadly arrows.

Jason was starkly afraid of any situation where he might not be the victor. He tried to avoid such situations, but now there was no way to avoid Josiah Gingerich.

Staying in control was Jason's sole security. He tried to prepare himself for the school term. He added more bricks to his wall and toughened his shield of defiance.

It would be a tough battle, but he wouldn't go down without a fight.

"HEY BOYS," JASON hissed at Allen and Philip. "I've got something to show you." He jerked his head toward the horse barn. His friends followed him to the wooden-sided door, where they stopped. "Come on inside," Jason urged. "Don't just stand there."

Philip glanced around. "Teacher Josiah said we're not supposed to go in there at recess without permission. Did you ask?"

"Of course not!" Jason scoffed. "Staying out of the horse barn is a ridiculous rule. I don't care what old man Josiah says. Besides, he kept some of the girls in to talk to them, so I *can't* ask. Now do you want to see what I've got or not?"

Allen and Philip looked at the schoolhouse, then they shrugged and let curiosity pull them through the door.

Jason scraped some hay aside and dug out the magazine he had carefully hidden that morning. He handed it to his friends. "It's Matthew's," he said, "but I know where he hides it, and I look at it all the time."

Philip was shocked. "I-I... Jason, you shouldn't – I mean, why did you bring it to school?"

"Because I can do whatever I want to." Jason's voice was hard. He had to be strong. He could never let anyone guess his weakness.

School was a tug-of-war between Jason and Josiah. It was exhausting, with both of them vying to be the strongest, each refusing to give in to the other.

Jason had been right in fearing his usual tactics wouldn't work with Josiah. He had tried them all – stirring him to pity, intimidating him, acting innocent, or even outright lying. But Josiah was tough; he was not cowed by Jason.

Ever since second grade, Jason had bent the rules to his convenience and gotten away with it. But Josiah's rules were like a shock collar – if he transgressed at all, then ZAP! It infuriated Jason to be forced into submission. He watched for ways to get back at Josiah, to prove that he, Josiah, wasn't the upper dog after all.

To break the rules and talk himself out of punishments no longer worked. But to break the rules and keep from getting caught? Jason poured himself into this new game. He thought he could get by with anything.

"Since it's here anyway, let's look at it."

Allen's voice jolted Jason back to the business at hand. He went over and peered through a crack in the wall. "I still don't see the girls," he said, "so it's safe."

Philip opened the magazine. Soon all three boys were absorbed in the pictures. They forgot everything else.

JOSIAH ENDED HIS session with the girls by asking them to remain inside and clean the classroom. When they were busy, he went out to check on the rest of the children. He felt tired. Teaching was rewarding, but it was also stressful and demanding. He hadn't known what great stores of emotional energy it took to meet so many children's needs.

They were all different. What worked for one child didn't work for

Bootprints

the other. Some needed praise. Some needed encouragement. Some needed firmness. Josiah rounded the corner of the schoolhouse and watched the game of Prisoner's Base. Children had so much energy. They chased and dodged and leaped and ran. All except Andy. Josiah noted the third grader standing peacefully on base and smiled ruefully. Andy needed motivation.

What did Jason need?

Josiah stifled a groan. He must never, ever give up on a child, but sometimes he felt like giving up on Jason. Jason was as uncommunicative as a fencepost, stubborn as Bermuda grass. He required more discipline than all the other children together, yet discipline seemed only to feed his rebellion. Josiah understood now why Lucy Mast hadn't been able to face another term with Jason. He was enough to give any teacher ulcers.

Josiah was surprised the game was going so well. It seemed whenever he wasn't out here, Jason stirred up some kind of trouble. By the way, where *was* Jason?

Josiah's eyes searched the milling crowd. His heart sank. No Jason. No Philip or Allen either.

Josiah checked the basement. He checked the grove of trees on the east side of the playground. Then he strode for the horse barn.

SILENTLY THE THREE boys watched their teacher stuff the magazine into a bag. "We'll take care of this after school." Josiah's voice shook a little. "I want all of you to stay."

Philip lifted brooding eyes. "Dad and I are going to town after school. He said he'll pick me up right at dismissal."

Josiah knew Deacon Henry. "He'll wait."

ALL AFTERNOON JASON tried to prepare himself. He knew he would receive the greatest punishment. He imagined all the things Josiah might do. He vowed to stay tough and defiant. If Josiah believed he wasn't sorry, he could still come out on top.

Josiah talked to them first. He tried to help them understand the harm of a magazine like that. They went outside and burned it.

Jason watched the ashes float away. A sense of loss gnawed at him. The magazine had acted as a band-aid. What would he do now, when he needed a boost?

They trooped back inside. Now the arrows would fly. Jason gritted his teeth. He was prepared.

"Let's pray," Josiah announced. He got down on his knees and motioned the boys to do the same.

Jason was dumbfounded. He was prepared for *anything* except *this!* His defenses wobbled precariously as he coiled his body.

Josiah began to talk to God in a quiet, earnest voice. He told Him what had happened today, and asked Him to cleanse the boys' minds. He prayed for Philip. He prayed for Allen. Then he prayed for Jason.

No one had ever prayed for Jason before, in his presence. He began to tremble. Josiah sensed his struggle, and put his hand on his shoulder.

Jason was used to punishments. He could handle the worst of its kind. But he couldn't handle this. The hand on his shoulder. It was a steady, warm pressure, and it did something no punishment had ever done. It reached into his heart – past the armor, past the walls – right into where the lonely, hurting boy hid himself.

Jason felt himself coming apart. He wanted to get up and run away. But the hand held him there. The hand and the voice.

Josiah's voice rumbled on and on in soothing waves, like spring thunder. He asked God to bless Jason, to help him grow up to be a worthy man. He asked God to minister to his struggles, whatever they were. The kind voice rained down over him, soothing away his hardness and anger.

No one had ever spoken to Jason so beautifully. All he knew was scolding. Degradation. Yelling. Starved emotions heaved in his chest. He listened to the voice, he felt the hand. He wanted to cry.

But Daddy said men didn't cry. Jason was six feet tall and his voice was changing. He was almost a man – too old to cry.

Bootprints

He choked back a sob. Swiped one tear. That was all. And nobody noticed.

Josiah ended the prayer. He squeezed Jason's shoulder, then went outside to talk with Deacon Henry.

Jason kept his eyes closed. The hand was gone, but the feeling lingered. He wanted it to linger forever. The feeling that for a brief capsule of time, somebody cared.

Josiah came back inside. He looked at Allen and Jason. "I want to talk to your fathers too, maybe on Sunday. But that's all for today. You are dismissed."

Jason stumbled to the horse barn. He wrestled the saddle onto Judy's back. Get out and ride. That's what he needed. Ride till he calmed down. This day was doing things to him, things he could not allow to happen.

First he'd wait till Deacon Henry left. He had tied his horse to the hitching rack behind the barn. Jason didn't want Henry to see him leave. He was afraid he couldn't stay strong, if Henry talked to him.

Jason could see through a crack in the wall. Henry was standing patiently beside the buggy. Philip came dragging out to meet him.

"Hi, son."

Philip's shoe scrabbled the ground. He did not reply.

"Seems like a talk might be in order."

"Yeah."

Henry pointed to a straw bale. "Let's sit."

They sat. Side by side, the man and his son. Philip did not seem afraid, only sad.

"Dad, I'm sorry." Philip's voice cracked. "I didn't mean to let you down."

Jason's breath labored in his throat. He waited for Henry to get mad, to shout at Philip, and tell him what a useless piece of junk he was.

But Henry didn't. He said, "I'm sorry it happened, son. There will be consequences. You disobeyed your teacher and that needs to be dealt

{64} *Bootprints*

with. About the magazine, I'm glad it's been burned, but you'll find the pictures won't just automatically erase themselves from your mind. You're going to struggle in dealing with that. You did some wrong things today, son. Nobody forced you. You gave in to temptation yourself, and you're going to have to take responsibility for it."

Philip's shoulders hunched beneath the weight of guilt. Deacon Henry continued, "You're my son and I care about you, but I can't do your reaping. Every man is accountable for his own sins. But this is what I want you to know. I can walk beside you. I want to support you through this. You're growing up and I can talk to you man-to-man. That magazine is going to affect you more than you know. You're going to have to fight for your purity. I want to help you be a victor. You don't have to be afraid to come to me, because I know how it is to be a man. I'll fight with you, son."

By now Philip was crying. Henry put his arm around his shoulders. Jason watched through the crack in the wall. He was astounded. Henry was crying too.

He was witnessing a sacred scene. He should leave, before he was discovered. But something held him transfixed. The power of that relationship. The rightness of it. The thing he had yearned for all of his life.

Jason's heart ached with an intensity that no words can describe. He didn't care anymore what Daddy said about a man not crying. He didn't care of he was a sissy. He stumbled blindly over to Judy and threw his arms around her neck. He buried his face in her mane, and wept.

JOSIAH TOOK PETER KAUFFMAN aside after church. "I'd appreciate your advice on how to handle this further," he concluded.

Peter shook his head, scowling. "I'll take care of it at home." He was enraged and grossly humiliated. *His* son stooping to such a vulgar act?! What a stain to his reputation!

The Kauffman buggy sailed home from church. Peter hustled Jason to the barn. "This is the limit!" he bellowed. "People will think I haven't taught you a thing!"

Jason was almost as tall as his father. He stared him silently in the eye.

Peter fairly danced with wrath. He snatched an old lawn mower belt and cracked it across Jason's legs.

Jason steeled himself. He was too old, too big, for a whipping. He stood rigidly as the blows lashed at his body. His muscles screamed with pain, but he refused to flinch. He would not allow Daddy to break him.

It was just as well that this happened. He had been really weak when Josiah had prayed and when he had spied on Philip and his father. Now he could be strong.

CHAPTER EIGHT

JASON FELT NO regret as he walked away from Echo Valley School with his diploma. He had learned there. Mostly he had fought with his teachers. It was a relief to sling his bag over his shoulder and jog out of the rutted lane for the last time.

While Jason was on his way home, his mother was busy in the kitchen, preparing a special graduation supper. She thought about Jason's first day of school. The little boy she had once held and rocked and sang to was becoming a man. She prayed he'd become a man of courage and honor. Like her papa had been.

Sarah's eyes glistened as she stirred the chocolate pie filling. If only Papa would have lived long enough for Jason to remember. He would have been a good example. Someone who depicted real manhood. Sarah didn't let herself think about why Jason needed that.

But then she thought of something Aunt Katie had once told her. A child's image of manhood is usually shaped by his father. If his father is angry and abusive, the child can grow up with a warped view of genuine, godly manhood.

Aunt Katie hadn't been talking about Peter, but her words stung anyway. Sarah knew Peter wasn't the example her sons needed. Papa would have been. But there was no use pining for what couldn't be changed. Sarah stirred the pie filling. She didn't have Papa, but she had God. She would trust her sons' welfare to Him.

The door slammed, heralding the arrival of the school children. Sarah pushed the bubbling filling – and her thoughts – to the back burner.

"Hi, Mom, smells good in here." Jason grinned. He dropped his Wal-Mart bag on the table and fiddled with the knot. His siblings pranced around him, vying for his school things. He gave eight-year-old Amy his crayons and pencil sharpener. He gave his ruler to Danny, and his scissors to Luke. He kept the pencil box.

The pencil box was old. It was dented and rusty. But it meant as much to Jason as it ever had. He gave it a place of honor on his dresser top. Maybe he could collect change in it, or use it to store his handkerchiefs. Maybe he would just let it sit there as a reminder of a day long ago, when Daddy had loved him.

JASON HAD MORE responsibilities now that he was out of school. Like going to the feed mill alone. Or driving the teams.

Peter kept a sharp eye on Jason the first few times he worked in the fields. He noted how much better the horses responded to Jason than they did to Matthew. Take Billy. Billy was not a large horse, but he was a contrary one.

Billy would not behave for Matthew. He would stop halfway around the field, and refuse to go farther. Matthew would rage and yell and pop the lines. If that didn't work, he'd fire dirt clods at him. Then Billy would snake his yellow teeth at Matthew. Or he would suddenly bound away, dragging the rest of the team and the cultivator behind him.

Billy was a lot like Jason, Peter thought. Thick-skulled and difficult to manage. He braced himself for a huge ruckus when the pair headed for the field.

But Billy behaved. Peter watched in astonishment as the horse marched along, looking not to the right hand, nor to the left.

And it wasn't just Billy. In the ensuing weeks, Jason proved his skills on more of the horses. Lazy Lillie became inspired. Grumpy Belle quit sulking. Rufus didn't nip the other horses as much.

"My boy's a real horseman," Peter bragged to the milk man and the vet and anyone else who came to the farm. "He sure is. He can make a model out of the most ornery horse in the county."

With the horses performing so well, Jason got a lot more done in a day than Matthew ever did. Peter was pleased, but he was careful not to say so to Jason. Praise would make him proud. Instead, he pointed out his flaws. The furrow over there was slightly crooked. That east corner was too rounded.

At first Jason was miserable at Dad's criticism. No matter how hard he tried, he was never good enough. But then Dad began assigning more and more of the field work to him. It was Matthew now who was left to get the milking done.

Jason's self-esteem crept out of the gutter. He reveled in the knowledge that Dad was giving him a vague sort of approval. Not with words maybe, but with responsibility.

Jason had always longed for words. *Good job, son. You're just the kind of hand I need.* But any approval was better than none. Jason bumped along behind the horses, and he was almost happy.

But the change in roles was tough on Matthew. He didn't like farming in the first place, and now he was being left with all the dirty work. Jason could feel his brother's resentment simmering below the surface. He tried to stay out of Matthew's path. If the volcano erupted, he didn't want to be around.

JASON DIDN'T MISS school, but he missed his friends. He often watched wistfully as Matthew dashed out the lane to attend youth gatherings.

It wasn't fair. Matthew could see his buddies all the time, while Jason couldn't see his except at church.

It was on one such evening when Matthew was gone and Jason was lonely that he came up with the plan. The more he thought about it, the more excited he became. He could hardly wait until Sunday to present it to Allen and Philip.

Of course there was the usual complication. It loomed over six feet tall, it had a six-inch beard, and its name was Peter Kauffman.

Jason wrestled. He plotted. He mapped out a course of action. It was a gamble at best, but it was worth a try.

Sunday finally came. Jason's friends loved the idea. "Camping! That's great, man!" Allen slapped Jason's back. "Where would we go?"

"You could come to our place," Philip offered. "We have the perfect place out beside the pond. Maybe we could catch some fish for our supper."

Fish?! Jason hadn't even thought that far. What a great idea! "Let's ask permission this week," he suggested, "then if it suits everyone, we can decide next Sunday when we'll go."

Allen and Philip didn't think getting permission would be any problem on their part. Only Jason was uncertain. Dad could be so narrow-minded. Maybe if he worked really hard this week…

Jason worked hard. He milked cows, mucked out the stables, cultivated the corn, and helped mow the first cutting of hay. He even mowed the lawn without being told.

Monday came and went. Then Tuesday. And Wednesday. Still Jason hadn't asked. On Thursday Dad took a load of calves to the sale barn. He was gone all day, so Jason couldn't ask.

All day Friday Jason tried to rustle up his courage. He watched Dad closely. It was important to ask when he was in a good mood. But Friday was not a good day for Dad. He was afraid they wouldn't get all the hay in before the weekend, and the forecast called for rain on Sunday. He pushed himself to the limit, and his sons likewise.

By Saturday morning Jason was desperate. He had to ask today, but there was still hay in the field, and Dad was grouchy. "This hay's got to be in the barn by tonight," he roared, "if we have to work till midnight! Now get going!"

Jason got going. He pitched bales on the wagon with all his might. His heart pounded – from exertion some, but mostly from anxiety. Dad had to say yes. But he wouldn't, not when he was in such a lather. Jason's only hope was getting the hay in on time. It was a slim one.

At dinnertime, Jason debated about taking time off to eat. Every minute counted. But he was hungry, and the horses needed a break. Reluctantly, he followed the others to the house.

"I put the mail on your desk," Sarah informed Peter after he'd washed up. "There's an envelope from the sale barn – probably a check for those calves."

Peter pounced on the envelope. "Eight thousand dollars!" he shouted. "That's two thousand more than I expected!" He came smiling to the table.

Jason watched Dad closely throughout the entire meal. He hadn't seen him so upbeat for a long time. This, he decided, was the moment he had been waiting for.

He waited until after dinner, when Dad was easing the precious check into his wallet. "Dad?"

"Huh?" Dad looked almost friendly.

"We boys, Allen, Philip and I, were talking on Sunday. You know we hardly get to see each other anymore. We thought it would be fun to go camping, so Philip invited us all over there one evening next week. Do you think I could go?"

"Hmmm." Dad gave the wallet a lingering stroke, then stuffed it into his pocket.

Jason's muscles quivered with suspense. "I wouldn't go until after chores."

"Well-" A scene from the past wormed itself into Peter's mind. He saw another boy, himself, standing in front of his father, asking permission to go swimming with his friends. He remembered clearly

Bootprints {71}

his father's answer. "The things you don't come up with! Swimming's a waste of time. Now get to your chores and don't let me hear another word of such childish notions!"

Peter remembered just as clearly his own feelings. Hurt. Disappointment. Rage. He looked at Jason's face in front of him. Expressionless, yet he knew the boy wanted to go. "Tell you what," he heard himself saying, "if we get the hay all in by tonight, you can go."

"Oh, Dad." Jason was seized by a wild impulse to fling his arms around his father's neck. Then he was seized by an equally wild impulse to laugh. Hugging Dad would be like hugging a tombstone. "Don't worry," he promised. "We'll get it in."

"I can go! I can go!" The chorus rang in Jason's mind all afternoon. He flung bales with a strength he didn't know he possessed. "Speed up the team!" he hollered to Danny. "We can go faster than this!"

The sun was just sliding beneath the horizon when Jason and Danny bounced up to the barn with the last load of hay. Jason was exuberant. They had done it!

AS SOON AS services were dismissed, the three friends congregated beneath a shade tree. "I can go," Jason blurted out before anyone else had a chance to speak.

"Me too," Allen said.

They looked expectantly at Philip. He grinned. "Dad said it's all right, if your fathers don't mind. He suggested Tuesday night. Is that okay with you?"

And so it was decided. Jason was thrilled. He had never in all his fifteen years gone camping. Or fishing. Now he'd get to do both in one evening. It was even more than he'd bargained for when he'd thought up the idea in the first place.

Jason thought Tuesday evening would never come. He fretted and stewed on Monday because it rained. What would they do if it rained on Tuesday? They hadn't even talked about that.

To Jason's relief, the rain clouds blew away during the night and the sun rose on Tuesday morning, beaming on the freshly-washed earth. And upon Jason who beamed right back.

JASON CLUTCHED HIS blanket roll under his right arm, and with his left he swung a bag of food. Mom had packed it and insisted he take it along. He sneaked a peek. Bread, a pack of hot dogs, ketchup, mustard, pickles. Jason grinned and walked faster. Henry's place was just ahead. Matthew had dropped him off at the crossroads on his way to a work bee with the youth. For once, Jason didn't mind that Matthew was going to a youth gathering again. He was going camping!

Allen had already arrived and he and Philip were loading a wagon. Sleeping bags, wood for a fire, fishing poles, baskets of food…

"Hey, Jason, it's about time you show up!" Allen called.

"I had to wait till Matthew was ready." Jason flipped his blanket onto the wagon. "But I'm here now and raring to go!"

Just then Henry came out of the barn. "Good evening, boys." He peered at the loaded wagon. "How long are you planning to stay? A week?"

They all laughed. "Well, Dad, we wanted to be sure we have everything we need," Philip explained.

"It almost makes me want to join you," Henry said. "Do you mind if we come back later for an hour or so?"

"Sure, come ahead," Philip said as he began to hitch the horses to the wagon.

The three boys didn't talk much as they rattled out the back lane. Jason, perched on Allen's sleeping bag, thought he had never seen an evening more beautiful.

They started the fire before getting the fishing gear ready. "That way it'll be just right if we catch any fish," Philip explained.

Fishing was even more fun than Jason had imagined. They all caught several and finally Philip decided it was enough for supper. "Let's get 'em cleaned and fried. There's nothing better than fresh fish!"

And there wasn't. No one had remembered to bring salt, but to

Bootprints {73}

the boys, the hot, flaky fish were sublime. They roasted several hot dogs and ate those too. Allen had brought chips and string cheese, and Philip's Mom had sent brownies and potato salad. Jason thought it was the best meal he had ever eaten.

They were finishing up the brownies when Philip's family emerged from the dusk. Henry strode over to the fire. "Good job on the campfire, boys. It's just perfect for these." He held up a bag of marshmallows.

Cheers erupted and the children scurried off to find roasting sticks. Jason watched in silence as the happy, chattering family clustered around Henry, asking for more marshmallows, or for help with the roasting. He noticed how Henry had time for them all – even the two-year-old. His rough hand gently held the little girl's as he helped her roast her very own marshmallow.

Jason stared into the fire and ate his marshmallow. He looked at the happy family clustered around him. He sighed.

He thought about his own family. The anger, the tension, the blame shifting. Laughter was rare, and they never did anything together, not like this.

Henry's voice broke into his thoughts. "Why don't we sing a few songs yet before we go back to the house?"

And so they sang. Jason helped the best he could, but he wasn't much of a singer. The only time he sang since he was out of school was at church. He watched Philip and his brothers and sisters. They sang lustily, and they knew all the words. Even the youngest one helped with "Jesus Loves Me".

Then Philip started one Jason didn't know. *O God, our help in ages past, our hope for years to come...* Jason closed his eyes and listened. How had God helped him in his past? He didn't know. He'd always been on his own, trying to survive. He wasn't good enough for God to get involved with him. Not that he wanted His involvement anyway.

Beneath the shadow of Thy throne, still may we dwell secure. What would it be like to be secure? Secure in God? Jason couldn't fathom it. God, he'd always imagined, was a lot like Dad. Tramping around heaven in his big boots. Peering down at the people on earth, ready to clap a punishment on anyone who wasn't toeing the line. Jason was afraid of God. Just like he was afraid of Dad. The words of the song were nice. But unrealistic.

O God, our help in ages past, our hope for years to come, Be Thou our Guide while life shall last, and our eternal home. The song faded into the darkness to be replaced by the occasional snap of the fire, and the rising chorus of cricket-song. A nameless longing flamed in Jason's chest. He wanted this moment around the fire to last forever. It was holy, almost. But Henry was rising to his feet. "Come children, it's time to go back. We'll let these young men rough it for the night."

Later that night, Jason lay wrapped in his blanket. It had been a good evening. Something he would always cherish, like the pencil box. But it had been sad too, a little. A reminder of what others had. Love and relationship. He longed for that, but it wasn't meant for him. He watched the stars dance across the velvety expanse of the sky. He was meant to be a loner. Someone who defended his territory single-handed. It was a tough life, and a lonely one.

So lonely…

CHAPTER NINE

JASON'S SIXTEENTH BIRTHDAY passed without celebration. Birthdays in the Kauffman family were like that. No gifts, no cake, no "Happy Birthday" songs.

Sarah did make chocolate pie for supper and was rewarded with a big grin from Jason. She eyed her tall son during supper. What did life hold for him? She knew his life, thus far, had not been easy. What would happen when he joined the youth group?

AT FIRST JASON felt strange to associate with the other youth. Most of them were older than he was, and he didn't know them well. He was relieved once Philip and Allen turned sixteen too. The three friends were often together at work bees, and sat beside each other at the Sunday evening singings.

That fall the boys received a special invitation to a wedding in Casey County. Two of their former teachers, Josiah Gingerich and Margaret Graber, were getting married.

Jason was excited. Allen and Philip, along with most of their former school mates and their parents, were planning to go. A large bus had been chartered.

But Peter Kauffman soon informed his family they could forget about going. "We've got to get the corn in," he said. "I can't see why *anyone* would decide to get married right over corn harvest, of all times! Besides, we don't have the money to go traipsing off to a wedding!"

They had to accept it. But Jason was mad. "Corn harvest indeed!" he fumed to Heidi. "What difference will one day make?!"

"I don't know," answered Heidi, "but he also said we don't have the money."

"No money!" Jason scoffed. "Heidi, Dad is probably the richest man in the whole community! He just plain doesn't want to go!"

"Well, at least Josiah and Margaret will be moving to our community," Heidi offered. "Then we'll get to see them more often."

"Huh." Jason wasn't interested in that part. What irked him was that they couldn't even take one day off to go to the wedding.

"WHY DON'T YOU come home with me?" Allen invited one Sunday after church. "We can walk back here for the singing."

Philip and Jason agreed and the three friends made their way across the field to Allen's home.

"You got all your corn in?" Philip asked Jason.

"Yeah."

"Well, you beat us," Philip laughed. "But then I think you do every year."

Jason shrugged.

"Hey, why didn't you go along to the wedding on Thursday?" Allen asked.

"'Cause we had to stay home and harvest corn, that's why!" Jason didn't even try to hide the bitterness in his voice.

"You mean you couldn't even take a day off for a wedding?" Philip was incredulous.

Bootprints

"That's exactly what I mean!" Usually Jason didn't talk about his home life. But right now he didn't care. "That's why we're always the first ones to get our field work done. Because we'd probably not get to take a day off, if it'd be our own funeral. The most important thing in life to Dad is his stupid work."

There was an awkward silence. "Well, that's too bad," Philip said. Then he changed the subject.

LATER THAT DAY Philip brought up another subject. One which was to hound Jason for months to come. The boys were comfortably sprawled in Allen's bedroom, munching popcorn. That's when Philip spoke. "Have you two thought anything about joining instruction classes next spring?"

Jason gaped at Philip in stunned silence. Then he looked at Allen. He looked almost as startled as Jason felt.

Allen was the first to find his voice. "I-I guess I haven't considered it. I mean, most of the boys wait until they are seventeen or eighteen."

"We'll be seventeen next summer," Philip reminded him.

"Yes, but…" Allen shrugged and fell silent.

Philip quirked an eyebrow at Jason.

"I-I haven't thought about it either," Jason admitted finally. "Are you going to?"

Philip smiled. "I'd like to. I'd like if we could do this together. We've done almost everything else together." He looked at his friends. "But I don't want to pressure you. This is an important step and we have to make our own decision."

Jason's thoughts were confused. Join church?! So soon? They were only sixteen! What was Philip's big hurry?

Allen asked him. "What made you decide to join so soon?"

"Well," Philip hesitated. "It's a long story, but I guess if you want to know…"

"We do," Allen assured him. Jason tapped his fingers nervously against his popcorn bowl. He nodded.

"For a while now," Philip began, "I've been feeling sort of confused and mixed up. Kinda lost even. And I hurt inside. It was an empty hurt. Have you ever felt that way?"

Allen nodded. Jason shrugged.

Philip took another bite of popcorn. "I felt really bad. I was terribly afraid the end of the world would come. I knew if it did, I would go to hell, because I'm a sinner."

Jason stared. Philip sinful? Philip?! Philip was better than he was.

"Then finally the other evening I talked with Dad. I told him how I was feeling, and I asked him a lot of questions." Philip took a deep breath. "I'm so glad I did. He – knew exactly how I felt, and explained everything."

Jason squirmed. "Just what has that got to do with joining church?"

"I'm getting to that in a minute," Philip said patiently. "Like I said, I felt so sinful and ugly. Dad said it was God, speaking through my conscience. He said the reason I felt so empty was because God placed a void in every person's heart that can't be filled with anything except God.

"He said people try to fill the void with other things, like popularity, sports, lust, drugs even. But as long as we don't surrender our lives to God and invite him into our hearts, we'll feel empty and miserable. And that is exactly how I felt. I was tired of it. I chose right then to give my life to God. I confessed all my sins and asked God to forgive me. And you know, boys, ever since then I've felt peaceful. The empty hurt is gone."

Something hot and fierce rose up inside Jason. It pressed his heart till he nearly gasped for breath. He had never heard talk like this before. He stared at Philip, bewildered. Why had this happened to a good boy like Philip? Would it happen to him? He cleared his throat and glanced at Allen, who seemed intent on cleaning his fingernails.

When his friends were silent, Philip continued, "That's why I want to be baptized now, because I accepted Christ. Dad explained to me that once a person experiences the New Birth, he will desire to receive baptism and be part of the church. And I do."

Bootprints

Finally Allen spoke. "Well, Philip, I'm glad for you, but I don't know about me. I must have some time to think it over."

"Me too," Jason agreed swiftly. "But hey, don't you think it's high time we head back to the singing?" He was grateful when the others agreed and the subject of joining church was dropped.

THE SUBJECT MIGHT have been dropped, but it didn't keep Jason from thinking about it. Not that he wanted to. He tried to forget. He couldn't. Not that evening, or the next day, or the next. It haunted him for weeks. Jason couldn't understand it. Philip's decision to join church was completely different from Matthew's.

Jason remembered distinctly the evening last spring when he'd heard Dad confronting Matthew in the milk house. "You joining church this spring?"

"Ah, probably not," came Matthew's uneasy answer.

"Why not?!"

"Well, uh, I-I'm just not ready yet."

Jason knew well enough why Matthew wasn't ready. He knew all about the parties Matthew and his buddies had Sunday nights after the singings. Smoking, drinking, girls… Matthew lived hard and wild. Jason wondered if Dad had found out about it.

"What?!" Jason heard Dad explode. "You're eighteen and not ready to settle down yet? Well, I'm telling you one thing, any boy of mine who doesn't settle down and join church at a respectable age won't get a cent of the inheritance! Not a cent!" With that he stormed out the door.

Matthew had joined church that spring.

THINKING BACK, JASON couldn't remember his Dad giving any other reason for joining church. It was just something you did at a certain age. Or else.

Jason sighed and rubbed his eyes. He was supposed to be fixing the fence, but it was too hard to concentrate. He pried a broken insulator off a post and tossed it into the fence row. "Can't understand why

Dad even wants us to join church," he muttered. "All he does is make trouble, then criticize the ministers when they talk to him."

Jason recalled the times the ministry had approached his father. Mostly it was about certain business deals, or his attitudes against other brethren in the church. Jason dreaded seeing the ministers almost as much as his father did. It always resulted in a heated tirade against the ministry at the dinner table.

"The trouble is, not one of them is a real businessman," he'd snap. "And only one of the lot is a farmer. And look at his farm! I'd be ashamed to live in a weedy dump like that!" His eyes bulged. "They just don't know how to use their heads and get ahead in life. A lazy lot if you ask me!"

Jason had seen his mother trying to stop the conversation, but Dad always ignored her. He kept right on ranting, and without fail he concluded bitterly, "This church is nothing but a heap of hypocrites!"

"Why would he think his children would want to belong to a church like that anyway?" Jason gritted his teeth and pulled the fencing tightly against the corner post. "It just doesn't make sense!"

He remembered Philip's explanation. *Dad explained to me that once a person receives the New Birth, he desires baptism. And I do.*

Jason shook his head. Who was right? How was he to know?

JASON TENSED AS Bishop Mose tottered to his feet. He looked at the wrinkly face and silvery beard and knew what was coming next.

"In two weeks we will be starting instruction classes," Mose announced. "If there are any young people who desire baptism, they can let one of the ministry know this week." He paused and glanced kindly at the young people. "We welcome all who desire to come."

Mose sat down and slowly Jason let out his breath. He shifted his feet beneath the bench and clasped his hands. What should he do? He knew what Philip would do. He would go, and gladly. He was so happy these days. It irked Jason sometimes.

Jason peeked at Allen. What would he do? The boys hadn't talked

{82}   *Bootprints*

about it since that time in Allen's bedroom. Jason had no idea how Allen felt by now.

He found out after church. "Have you decided yet what you'll do?" Allen asked as they stood waiting until dinner was ready.

Jason shuffled his feet in the gravel. "Not for sure."

"Well, I decided last week I'll join," Allen announced. "I told Dad and he was real pleased."

So Allen and Philip were both joining. Somehow Jason felt left behind. Left out. If they joined and he didn't, would they still be friends? Or would things be different? Jason didn't like the idea. Maybe he should join too, if his friends were going to.

MAYBE HE SHOULD. Jason wrestled with it all week. On Monday he decided he would. On Tuesday he decided he wouldn't. On Wednesday he didn't know. Jason knew he had no desire to join this church. Wasn't it full of hypocrites? But he knew if he didn't join this year his father would same as force him to next year. Or the next. He'd rather do it on his own accord, when his friends were joining anyway.

By Saturday Jason had once more decided he would. He'd talk to Deacon Henry tomorrow morning before church and tell him. Should he talk with Dad too? Allen and Philip had talked with their fathers.

Jason dreaded to do it, but he knew he should. He dawdled in the kitchen until the other children had gone upstairs. He took a long drink, trying to ease the thumping of his heart. He walked into the living room. Dad's face was hidden behind the voluminous pages of *The Budget*.

"Uh-- Dad?"

"Huh?" The voice was distracted.

Jason took the plunge. "I decided to join church this spring."

Dad's head shot up like a bullet. "Whatever for? You're only sixteen!"

"Allen and Philip are joining."

"You're too young to understand what it's all about."

A surge of anger gave Jason a sudden boldness. "Well, what *is* it all about?"

Bootprints {83}

Dad cleared his throat and rattled *The Budget*. "The ministers explain that in the instruction class." He blinked at Jason. "I guess you can join if you insist, but I still think you're pretty young. I just hope you know what you're doing."

Jason stumbled up the stairs.

JASON AWOKE THE next morning feeling sick. His head throbbed and his eyes burned. There was a dull ache in his chest. He groaned. He knew he hadn't slept more than two hours. He had battled all night, trying to make up his mind. This morning he still didn't know.

"Jason!" His mother's soft voice drifted up the stairs. "Are you awake?"

"Yeah." Jason got up, fumbled with his clothes, and staggered down the stairs.

Mom met him in the kitchen. "Jason, it made me very happy to hear you want to join church. I don't think sixteen is too young." She looked at him with concerned eyes. "Don't let what Dad said change your mind."

Jason nodded as he pulled on his boots. Relief came strong. He felt a little better as he headed toward the barn. "I'll go through with it," he muttered. "Nothing Dad says can stop me."

JASON ARRIVED AT church early, the same time as Henry. He followed the deacon to the barn. "Um, I'd like to join church too," he croaked in a near whisper.

Deacon Henry smiled. "I'm glad to hear that, Jason. Nothing makes us happier than seeing young people dedicate their lives to God. It's the most important choice a person can make." He placed a hand on Jason's shoulder. "God bless you, son."

Jason struggled with his emotions as he left the barn. Henry's response did something to his heart. He stood behind his buggy and brushed away several tears. Why couldn't Dad be more like Henry? Henry always made him feel good. He knew he liked Henry, even if his father didn't.

Bootprints

Jason blew his nose. Then he squared his shoulders and walked toward the house. He would do it. He would! Even if he didn't understand. Mom believed in him, and so did Henry.

MARGARET GINGERICH SAT with the other young women and watched the ministers file out of the church room. She waited. Philip stood. So did Allen. And… and then Jason! The three young boys followed the ministers out of the room.

Margaret closed her eyes. Her pupils, her children, taking this important step. Her heart overflowed with joy. Somehow seeing Jason's choice made all her efforts with him worth it. "Help them, Lord, to be true," she whispered as two shiny drops fell on her lap.

CHAPTER TEN

JASON SHIFTED THE sweaty harness from Billy's back and heaved it onto its hook on the wall. Billy stamped his foot and shoved Jason's shoulder with his head. "Patience," Jason grunted, sinking the feed scoop into the barrel of oats. "I'm hungry too, but I don't act like that!"

Tall gray shadows swooped at Jason as he came out of the barn. His boots, bigger now than Dad's, clopped for the house. He could hardly wait for supper. Chicken salad. That's what Heidi had said they were having when she brought him a drink. Chicken salad and rhubarb dumplings.

Mom's dumplings were the best in the country. Tender biscuits wrapped around fresh rhubarb, floating in a pan of syrup – Jason hurried. Past the barn. Past the granary. Around the corner of the milk house.

A puddle of light oozed from the milk house. Was someone still out there? Or had one of the younger boys forgotten the light – again? They could be so careless…

Bootprints {87}

Jason's boots grumbled to the milk house. He had no time for delays. He was tired and hungry.

He ducked his head as he went through the doorway. What was that noise? He stopped short.

Dad was beating Luke with a broomstick. *Whack!* Luke was small-boned and slender, like Mom's side of the family. Hunched in the flickering light, he looked frail. *Whack.* The sound bounced across the walls.

Luke's lips were pressed in a thin, hard line, struggling to hold back the screams. His dark eyes bulged in his white face. *Whack.* Sweat dripped from his forehead. He swayed.

"STOP!" Jason lunged suddenly at his father. "Stop right now!"

Dad whirled around, yanking his arm free from Jason's grasp. "Who do you think you are?" he shouted. His eyes blazed. He flailed the broomstick.

Jason ducked, a second too late. The broomstick smashed into his face, just below his left eye.

Jason staggered. His teeth rattled. He looked at Dad, disbelieving.

Dad was panting. "That'll teach you to interfere!" But his voice had lost some of its bite. He flung the broomstick to the floor. "Get out of here. Both of you!"

Jason stumbled to the house. *He hit me!* Gingerly he touched his throbbing face. *Me! And I'm seventeen years old!*

Mom and the girls were busy in the sewing room. Jason slipped through the empty kitchen. He glanced at the table. His place was neatly set. A chicken salad sandwich lay folded in a napkin. The half-empty pan of rhubarb dumplings and a pitcher of milk waited beside his plate. He turned his face aside and kept walking. He wasn't hungry.

He headed through the living room and up the stairs. "I hate him!" he thought.

"I hate him!" the steps creaked under his heavy feet.

{88}   *Bootprints*

PETER KAUFFMAN PACED back and forth. Had that really happened? He hadn't meant to hit Jason. Not in the face. Not that hard. Suppose he'd broken his jaw? His own boy. People would never forgive him, or let him forget. He'd be marked, like Cain in the Bible.

It was all Jason's fault. If he hadn't interfered, it wouldn't have happened. Jason had no right to stick his nose into affairs that were none of his business. The boy needed to be taken down a notch.

Peter kicked the broomstick, and it rattled against the wall. Why did he always have to lose his temper? He was almost fifty years old and still couldn't control himself. Peter shook his head in misery. He was a failure. He would never amount to anything, just like his father had said.

His father had always liked Leroy better. Leroy was older. Leroy did everything right. He had lots of friends. Leroy was a money-maker; he could squeeze a profit out of thin air.

"You need to be more like Leroy," his father would say.

All his life Peter had tried. He was determined to be successful, no matter what the cost. He would show his father. Leroy too.

Today, Peter's farm was a success. His children were not.

Peter couldn't understand. Hadn't he trained them right? Hadn't he been faithful in the use of the rod? Yet his sons were all so stubborn. Rebellious even. They didn't respect him.

Peter dropped his head. What good did a nice farm do, if he didn't have his family under control? Or his temper?

Peter hated himself every time he flew into a rage. He'd always been angry, as long as he could remember. Angry at his father and brother. Angry at his schoolmates, who mocked him. Angry- at life.

Peter was a strong man, but he wasn't strong enough to overcome his anger. He felt trapped. He was a failure.

Peter shuddered to remember the bone-jarring thud against Jason's face. Maybe he should tell him he hadn't meant to do it.

No, an apology was a sign of weakness. He had enough of a struggle to maintain his position without telling his children he was sorry.

They'd never respect him then.

Peter Kauffman sighed. He turned off the light and started for the house. The house was dark too.

JASON LOCKED THE bedroom door. There was a mirror above his dresser. An ugly bruise stood out on his cheek. He probed carefully along his jaw. Was it broken?

Only bruised, he decided. It hurt. He turned away from the mirror. Walked to the window and stared into the darkness. Crying was for babies. He thought of his father and rage choked him. What kind of father would hit his son in the face with a broomstick?

Sometimes Jason wondered if Dad had any heart at all. He was like a monster sometimes. Jason hated that man.

His thoughts were interrupted by a clatter of hooves outside. Who was coming? Jason flopped on the bed. He didn't care. He groaned as pain shot through his face. Maybe he should ask Mom for some Tylenol. He needed something to numb his heart too.

Footsteps sounded on the stairs. Then a knock at his door. Jason sat up. "Who is it?"

"Me. Allen. Can I come in?"

Jason tried to smooth his hair as he headed for the door. He winced at himself in the mirror. What would Allen think?

Jason opened the door. "Come on in."

"You weren't in bed already, were you?"

"Nope. Just lying here thinking."

"Well, I won't keep you long… Hey! What happened to you?"

Jason looked away. Should he tell? Who was he protecting anyway? He looked at Allen. "Dad walloped me a good one."

Allen looked horrified. "Wh – why?"

"'Cause he was mad at me, that's why!" Jason stalked to the window and stared out. "I'm telling you, Allen, you have no idea how it is to live with a father who doesn't love you. Sometimes I just feel like running away from home!"

Bootprints

There was an awkward silence. Allen cleared his throat. "Well, I know how you could leave for a few days."

Slowly Jason turned around. "How?"

"My uncle John's family is leaving day after tomorrow to visit some friends up north," Allen explained. "They'll be gone for a week and wondered if I could round up some boys to help with their chores while they're gone. They said it'll take at least three of us. Philip's going to help. Thought it'd be fun if you'd come too."

Jason nodded. "I'd like to, but I don't know what Dad will say. He's pretty tightfisted with his favors."

"Well, let's go ask him now," Allen suggested. "If you can't go, I'll have to ask somebody else yet."

The boys tramped down to the living room. Peter saw Sarah draw in her breath when she saw Jason's face. He shifted uneasily. He wondered if Allen knew what had happened.

Jason told him what Allen had said. "Do you think I could help?"

Peter scratched his head. He didn't approve of people traipsing over the country, leaving their work for other people to do. Shiftless, that's what it was! Peter looked at his son, trying to ignore the bruise. It was getting darker. It glared at him, and Peter found he couldn't say no. He didn't say yes either. "Suit yourself."

"GUESS WHAT!" ALLEN announced as he walked into the barn Friday evening.

Jason and Philip paused in their milking. "Must be something pretty exciting the way you look," Philip grinned.

"It is. You know Ken Walker, the boy who works on our crew? Well, he offered to take us to Clearview tomorrow night."

"What's at Clearview?"

"The race track. They have horse races every Saturday night during June. Won't that be cool?"

"Say, wouldn't it!" Jason was all for it. "But what about the chores here?"

Bootprints

"No problem. We wouldn't go till six-thirty and if we start chores early, we can be done by then."

"But that's Saturday evening," Philip protested. "Would our parents let us do that?"

"They don't have to know," Allen assured him. "We'll be here for the night anyway to get an early start with the chores Sunday morning. Why would they care? There's nothing wrong with it. We drive horses. What's wrong with us going to watch other people drive theirs?"

Philip was still uneasy. "I don't suppose watching the horses would be wrong," he said hesitantly, "but what about the betting, drinking, smoking…"

"C'mon, Philip," Jason was getting irked. "We wouldn't do any of those things! All we'd do is watch the horses."

"I know, but…" Philip paused. "I don't like doing things behind my parents' backs."

"Hey, that's the only way to have fun sometimes!" Jason was impatient.

A hurt look flickered across Philip's face. He turned and went outside to feed the calves.

Jason rolled his eyes at Allen. Allen grinned and opened the door to let in another batch of cows.

As Jason tore off some paper towels, he saw Allen pulling something out of his pocket, a little round can. Jason stepped closer. Now what was that? *Skoal,* it said on the lid. Where had Allen gotten that?

Allen flicked off the lid. He withdrew a pinch of something and dropped it inside his lip. He held out the can. "Want some?"

Jason didn't reach for it. "Where'd you get it?"

"Ken got it for me. Sure you don't want some?"

Jason shook his head. "No, thanks." He was keeping busy with the cows.

"Suit yourself. It's good stuff." Allen winked. He stuck the can back into his pocket and grabbed a milker. "Just don't be like Philip," he warned.

JASON WASN'T LIKE Philip. He was going to the horse race. On Saturday evening he arrived at John's fifteen minutes early. Allen had already brought the cows in. He grinned at Jason. "You in?"

"You bet!"

Philip was quiet when he showed up. He barely said hello.

"What's wrong with you?" Allen asked. "You sick?"

Philip was busy. "No."

"Well, what's the problem? Aren't you excited about tonight?"

"I'm not going."

"Why not?"

"I just don't think we should."

"Well." Allen raised his eyebrows at Jason and Jason shook his head. "Your loss, Philip."

Philip went on milking.

"You sure?" Jason prodded. "Nobody has to find out."

Philip shook his head. "I just don't feel right about it."

"I feel just fine," Jason said to Allen. They grinned.

JASON AND ALLEN finished choring and raced to the house to shower. They were waiting when Ken drove up. Jason caught a glimpse of Philip at the window and felt bad. Why couldn't he just go along? Ever since they'd joined instruction class, Philip saw danger everywhere. He was no fun anymore.

Ken and Allen chatted all the way to Clearview. Jason liked Ken's fresh haircut and easy laugh. His hat was cool too.

The racing grounds were already full of people when they arrived. Jason and Allen had no idea where to go, but Ken did. They stood in line to buy tickets, then followed him to their places in the stands.

While they were waiting for the race to begin, Ken fished a little round can from his hip pocket. He dropped a wad inside his lip and handed the can to Allen. "Need a buzz?"

Allen reached into his pocket. "Got my own."

"Oh, yeah, sure." Ken offered the can to Jason. "You dip?"

Bootprints {93}

Jason hesitated. Should he? The can loomed in front of him. He shifted uneasily. "Uh, no, thanks."

"Sure." Ken put the can away, but not before Jason caught the look he flashed at Allen. His hands tightened around his can of soda. He wanted Ken to like him.

Soon they were caught up in the excitement of the race. Jason found himself screaming and yelling as the horses thundered around the track. All too soon it was over. He popped open the lid of his soda and guzzled it down.

When the races were over they didn't go straight home. Ken pulled into a Shell station and got out to pump fuel. "I'm going to pick up some more dip," he told them. He glanced at Allen. "You need some more?"

"Might as well get some if we're here anyway."

They followed Ken into the service station. Allen elbowed Jason. "Come on, man. Why don't you let Ken get you a can. You can always ditch it later if you don't like it."

Ken's boots were sharp. Jason had seen boots like that in a magazine. He found himself nodding. "Okay – whatever." Dip made you feel good, Allen had said. Well, he'd see. He'd make up his own mind. Maybe he wouldn't like it.

He pushed the can into his pocket as they drove away from the station. Maybe he would try it out tonight yet.

As they neared Ken's apartment on the edge of town, Ken checked his watch. "Hey, guys, it's not late yet. Want to stop in and watch a movie or something? We could see that new one I told you about, Allen."

Allen and Jason glanced at each other. Jason wanted to go home. He was already feeling uncomfortable about the race. That, and the can in his pocket. But Ken was nice. He didn't want to offend him. He didn't want to be an oddball. "Sounds like fun to me," he answered lightly.

"Just great," said Allen.

Jason dragged himself out of bed and fumbled clumsily with his clothes. His head pounded and he felt sick to his stomach. He groaned as he stumbled toward the barn. The movie had reminded him of those magazine pictures he'd been trying to forget for years. A couple of times he had tried to think of something else, but it was no use. He had wanted to look.

This morning he was miserable, but maybe he could have felt worse. At least he hadn't taken the beer Ken had offered.

Allen and Philip were in the parlor already. Allen looked as wretched as Jason felt. Jason resented Philip's happy expression.

"Did you have fun at the race?" Philip asked.

Jason couldn't remember much about the race. "It was okay, I guess," he mumbled.

"I didn't even hear you come back," Philip said. "I waited up till ten o' clock."

"Yeah, it went later than we expected." Jason wasn't about to tell Philip they hadn't come home till one-thirty this morning.

"I don't want breakfast," Jason yawned as they walked to the house after chores. "I'm going to take a nap before it's time to head for church."

"Me too," agreed Allen.

"I won't bother making breakfast for just myself," Philip decided. "I want to study the articles we'll be having today anyway."

Jason rolled his eyes at Allen as they tramped up the stairs. "I never bother," he muttered. "It's the ministers' job to explain them."

Allen nodded and fell onto the bed. "Think he'll tattle on us?"

"I don't think so." But Jason wondered. Suppose he did? "Well, don't give him any details or he might. We don't want that to happen."

On Thursday evening Jason looked up from cleaning out the horse stalls to see Dad scowling in the doorway. With a jerk of his head he motioned for Jason to follow him.

Jason propped his pitchfork against the wall. What was Dad mad about now? Did he know? He stepped outside. The sun blinded him at first. Oh no. What were Bishop Mose and Deacon Henry doing here? Had they – ? Did they – ?

"Hello, Jason." That was Henry.

Jason fought down the urge to run away. "Hi."

Mose prodded a clump of grass with his cane. "We need to talk with you, Jason. Your father too."

"No!" Jason screamed silently. "Whatever you've got to say, *don't* say it in front of my father!"

But they did. They had found out about the horse race. They warned him about the evil of such places and asked Peter if he knew anything about it.

Peter didn't, but he hated to admit it. How had his boy managed to sneak off to a horse race without his knowing it? He quivered with rage and humiliation, and the effort it took to suppress it in front of the ministers. He could hardly wait for them to leave.

"I know you're not a church member yet, Jason," Moses said. "But since you're in instruction class, we needed to address this." Jason stared silently at his feet. He refused to look at the ministers. Refused to look at Dad. Philip must have tattled. He wanted to hit him. The rat. Just see if he ever found out anything again.

WITH A LAST glance at Jason's sullen face, Henry untied the horse from the hitching rack, then climbed into the buggy beside Mose. For awhile the two men jostled along in silence.

"I just don't have a good feeling about our visit," Mose ventured at last. "I had hoped we could resolve this problem, but somehow I think we've made it worse."

Henry nodded. He had felt the tension too. "I want to be careful not to pass judgment," he said, "but I've picked up over the years that the relationship between Peter and his sons isn't the best. I suggest after this we talk to them separately. It might bring better results."

"Hmmm, maybe you're right." Mose stroked his beard. "Maybe Peter is part of the problem."

"It wasn't Philip," Allen told Jason that Sunday after church.

Jason scowled. "What do you mean it wasn't Philip? Who else would it have been?"

"Blame Ken. He asked me at work if we'd like to go again this Saturday. Said there'd be lots of pretty girls there. I tried to get him to shut up, but he was too dense to get it. Dad heard him, and so did Uncle Joe. Joe's the one who trotted to the ministers."

Jason felt like someone had knocked the wind out of him. Ever since the ministers' visit, he felt like he hated Philip. This morning when Philip had come around shaking hands, he had felt more like slapping his hand than shaking it. He hadn't been able to meet Philip's eyes or return his smile.

Now Allen was claiming that Philip was innocent. Jason was disgusted. Disgusted at Ken and even more disgusted at himself.

As if on cue, Philip came ambling across the yard. His face was friendly, but uncertain. "Mind if I join you?"

"Of course not," said Allen.

Philip folded his frame beside Jason's. Jason gave him a quick smile. Just to let Philip know it was okay now.

Or was it? Philip hadn't tattled on them. But just knowing how he'd felt about the horse race in the first place kept a little resentment alive in Jason's heart.

CHAPTER ELEVEN

JASON FUMBLED UNDERNEATH the buggy seat. Where had he put it? He groped to the right. Nothing. To the left. He touched the little round can and drew it out. The lettering glinted in the sun. *Skoal.*

He liked it now. The first few times he'd tried to like it, but it had made him a little sick.

"That's normal," Allen had told him. "You'll soon get used to it – be riding high like me. Hey, you know what Ken said? The company mixes in tiny pieces of metal so it rubs your lips open and goes straight to your bloodstream. Kinda smart, huh?"

Jason set the can beside him. It was almost empty. With a slight tug on the reins, he drew Starburst to a halt at Bonner's Crossroads.

A dump truck rattled past in a flurry of coughing, then a little blue car. Jason glanced at the can on the seat. He shifted nervously and checked the road. "Get up, Starburst."

Jason's fingers tapped tensely against the lid. It had not been a good morning. Sunday mornings never were. They had to hurry so they wouldn't be late for church. Hurry through the chores. Hurry through breakfast. Hurry out the lane, just as fast as the horses could trot. This morning Jason hadn't felt like hurrying. He dreaded the scheduled baptismal service. Getting down on his knees in front of all those people. The thought was unnerving.

Jason had dawdled with the milking. He wondered if there was still a way to back out. He could tell Mom he was sick. His stomach did feel queasy, and if Mom knew, she would likely pour some Pepto Bismal down his throat and send him to bed.

But Mom was so happy he was going to be baptized. It seemed everyone was happy for him.

This past week he had received a card from Josiah and Margaret, telling how they rejoiced at his decision. Deacon Henry had talked to him several times this summer, saying how wonderful it was to see young people find joy in serving the Lord.

Where was the joy, Jason wondered grimly. He sure hadn't experienced any so far. And what was the big deal about being baptized? He could hardly wait to get it over with.

"Get a move on, boy. Have you forgotten it's Sunday?"

Jason had jumped at Dad's impatient voice. He fumbled with a milker. "So what?" So what if he dared to talk back to his dad. "I'm not planning on leaving early this morning anyhow. The other boys don't arrive until five minutes before the services start."

"You will leave at the usual time!" Dad's voice rose. "We always get there right after the ministers. People expect it."

"I don't care what people expect." Jason straightened his back and looked down at Dad. "You can't force me."

He couldn't explain to his dad, of course, his phobia of having the men swarm by this morning to shake hands. Smiling solemnly and saying what a blessing it was to see the church grow. How they certainly hoped he would be a good, strong pillar, supporting the rules and everything.

"Do you call yourself a Christian?" Dad demanded. "Talking back to your father like this! You're not fit to be baptized!"

{100} *Bootprints*

A piece of plastic crackled in the ditch. Starburst shied, jolting Jason back to the present. The yellow lines on the road flashed under the buggy wheels. He didn't want to be baptized. But to have Dad scream in his face he wasn't fit? Jason clenched his jaw. He fingered the can. What would Dad say if he knew about this?

Not that it mattered. If he wasn't a Christian anyway… Slowly he removed the lid.

BISHOP MOSE WAS preaching. "I like to think of it this way. While we are sinners, we are like a thorn in Jesus' crown. But once we turn our backs to the devil and become saved, we are like a star in Jesus' crown." He smiled. "This morning I trust these three boys are stars."

Jason picked his fingernails. Mose was old and senile. Even his sermons sounded like it. Whoever heard of being stars and thorns in Jesus' crown?

He sneaked a peek at the clock. Would it ever be time for the ceremony? His stomach was in knots and his suit coat was stifling. He watched a fly buzz against a window pane. Listened to the shrill howls of a baby. Counted the number of buggies he could see through the window. Why did so many people from the other district have to flock in today?

Finally the time came. Somehow Jason got himself folded in the correct position on the floor. "Yes, I believe that Jesus Christ is the Son of God," he said. He looked at Mose's shoes in front of him and wondered if they were as ancient as he was.

Deacon Henry poured the water from a little tin cup. Jason felt an unexpected burst of emotion. "Maybe," he'd thought last night, "once I'm baptized I'll feel the joy and peace everyone keeps talking about." He found himself holding his breath. Waiting.

The water trickled down his neck. Splashed on the floor. There was silence in the room. Silence in his heart.

SARAH BLINKED AS the door closed behind Jason. He looked so tall, heading for the barn. Her mind was still spinning. She turned back to the cake she had been mixing when Jason had unexpectedly stepped into the kitchen. His question had been abrupt. "Mom, do you have time to talk?"

"Of course." She'd laid down her spoon, puzzled. What would her eighteen-year-old son want to talk about to her in the middle of the day?

"I'd like to have a date with Lori Byler. Is that okay with you?"

"Oh." Sarah nearly dropped her measuring cup. Lori Byler? Lori? She was a pretty girl, close to Jason's age, but… Sarah realized that was all she knew about her. The family had moved into the community only a year ago. "I don't have any objections, Jason, though I don't know her very well. But I'll talk to Dad about it and see what he says."

"Okay." Jason nodded self-consciously. He took a drink, then left.

Sarah watched him now. Her son had grown up. Her heart gave a strange little twist. Here Matthew was making wedding plans and Jason wanted to date. Already. Her sons, wanting homes of their own. "I wonder what kind of husbands they'll make?" Sarah wondered suddenly.

The door slammed and Sarah jumped. She must get busy. Suppose it was Peter? He did not like to come into the house and find her not working. She scurried to her cake.

It was Peter, sure enough. "What was Jason doing in here?"

Sarah clutched her spoon, trying to calm herself. "Oh, uh, just talking, I guess."

"Talking!" Peter's voice clattered through the kitchen. "Of all things! Taking off from work to *talk!*"

Sarah stabbed her spoon into the batter. "He had a question for me." She glanced at Peter out of the corner of her eye. "For you too."

Peter looked blank.

"He wants to date Lori Byler and – and wondered if we have any objections."

Bootprints

He blinked. "Lori Byler? Who's that?"

"Levi's daughter. You know, they just moved -"

"Oh, yes. Well. I don't see any reason why he has to take off from work for that. The boy's never going to get ahead in life if he's not a little more aggressive." Peter's face was stern. "What did you tell him?"

"I told him I don't know her well, but that I'd talk to you."

"Hmm."

Sarah began stirring the batter again. She heard Peter shuffle his feet on the linoleum. Tap his fingers against the counter top. Now where was she? Eggs. She must have two eggs. Peter's tapping made her nervous. What was he thinking? She wanted to look at him. Instead she went to the refrigerator and took out two eggs.

"I don't know Levi well," Peter said, "but from what I've seen he's a good manager. He bought a big farm and has fixed it up pretty well already. They say he owns two more farms back in Pennsylvania. I guess if his daughter is anything like him, she ought to be okay."

Peter clomped to his desk, took out his checkbook, and went back outside. Sarah sighed with relief as she finally slid the cake into the oven. Now to sweep up the mud that Peter had tracked in…

JASON TRIED TO act nonchalant at the supper table. He felt his mother's eyes on him from time to time. Had she talked with Dad already? He wasn't hungry, but he helped himself to a piece of cake. He frowned when he saw it didn't have frosting again. Frosting made a cake better, but Dad didn't approve of frosting. "It's extravagant, all that sugar," he'd say. "Sugar prices are outrageous."

Jason chewed on the cake. It stuck in his throat, stirred the jitters in his stomach. "Hey, Heidi." He held up his glass. "Pass the milk."

After the evening prayer, Jason hurried upstairs. He didn't care to stay in the living room. It was unsettling, not knowing whether Dad knew or not.

Jason knew he should have talked to Dad, but he had been trying to get up the nerve for at least a month and hadn't been able to. Dad was so

Bootprints

unpredictable. Suppose he told him right off that Lori wasn't an option? Or that he was too young? Maybe eighteen was a bit young, but he was almost nineteen. Allen had been dating for several months already.

Lori was prettier than Allen's girlfriend. He pictured Linda – red hair, freckles, a little bit dumpy. He couldn't understand how Allen could act so proud of a girlfriend like Linda.

Lori now, she would make any boy proud. Dark hair, deep blue eyes, and a perfect figure. Suppose she wouldn't accept him? Jason got up and paced back and forth. No, he wouldn't even worry about that until he had his answer from his parents.

It irked Jason that he had to ask his parents in the first place. But the church required it, and Jason knew Dad would be furious if he didn't. If only his parents would be easier to talk with.

What would Dad say?

HE FOUND OUT the next morning. Mom met him in the kitchen as he was getting ready to go chore. "Dad and I have no objections to Lori," she said softly. "Like I said, we don't know her that well, but Dad thinks a lot of her dad."

Jason fingered his hat. He wanted suddenly to be a little boy again. Feel Mom's arms around him as she sung him lullabies. Stroked his hair. Soothed away his hurts. In the dark, chilly memories of his childhood, his mother's love shone. Jason swallowed. He nodded at Mom. "Thanks. I'll probably ask her Sunday then."

BUT HE CHICKENED out. He got her brother William to ask her for him. He waited nervously beside his buggy while William was gone. He swiped a speck of dust from the oilcloth. Yesterday when he'd washed and polished it, he'd been full of anticipation. Now he was uncertain. Suppose she didn't want him? Worthless Jason Kauffman. His throat tightened as he stared at the house. What was taking William so long?

By the time William came back, Jason's shirt was damp with sweat. He waited.

"She said she'd like some time to think it over. Is that okay?"

"Uh... sure." Slowly Jason let out his breath. At least it was better than a flat no.

"She said she'll try to have her answer ready by next Sunday. I think she was pretty surprised." William flashed him a grin.

LORI WAS SURPRISED. For one thing, she was barely eighteen. For another, she barely knew Jason Kauffman. She tried to picture him the next morning as she hung out the laundry. He was tall, had dark hair, and his eyes... they were brown, weren't they? He was really handsome, now that she stopped to think about it.

Try as she might, she couldn't remember anything noteworthy about him. He kept to himself and drove a nice horse. But otherwise... Lori shrugged and pinned an apron on the line. Maybe William could fill her in.

But William shook his head when she asked. "Jason doesn't talk much in a group. And he's quiet even if you talk to him alone. Sorry, Lori, I'm not much help, am I?"

"Keep praying about it," her father advised. "Take your time and don't rush into it."

Lori prayed. She debated. She thought. In the end, she told William to tell Jason he could take her home.

"CONGRATULATIONS, JASON!" PHILIP slapped his friend's back.

Jason grinned. In the past week he had received lots of congratulations. He enjoyed it, especially since they meant that Lori Byler, the prettiest girl in the community, was his girlfriend. "Thanks. So -" Jason raised his eyebrows, "it's your turn now. When are you going to ask a girl?"

Philip chuckled. "Probably not for a while yet. I'm in no hurry. Besides," his face turned sober, "there are lots of areas in my life I need to work on before I ask any girl. I still have some growing to do, especially spiritually."

Growing spiritually? Philip? Jason was bewildered, but he covered it with a quick nod. "Well, see you later." He turned and walked away. It seemed Philip became more odd the older he got.

"I can just see him becoming a preacher some day," Allen snorted when Jason repeated their conversation. "Have you ever heard such rot? By the time he gets around, all the girls will be gone!"

They laughed.

"Well, at least we got the ones we wanted," Allen stated. "I sure did."

"Uh-huh, me too."

Jason shook his head and wondered again how Allen could be so happy with Linda. Linda wasn't even pretty. Not compared to Lori.

JASON SOON DISCOVERED that Lori's beauty went beyond her face. The more time they spent together, the more he enjoyed being with her.

She would hurry out to greet him the moment she heard his buggy. "Hi, Jason!" Her smile would flash across her face, welcoming him.

Lori always tried to make their dates special. One time she fixed brownie sundaes in stem glasses. Another time she served tiny heart shaped taco tarts. The tarts were a calamity. Jason fumbled one from the plate. It crumbled across the starched tablecloth and collapsed in his hands. A blob of sour cream toppled down on his shoe. Red-faced, he looked at Lori.

"I guess they're kind of small for your hands," Lori apologized.

Jason couldn't fathom how such little things could be so difficult to transport to his mouth. Nor could he fathom why Lori hadn't made them a decent size in the first place. He sighed with relief when she put the tarts away and they settled down to talk.

Sometimes it was easy to keep the conversation moving. Other times there were gaps. Lori filled the gaps by asking questions. She wondered about Jason's daily life. His past. His family.

At first Jason was scared. What would Lori do if he told her about his dad? Would she believe him? Would she think it was his fault? Would she still want him?

Nobody had ever accepted him like Lori did. She'd given him a card two weeks ago. "I'm so thankful to have you for my special friend," she'd written. "You're a blessing to me."

Jason cherished that card. He took the pencil box off his dresser and put the card there instead. Every night before he went to bed, he picked it up and read it. Lori wanted *him* in her life. Who had ever wanted him before?

But there was so much Lori didn't know. His struggle with lust. Tobacco. Dad. Surely Lori wouldn't want him if she knew who he really was.

Jason sensed a wholeness in Lori. A freedom in her spirit. Her face was full of light and innocence.

How could he snuff that out by telling her about himself? Jason knew Lori had a good family. She'd never been scarred by his type of experiences. He could imagine her repulsion if she discovered the boy behind the walls. Her rejection of him.

Jason couldn't bear to think of losing Lori. She made him a person. A real human being. Not the worthless trash he'd always believed himself to be. He loved her. *He needed* her.

Lori kept asking questions. Probing into his life. His heart. Sometimes he told her a little, the things that didn't matter so much. Most of the time, he was evasive. It was too frightening to expose himself.

LORI TRIED TO figure out Jason. William was right, she decided. Jason was hard to get to know. Oh, he talked, but only about surface things. The horse he couldn't drive because of bowed tendon. The weather. The crops. Always the crops.

Lori knew these things were important. They were part of life. But she longed to go beyond that. What was he feeling? What were his goals and ambitions? How was his relationship with God? With his family? She asked him questions sometimes. She was puzzled when he didn't answer. Didn't he trust her?

"Don't push him," her mother advised. "Give him time to feel comfortable and safe. Maybe his family isn't used to sharing as openly as we are. If they aren't, it will probably take a while till he's ready to open up."

Lori tried to be understanding. But the longer they courted, the more she desired to know the man behind those eyes. What was it about those eyes that made her want to cry? They were too serious. Too full of... pain? Yes, it was pain.

Jason was hiding things from her. Lori was convinced of that.

HE STILL HADN'T shared anything with her when they found the puppy. They found it beside the road on the way home from the singing. "It must have been hit by a car," Jason said, as Lori worked over the puppy. Probing. Soothing. Murmuring reassurances.

She gathered the crumpled body into her arms. "I'm taking it home. We can't just leave it here."

Jason touched the curly head. Looked away at the shadowy tree line across the field. He couldn't stand it. The puppy's eyes. They begged up at him, frightened, helpless, and hurting. Hurting above all.

"Jason?"

Jason struggled to control himself. He glanced at Lori. At the puppy. He didn't really want the ugly thing. But he nodded reluctantly. "Come along."

A tiny smile flickered across Lori's face. "Thanks." She carried the puppy to the buggy.

At home, she carried it to the barn. Not caring about her good dress, she knelt on the floor, fixing a soft bed for it in the bottom of an old box. Jason thought he'd never seen his girlfriend more beautiful. Pouring herself out on a dog, a homely little mongrel she didn't even know.

A bird twittered sleepily from the eaves. A horse stamped. The puppy whined.

"He's in such pain, Jason." Lori looked up briefly. Jason was startled to see tears in her eyes. "I can't bear to see him suffering like this!"

Jason's throat tightened. He was seeing a side of Lori he hadn't seen before. She cared. She didn't need to – the puppy wasn't hers. It was

Bootprints

repulsive in its pain. Jason didn't want to look at it. It was too raw. Too nearly like the boy behind the walls. How could Lori get down on the floor and hold it?

If she cared that much about a dog… would she care about him too?

"I've always been scared of my dad," he told her later that evening. The words lurched from his throat. He forced himself to continue. "One time I hid from him." He told her about Barabbas, the way the floor had shaken beneath his hooves. How he had been scared a little bit of the bull, but more scared of Dad. He was still scared, even though he was now bigger and stronger than his father.

Silence fell over the kitchen when he finished. Jason stared at the tabletop, tracing and retracing the pattern on the tablecloth. What was Lori thinking? Would she still like him? He thought of the puppy. It was a lot like him. Forgotten, smashed, and unloved. But the puppy was only a puppy. He was Lori's boyfriend. Would she want a boyfriend who was weak and hurting like that?

Jason berated himself for having softened. For having allowed Lori to discover he wasn't the perfect man she thought he was. Fear stiffened him. She held in her hands a piece of his heart. He'd never given that to anyone before. He felt shaken and exposed.

Miserably he thought of Lori's eyes. He loved everything about her, but he loved her eyes most of all. He'd seen trust reflected there. Admiration. Love. Now he'd see rejection. He sat there in misery. The beautiful blue eyes, not wanting him any longer.

She deserved someone better. Someone who was strong outside, and inside too. He was weak. Insecure. Why had he asked her in the first place? Now he had to let her go. He wanted to tell her it was okay, but he couldn't. It *wasn't* okay.

The silence deepened into a roar. Finally he could stand it no longer. Using every ounce of his strength, he lifted his gaze.

Lori sat across the table. For the second time that evening, her eyes were filled with tears. Not only filled, but rolling down her cheeks.

CHAPTER TWELVE

JASON AND LORI had been dating for over a year. At times Jason couldn't believe he was still the same boy he used to be. How could a mere girl make such a difference?

But then Lori wasn't a mere girl. She was... *Lori*. She believed in him and no one had ever believed in him before. She looked up to him. Physically, because he was head and shoulders taller than she was. Emotionally because... Jason wasn't sure why. What did she see in him? Two other boys had requested her friendship before he had, and she could have chosen either of them. But she'd chosen him. It was still puzzling, even after a year, but it was thrilling too. To be accepted. Loved.

It was not as hard now to make it through the week, because at the end of it there was his visit with Lori. Being with Lori felt good. Not the kind of "happy good" he felt after dipping, but a nice, comfortable, satisfying good.

Lori was always concerned about him, ever since he'd told her about

Dad. "Did anything happen this week?" she'd ask.

It had, most times. Sometimes Jason told her about it and sometimes he didn't. What would she think if she knew how bad it *really* was?

There were other things he didn't tell Lori. He didn't tell her about the horse race, and he certainly didn't tell her about his dipping.

"I don't want to hurt her," he told himself. It was true, but not the whole truth. He didn't want to lose her. It was the most terrible thing he could think of. Lori walking out on him because of his addiction. If he could just keep it hidden until after they were married.

"Actually, it's not an *addiction*," he thought. "I only use it when I need it. Which reminds me, I'm almost out again. I must get some the next time I go to town."

He felt guilty thinking about it, as if he were betraying Lori. Maybe he was. But Lori didn't know how it was, living with a dad like his. And he only had her on Sundays. During the week he needed something else.

JASON HERDED THE grocery cart down the aisle. He detested grocery shopping. How was a man supposed to find what he needed amongst hundreds of other grocery items? He'd circled the store twice already in desperate pursuit of vinegar. Maybe he'd just have to skip it. But no, Mom was canning pickles, and the last thing she'd told him as he headed out the door was, "Now don't forget the vinegar."

Where would they keep it? He checked the cereal aisle and the snack aisle and even the toilet paper aisle. He felt clumsy, navigating his cart around so many people with their loaded carts. It was a zoo almost. If it weren't for the items he needed himself, he would never have offered to get Mom's groceries.

Finally the vinegar appeared beside the salad dressing. Jason seized a jug and loaded it gratefully into the cart. He had never been so glad to see something in his life. He scanned the list. That was all, for Mom. He needed shaving cream yet, and… why did he have to think of Lori now?

His heart hammered as he headed for the checkout line. Suppose

{112} *Bootprints*

Lori walked in and caught him? Maybe he should skip it – this time. But he needed it! Had needed it ever since Dad's chewing-out this morning. And he'd come all the way to town for this.

Jason's breath came quickly as the silver-haired lady in front of him fumbled with her pocketbook. It was almost his turn. He was disgusted at himself for being so paranoid all of a sudden. He'd done this before, dozens of times. His eyes darted around the store. No plain clothes in sight.

He pushed his cart to the counter and began unloading. He placed the vinegar on the counter. *I'll do it!* Baking soda. *I won't!* Brown sugar. *I will!* Cheese…

"Will that be all for you?" the cashier asked.

Desperately Jason scanned the store again. "Uh, yes, er, add two cans of *Skoal*, please. Mint flavored."

She was turning around, reaching for the cans, when Jason saw the hat. It bobbed briskly around the corner and headed straight toward him.

Mosie Bontrager's beady eyes pierced into Jason's as he walked past. The cashier placed the cans among Jason's other purchases. "That will be thirty-two even, sir," she said.

"Uh," Jason stuttered, "I, uh, I changed my mind. I don't want the tobacco after all."

"You what?"

"I-I guess I don't want it. Just take it off." Jason could feel the heat washing over his face. And where was Mosie?

The cashier gave him a queer look as she placed the cans back on the shelf behind her. Feeling breathless, Jason paid for the groceries and fled from the store.

Surely Mosie hadn't seen. He'd been too far away. Or hadn't he? He hoped Mosie would stay in the store until after he left. He did not want to speak with Mosie outside, alone.

Mosie stayed in the store, but that didn't stop Jason from worrying. He worried all the way home. How much had Mosie seen? And when

Bootprints {113}

had he sneaked into the store? It wouldn't have been so bad, had it been anyone except Mosie Bontrager. Mosie's sharp eyes and his habit of galloping to the ministers about every trivial issue had earned him the name "Nosy Mosie." Jason thought it suited him just right.

It seemed like a long time until Starburst jogged in the lane. Jason unhitched, then carried in the groceries. He did his chores and went to bed. The question stalked him every step of the way, like a cat stalking a mouse.

What had Mosie seen?

NOT THE TOBACCO, Jason decided at last. It was over a week later and he hadn't heard anything further concerning his harrowing encounter with Mosie. He started to relax.

Then the buggy came. The Kauffman family had just started supper when they heard it arrive. Jason glanced uneasily out the window. It had been here before. The same homely rattletrap, leaning perpetually to the right.

Jason scooped a bite of casserole into his mouth. Maybe they had come to talk with his father.

But they hadn't. Peter stormed back into the house. "They want to talk to you." He scowled at Jason.

"Me?" Jason tried to sound surprised. "Wonder what for?"

He took his time pulling on his boots. He watched the two men standing silently outside the house. Josiah was with Henry this time. Jason still wasn't used to seeing his former teacher with the ministers. He had to grudgingly admit he wasn't bad when it came to preaching, but…

"Good evening, Jason," they greeted as he stepped outside.

Jason nodded. He listened politely to their pleasant remarks about the weather and the crops. He wished they would get to the point. He had his answer ready.

"No, I didn't buy any tobacco," he answered in a bewildered voice when they told him what a "concerned brother" had said. "Now which store did you say that was supposed to have been?"

"Carver's Grocery." Josiah's keen eyes bored into Jason's.

"I was there last week," Jason said thoughtfully. "But I only got some groceries for Mom."

"Well, we're sure glad it's not true," Henry said warmly. "We hoped it wasn't."

Jason snorted as he watched them drive away. "A 'concerned brother' indeed! Well, Mr. Nosy, your concerns are empty this time." He laughed a short, hard laugh as he opened the door.

JASON WASN'T LAUGHING the next Sunday evening as he headed for Lori's place. What if she had heard the rumor too? What would she say? He imagined her blue eyes cloudy with disappointment. Would she think she'd made a mistake by choosing him instead of David? Or Mark? Mark was a good fellow. Maybe after tonight Lori would want him. Jason imagined the two of them together. Mark and Lori. Lori looking at Mark the way she looked at him.

No! Anger raged through him. Lori was his! He would fight for her with every ounce of his strength. But – his shoulders slumped – he couldn't force her.

Jason dreaded facing Lori. He slid his fingers behind the buggy seat and pulled out the little can. He'd gotten it yesterday, when he couldn't stand the craving any longer. He unscrewed the lid and looked at its contents. Miserable stuff, threatening his courtship. But he needed it – needed it now.

Lori's dad was in the barnyard when Jason drove in. He came to help Jason unhitch. "No singing tonight?"

"Not tonight." Jason tried to hide his nervousness. Why was Levi out here to meet him instead of Lori? Lori never saved her enthusiastic welcomes until he came inside. She was right there the moment he arrived. "Because"- her eyes would sparkle at him – "every moment counts!"

"Lori's finishing the supper dishes," Levi said. "Said to tell you to come on in."

Lori didn't turn from the sink when he entered. Methodically she placed a roasting pan into the drainer. Then a bowl. She glanced toward Jason, but didn't meet his gaze.

Jason tensed. This was not a good sign. He wished the rest of the family would stop being so friendly and leave them alone. He must bring up the subject before Lori did and explain how it was.

Slowly Lori hung up her dish towel. "Mom said we can visit on the sun porch as long as it's still daylight." Silently she led the way.

Usually Jason liked the sun porch with its wicker furniture and potted plants. But tonight he couldn't care less. He would gladly sit in a … a pig pen… if only Lori would stop being so frosty. He noticed two bowls of popcorn and two glasses of lemonade arranged on the table. Lemonade made with real lemons. Lori knew it was his favorite drink. Why had she made it if she was going to end their relationship within the next hour?

Jason felt paralyzed. *Suppose she would?*

An awkward silence brooded between them. Jason cleared his throat. How should he begin? "You're quiet tonight," he said finally. "Is – is something wrong?"

Lori looked at Jason. His handsome face, those brown eyes that had captured her from the first. "It can't be true," she thought. "It can't! But I must find out for sure, because if it is -"

"Well," she began. Her voice trembled. "Mosie Bontrager stopped in the other day to talk with Dad." She saw Jason's eyes narrow and stopped.

"So he passed that rumor on to you too?" His voice was harsh, almost.

"What rumor?"

"About me having bought tobacco at the grocery store."

"Then – it was just a rumor?"

"It sure was!" Jason leaned forward. "The ministers came to talk to me about it. But I'll just tell you what I told them. I bought groceries for Mom. That's all." He gazed into her eyes. "Please believe me, Lor. I did not buy any tobacco!"

He saw the tautness on Lori's face relax. "Oh, Jason, I'm so glad. Mosie claimed he saw you get it himself, but I didn't want to believe it. I just couldn't imagine you'd do something like that!"

Guilt hammered at Jason's temples. She believed him! And he was lying to her. He felt like a dirty, lowdown scoundrel. If he could just confess everything. But that would be even worse than if he'd told her right away. He looked at her. His girl. This was it. He'd stop dipping. If she believed in him, he would be man enough to resist it.

JASON TRIED HARD. He didn't chew on Monday or Tuesday. On Wednesday he had a fight with Dad. Desire tortured him. He opened the can and smelled it. This was the answer. Maybe he could taste it just a little. Surely a little pinch wouldn't hurt.

"No!" Jason's fingers twitched as he replaced the lid. "I won't!" Viciously he poked the can into its secret place beneath the buggy seat. Lori's face on the sun porch burned in his mind. He marched from the buggy shed, his jaw set.

A week passed, then two, three, and four. Four harrowing weeks. Jason couldn't forget the can on the buggy. But he didn't give in – not more than once or twice. "As long as I stay in control of it, it's not that bad," he reasoned.

One evening on his way to the house his ears caught a sound from the buggy shed. It sounded like a buggy door slamming. He hesitated, then walked toward the shed. He'd thought the others were all eating supper already. Maybe Allen had stopped by with that book he wanted to read.

But it was Dad, not Allen, whom he met in the shadowy doorway. Jason saw two things at once. Dad's stormy face and the can of tobacco in his hand.

"Who…? What…?" Jason's mind reeled. What had Dad been doing snooping through his buggy like that? Panic flooded him as he stared at his father.

Dad stared back, silent for a minute. Then a triumphant grin spread across his face. "Thought you could fool me, didn't you? Well, let me tell you one thing, I'm not as dumb as you think I am!" His grin faded and his voice thundered. "What do you think you're doing with this filth? Trying to get in trouble with the church and smear the Kauffman name?"

Anger tore through Jason like a swarm of red wasps. His father had been snooping! "What were you doing in my buggy?" he hissed.

Peter grinned again. Tauntingly. "It's my responsibility to see after my boys. And deal with their folly."

Would he tell the ministers? Jason wondered in horror. But surely not, if he was that concerned about his name being ruined. He looked at the cold smirk on Dad's face and his fury rose.

Jason took a fast step toward his father and ripped the can from his hands. "You think you're smart, don't you?" he shouted. He was pleased to see the grin wobble and disappear. "Well, let me tell you one thing. I bought this a *long* time ago, when I was younger -" (Hadn't it been a month already?) "But I didn't try it more than once or twice -" (He hadn't!) "and I haven't had any for I don't know how long. So there!"

Anger made him bold. He towered over his father, glared down at him. The man he hated. He raised the can, held it an inch from Peter's face. "You want to know how much I care about this stuff?"

He was gratified to see Peter take two hesitant steps backward. Jason followed. "I'll show you!" With one quick jerk, he wrenched the lid from the can and flung the contents at Peter's feet. He glared at his father, then tossed the can at him and spun on his heel. The empty clatter of the falling can followed him. Then silence.

PETER WATCHED HIS son disappear into the darkness and realized his legs were shaking. Anger flared and he started to follow Jason. Just as suddenly it died, and he stopped. What was the use? Jason was bigger now than he was. And stronger. Peter realized this as never before. He felt defeated suddenly. Weak. What had happened?

Peter blinked, then slowly, deliberately, allowed himself one more question. Why were his children turning out like this?

JASON WAS STILL seething the next morning. He wished fervently he hadn't destroyed his tobacco. He needed it. He had to go to town today. He went. He told Dad he'd check to see if the corn planter part had come in. It hadn't, but he didn't care. He hurried to the grocery store. He walked every aisle, checked every square foot of the store. No straw hats. No Mosies. He walked to the front counter. Asked for one can. Then two.

On the way home he tucked a wad inside his lip. The buzz in his head was good. It was a relief not to fight it. To give in and let it be his friend. He touched the can. *I can't do without it,* he thought. *Why did I think I could?*

But on Sunday evening when he sat beside Lori, his conscience smote him. He had failed her! His girlfriend. His best friend. The only one in all the world who cared about him.

Of course Lori didn't know about it. But that only made it worse. Jason knew she trusted him. And he was deceiving her. He hated himself for that. He longed to tell her everything. He tried several times, but the words wouldn't come.

They made wedding plans instead.

{120} *Bootprints*

CHAPTER THIRTEEN

CAREFULLY LORI WIPED the last of the silverware – two spoons, two forks, two knives – and placed them in the drawer. She hung up her tea towel and looked at her kitchen. Her very own kitchen with its ivy accents and bay window.

Lori liked every room in their house. The airy living room, the square bathroom, the cozy bedroom. But she liked the bright kitchen with its bay window best of all.

Lori walked to the cupboard and took down her little stack of cook books. She had five, all wedding gifts. On the covers were gorgeous desserts, steaming pizzas, perfect pies. Could she ever learn to cook like that? Or – Lori allowed herself a sigh – was Jason doomed to everlasting flops? If only he weren't so particular. And now he wanted chocolate pie for his birthday supper.

She'd *asked* him what he wanted of course. She'd hoped he'd say banana pudding. It was one thing she *could* make, and with those two boxes of instant vanilla pudding left from their grocery shower, it would be even easier. "I have some bananas that should be used," she had stated hopefully.

Jason shook his head. "I'd rather have chocolate pie."

Lori stared dismally at her cookbooks. She hadn't had the courage to tell Jason she'd never made a pie before. A birthday should be special and if he wanted pie instead of banana pudding…

She'd try. At least she'd try.

Lori began to hunt for crust recipes. She found nine, all in the first cookbook. Her head whirled. How was she to know which one was best? She compared and debated and finally settled on Never-fail Pie Crust. It seemed like a safe option. *Never fail.*

So far Lori's cooking had failed. Her bread had failed. It had taken Jason's mighty hand to carve through the dense, sunken loaves, and then he hadn't liked it. The cats had agreed with him. They came sniffing to the garden where she'd pitched the last loaf, and they'd buried it. Buried the bread in the garden. She doubted the worms would eat it.

Her eggs had failed. Some mornings she got them too soft, and Jason hated egg whites shivering across his plate. Other times she got them too hard, and Jason grumbled when there wasn't enough yolk left to dip his toast into.

Her lasagna had failed and her biscuits had failed. But *never-fail* pie crust. Maybe this time she would taste success. Maybe Jason would even brag on her a little, like Mark bragged on Elaine.

Lori measured and stirred. She floured the counter and rolled out the dough. But when she tried to slide it into the pan, it fell apart. Just like that, into long, ragged pieces.

Determinedly Lori pushed the pieces back into a lump and rolled it out again. She had to pick it up now. Maybe if she moved quickly she could whisk it into the pan before it had time to tear.

Her fingers flew, but the crust flew faster. One piece hurtled into the drainer and another spiraled to the floor. Woefully Lori collected the pieces. *What was wrong?* She was sure she had followed the directions. She thought for a minute, then plopped the whole lump into the pan and patted it out. Who said it had to be rolled? It was a little thick and lumpy, but no one would notice once it was finished. At least it was in the pan.

Now for the filling. Lori paged through her cookbooks again. She stared in alarm at the huge selection of chocolate pie recipes. There was chocolate fudge, chocolate custard, Dutch chocolate, caramel chocolate, and chocolate cream. Which one was Jason's favorite?

Finally she decided on chocolate custard. Once she had made plain custard for Grandma Byler and it had turned out… not exceptional, but… *okay*. She would be thankful if she could only serve Jason an *okay* pie. She was so tired of flops. She knew Jason was, too.

Lori pored over the directions. She knew how particular you had to be with custard. The eggs had to be beaten just right – not too stringy and not too foamy. The milk had to be exactly the right temperature.

Finally the pie was in the oven. "Please turn out right," Lori whispered as she closed the oven door and set the timer.

While the pie baked, Lori began peeling potatoes. Through her bay window she could see Jason plowing the back field. He was in a rush to get it plowed before planting time. "This is taking a long time," he'd grumped to her that morning. "Mr. Cain always no-tilled it. It hasn't been plowed in years."

Lori reached for another potato. Jason was a real farmer, there was no doubt about it. He was a hard worker too. Lori knew their debt put a lot of pressure on him, but sometimes she wished he wouldn't work quite so hard. Or so late. It seemed they never had time to do things together like other young couples did. Like taking walks, going on picnics, or inviting friends over for supper.

Mark and Elaine did such things all the time. Lori tried not to be jealous. After all, Marks weren't buying a farm. They didn't have a thousand and one things to do in a day. Every day. Still…

If she was really important to Jason, wouldn't he make more time for her? She missed their talks, the heart-to-heart kind they used to have during courtship. Maybe they could talk tonight. After Jason's birthday supper, they could snuggle up on the love seat with some popcorn and lemonade – she still had a few lemons, didn't she? – and talk. She longed for that, but Jason was always too busy.

Did Jason even like her anymore? Lori liked how he looked, riding behind the horses. She thought of something Deacon Henry had said at their wedding. A married couple should tell each other *I love you* at least once a day. Maybe Jason hadn't heard that. Maybe he didn't think it was important. He seemed to appreciate it when she said it to him, be he never said it to her. Did he?

Lori sighed. Married life was harder than she had imagined. Would it have been if she'd married Mark? No, she mustn't think that. Not even for a minute. It was just that her parents had never quite approved of Jason. They had liked Mark. And now Mark and Elaine seemed so happy. Did they have something she and Jason didn't?

"I mustn't compare," said Lori. She said it aloud, to make it more real. "Jason is my husband and I will accept him the way he is. I-I love him."

She did. But did he love her?

The timer buzzed on the counter. Lori snapped out of her reverie and scurried for the oven. She took out the pie. The crust around the edges was nicely browned, but the center jiggled alarmingly. Should she bake it some more? No, the directions said thirty-five minutes and she'd better stick to that. She scooted the pie into the refrigerator. Hadn't Grandma said that custard set up as it cooled?

JASON WAS TIRED of plowing. These tough, rocky, old fields! Dad had been over this morning to check on him – as if he needed checking on – and worked himself into a huge lather. He was still plowing when he should be *planting!*

Jason scowled. Of course he was plowing! Couldn't Dad see his fields were a mess? At home Dad could rip through the fertile soil in no time, but this. This was a different story.

Dad had excitedly paced around him as he hitched the team. "When

I bought you this farm I did not intend to give it to you. How do you expect to keep up with your payments if you keep idling around? You should've been in the field an hour ago and here you're only getting started. As bad as Deacon Hen-"

Jason's blood boiled. "If all you came for is to chew me out –" he spat the words – "then you can just go straight back home!" He clucked to the horses and rattled out the field lane. Of all things. Treating a grown man like a… like a five-year-old! He hurled a baleful glare at Dad over his shoulder, just before a curve swallowed him out of sight.

Jason plowed furiously. The horses strained in their collars. He would get this field done by tonight if he had to get Lori out here with a flashlight.

Lori would do it, too. Jason softened as he thought about his wife. He'd sure gotten a good one. She helped him whenever she could, and she supported him – a lot more than Matthew's wife supported him. Jason felt sorry for Matthew at times. Hannah made it no secret that she didn't approve of Matthew's work.

Matthew had never enjoyed farming. He'd never gotten along with animals either. But when he had announced that he was thinking of joining Amos Peachey's carpenter crew, Dad was incensed. "What?!" he shouted. "I didn't raise my boys to be lazy, shiftless carpenters and you're not going to be one! I won't have it!"

Matthew had ignored Dad and gone on to turn in an application. Dad still hadn't forgiven him. Hannah hadn't either.

Jason knew Dad was relieved when he chose to farm. When a neighboring place came up for sale, Dad made the down payment, his wedding gift to them. "The place is yours," he told Jason. "If you can keep it."

Jason knew it would take years to pay off the debt, but he knew he could do it. His own farm. It was a little run-down, but it was nothing that hard work and time wouldn't fix. If only Dad would stop poking his nose into everything and finding fault!

Dad had told him how he should manage. "You've got enough fields to raise a decent amount of crops," he'd informed Jason. "And a lot of good pasture land. Put a herd of beef on the pasture and farm the fields. Don't think about milking now – it'll cost too much to get fixed up. Once your debt's paid off and you've got boys to help chore, then you can milk."

Jason knew it was a reasonable plan, but he resented the advice. "Dad can't control my life forever," he complained to Lori. "I'm a married man now with my own farm and I can make my own decisions!"

"But the advice sounds good," Lori said cautiously. "Don't you think he'd feel honored if you'd take it?"

"Lori." Jason laid down his spoon. "Dad doesn't have any feelings like that. All I am to him is a business asset. If I take his advice, it's because it's a good idea, not because I want to – *honor* him."

"Oh." Lori looked a little stunned. She covered it quickly with a smile. "Don't worry, Jason. I'm sure we'll do alright here." She pressed his hand. "I can already see you're a good manager."

Her words had given him confidence. They gave him confidence now as he lurched behind the plow. Lori was perfect.

Almost. Jason grinned wryly. Her cooking was kind of… shocking, but he didn't mind, not too much. He'd just keep telling her how he wanted his things fixed and one of these days she'd learn. She was so eager to please him.

LORI SAW HIM coming. Her heartbeat quickened as she surveyed the table. The china and silver sparkled in the candlelight. The water glasses were filled and ready. Beside Jason's plate lay a tissue-wrapped gift.

Lori smoothed her dress. She'd put on a good one for tonight. Would Jason notice? She hurried to the stove and ladled the corn and scalloped potatoes into serving bowls. She poured dressing over the individual salads and set them on the table. The pie. She mustn't forget the pie.

Lori rushed to the refrigerator as Jason clomped through the entrance. She lifted the pie. It was set around the edges, but the center was quivery. She'd worked all afternoon to make that pie. Was it supposed to act like that? Had Grandma's custard quivered? Lori couldn't remember, but she hoped so.

"What's all this about?"

"Oh." Lori whirled around, nearly dropping the pie. "Why-why, it's for your birthday." She set the quaking pie on the table. "Happy Birthday, dear!"

Jason didn't know what to think. At home birthdays had passed almost unnoticed, and here Lori was making it seem like Christmas or something. All the candles and fine dishes. He smiled at her and settled awkwardly into his chair. "What's this?"

"It's a little birthday gift." Lori watched his face anxiously.

"Hmm." Jason's big fingers ripped the tissue paper. "Oh. A shirt. Thank you." He nodded at Lori.

Was that all he was going to say? "Do you like it?" Lori asked timidly.

"Yes, it's okay. Did you make it?"

"I worked on it for two days. It matches my new dress."

"That's nice." Jason laid the shirt aside. "Can we eat now?"

"Uh – yes, everything's ready." She sat down beside him and tried not to notice how she was feeling. But she did. Some of the joy and anticipation was leaking out of her. She felt as flat as the last cake she'd made.

Jason took a drink. "This water's warm."

Lori jumped to her feet. She carried his glass to the sink and filled it with fresh water.

"You should wait to fill the glasses till last," Jason said. "Mom always did, to make sure our water was still cold."

"Oh. Whatever." Lori set the glass in front of him. She felt suddenly tired. She served Jason, took tiny portions herself, and they ate.

Too soon it was time to cut the pie. Slowly Lori pulled the pan toward her plate.

Jason was staring at it. "You call that chocolate pie?"

"What else would it be?" Lori mumbled. She began to cut.

Bootprints {127}

"Where's the whipped cream?"

"The recipe didn't call for any." Lori concentrated on the pie.

"Well. Mom always put some on hers."

Without answering, Lori carefully eased a shivering slice onto Jason's plate. It sat there, and she sat there, holding her breath. Slowly it leaned. Lori closed her eyes, then wrenched them open again. She watched the pie run into a sad little puddle.

Jason laughed. "You should get Mom's recipe. She's a real good cook."

Lori nodded and busied herself cutting a piece for her own plate. She had tried so hard to please him. Make him feel valued with this special meal. How could he be so ungrateful?

"You might want to get Mom's crust recipe too," Jason commented. "This one's kinda sawdusty." He laughed again.

Lori looked at the pie sprawled across her pretty china plate. Suddenly she knew she couldn't eat it. Not one bite. She stood quickly. "I don't feel well," she croaked.

Jason watched in amazement as his wife fled to the bedroom. What was wrong with her? She had seemed just fine when he came in for supper. All gay and sparkly. Thoughtfully he ate his pie. Was it something he had said? Maybe his remark about the pie crust? But it was the truth. If he'd purse his lips and blow, crumbs would fly all over the table. Mom's crusts were great. What was wrong in asking Lori to get the recipe? She was touchy sometimes, even if she was a good wife.

Jason looked at the table. The pretty dishes, the candles, the leftover food. She must've spent a long time getting ready, he suddenly realized. And she'd made him a birthday gift. He picked up the shirt again and fingered the fabric. It was the first birthday gift he'd ever had. He wished he could tell her how much it meant, but he didn't know how. How do you say a thing like that?

He hung the shirt on the back of a chair. He had some fence to fix tonight. Should he tell Lori where he was going? He started for the bedroom, then stopped. She might be sleeping. He'd leave her alone.

He felt bad, but he knew she'd get over it. He headed out the door with a feeling a lot like relief.

LORI DIDN'T HEAR him leave. Her face was still buried in the pillow. What was wrong with her? She was sure Jason didn't mean to be cruel, but she had tried so hard. It was too much. Lori stuffed the pillow into her mouth and sobbed. Could Jason hear her?

He was not fair. How could he expect her to cook as well as his mom? She had forty-some years of experience, and Lori was just learning. She wished fervently she would have learned before she was married. Her family would at least have appreciated her efforts.

Would Jason come looking for her? Lori hoped so. She hoped he would come see what was wrong, take her in his arms, and hold her until she felt better. Until they both felt better. Surely he was having a hard time, too.

Finally Lori realized the bedroom was growing dark. How long had she been in here? Where was Jason? She lifted her head. Silence.

She got up and eased open the bedroom door. Maybe she needed to take the first step. She'd go to him, tell him she'd forgiven him, and apologize for having run away. She went to the bathroom and washed her face, then headed for the kitchen.

She stopped, taking it all in. The candles had burned to stubs, their flickering flames throwing eerie shadows across the table. Melted wax had created hard red puddles on her linen tablecloth. The china was dirty. The food cold.

Jason was nowhere in sight.

Lori tried to keep back her tears, but still they came. How could such a special evening turn out like this? And oh, where was Jason? Lori wanted to go look for him, but another glance at the table kept her inside. This mess. She could clean up the table, but what about the mess in her heart?

She was drying the last of the dishes when Jason came in. "Feeling better?"

Bootprints {129}

Was that a touch of kindness in his voice? She kept her back turned. "A little."

Jason studied her. She still wasn't quite herself. He couldn't quite shake the uncomfortable feeling it was his fault. He felt bad, but he didn't know what to do. How was a man supposed to make up with his wife after hurting her? Hesitantly he walked over and stood beside her "Shall – can I help you?"

Unexpected warmth came into Lori's battered heart. Jason had never offered to help her wash the dishes before. He was sorry – surely he was sorry. She leaned her head lightly against his shoulder. It felt so good, connecting instead of being at odds. "Thanks, hon, I'm just finishing up."

"Okay. Well…" Jason headed for the living room and picked up a farm magazine. Maybe things were all right, after all.

CHAPTER FOURTEEN

BUGGY LIGHTS BOBBED out the lane and receded into the dusky twilight. Jason shook his head as he reached down and hefted a sack. He could've known Dad wouldn't drop in just to visit.

He carried the sack into the barn and heaved it into an empty stall. Three more trips and all the salt was under cover. The sacks made a neat stack in the hay. Dad was his worst enemy, but Jason supposed he'd better listen to him.

"Tomorrow I'll bring the cattle into the corral," Jason thought. "I'll start them on the salt then." He was on his way to the house. Through the bay window he could see Lori putting supper on the table. He watched her slow movements. Tired again. She was always tired these days. Was she lazy? He couldn't remember his mother ever lying around in the middle of the day like Lori did. Nor had she ever talked Dad into cleaning the garden because she "just didn't feel like it."

He hadn't felt like it either. Swinging a hoe was for women and children. But when Lori insisted the weeds would choke out the vegetables if they didn't do something about them, he had grudgingly given in. Halfway through, he had heard a buggy coming up the road and had bounded into the corn patch. He peeped through the scratchy stalks. Allen! No way was he going to let Allen see him in the garden. He hunched his broad shoulders out of sight until the buggy rolled over the hill.

"I saw you run into the corn patch," Lori said later. "Was there a coon in there? I've been so worried the coons will get all our corn."

Jason was embarrassed. "Of course not!" he snapped. "Would a coon come out in broad daylight while I'm out there?"

"I-I don't know." Lori sounded hurt. "I just thought you might have seen something when you ran so fast. What was it?"

"Nothing!" Jason shouted. He wanted to say more. Tell her that if she expected him to clean the garden, she needn't ask such stupid questions afterward. But he saw her flinch and stopped. Was she afraid of him?

He had reached for her hand. "Ah, forget it, Lor. Come out to the barn with me."

Lori hadn't gone, though. "I'm sorry, Jason. I'm just so tired."

It was always her excuse. Now he could see her through the bay window, sitting there waiting for him. He missed his wife! She never helped him anymore. She didn't come to meet him the minute he walked through the door. She barely noticed he came in, sometimes. More than once he'd run out of clean clothes before she'd gotten around to washing. He might as well be a fence post, no more than she cared about him.

Was she thinking about Mark?

Jason didn't like that Lori was such good friends with Elaine and Mark. He could never forget that Mark had wanted Lori too. Last week when Marks stopped in with some food, he had watched Lori closely. She had smiled at Mark! When had she last smiled at him?

So now he knew. Lori's problem was more than just not feeling good. She was sorry she'd married him. She had wanted a good husband and what had she gotten? A louse. He'd hurt her more often then he could count. Did Mark ever hurt his wife? Oh no, he was perfect.

Jason couldn't stand Mark. He was always hovering over Elaine, catering to her. What was it Lori had said to him? He helped Elaine can her tomatoes. *Can tomatoes!* How sissy was it possible for a man to become?

Yet Lori had said it with such a wistful look. She had eyed the bushel of tomatoes in the corner of the kitchen, as if willing him to get the hint. He'd clamped his hat on his head and slammed out the door. No way was he going to help Lori do that! Cleaning the garden? Washing the dishes occasionally? He would stoop no lower. Lori was not going to make a woman out of him!

What did Lori think of Mark? Jason wanted to put him out of her sight forever. He did not want to be compared with Mark. Mark was the perfect husband. He would never – Jason thrust his hand abruptly into his pocket. He'd almost forgotten. What if Lori had found it? His knees shook as he whirled and hurried back to the barn.

Underneath the work bench was a pack of shingles on a pallet. Jason slipped the can under the pallet. It made a good hiding place.

Those shingles were another of Dad's unsolicited schemes. "Saw you need to replace some shingles on your roof," he'd announced as he unloaded the pallet. "It's cheaper to do it yourself. Hiring a carpenter costs an arm and a leg."

Jason kicked at the shingles. Dad had no business buying them, then demanding that he pay. Now he had to pay for all the salt, too. His money seemed to disappear faster than he made it. His life was a mess. Money. Dad. He'd felt like hitting Dad when he climbed off the buggy with those salt bags. But he claimed they were a good investment. Were they?

Jason shrugged helplessly. For the second time he left the barn and headed for the house.

"WHO WAS HERE?" Lori asked as she set a kettle of chicken soup on the table.

"Dad."

"Your dad?"

"Uh-huh."

Lori waited a moment. When Jason didn't offer any more information, she asked, "Did he – did he want anything in particular?"

Jason crumbled crackers in his soup. "Dropped off some bags of commercial salt."

"Oh?" Lori raised her eyebrows. "Had you asked him to get some?"

"No!" Jason banged his fist on the table. The dishes jumped. "He's got this big notion if he doesn't control my every move, this whole farm is going to pot! He doesn't trust me further than he can throw me–" Who did? Not even Lori! "-and I'm twenty-three years old!"

"But, Jason," Lori put out a hand to touch him. "*I* trust you."

Jason frowned. Was she joking?

"You're doing a good job with this farm," Lori said staunchly. "We don't have a lot of money, but we're surviving." She stepped to the counter for the cake. "I thought about leaving off the frosting – to save sugar, you know – but I know how much you like frosting." She set the cake in front of him and smiled.

She smiled! *Tiredly*, thought Jason. He cut a slice of cake. "Are you… feeling okay?"

Lori propped her head in her hands. "Exhausted."

Jason nodded. Looking at her now, he couldn't imagine he'd accused her of being lazy, even to himself. She trusted him! She hadn't said anything like that for the longest time. He'd assumed she didn't like his way of doing things. He'd been envying Mark, who seemed to be rolling in greenbacks. Had he been mistaken?

"You're doing fine," Lori said. "I'm the one who's not. I'm tired of not being able to do my work. I'm tired of" – tears rushed to her eyes – "not being a better wife."

Jason could only look at her.

Bootprints

"I love you, Jason, but the last while I'm so sick I can't let you know it. I can barely even be civil." Her voice choked. "Today I was thinking about it, and I'm so afraid you're feeling neglected. That's why-" she dabbed at her eyes – "that's why I made you this cake. I was determined to do something special for you today, no matter how terrible I felt. I don't want you to forget that you're still the most important person to me in the world."

So she wasn't wanting Mark. Jason felt weak with relief. She'd made him a cake. A good one! "Lori." His voice was gruff. "You go to bed. I'll do the dishes. Yes." He pushed her gently toward the bedroom. "I will."

The dishes took a long time. Not that it mattered – he needed time to think. Lori trusted him! She loved him! He felt better then he had in ages. Then he groaned in sudden guilt. Would she have said that if she knew what was under the pack of shingles? If she knew what the salt was for? His shoulders lost their square. *Would she?*

THE NEXT MORNING Jason carried a bag of salt out to the corral. He dumped it into the feeding troughs and mixed it with the grain. He filled the water tank. "Make sure it stays full," Dad had said. Jason closed and latched the gate. What if the steers didn't bring enough? He had another farm payment coming up. The barn needed repairs. And Lori's doctor bills! Jason grimaced as he strode for the barn. He needed money!

Beef prices were up right now. His steers were healthy and looking prime. If only Dad's idea would work…

Jason kept a sharp eye on the feeding troughs and the water tanks. He refilled them twice. By the next morning the steers' stomachs looked a little swollen. Jason peered into the loaded cattle trailer and grinned. "Let's go!" he told the driver jovially.

Jason had done some careful figuring the night before. At a dollar-fifty a pound, he ought to get at least eight thousand dollars for his load. That should be enough to scrape by another few months, even with Lori's doctor bills.

The sale barn was noisy and hot. Animals bellowed. Flies swarmed.

But when Jason headed home he was exultant. Almost nine thousand dollars! The salt and water had made a difference! Jason felt friendlier toward Dad than he had in years.

FEELING RATHER SHAKEN, Jason stood beside the hospital bed. Lori was propped up in bed with a bundle in each arm. "Hello, Daddy," she said softly. "Would you like to hold one of them now?"

Jason sat cautiously beside his wife. He stared at the babies, the red wrinkled faces and spindly bodies. He took a deep breath. These puckered creatures were actually his sons?

"Aren't they adorable?" Lori whispered rapturously. She held out a squirming bundle.

Gingerly Jason took it. Its head! It wasn't on tight! Frantically he looked at Lori who already had a hand under the baby's head.

"Don't you know how to hold a baby? You have to support its head. Like this." She cupped Jason's hand around the bald little dome.

Stiffly, Jason held his son. He didn't want to break him. Those flailing arms looked as though the slightest effort could snap them in half. No thicker than his fingers!

"We need to decide on names," Lori said. "We had talked about Kenneth. Do you still like that?"

Jason nodded. "What about the other one?"

"What would go well with Kenneth?"

"I don't know." Jason wracked his mind. "What about… Harvey?"

Lori frowned. "I don't really like Harvey. Besides, it should start with a "K", same as Kenneth. What about Kevin?"

Jason said the names out loud. Kenneth and Kevin. They sounded nice. He smiled at Lori and bent over the baby in his arms. "Hey, Kevin. It's me. Your daddy."

As if he understood, Kevin reached up and grasped Jason's finger. Jason was mesmerized. The tiny hand clutching his own. He had a sudden, burning revelation. He was a father! Responsible for two little boys! It staggered him.

Bootprints

These babies would be little boys someday. Jason flinched from the memories of his own childhood. A little boy, alone and afraid. Always afraid of the man in the big boots. His arms tightened around the bundle in his lap. The baby was holding his finger with all its might. Would Kevin ever be afraid of him? Would he hide in terror at the sound of his boots? His throat swelled. His little family trusted him. He leaned against Lori and she leaned against him. They each held a son.

The sterile hospital room was almost sacred, Jason thought. He closed his eyes. He could still feel the pressure on his finger. *Had his Daddy ever held him like this?*

LIFE IN THE Kauffman was turned upside down after the twins came. Jason was constantly tired. How was a man supposed to get his rest if the babies insisted on howling all night long? It seemed Lori was never in bed. At times she even asked him to rock one of the boys for awhile.

If Jason had felt fatherly in the hospital room, he did not feel so now. Jostling a squalling baby in the middle of the night grated on him. His body needed sleep and there was nothing to do about it – unless he unrolled a sleeping bag in the kitchen. On the dirty, grimy floor. But leave Lori alone with these two shrieking sirens? Jason's rocker thumped noisily. No. He would not shake the little boy in his arms. But why – *why?!* – couldn't he shut that gaping, toothless mouth and go to sleep like a normal person?

The days were almost as bad as the nights. Jason never knew when to expect meals. Nine times out of ten supper wasn't ready when he came in. Last night Lori hadn't even started peeling potatoes yet at seven-thirty. And the house was a wreck. Mom's house had never looked like this!

Lori shuffled out of the pantry with a bowl of potatoes. "I'm sorry, Jason. The babies-"

"Yes, yes, it's always the babies. Well, might as well go on working until dark. Maybe supper will be ready by then." He had slammed the door behind him.

It was still light enough in the barn to mend the broken door on Starburst's stall. Jason felt a little ashamed of himself. He hadn't meant to snap at Lori like that. But enough was enough. He hardly had a wife anymore, she was that taken up with those babies. Why didn't she just lay them on the bed and let them scream, if that's what they liked to do?

Lori had been horrified when he suggested it. "Jason! The poor things have tummyache. What kind of mother do you think I am?"

A good one, Jason thought grimly. Utterly patient, with not a speck of time left for him. He was her husband, wasn't he? What did she do for *him*?

Still, he shouldn't have talked to her like that. He worked a while longer, then allowed his conscience to send him back inside. The babies were still crying. Or was it again? And Lori was crying too. Jason was struck by a compulsive urge to join them. Instead he folded the mountain of diapers on the table and swept the floor. Had Lori swept it even once since the maid left?

Maybe he should have let her have a maid for longer than a month. Her mom still came at least once a week. Wasn't that enough? Besides, he had been tired of having someone else underfoot all the time. Jason sighed. How would he ever provide for his family? He watched Lori stir the potato soup. He didn't know if he wanted any. All he wanted was peace and quiet. And a big pinch of *Skoal*.

JASON GUIDED STARBURST into his parents' lane. He dreaded this meeting, but he had no choice. Dad came out of the barn as he drove up. "Now what?"

Jason scowled. Why must Dad always be so abrupt? "I wondered if Luke or Danny could help me with corn harvest this week?"

"You managed by yourself last year."

"Lori helped. This year that's not going to happen. Besides, I've got more corn."

Dad narrowed his eyes. "You'll be losing money if you pay someone else. If you'd put in a little longer da-"

{138} *Bootprints*

"I work hard enough!" Jason didn't wait. He slapped Starburst with the reins. If Dad wouldn't help him out – fine. He would not stoop to begging.

But early Friday morning, Dad drove in with Luke. Jason dumped Kenneth into Lori's arms and hurried outside.

"What!" Dad exclaimed. "Still in the house at this time of the morning?"

Jason's relief turned to disgust.

"I see you still haven't replaced those shingles," Dad said next.

"Haven't got time."

"You have to *make* time. Next thing the roof will be leaking and you'll have to fix that too."

Jason was tired from another sleepless night and this was positively too much. "Why don't you come and do it yourself if you're so anxious to have it done?!" he roared.

"Got my own work to do and now you're stealing my help!" Dad's voice was just as loud.

Jason jerked his head at Luke and stalked toward the barn, as Dad clattered out the lane in a cloud of dust.

"Dad thinks he can control every little thing on this farm!" Jason fumed as he threw the harnesses on the horses. It was time that he, Jason Kauffman, showed some backbone.

Those shingles, for instance. He had not the foggiest idea how to go about replacing shingles! It was all Dad's idea. It wouldn't cost him *that* much to get a carpenter crew to replace a few. And Matthew might do it for free, or at least a reduced price. He started out the field lane, tall and determined. After he collected the money for his corn…

MATTHEW CAME ON a Saturday in mid-October. "I'll charge you a little for my labor," he told Jason. "Hannah would have a conniption if I didn't."

"That's fine." Corn prices had been high this year. Jason still had some money left, even after a significant farm payment. Besides, another batch of steers was almost ready for the sale barn.

"Don't mention this to Dad," Jason said later as he handed Matthew a check.

"Oh?" Matthew grinned a little. "He didn't want you to ask me to do it?"

"He didn't want me to ask *anyone* to do it. Thought I could do it myself to save money."

Matthew nodded. "Dad's still trying to keep you under his thumb, huh?"

Jason scowled.

"Look, you don't need to let him do it. Once I just dug in and did my own thing, no matter what Dad said or did, hey, it was a different life."

Jason nodded. It had been freeing to make his decision about the shingles — against Dad's wishes. "But wait, Matt. Don't tell him anyway."

"I won't," Matthew promised.

HE DIDN'T, BUT somehow Dad found out anyhow. "You mean to tell me you hired your no-account brother just to replace a couple of shingles!" he yelled. "And just what did that cost you?"

"Not much." Jason wasn't about to tell Dad he'd given Matthew seventy-five dollars. He'd pop a blood vessel.

Jason let him rant. He let him rave. For once he didn't care. He could do what he wanted and there was nothing Dad could do about it. He smiled inside. As soon as Dad left, he'd have a pinch of snuff to celebrate.

CHAPTER FIFTEEN

LORI GAZED AT her sons. She always loved them when they were sleeping like this. Not that she didn't love them otherwise, but they wore her out. They were so energetic. So everlasting bent to mischief. If their Daddy knew…

Lori kissed Kenneth's nose and brushed Kevin's hair out of his eyes. Their daddy wouldn't know. She tiptoed from the room and scurried to find the slop pail. She'd make sure of that.

Lori pulled the plastic pail from under the sink and hustled to the refrigerator. She took out a pan of cherry cobbler. With a swipe of her spatula, it smacked the bottom of the pail. She delved back in for the macaroni and cheese. Their dinner for tomorrow. She flipped the container upside down and watched it plop. The little red cherries and the macaroni.

A jar of pickles. Two slices of meatloaf. A half gallon of milk. The pail became a pond. A chunky, slurping pond with pickles dodging cherries. Lori peered into the refrigerator. No more pickle-relish-mustard infested dishes. Stiffly she rose and carried the empty containers to the counter. She shoved the breakfast dishes aside and stacked the dinner dishes higher. Yes, there was a tiny space for her containers.

She must get at the dishes. There weren't enough clean plates for supper, nor glasses. But supper was swimming in the slop pail. Sadly Lori remembered the cherry cobbler. Should she have spanked the boys?

Jason would have. Lori winced as she picked up the slop pail. She glanced out the window. Still raining – too hard for a trip to the garden. It was just as well. Jason might see some things he shouldn't, and – Lori bit her lip. It wasn't that she didn't believe in discipline. It was just that Jason's methods seemed kind of brutal to her. She didn't tell him half the scrapes the twins got into. How could she, when he punished them so severely?

Lori toted the sloshing pail to the bathroom. She watched silently as the commode swallowed the pond. Out of sight. Out of reach. Would Jason remember she'd planned on cherry cobbler for supper? He still grumbled about some of her cooking, but he liked her cherry cobbler. Maybe if she hurried with the dishes, she could still make a new one.

Lori hurried. But the dishes were a crusty, towering mountain. She should have done them hours ago, if only the twins had given her a chance.

Lori wondered who was more tired of the rain: Jason who couldn't get into the fields, or the boys who had to stay penned up inside.

Not that they'd been inside all day. Once she'd looked out the bay window to see their two sturdy figures in the yard. Side by side they stood, dark heads tipped toward heaven, mouths wide open.

Horrified, she dragged them inside. "Sorry, Mommy," Kevin begged as she peeled off their soggy shirts. "We wanted a drink of rain."

Lori had told them to stay inside. She punished them for their disobedience, then helped them set up their farm animals. Once they were playing nicely, she hurried to the basement to hang up a load of laundry. She disliked hanging laundry inside – it took so long to dry –

but she had no choice. It had rained three days already.

While she clipped denims to the makeshift line, Lori eyed the potato bin. There were a few rotten ones and they needed sorting – should she take time to do it? She listened to the boys' prattle. It sounded like they'd moved to the kitchen, but they were happy enough. Briskly she delved into the potato bin.

When she finally ascended the stairs, she was startled to see the refrigerator door wide open. Was she dreaming? She had to be. Kenneth clutched a quart of pickle relish, and Kevin a pint of mustard. They had stirred some of each into all the containers and bottles they could reach.

Lori bolted to the fridge. "Boys! What are you doing?"

"Cooking, Mommy." A blob of pickle relish dripped from Kenneth's hair.

"It's yummy for Daddy." Kevin had pounded holes into the cherry cobbler and filled them with mustard. "Like you make, Mommy."

She felt utterly helpless. Laugh, cry, scold, or pardon? The boys stared at her with round, chocolate eyes.

"It's naptime," she gasped. She swiped at the tears on her cheeks and washed the mustard from Kevin's face. "You're going to bed."

They were sleeping now. Lori rinsed the pickle jar. She hoped they'd sleep till supper time. She was frazzled and tired. Tired of being in this stale house with rain drumming on the roof. She needed a change of scenery. A little break from the demands of motherhood. She was too grumpy these last few days. Was that why the twins were so hard to handle? They sensed her restlessness. If she could just get out of the house for a bit.

Why couldn't she? Lori's face brightened suddenly. She could take some cookies out to the barn for Jason. Maybe an apple, too. It would be like a date. Just the two of them.

It seemed they rarely had time for each other these days. Jason was busy with the farm. She was busy with the boys. Recently she'd looked out the bay window and thought, "That man is my husband." It jolted her. Had they actually grown so far apart they were almost like strangers? She resolved to change things. Try harder. This wasn't working.

But Lori and Jason had fallen into a rut. Lori made several attempts to get out, but it was hard. How could they focus on marriage when the twins and the farm were so demanding?

Lori swished the last of the silverware through the water and pulled the plug. This was her chance, with the twins sleeping so long. But she should sweep the floor, get the cobbler into the oven, and snatch the opportunity to sew uninterrupted. She was always behind – but Jason! Lori longed for him with sudden, fierce intensity.

She hurried to the cookie jar and searched for several cookies the twins hadn't taken bites out of. Then she donned her coat and scarf and splashed through the rain to the barn.

Jason was at his workbench, measuring and marking two-by-fours. "Hello, dear!" she called.

Jason whirled, knocking a board to the floor. "What are you -"

"Don't be scared, Jason – nothing's wrong. I just brought a snack." Lori tugged the bag from her pocket.

"What? Oh." Jason looked confused. He picked up the board and slipped something into his pocket. "Let me – uh, let me go wash my hands first."

Lori clutched the cookies as he disappeared around the corner. She had forgotten the apple. But maybe he had one. She had seen him chewing something. Why did he act so jumpy and nervous? Did he wish she hadn't come?

"I hope I'm not bothering you," she said as he reappeared. "I thought you might be hungry, but -" she searched his face. "You were eating?"

"Me?" Jason bent to brush some sawdust from his pants. "I wasn't eating anything." He brushed vigorously. Tossed Lori a smile and bit into a cookie. "You left the boys by themselves?"

"They're sleeping." Lori ached to tell him about her day, but he'd probably rather not hear it. Instead she asked, "What will you do with those two-by-fours?"

{144} *Bootprints*

Jason reached for another cookie. "I'm trying to get the barns fixed up. You know I'd like to start milking in a year or two. But there's still so much to be done."

Lori looked around. She hadn't been out here much since the twins came.

"To make matters worse, Dad keeps hounding me about it every time he comes. Fix the mangers! Replace the broken windows! Get the parlor redone!" Jason's voice cracked. "He claims if I wouldn't be so shiftless and lazy, if I'd just dig in a little more, I'd have it all done."

"Jason!" Lori was shocked. "That's not true!"

Jason hung his head. "You sure? Dad thinks so, and our bank account sure looks like it. If I'd start working twenty-fours a day, maybe – I could get us out of this hole."

"Oh, Jason." Lori had never seen him so discouraged. She had a sudden, powerful feeling it wasn't chance that brought her out here. She reached for him, her husband. Why didn't they share their problems more often? They needed each other. It was too lonely, too hard, to walk separately.

"Look, Jason." She spoke earnestly. "It's nothing to be ashamed of that we're not as rich as your Dad. It takes time to get established. And you've done a lot to this farm already. There's not a lazy bone in you." She could feel him shaking a little. Her heart ached for the little boy inside this big man. He still craved acceptance from his father. Still didn't get it. "You're not a failure, Jason." Her voice wobbled. "I'm your wife, and I *know.*"

They sat on a dusty crate side by side. Rain drummed on the roof. Lori wished she could preserve this moment. This was what it meant to be... *married.*

Jason stirred. "I don't know why it's bothering me so much today."

"You're all by yourself out here, with too much time to think. Why don't you come in a little earlier tonight? It'd be nice to have a relaxing evening once."

Jason shook his head. "It'd just put me further behind than ever." He handed the empty cookie bag to Lori and reluctantly stood. "Thanks for coming out, Lor. I better get busy again."

BUT HE DIDN'T. He stood at the window and watched her hurry back to the house. She had come through the rain, just to bring him cookies. And he'd stormed into her with that tirade. He shouldn't have – now she'd worry – but she was so warm and comforting, and the barn so bleak.

He could still feel the warmth of her touch. He had a good wife. Was he a good husband? Jason groaned. He pulled the little round can from his pocket. He had lied to her! No, not lied. She had asked him if he was eating something, and he wasn't. You didn't eat tobacco. But he'd duped her, misled her. He wasn't honest.

He clutched the can. *Skoal.* He was looking to *Skoal* for comfort, with a wife like Lori? He felt nauseated. He'd dump this stuff out. Out in the rain, and let the rain wash it away. He was no slave. He could stop now, this minute.

Can in one hand, lid in the other, Jason headed for the door. He stopped, stood in the open doorway. He was going to do it. This was for Lori. She would be so happy.

Jason took one last pinch of Skoal and tucked it into his lip. He brought the can to his nose and breathed the sweet, familiar smell. What was he thinking? He'd paid money for this stuff. What a stupid waste of money to throw it away. He put the lid back where it belonged, pounded it down with his fist.

He put it back in its new place behind his ratchet set. He'd finish this one last can; it was wrong to waste money. But that was it. He'd never buy another one. He was glad to be quitting.

Jason took a look under the workbench. The shadows and the ratchet set were all he could see. He ought to get busy again, but he kept thinking about Lori. She had come through the rain to see him. She was good for him, better than dip. He was definitely going to quit.

Why hadn't he gotten a wife like Hannah? Hannah made Matthew's

{146} *Bootprints*

life nearly as miserable as Dad had. Jason deserved someone like Hannah, but he'd gotten Lori. She was so good, it tortured him sometimes. It tortured him now. He was a worthless farmer, and an even more worthless husband.

Rain slashed against the window. Jason groaned. "Men"- the word was ripped from his throat – "don't cry."

And he did not.

IT WAS SCARCELY a week later when Lori heard a strange sound. A roar and a clatter. She hurried to the window and gaped as Jim Conway throbbed to a stop in front of the barn with… was it a tractor? She'd never seen such a big one, up close. And what was it pulling? A disk? Did they make them that big?

Lori watched as their next-door neighbor climbed down from the tractor. Jason came out of the barn to talk to him. Lori saw him motion and wave his arms. Then Jim climbed back into the tractor and the enormous rig clattered out the field lane.

Lori frowned. Something wasn't right. Should she go out and ask Jason what was going on? Would that make him mad? She hated to make him mad. She'd better not risk it. But what-?

"Mommy! Mommy!" A grubby hand tugged at her apron.

Lori tore her gaze from the window. "Yes, Kevin. What do you want?"

"A drink. With ice, Mommy."

"Me want ice too!" Kenneth yelled.

Lori tried to push the tractor out of her mind. She dropped three ice cubes into Kevin's sippy cup, and three into Kenneth's. "Careful now." She smiled pensively as they noisily rattled their ice cubes. They wanted their water cold, because Daddy liked his cold.

She wished Jason would take more time for them. He rarely gave them attention unless it was to scold or punish them. Would they grow up to fear him, like he feared his own dad?

Lori sighed and set a saucepan on the stove. It was too troubling to think about. She glimpsed Jason through the bay window and sighed again. That tractor…

It roared out the lane as they were eating dinner. The boys bounced in glee. "Tractor!" Kenneth shouted.

"Big, big tractor!" Kevin echoed.

Jason scowled. "Quiet! Eat your food."

Lori spread apple butter on a slice of bread. She hardly dared ask, but she had to know. "Jim-" her heart thudded. "What did he want?"

Jason picked up his glass and took a long drink. He poured gravy over his potatoes. "Helping me out, like the good neighbor he is."

Lori looked sharply at Jason. He was concentrating on his meal. "But… how?"

"He's offered several times to help me if I get behind in my field work. I was behind the way it was, by Dad's standards, and that rain last week really set me back. So when he said something again yesterday, I told him I'd let him disk the back fields."

A queer, uncomfortable feeling settled into Lori's stomach. "Surely he won't just do it for… nothing?"

"Well, no, but I figure with the time it'll save me, I'll still come out on top."

"But Jason-" Lori hesitated, looking first at the twins' curious faces, then Jason's stony one. Maybe they ought to wait to discuss this until they were by themselves. Hadn't she heard that parents should never argue in front of their children? But they weren't arguing. Not exactly. She would ask one more question. Just one. It had to come out. "But Jason, what about the church? I mean, well, is it okay? You won't get in trouble?"

"Listen, Lor." For the first time Jason looked at her. His eyes were very dark. "*I'm* not farming with a tractor. There's no need to get all up in the air because I let Jim help me once. It's not like I'm planning on doing it regular or anything." He turned back to his plate. "You ask too many questions."

Blindly Lori turned to help Kenneth with his meatloaf. She was

{148} *Bootprints*

cut to the core. It was one thing to hear Jason berate the cows. It was another thing to hear him berate her. A dumb, pestering child. That's what she felt like. "No, Kenneth." Her voice was a strained whisper. "You mustn't put potatoes in your water."

JASON DIDN'T INTEND to make a habit of hiring Jim with his tractor. But when he saw how much Jim could get done, he saw it as a way to get ahead. He had a family to feed, and debts. Beef prices were coming down. He had to do something. What would people say if he couldn't make it on the farm?

Jason figured it this way. Jim could do in a few hours what took him a few days. With grain prices sky high, wouldn't it make sense to get rid of one of his fields of cattle and plant corn there instead? The extra time wouldn't be a problem with Jim to help, and the extra money…

Of course there was the thing about what Dad would say. Jason tried to brush the niggling worry aside. It was his farm. His decision.

Jason got Jim to plant corn. Then he let him spray the fields. He always sent Jim to do the back fields and did the front one himself. There was no sense in giving some busybody a chance to stir up trouble in the church.

PETER WAS SURE he wasn't seeing right. The fence around the north beef pasture – he shaded his eyes with his hands – it was gone. The cattle were gone too. He had come to check up on them, had made a special trip, and all there was – he stepped closer for another look – were rows of young corn marching across the entire field.

Peter looked for a fence post to lean on, but it wasn't there. That boy. Always up to some kind of nonsense the moment he turned his back.

Inside the barn, Jason saw him coming. He gripped his hammer. He was ready.

Peter hurtled through the door. "I'd like to know what's going on around here!" he announced. "The fence. The cattle – where are they?"

Jason tapped his hammer against the workbench. "I took the fence down. Sold the cattle."

"Whatever for? You didn't even ask my permission!"

"Why would I? It's my farm."

Peter glared. "Don't forget it's not paid off yet," he snapped.

"It'll be a lot closer by fall." Jason grinned at his father. "Got an extra field of corn out there, you know."

"But – but -" Peter slammed his fist on the workbench. "Why did you sell the cattle?"

"The bottom's dropped out of the beef market and I figured I could do better by raising more crops." Jason laid his hammer down and rifled calmly through a box of screws.

Peter turned away, feigning interest in a chainsaw. It wasn't a bad move. A good one, actually. But Jason was too cocky, not even considering his opinion. He spun back. "You should've asked me first," he barked. "Since you didn't, well, guess you'll have to take the consequences."

Trying to scare me, thought Jason. He shifted the wad in his lip. He wasn't scared.

THAT FALL JASON didn't ask Dad for help during corn harvest. Jim combined the back fields while Jason did the front one. It was a good year. Plentiful rainfall produced a bumper crop. Prices were good. As Jason sat at his desk and worked out his figures, he couldn't wipe the smile from his face. The decision to hire Jim and farm an extra field was coming off with substantial dividends. If he'd keep doing this… well, whatever consequences Dad had been referring to, they weren't bad.

THE NEXT SPRING Jason got Jim to help him again. This time he took things a step further. He learned how to drive the tractor himself. It was all part of being an efficient businessman. If he wouldn't have to pay Jim for his time, he'd be that much further ahead in the end.

Jason loved the thrill of riding high above the ground. The powerful throb of the motor filled the air-conditioned cab. Wouldn't the twins love a ride! But Lori wouldn't like it. She didn't approve of the whole thing. Not that she said much. She just looked at him with a sad, drawn expression. It irked Jason. Couldn't she appreciate his efforts at providing for her? Last week she'd spent sixty-five dollars on fabric. How could she fling money around like that, then be so stuck up when he wanted to use the tractor?

JASON SCOWLED AS the buggy-leaning-to-the-right rattled out the lane. "Of all things!" he spouted. "How in the world did they find out about that? Probably Nosy Mosie's got a hand in it somewhere!"

Jason clenched his fists and stomped to the house. He let the door slam noisily behind him. Lori shot him a grieved look, but he didn't care. He marched to his desk.

Lori moved quietly around the house. Had the man in the buggy brought bad news? "Shh," she told the twins. "Don't disturb Daddy. Maybe tomorrow you can show him your pet frog." She took them to the bedroom to put on their pajamas. "Sleep good now. Mommy loves you."

"Mommy?"

"Yes, Kenneth."

"Does Daddy love us?"

"Why – why -" Lori's throat choked as she looked into the doubtful brown eyes. Did he? She didn't know. He didn't act like it very often. Just today, when the twins hadn't come to the dinner table fast enough, he had snatched a book and given them a good wallop across the seat. Was Kenneth remembering? She bent over and stroked his hair. "Of course, Kenneth, Daddy loves you -" he had to! They were his flesh and blood – "but sometimes I think he… forgets."

"I'm glad you don't forget, Mommy."

"I am too. But listen, I hear Emily crying. Good night, boys."

Lori hurried to the living room and picked Emily out of her infant seat. She sat down to rock. Jason was still at his desk. His calculator

Bootprints {151}

clattered as he punched in numbers and his pencil made sharp, scrawling noises as it raced across the notepad.

What was wrong? She wanted to ask him, but the look on his face stopped her. She rocked in silence. A mouse scurried back and forth in the doorway. She shuddered but made no sound. The clock ticked off the minutes, and finally, hours. She shifted the slumbering Emily. "Jason?"

Jason's fingers thumped the calculator.

Lori waited.

At last he threw down his pencil and rubbed his eyes.

"Aren't you coming to bed, Jason? It's eleven o'clock already."

He snorted. Shook his head and slammed the calculator into the drawer. "Couldn't sleep anyway."

"Why not?"

"Could you, if the whole community was trying to force you to go bankrupt?" He glared at her.

"What – what are you talking about?"

"Just that! You know how hard it is for us to get ahead financially. But since I've been using Jim's equipment and farming an extra field, I've stayed on top. Now some busybody had to go and blab to the ministers about it, and they trotted over here tonight to tell me I have to stop it!"

When Lori didn't answer, he plunged on, "I tell you, Lor, I tried to explain nicely how it was, but do you think they'd listen to reason? No! Just prattled off a long, pious row about supporting the church. I think I'd better support my family first!"

Jason pounded his fist on his knee. "They just don't understand. They're not farmers and don't know how it is. Without that tractor, we'll be going right down the drain again!"

Jason ranted on and Lori listened. When they finally went to bed it was Lori and not Jason who lay sleepless.

CHAPTER SIXTEEN

"ARE YOU ABOUT ready?" Jason poked his head in the kitchen door.

"Soon," Lori called in a muffled voice. She shone the flashlight under the couch. She saw a pair of rolled-up socks, some stale popcorn, Emily's missing pacifier, and Kenneth's toy tractor.

Jason's heavy feet marched through the kitchen. "We don't have all day. I thought surely –" His impatient voice stopped in surprise. Lori was lying on the floor. Was she sick?

"I'm looking for Kenneth's left shoe and Kevin's right one. I thought they might be under the couch. There's about everything else under there, but –" Lori stood up – "no shoes."

Jason eyed the clock. "You should teach them to put their shoes where they belong."

Lori gave him a look that spoke volumes, only Jason wasn't quite sure he knew how to read it. She scurried around, checking the toy box, the wood box, behind doors, corners, anywhere that shoes might be hiding. "The boys' coats are on the table," she told Jason. Surely he

Bootprints {153}

could help them with their coats instead of standing there so helpless and expecting her to do all the work.

Grudgingly Jason stuffed Kevin's arms into his little gray coat.

"Daddy! My shirt feels yucky," Kenneth wailed.

Lori spied a shoestring hanging from a cupboard door. Gratefully she hauled out the shoe and tossed it to Jason. "Here's Kevin's shoe. And Kenneth put his shirt on inside out. I forgot."

Jason muttered something under his breath. Lori continued her search for the shoe. It was good for Jason to see what she dealt with all the time, she thought. If only he'd enjoy his sons, instead of sitting there with that martyred expression.

Finally the little family was settled into the buggy. Kenneth proudly wore his Sunday shoes since Jason had declared they were leaving at once, or else.

Jason picked up the reins and clucked to Starburst, and it was then that Lori remembered. The grocery list. "Wait," she gasped. She jumped off the buggy and ran for the house, as fast as it was possible to run with Emily jiggling in her arms. By the time she puffed back out, Kevin was sobbing heartbrokenly. "I want my Sunday shoes too," he wept. Lori looked at Jason. "Shall we give up going to town?"

Jason jerked his head at the empty space on the seat. Lori climbed up and they drove out the lane. Kenneth loftily held his feet in front of Kevin, reminding him about the shoes.

"Sunday shoes!" howled Kevin.

"Maybe we should leave the boys with your mom," Lori suggested loudly above the racket. "Do you think she'd have time to look after them?"

Jason rolled his eyes. "I hope so."

But the Kauffman home seemed deserted. No one came to the door when Jason knocked. He knocked a second time and looked at the twins. One gloating with Sunday shoes, the other sniffling with everyday shoes. What would they do if no one was home? It was like a circus, shopping with three children.

Jason glanced at the buggy where Lori was waiting with Emily. He decided to try one more time. He knocked, then opened the door. "Anybody home?"

Footsteps shuffled toward the entrance. "We're on our way to town," Jason began as the door cracked open. Then he stopped. Mom's face was tear stained and she clutched a soggy handkerchief. Graying strands of hair hung limply across her forehead.

"Hello, Jason." Her voice was quiet. Sad.

"Is something – wrong?" Jason stepped inside, pulling the twins behind him.

Mom's eyes filled. "Yes, Jason. I'm sorry to tell you, but Luke and Danny –" Her voice broke and she pressed the handkerchief to her face.

Jason's heart raced. What had happened? Had the boys been in an accident? He'd heard an ambulance this morning. Maybe they were unconscious in the hospital. Maybe they were dead.

"What happened, Mom? Tell me!"

"The – the boys." She blew her nose and tried again. "The boys left home last night."

Jason was momentarily relieved. At least they weren't lying in the morgue. Would they have been ready to die? He brushed the uncomfortable question aside as reality sank in. His brothers had left home.

"Do you know where they are?"

Mom looked very old. "No, we don't know," she sobbed.

Jason shook his head, trying to clear it. "Are you sure they left for good? Maybe they're just at a friend's house." He was grasping at straws.

"No, Jason." Mom drew a note from her pocket. "They left this."

Jason stepped closer. The handwriting was square and precise. So *Luke.* "Don't look for us," he read, "we're going out of state and we won't be back."

It was a cold, cruel note. Still, Mom tucked it carefully back into her apron pocket. It was the last thing she had from her boy. "I think I just can't bear it," she whispered.

Jason wished Lori had come inside with him. He was no good at this. He looked around the entrance. Luke and Danny's boots were still beside

Bootprints {155}

the door. It was strange, incomprehensible, that they could be gone.

But they were. No one was here but Mom. And Dad. Where was Dad?

Kenneth pulled urgently on his hand. "Daddy! I want to play with the blocks."

Jason shook his head. He couldn't leave the twins here now. Maybe they'd just go home. He didn't feel like going to town after all.

But Mom was finally noticing the boys. She tried to smile at them. "What – What?" She looked at Jason.

"Lori and I were planning to go to town and had wanted to leave the boys here," Jason explained. "But don't worry about it. We'll take them along. I – we didn't know."

"No, go ahead," Mom said. "Just leave them here. I think it might… be good for me."

"You sure?"

She nodded and stuck her handkerchief into her pocket. "Come, boys." She reached for their hands. "Let's see if we can find you some cookies."

Jason turned to leave, then called over his shoulder, "Where's Dad?"

Mom's face clouded again. "Still trying to finish the chores. He had no help this morning, you know."

Jason's mouth dropped. *His* father still choring at eight forty-five in the morning?

"Amy's helping Heidi this week, so he didn't even have her," Mom said.

Dazed, Jason headed for the buggy.

IT WAS SUNDAY morning and the Kauffman family was on their way to church. The twins chattered, Emily cooed, and Lori patiently answered questions. "That's a cow, Kevin, not a bear. Yes, Kenneth, we're glad God didn't give us tails like a horse. Think how much it would get in the way."

"I'd like a little tail," Kenneth imagined. " A bunny tail wouldn't get in the way, would it, Mommy?"

Jason sat tall and silent. The wad in his lip eased only a little of his

{156} *Bootprints*

dread. How would people treat him today? What would they say? He glanced sideways at Lori. This was the first time he'd used dip when he was with her, but she too taken up with the children to notice him. He was grateful. He needed this.

He wondered about Dad. Would he have the courage to come today? Luke and Danny's disappearance was a terrible blow to his pride. It had always been important to him that his family looked good in public. He'd be worrying about his reputation.

Jason unhitched on the far side of the barn. For a minute he considered holding on to his dip through services. But after Nosy Mosie led his swaybacked gelding past him, and his sharp eyes raked Jason's face, Jason spit the dip into a patch of tall grass.

The atmosphere was deathly somber, Jason noted as he approached the group of men. Nobody smiled. Nobody talked. Jason imagined the knowing looks being cast at his back as he moved around the circle, shaking hands. He was relieved when it was time to go in and sit down. He was even more relieved to sit in a back corner of the room, away from curious, probing eyes.

Jason could see both his parents and Heidi. His father sat rigid, unmoving, all through the service. Mom and Heidi kept wiping their eyes. He glimpsed Lori sitting beside Elaine. She was crying too.

Jason's fingers rested on his can of Skoal. It was hidden in his pocket, but he could feel it. The hard plastic reassured him. He could endure the service, knowing it was there. He'd have some as soon as he could.

He wondered where his brothers were. Were they safe? Suppose something happened to them? Would anyone find out? What would they do for a job? Where would they live?

There was no question why they'd left. Jason glanced at Dad. He couldn't blame his brothers. Hadn't he wanted to do the same thing when he was still at home? Anything – even a New York slum – held more appeal than living with Dad. Not that he'd known anything about slums, but at least Dad wouldn't have been there to beat him up.

His brothers had more guts than he had. Packing off in the middle

Bootprints {157}

of the night. Jason admired them, but he was embarrassed too. It put a blot on their whole family.

The ministry obviously felt the loss of the boys too. They preached moving sermons, stopping often to regain their composure.

Jason tried to block out the stories of the prodigal son and the lost sheep, but it was hard. All around him men were blowing their noses and women were wiping their eyes. He looked at Dad. Dad wasn't crying. He straightened his shoulders. Neither would he.

LORI DIDN'T ALWAYS wash Jason's Sunday pants, but this time they were muddy at the cuffs. She picked them up and checked the pockets. She found his comb and smiled a little. He was always so concerned that his hair was groomed just right. What was that? Something round and hard. She drew it out, expecting to see the can of Altoids Jason sometimes took to church. Instead it was… well, what *was* it? Skoal. What was that? She took off the lid and looked at the contents. A sudden, horrible feeling, a dizzying weakness, drove her to the floor.

"No!" It was an inaudible scream. "Jason would not do that! He wouldn't! It's not –"

"Mommy, Mommy! What? You fall down?"

The boys hovered anxiously over her. She forced herself to sit up. "Mommy is very sick, boys." She had never felt so sick in her life. "Please play nicely with your toys while Mommy lies down. Try to be quiet so you don't wake Emily." She clutched the can and stumbled to the bedroom.

Their bed, hers and Jason's, swallowed her into its depths. How long had he been doing this? And why? Why hadn't she suspected? That peculiar smell on his breath sometimes. It must've come from this. This filth. She plunged the can beneath his pillow. She buried her face in her own and sobbed.

JASON WAS THIRSTY. Hungry, too. It was a major job splitting enough wood to feed their outdoor furnace. He decided to take a break. Go to the house and see if Lori might make him a sandwich.

Bootprints

The twins came tiptoeing to meet him. "Quiet, Daddy," Kenneth whispered gravely. "Mommy's terrible sick. I think she's dying."

"Mommy's going to heaven." Kevin's face was sorrowful. Just last night Mommy had read them a story about someone who had gotten sick and gone to heaven. "Will Mommy be an angel, Daddy?"

A big, black fear seized Jason's throat. In an instant he remembered the history of heart disease in Lori's family. Two uncles and a cousin had died suddenly from heart attacks. "Where is she?" he demanded.

Kenneth pointed to the bedroom. Jason bounded through the kitchen, wrenched open the door. "Lori!" She was face down on the bed. He grabbed her shoulder and shook it.

Lori shuddered. What was he doing? She wasn't ready to face him yet. Could she ever face him? He pulled at her, and his breath was hot on her face. She turned aside.

"Lori, are you okay? Shall I call the ambulance?"

The what? She pushed herself from his grasp and pulled the covers around her shoulders. She'd rather have the covers than him. "No." Her eyes were gritty. Swollen. "I'm not okay."

"Is it your heart? Tell me, Lori."

Lori tried to focus. This was Jason – broad shoulders, tanned, chiseled face, worry in his eyes. Could she be wrong? She'd never seen tobacco before. Maybe it was something else. Maybe it wasn't his. Surely he'd have a reasonable explanation if she asked him. Her fingers reached under the pillow. It was still there. She clung to hope. She loved this man. He wouldn't betray her, would he?

Slowly she drew out the can. Into the light. She raised it to him, on the palm of her hand.

Jason's face blanched. He stared. There was nothing to say.

LORI'S KNIFE CUT into the apple. She halved it, quartered it. Methodically dropped the slices into a plastic sandwich bag. She slid open a drawer and took out a candy bar. As an afterthought, two.

Lori didn't know whether it was a good idea to visit Jason's parents

Bootprints {159}

today or not. They hadn't been there since the boys left home, but was Jason strong enough to handle a day with his father? And she – could she forget her own pain long enough to comfort Mom in hers?

Emily prattled and cooed as she waved at her beads. Lori picked her up and squeezed her tight. "My little pumpkin," she said softly, so Jason wouldn't hear from his desk, "you're the only one that's happy these days, aren't you?"

Jason's chair scraped the linoleum as he dragged himself to his feet. "Guess I'll go out and get Starburst ready." He stuffed the apples and candy bars into his pocket. "Think you'll be ready by the time I hitch up?"

Lori set Emily down and reached for the diaper bag. "I'll try," she answered. Jason was being nice again. Asking if she *could* be ready, instead of demanding that she *was* ready. No doubt by tonight he'd be back to snarling and snapping at them all.

The ride to Peter Kauffman's was a silent one. Jason and Lori were lost in their own worlds, and the twins, sensing the heavy atmosphere, contented themselves with watching the scenery.

From time to time Lori jostled against Jason's arm. Why had she married him? She tried to think. She'd loved him – of course she had.

Or had she pitied him?

Always, ever since she was a little girl, she hadn't been able to stand suffering. Not in birds, animals, or people. People least of all.

"Are you sure about this?" her mother had asked when Lori confided her engagement to Jason. "He seems like a – a rather troubled young man."

"Jason's fine, Mom." Lori resented her mother's constant worries about her boyfriend. "He's been hurt a lot, but that's not his fault. Once he's married and away from his dad, he'll be different."

Looking back, Lori could see she had ignored things she shouldn't have. Jason's disinterest in spiritual things. Had he ever mentioned God in their courtship? Had they ever read the Bible or prayed together? She had sensed a hardness in him too. It bothered her sometimes, but she blamed it on his hurts. She blamed everything on his hurts.

"Mark is such a stable, decent boy," Mom had said next. "Sometimes I still wonder if you wouldn't be better off with him."

"He's boring," Lori had snapped. She wanted no one but Jason. Why couldn't Mom focus on his good points once?

"I can't wait to be married," she had told Jason the next Sunday. His slow grin was reassuring. He had needed her. Did he still?

In the last few weeks, she was tortured with the thought that it had all been a giant mistake. Marriage hadn't changed Jason at all. Living with a wounded man was far different than dating one. Worst – there was no escape.

Would she escape, if she could? Lori stared at the rhythmic sway of Starburst's hindquarters. There were moments when she thought yes, she would. All these years she had trusted Jason, and he had deceived her. The liar. What other sins was he hiding that she hadn't discovered yet? Would this feeling of betrayal and hopelessness ever leave?

The future looked bleak. She was trapped with a man she no longer believed in. Didn't love.

Or did she? Lori didn't know. So often she was angry, wanting to lash out at Jason. He was supposed to be her protector and leader, but he abused his position in every way.

But there were other moments too. As she watched Jason wrestle with withdrawal, she loved him more fiercely than ever. He was trying! He had promised her with tears he would never touch a can of dip again. Couldn't she at least give him a chance? Do all she could to help him through this?

This deep, wide valley of withdrawal. How had Jason described it? Something about long, black arms snaking out to get him. Lori shivered. She knew the grip of those arms. Nervousness, depression, rage. Would Jason ever break free? He ate constantly – candy bars, fruit, jerky, cookies… anything to chew on that might lessen the craving.

Lori hugged Emily against her chest as Starburst clopped in the lane. She was all mixed up. First she couldn't stand Jason – she could walk out on him and not care less. His rages terrified her. Yesterday he had kicked a chair so hard it broke off one of the legs. What if he hurt her sometime? Or one of the children?

But sometimes he was sorry for his explosions. He would creep about trying to be extra nice, and Lori, catching the pathetic look in his eyes, would soften. He needed her now more than ever. She would stick with him.

Back and forth. Up and down. Lori was tired. Maybe a day away from home was what she needed after all.

JASON AND HIS father worked in silence all day. Jason wondered what his father was thinking. Neither of them mentioned Luke or Danny. It was obvious to Jason that his father was starting to get behind in his work. Watching him, Jason understood why. He didn't move as fast as he used to, and he stopped more often to rest. Dad's bushy hair was threaded with gray, his shoulders a little stooped. It was a queer feeling for Jason, realizing his dad was getting old.

Jason was surprised when Dad helped him hitch up to go home. He had never done anything like that before. Was it his way of thanking Jason for helping? Jason studied his father from the corner of his eye, but his expression was unreadable.

Then as Lori came out the door with the children, Dad came to the point. "You don't want this farm, do you?"

Jason's hands stilled. "What?"

"This farm. You want another one?"

"But – but the other one isn't paid off yet." Jason could hardly believe his ears. Dad wanted to sell the farm?

"I'd give you a decent deal. I had thought one of the younger boys might –" he stopped. Scuffed his boot in the gravel. "I need to do something with it in a year or so. Can't keep up by myself. Think about it." He turned and disappeared into the barn.

Jason shook himself. Slowly he turned and realized that Lori and the children were waiting for him. He climbed onto the buggy and they started out the lane.

CHAPTER SEVENTEEN

JASON SHIFTED HIS weight. Another service to endure on a too-low, leg-cramping, tailbone-punishing bench. He flinched when the bench squeaked noisily, and Mosie Bontrager turned to gaze rebukingly at him. It was like a prison cell – you couldn't even change positions.

There was a quiet rustle as the boys began filing into the church room. Jason forgot the bench momentarily. There was Philip, in the lead. At twenty-six, he was still not married. Jason had begun to think he'd be a permanent bachelor, but now he had a girlfriend, at last. Some Mary Kanagy from Ohio who was even older than he was.

Jason had seen her only once. "She looks like a grandma, that huge covering and all," he joked to Lori.

Lori was not amused. "I think they make a good couple," she said reproachfully. "I visited with Mary the Sunday she was here, and she couldn't be nicer. You ought to be glad for Philip."

He was, thought Jason. He was also glad Lori didn't look like she'd stepped out of the 1700's. But that was just like Philip. Showing up with some homely spinster and managing to be overjoyed about it.

Behind Philip trailed a long row of younger boys. Jason was acutely aware of two missing faces. Where were Luke and Danny today?

The song leader announced the first hymn. Jason paged through his songbook. Why didn't his brothers let them know where they were? Didn't they realize their family would worry, after four months of silence? Maybe they were trying to get back at Dad.

Jason didn't think it did Dad any harm, not knowing. But what about Mom? Mom was worrying herself into her grave, Heidi had told Lori. Jason could see Mom across the room. She did look pale and sad. Old, too.

A small fist pounding his knee brought Jason back to attention. Kevin squirmed urgently on the bench beside him. "I have to go potty!"

Jason frowned. Surely not already. Church had barely begun. He started to shake his head, but the anxious brown eyes portrayed real need.

Resignedly Jason plunked his songbook on the bench and grasped Kevin's hand. His face felt hot as he threaded his way across the room. He hustled Kevin through a side door and out to the barn. "Now hurry!" he barked.

Jason sighed with relief when they finally settled into their places again. He fumbled with his songbook, managing to locate the correct number just as the rest of the congregation stopped singing.

A hush fell over the room, then – "Daddy!" A piercing whisper shattered the silence. "Daddy, I have to go potty, too!" Kenneth bounced up and down on Jason's other side.

Chagrined, Jason clapped a hand over Kenneth's mouth. "Shh! Wait," he mouthed. He was intensely aware of people turning to look in their direction.

"Daddy, I can't wait!" Kenneth bounced desperately. "I have to go bad!" His whisper was shriller than ever.

Now people were smothering grins. Jason wanted to disappear. He couldn't go out again, not barely five minutes after the first time.

Bootprints

People would think he hadn't taught his boys a thing. And surely three-year-olds didn't have to be trotting out all the time. He shook his head firmly at Kenneth and stared at his shoes until the next song began.

Halfway through the song, Kenneth pounded his knee. "Daddy, I *have* to go!"

Jason debated about sending him out alone. But no, he remembered distinctly three weeks ago when he'd sent him out alone. After ten minutes, he had finally gone to look for him. To his dismay, he found him cruising calmly up and down the walks on a little red tricycle. He had spanked him soundly, but it was hard telling what he would come up with this time.

Jason stood and hauled Kenneth off the bench. He'd take him this once, but it was high time these boys learned it wasn't necessary to be trotting out every Sunday.

Jason kept a stern eye on his sons the rest of the service. He pinched Kevin twice and Kenneth once for turning around. He poked them when they wiggled too much, and glowered at them when they whispered.

Halfway through the main part, Jason finally relaxed. Josiah was preaching and he had a way of holding people's attention. He did more than quote lengthy passages of scripture in German that Jason couldn't understand anyway, and he didn't repeat Bible stories he'd heard hundreds of times before. He made God seem... nice almost. Like you could relate to Him on an everyday level. *Was God really that way?* Jason wondered. Somehow...

A small scuffle beside him jerked his attention back to the twins. The snack container was making its rounds and someone had just passed it to the twins. Only one chocolate chip cookie was left, and both boys were trying to claim it. Before Jason could intervene, Kenneth gave an indignant jerk and the cookie broke in half, scattering a shower of crumbs all over the place. Jason watched in horror as the cookie slipped from Kenneth's fingers and hurtled through the air. It skimmed Chester Miller's bald head and landed with a plunk right on Mosie Bontrager's lap.

Bootprints {165}

Jason sat frozen on the bench. In slow motion, Mosie picked up the cookie and stared at it with unbelieving eyes. Then he shifted his lean frame on the bench and slowly turned his head back and forth, trying to figure out where it had come from.

Before he could turn in his direction, Jason ducked behind Solomon Graber's portly form. He snatched the cookie container and hastily passed it on. His boys would not get any cookies today. Or ever again during church. They were three years old and able to do without.

When Jason finally dared to peek out from behind Solomon's back, Mosie had turned around again. No one else seemed to be watching him either. But for Jason the day was ruined. He could hardly wait till it was time to go home.

Jason could imagine Mosie hustling the chocolate chip cookie to the ministers with a concern about the games being played through church. Maybe the ministers would come visit him. Jason wondered how he'd feel. Standing in front of the ministers while they told him what a poor father he was. He fidgeted, and the bench squeaked again.

"Shh!" hissed Kenneth sternly.

It was too much. Jason leaped to his feet, yanking the boys behind him. This time he didn't care when people saw him leave. They could know. Jason Kauffman was not a father who winked at his sons' transgressions!

"Where are we going?" Kevin asked as they scuttled to the barn. "Do you have to go potty, too, Daddy?"

Jason ground his teeth. In the shadows of a far corner, he finally let fly his rage and humiliation.

The boys sobbed convulsively. "Be quiet!" ordered Jason. "People will hear you." He did not let their terror move him. They had made him look like a fool. Like a father who did not train his children.

There was a rustle as someone approached. Jason stiffened. Of all people, what was Mosie Bontrager doing out here?

Mosie eyed them curiously as he filled a pail with water at the hydrant. He kept glancing at the twins who were still sniffling jerkily.

Bootprints

"We were having a little problem with the boys not sitting still." Jason stepped forward. He felt a pressing need to explain to Mosie. "I don't think it's right to just ignore disturbances, do you?"

Mosie shook his head vigorously. "Indeed not! I was made aware just this forenoon how much our children lack reverence. It's appalling, the things that take place in church these days. Throwing cookies around." He set the brimming pail in front of his gelding. "Simply appalling," he repeated. He nodded as he looked at the twins. "I'm glad we still have some fathers who take their responsibility seriously."

Jason took the twins' hands and they started back to the house. He felt better.

LORI DIDN'T KNOW what was wrong with the twins. Ever since they'd come home from church, they were grumpy and out of sorts. She fixed an early supper, then put them to bed. Maybe they were just tired.

Jason sat on the couch, reading a magazine. Lori sat down beside him. "I talked with your mom today. They got a postcard from Luke and Danny on Friday."

Jason's face shot out from behind his magazine. "What did they say?"

"Not much. They're somewhere in Kansas."

"Kansas!" Jason's magazine thumped to the floor. "Whatever are they doing there?"

Lori was glad to see Jason's interest in his brothers. He had not mentioned them recently. "They're following the wheat harvest."

Jason shook his head. For so long they hadn't known anything. All kinds of worries had come to mind. Were they safe? Did they have anything to eat? They could be stuck in some dingy apartment in the middle of town. What if they got involved with a gang?

It seemed strange to finally know. His little brothers were in Kansas, on a harvest crew, hundreds of miles away.

"They didn't send any address because they're moving around all the time," Lori said. "It's hard on Mom that she can't write back."

Bootprints {167}

Jason nodded. "Was that all they wrote?"

"One more thing." Lori's eyes filled with tears as she remembered Mom Kauffman's face. "They have no intention of ever coming back."

THAT PIECE OF news convinced Jason even more he ought to take over Dad's farm. Dad had mentioned it again last week. Said they'd build a *doddy* house on the other side of the driveway so Lori and Jason could have the big house.

Jason knew his father would never offer to sell the place unless he had to. He must have realized he was not able to handle the farm alone.

Jason dreaded the thought of going deeper into debt, but another farm would be a good investment. If he'd rent this one out, it would help make the payments.

Dad's farm had advantages. For one thing, for all the work Jason had done on his barns, he was still a long way from being ready to milk. Wouldn't it be more practical to take on Dad's set-up than to spend huge amounts of time and money establishing his own?

There was the house, too. A house the size of a postage stamp was okay for newlyweds, Lori said, but not for a family. Jason had to admit they were crowded. There were only two bedrooms, and one was used for storage and a sewing room. Now the twins slept in there too, and the only clear space was a narrow walking trail.

If they stayed here, they would need to build an addition before long. If they moved to Dad and Mom's place, they'd have room to spare.

"Overall, I think it'd be a wise move," Jason told Lori.

"But I'm not sure it's wise to live on the same place as your dad." Lori looked anxiously at Jason. She was worried about this. She wasn't sure she wouldn't rather wiggle through a house on narrow trails than live on the same farm as Peter Kauffman. There was their privacy to consider, too, and –

"Dad is not going to run over me!" Jason's voice was firm. "Of course he'll try and control everything – at first – but he's going to find out pretty quick. I'm putting my foot *down!*"

{168} *Bootprints*

Lori wasn't convinced. Peter could be mean when crossed. She didn't want Jason to get hurt again. She knew what happened when he was hurting, how he acted. It was hard on the children, and on her too. She didn't want him in a situation that constantly tempted him. She knew he wasn't strong enough for that."

But Jason kept leaning more and more toward moving. By fall he gave his word to Dad, and his parents promptly began work on the *doddy* house. They hoped to be done by spring.

"Guess I'd better start looking for renters," Jason told Lori. But before he got a chance, he had an offer from an unexpected source. Philip came driving in the lane one day in early November. "I heard you want to rent out this place," he began.

Jason nodded. "Are you interested?"

"I am. Or rather – we are." Philip laughed a little self-consciously. "Mary and I are planning to get married in February. We'd like to live in this community if we can find a decent place to rent. I told her about this place, and she remembered it right away – said something about the house having a bay window." Philip smiled. "She's always liked bay windows. The only thing is, we're just interested in the house and barn. I didn't know whether you'd consider renting the fields separately from the buildings or not?"

"Well," Jason thought about it. "Maybe if you'd see after the beef cattle, I would. But I don't know if we could be out by February. It all depends when Dad gets the *doddy* house done."

"Oh, that shouldn't be a problem," Philip said. "We want to stay in Ohio a month or two after the wedding anyhow, to make the move easier on Mary. And the cattle shouldn't be a problem either. I get off work at the pallet shop by four o'clock, so that leaves plenty of time for chores. How much are you asking?"

"How about four hundred fifty a month?"

Philip nodded slowly. "We might be able to swing that. I want to talk with Mary first, but we'll let you know within a month. If that's okay."

"Uh-huh. Sure." Jason was busily calculating.

Bootprints {169}

Philip smiled as he picked up the reins. "Thanks, Jason. I hope you can come to our wedding."

"Wedding?" asked Jason. "Oh – your wedding. Well, sure we will." He was still figuring. Had he asked enough for rent?

IT WASN'T UNTIL a week before the wedding that Jason realized it came right over the time he'd planned to spread manure on the fields.

"But surely you can wait another week," Lori protested. "You don't want to miss Philip's wedding, do you?"

Jason's mind flashed back to another time. Another wedding. They couldn't go because Dad said they were too busy. Jason could understand Dad's viewpoint a little better now. He could also remember the anger he'd felt at not being able to go.

"We'll go," he heard himself saying. "I'll work something out."

Jim agreed to spread manure on the fields during the time the Kauffmans were in Ohio. He also promised to consider Jason's offer at renting the fields.

"If he decides he wants the fields, he might as well start working them now," Jason informed Lori. "It makes perfect sense."

IT MIGHT HAVE to Jason, but it didn't to everybody. A week after the wedding, the buggy-leaning-to-the-right came rolling in the lane.

"Disgusting," Jason muttered as he peered out the barn window. He berated himself for not having already coaxed a commitment out of Jim. If Jim was going to rent the fields, no one would have any objections to his hauling manure. As it was…

"Good evening, Jason." It was Henry and Josiah again.

"Evenin'."

They came to the point. "Someone said you were using Jim's tractor again last week. We just came to find out if it's true."

Jason raised his eyebrows. "Me? Why no, I wasn't. I haven't used it since you asked me not to. And I wasn't even home last week. We went to Philip's wedding, you know."

{170} *Bootprints*

"That's true," Henry said. "I remember that. Well, we just thought we'd drop in and check it out."

Jason nodded. "We sure enjoyed our trip to Philip's wedding." He grinned at Henry. Anything to get his mind off the tractor.

"Yes, we enjoyed it too," Henry said. "But we'll miss Philip at home."

A little later, Henry's horse ambled away from the barn. Had his father missed him when he left? Small chance.

JOSIAH WAS SILENT on the way home. Somehow he had the feeling that Jason had led them around a stump. He remembered well, too well, how Jason had been in school. His way of smoothing things over. Lying, without lying exactly. So he wondered.

{172} *Bootprints*

CHAPTER EIGHTEEN

SOFTLY LORI CLOSED the bedroom door and hurried to the kitchen. It still felt strange. All these years this had been Mom Kauffman's kitchen, and now it was hers. She missed the bay window in her old kitchen, but here she had more cupboard and counter space. Lori liked elbow room. She also liked that dishes stacked up on a large counter didn't look as overwhelming as dishes on a smaller counter.

There were dishes on the counter now, hiding the ivy canister set. Lori began filling the sink. She wanted to keep the counter clean and uncluttered, so Mom Kauffman wouldn't faint when she came to visit. Mom had always kept this house achingly clean. Lori felt responsible to do her best, too. She could imagine how Mom's tidy soul would shudder to step into her former home and find it overrun with dirt and clutter.

As the dinner dishes swept through the water, the ivy canisters merged back to existence. Lori was thankful for their familiar shape. They made the kitchen seem more familiar, as though she might be the mistress after all, not just a guest or a maid.

The children were still sleeping when she hung up her dish towel. Through the window, round, puffy clouds chased each other across the sky. The grass was green, the apple trees blooming. Suddenly Lori had an urge to explore. Go see what flowers were coming up on this place.

Their other farm hadn't had much landscaping. With the children, Lori didn't have time for much either, but she could never get used to such a bare yard. Surely here Mom would have some beds established that she could enjoy. Lori found a spade and a pruning shears and started around the house.

There were two shrubs beside the porch steps. A bit of ivy on the shady north side, and two straggly rosebushes on the south. "Is this all?" Lori cried. She searched the yard. No beds anywhere. No tender green perennial shoots.

"I can't bear this," thought Lori. "I can't live on another drab, colorless farm." She remembered their farm at home. Her mother had been an avid gardener who believed the adage that flowers were therapy for the soul. Splashes of color had spilled across her yard, rioting for attention all summer long.

Lori knew it was unreasonable to think she could manage that many flowers while the children were young. But surely she could keep up with a few, enough to add some color. A home without flowers gave an unfriendly appearance, like a face without a smile.

Maybe Mom would have some perennials she'd be ready to divide. Perennials wouldn't take up her time. They came up every year and fended for themselves.

Then there was her birthday money. She could use that for a few annuals. There was nothing like annuals for putting on a show.

Lori smiled as she began pruning the shrubs. Jason had been utterly indignant when, the first year after they were married, she had pulled a crisp twenty dollar bill from her parents' birthday card.

"They must think I'm not providing right," he sputtered. "Listen, Lor, you give that money back and tell them I can take care of my own wife."

"Oh, but Jason, that's not the way it is," Lori had explained. "My parents always give their married children twenty dollars for their birthday."

Eventually Jason had accepted it, and he even allowed Lori to use it as she pleased. One year she'd gotten a new dress. Another time she'd bought a cheese slicer to replace the broken one. And once she'd gotten Jason's favorite candy at the bulk food store. She'd smuggled it home and put it in the drawer with his socks.

"A little surprise," she grinned when he found it. "All yours."

The next time Lori put his clean socks away, the sour gummies had disappeared. Jason hadn't said much, but Lori knew he was pleased she'd thought of him, when spending her birthday money.

"This year I'll buy flowers," Lori determined. She knew exactly where the money was, in a little pink envelope at the bottom of her sewing basket. Two ten dollar bills.

CAREFULLY LORI TUCKED a pack of ageratums into her tray. Surrounded by hundreds of colors and varieties, it was hard to decide which flowers to choose. She'd love to try that new kind of geranium yet, and those raspberry ice petunias. But no – she looked at her tray and mentally figured up the cost – she already had her twenty dollar's worth, and she must not use a cent of Jason's money.

"I'll stop at Mom's and see about some perennials," Lori decided as she loaded her flowers and the twins into the buggy. She was grateful Jason's mom had offered to babysit Emily. How she would have managed with a toddler yet was beyond her. It was enough of a circus with the boys prancing around and exclaiming about every flower in sight.

"May I help plant my flower, Mom?" Kenneth chirped as they headed down the road. He squeezed a scarlet salvia tightly by its throat.

"Sure," Lori smiled. "Here, hold your flower like this." She guided his hands to the base of the plastic pot. "Now it can breathe."

"Am I holding mine right?" Anxiously Kevin waved his brilliant yellow snapdragon.

"Keep it on your lap," Lori gasped as a chunk of potting soil hurtled past her nose. She guided Starburst around a curve. "Look, there's the roof of Grandpa's house. Can you see it?"

Lori's mom was delighted to see them. She set out some frosted cookies and milk for the boys, then she dug up three boxes full of plants for Lori. Black-eyed Susans, echinacea, several kinds of daylilies, tansy, daisies, and a few other things Lori couldn't remember the names of. It made quite a conglomeration when she unloaded it on the porch at home.

"How much of my money did you spend on that stuff?" Jason asked sternly.

"None!" Lori was triumphant. "I used my birthday money for those. And all these," she motioned toward the boxes, "my Mom just dug out and gave me."

"They look like weeds." Jason frowned into the boxes. "Not a speck of color. I thought that's what you wanted. Color."

"Oh, they're just not blooming yet," Lori explained. "But they will. The first thing you know, this place will look like a park."

"Hmmph." Jason sniffed and disappeared through the door.

"He'll like them once they bloom," Lori assured herself the next day as she dug holes and carefully planted her flowers. "Who wouldn't?"

Lori had a few perennials left after planting around the house. She put a clump of black-eyed Susans beside the woodshed, and some lilies around the gas tank. She debated about the last two clumps of daisies, and finally carried them across the lane. There she dug two holes, set the clumps in place, and smoothed down the soil. She imagined how nice they'd look. The breezy white daisies against the red barn.

PETER EXAMINED THE strange clumps beside the barn. What kind of weed was this? It was queer he hadn't noticed it before. He went into the shop and got the weed eater. No weeds ever cluttered the sides of Peter Kauffman's buildings if he could help it.

Jason came around the corner of the barn, just as Peter was ready to start the weed eater. "What are you doing?"

"What does it look like? Taking care of these fool weeds." Briskly Peter jerked the starter rope.

"Hey, wait." Jason stepped closer. "That's not weeds. That's flowers."

"Flowers!" Peter spluttered. "You explain to me what flowers are doing here. Of all the ridiculous things!"

"Lori planted them, and you will leave them alone."

"I will NOT" – Peter yanked the rope again and the weed eater coughed to life – "have flowers beside my barn!" In five seconds the daises lay shredded on the grass. Triumphantly Peter shut off the weed eater. "And you can tell your wife that!"

Jason shook a fist in front of Peter's face. "You-had-no-right-to-do-that!" he hissed. "She's my wife and I will not have you interfering. You hear?"

Peter smirked. "Got your dander up, huh?" He took a step backward, away from the fist. His voice hardened. "Just how much money did that – woman – throw away on them things? I say once she has to plant flowers beside the barn, she has way too many! You watch her, or she'll spend every cent you -"

"Her Mom gave her most of those flowers -" Jason broke off. Peter was halfway to the shop.

"COME ON, BOYS." Lori bounced Emily on her hip and opened the back door. "Let's go see what Daddy is doing."

"Yay!" The twins raced for the door and tumbled out ahead of Lori.

"Get your wagon," Lori called, "and I'll give you all a ride." She stood still, breathing in the fresh air. She had thought of sending the boys out to Jason by themselves, but if she went along, it would give her a break.

Emily waved her arms, happy to be outside. "That's my girl," Lori praised. She could hardly wait till Emily got that tooth pushed through. After three days, the rocking chair was getting monotonous.

Lori stepped down from the porch to check on her flowers. Transplanting had set them back, but now they were lush and green.

The echinacea even had some tiny buds already.

Lori glanced at the gray-shingled house across the driveway. Just as quickly she glanced away. Peter was not worth a thought. He had murdered her daisies. It still smarted every time she thought about it.

The boys came careening around the corner, narrowly missing her daylilies. "We couldn't find the wagon at first," Kenneth panted, "then it was -"

"Under the grape arbor," Kevin said as he bounced into the back. "Be the horse, Mom. Get up, horse!" He slapped imaginary lines.

Slowly Lori pulled the loaded wagon across the gravel. She wasn't sure where to find Jason. Would he be in the shop or the barn? She knew he was trying to get the planter ready so they could start planting corn tomorrow.

Halfway across the driveway, Lori heard loud voices coming from the shop. She gripped the wagon handle. Should she turn around?

"...old enough to be responsible and apply yourself!" Lori recognized Peter's voice. But who was he scolding? Surely not -

"Listen, Dad." That was Jason and he sounded hurt. Angry, too. "I told you the alarm -"

"Alarms work if you set them! You can't keep up with your payments if you idle around like a good-for-nothing. I've got a notion to -"

Lori jumped as the door burst open and Jason came boiling outside. His eyes blazed, and his face was livid. His boots rang on the hard ground as he stomped toward the machinery shed. Lori listened until his footsteps faded. There was no sound from inside the shop.

"Mom, Daddy went that way." Kevin pointed toward the shed.

"Yes, son." Lori tugged at the wagon. She was seldom angry, but she was angry now. She trembled with its intensity. How dare Peter treat her husband like a lazy little boy? It was none of his business that they'd forgotten to set the alarm this once. She pulled harder, walked faster. She must go to Jason.

But Jason might not want to see them, Lori realized suddenly. She stopped at the door of the shed and peered into the dim interior. Jason

{178} *Bootprints*

was under the planter, doing his work, getting it ready for planting.

She hesitated. Finally she lifted Emily from the wagon as the twins scrambled out. Jason glanced up, then went on with what he was doing.

"Let's go find some baby mouses," Kenneth announced. He and Kevin pelted away to the back end of the shed, where a stack of old feed bags was stored.

Last week the boys had discovered a nest of pink baby mice. They had carried them into the house, wanting to keep them for pets.

Lori shivered, remembering those gruesome creatures wiggling in her sons' hands. As she carried Emily over to the planter, she hoped the mice mamas had moved out of the feed bags. Why had God created mice anyway? The thought startled her, because – why had God created Peter?

Lori stood beside the planter and watched in silence for awhile. She could tell by Jason's actions he was still upset.

"Jason, I heard your dad in the shop." Now she better understood the struggle he'd had with dipping. He was under so much stress. Was he wanting to dip now? She eyed him anxiously. Maybe if he knew she cared, he wouldn't need his dip so much. "I'm sorry, Jason. What he said was all wrong. He doesn't -"

Jason sat up. "He has no right to treat me like that!" he exploded. "He won't even listen to what I say. Treats me like a five-year-old-"

Nervously Lori patted Emily. Jason was terribly upset.

"He makes me so mad!" Jason threw down a grease gun. "It was no big deal. We forgot to set the alarm once – just ONCE – and he's ready to send me to hell for it."

Lori smothered a gasp. In all his outbursts, Jason had never come this close to profanity. Her sympathy was fading. Why couldn't he control himself better?

"I've had it with him! He's completely unreasonable!" Jason picked up the grease gun and crawled under the planter.

"I – I think I'll go back to the house," Lori said weakly. "I was going to leave the boys out here, but if you'd rather not -"

Jason shrugged. "They can stay. But they better leave my tools alone."

LORI HAD BARELY disappeared when the twins peeked under the planter at Jason. They never got tired of watching him work on the farm equipment.

"What are you doing, Daddy?" asked Kevin.

"Greasing the planter." The words came out in a grunt.

"Why?"

"So it works better."

"It didn't work?"

"It was squeaking and didn't turn right."

A short silence.

"Daddy?" This time it was Kenneth. "Where's Grandpa?"

"I don't know."

"Was he mad?"

"Maybe."

"I don't like Grandpa. Do you like Grandpa, Daddy?"

Jason hesitated. "Go play, boys." His voice was gruff. "Don't even think about touching my tools either, you hear?"

Jason squeezed the handle of the grease gun. What he needed was a lip full of dip. He needed it bad. Maybe he should keep some on hand, just for emergencies. Would Lori believe him if he said he needed some things in town today?

A shadow fell across the doorway. "Come help me fix the manure spreader," Peter ordered. "I need it right away."

Whose farm was this anyhow? Jason ground his teeth. Briefly he considered not going. That would show he was his own boss. But every time he stood up to Dad, it ended in a fight. Could he handle that? Jason put his grease gun down and went. He wanted dip.

KEVIN AND KENNETH were tired of playing. They had rustled through all the feed bags without finding any mice. They wandered back to the planter. "Where's Daddy?" Kenneth asked.

They lay on their tummies and peered under the planter. "Daddy!" There was no answer.

{180} *Bootprints*

"Look! Here's his greaser." Kevin picked it up.

"I know how to run it," Kenneth boasted.

"How?"

"Like this. I saw Daddy do it." Using both hands, Kenneth squeezed. Grease wiggled out. He wiped it against the wheel of the planter.

"Hey! Let's grease the wagon!" Kevin shouted. "It squeaks. Daddy said grease is for squeaks."

The boys went to work. They coated the wheels. They squeezed some grease on the handle, so that wouldn't squeak either. Kevin was dabbing it on the racks when it stopped coming out.

"Here, let me." Kenneth grabbed it away. He squeezed hard. Nothing. Had they used it all up?

They looked at each other.

"WHERE'S MY GREASE gun?" Jason looked all around the planter. "I know I left it right here." He checked under the planter. On top of it. Finally he saw the wagon. Grease! "Boys!" The yell echoed through the shed.

Silence.

"Kevin! Kenneth!"

The only sound was the excited chatter of a sparrow near the roof. Jason kicked the wagon and fired the empty grease gun to the floor. He headed for the house. "I'm not putting up with this! Running to hide behind Mama's skirts!" He wrenched the door open. "They've got it coming now."

LORI LISTENED IN horror to the screams coming from the entrance. What had the boys done? Jason had stormed into the kitchen and hauled them off their chairs, where they were waiting for supper.

"Thought you'd get away with it, huh?" he'd roared. "I told you to leave my tools alone!" He shoved them into the entrance and slammed the door.

Emily whimpered, and Lori carried her into the living room. What had the boys done?

Bootprints {181}

Lori heard Jason bark a command and then the outside door slammed. She got to her feet. She had to find out what happened.

But it was Jason, not the twins, who came into the kitchen. Lori stopped short at the sight of him. His face was red and his eyes dark. His breath came quickly.

"Wh – where are the boys?"

"I sent them out to clean up the mess they made! They're not getting any supper until they do."

"What – what did they do?"

"They got my grease gun, after I told them *not to touch my tools,* and squirted grease all over their wagon. Used up the entire tube, too, the last one I have. Dad's going to have a fit if I don't have that planter in shape for tomorrow."

Lori felt sick. He feared his own dad's wrath, and took it out on his sons. "Do the boys know how to clean it up?"

"Let them figure it out! They know where my grease rags are. I'm ready to eat."

"But the boys -"

They can eat a cold supper, but I'm not going to. Sit down.

Lori gripped Emily tighter. "I – I think I'll wait on the boys."

"You'll do no such thing! Eating alone is part of their punishment."

Lori set Emily into the highchair and sat down. Jason was being totally unreasonable. Lori scooped a tiny mound of mashed potatoes onto her plate. Earlier today, she had heard Jason call someone else unreasonable.

She took a bite. Forced it down. The empty chairs across the table tormented her. Jason was shoveling in huge bites of potatoes and meatballs. *Jason is just like his father.* The thought flew into her mind and stuck. *He is. He hates his father, but he is just like him.*

Suddenly the future looked bleak and discouraging. If Jason followed his father's footsteps, the rest of their lives would be unspeakably miserable.

Lori took another bite of mashed potato and blinked back a tear. She could see no way out.

Bootprints

CHAPTER NINETEEN

LORI FUMBLED THE covers away from her body. She staggered to the bassinet and picked up her wailing baby. "Shh." She bounced her gently, hoping Jason wouldn't hear. He'd already scolded her once tonight, told her to "shut up that little siren." Said if Lori couldn't keep that baby quiet, she could haul her out to the living room and let her screech, but he needed his sleep.

"As if I didn't," Lori moaned as she tiptoed from the bedroom. She hugged Beth against her chest, stung by Jason's brusque referral to "that baby." Was that all that Beth meant to him? Just another child to get in his way and slow him down financially?

"If he'd hold you more often, he'd find out how sweet you are," Lori whispered. She felt a need to reassure Beth. Or maybe she needed to reassure herself. "You're his baby, too. He cares, he really does." Did he? She hoped so. "He's just frustrated because you cry and cry and cry. Why do you cry so much, Beth? If only you could tell me what's wrong."

Bootprints {183}

Everything blurred together in a fuzzy haze. Lori leaned her head against the back of the rocker and let the tears come. How many times had she been up tonight? It really didn't matter. She was tired. Tired to the very core of her being.

Tomorrow she must can applesauce. Or was it today? Lori's eyes strained at the clock. Two forty-five. Today she must can applesauce. How would she get all the apples cut up with a colicky baby and three preschoolers? It made her weary to even think about it.

If only Peter would allow Amy to help. But he said living next door was no excuse for Lori to come begging for help at every turn. If she really needed help – which she probably wouldn't, if she'd stop playing around with those children all the time – then she could treat Amy like any other maid and pay her fifteen dollars a day.

Fifteen dollars a day was too much pay, said Jason. But Lori kept track of the balance in the checkbook and knew an occasional fifteen dollars would not send them to the poorhouse. Jason just didn't like forking out money to his father. Lori understood that, but couldn't he see how much she needed help? It was only a few measly dollars. Was she just "the wife" as Beth was "the baby"?

Lori shook her head, trying to reason through the fog on her brain. Apples. How would she do the apples? Maybe she could send the twins out with Jason, and Emily over to Grandma – at least if Peter didn't consider it taking advantage. But that still left Beth. How would she cope if Beth kept crying for hours?

There were only two and a half bushels of apples, but it might as well be ten. If only Jason –

Lori closed her burning eyes. She wouldn't even think about that. Maybe she could sleep on the rocker.

THE APPLES WERE small. And every other one was wormy. Lori dropped another slice into the tub of salt water and glanced at the clock. Eleven-thirty! She scrambled to her feet and began tossing bologna sandwiches together. No doubt Jason would complain about such a meager dinner, but if he'd let her have a maid, it would be different. She'd just tell him that.

Lori slapped the plates on the table, trying not to look at the baskets of apples in the corner. She hadn't even cut up half a bushel yet. But then, Beth hadn't settled down till forty-five minutes ago. She breathed a quick, desperate little prayer that things would go better this afternoon.

They didn't. Beth woke up with a lusty howl while they were eating dinner, and Emily, disgruntled at being sent home from Grandma's, howled too.

"Quiet!" Jason pinched Emily's arm. For a second the little girl was startled into silence. Then she scrunched up her face and howled louder than ever.

"Here." Lori thrust Beth into Jason's arms. "Hold her while I put Emily to bed." She hustled her sobbing daughter into the bedroom before Jason's annoyance could result in a spanking. "Shh, Emily, Grandma needs to go to town this afternoon. Look, here's your blankie. Do you want your teddy, too? There. Now lie down and close your eyes. That's it."

Lori gave Emily a quick pat, then scurried from the bedroom. She was dismayed to find Beth on the couch, hoarse from crying. "Daddy said he has to go," Kenneth announced soberly.

"And we can't go with him this afternoon, 'cause we're a bother," Kevin added. "Are we a bother, Mom?"

"You will be a help if you clear the table for Mom." Lori tried to smile. She picked up Beth and sat on the rocker. She was at the point of collapse. She'd tell Jason they'd do without applesauce this year.

"Mom!" Kenneth's face was grieved. "I was going to take your plate to the counter, then Kevin took it."

"What?" Lori struggled to focus. "Never mind, Kenneth. You just take my glass." What was that? She lifted her head and listened. A knock.

Lori looked wildly around the kitchen. The dirty dishes, the apples,

Bootprints {185}

the boys' Legos on the floor. She stumbled through the mess. Whoever it was needed to stay outside. She was more of a wreck than the house.

Mary stood on the steps, holding a casserole and a pail of cookies. "Philip dropped me off on his way to town," she explained cheerfully. "So I'm here to help till he comes back."

Lori stared blankly. "Come in," she said finally. She held the door open, hiding her stinging eyes.

"Oh, you're doing applesauce," Mary exclaimed as she slid the casserole into the refrigerator. "Hi, boys. Would you like some cookies? They've got raisins in them, see?"

"I haven't gotten very far," Lori mumbled apologetically. She jostled Beth in her arms.

"That's quite understandable, with the baby so fussy." Mary looked at Lori in concern. "I can see you're tired. Why don't you go take a nap and I'll just take over here? You'll help me, won't you, boys?"

The boys beamed as they stuffed raisin cookies into their mouths. Of course they would help someone as nice as Mary.

Lori fed Beth, then dropped into bed. "Thank you, God…" the words faded fuzzily into oblivion.

By the time Lori awoke, Mary had the apples all cut up, and several batches cooked and put through the strainer. With her help, the boys had washed the dishes and picked up the toys from the floor.

Lori rubbed her eyes. "Mary, there's just no way I'd have gotten this done without you." She stirred a kettle full of apples on the stove. "I – I was feeling rather discouraged today."

"Then I'm extra glad I came. Philip and I really appreciate you letting us rent your other house. We were talking about it last night, and wished we could do more to help you."

"Before you came, I had made up my mind to give the apples away and do without applesauce for a year." Lori put the lid back on the kettle. It felt good to have another woman to talk to. Someone who listened and cared. Jason didn't seem to care about her struggles. If she confided anything, he usually just told her to work harder. As if he

{186} *Bootprints*

expected her to be like God or something. "You saved my day, Mary. The boys do like applesauce."

Mary paused in her sweeping. "I enjoyed this, really I did, Lori. My days get long. It was a treat to go away today."

"My memories of having long days to myself are pretty dim and dusty," Lori said, and the two women laughed together.

"Evenings are my favorite part of the day," Mary confided. "Philip and I often grill our supper over the fire pit, or work in the garden, or just relax. We take walks, too. I've always enjoyed birding, and we like to see how many birds we can spot to add to my list. I know I'll really miss all that 'together time' once we have children."

"That certainly changes," Lori agreed. *Not that we ever did much together anyway,* she mused wryly.

The applesauce was mostly in jars by the time Philip came for Mary. Lori watched as Philip gave Mary his hand, to help her into the buggy. They looked like such a happy couple. How would it be if…

Lori turned away from the window. There was no use dwelling on what couldn't be.

"BOYS, HAVE YOU fed the chickens yet?"

"No -" The boys looked up from the sandbox guiltily.

"Then it's high time you get at it. Now scat."

"But – but Daddy, the rooster."

"How many times have I told you that rooster won't hurt you, if you just show him who's boss?"

"He's mean, Daddy. He chases us." Kenneth was begging.

"So? You chase him!" Jason turned and stalked toward the barn. Imagine being scared of a measly rooster! He was about tired of this fuss.

Kevin and Kenneth frowned at each other. "I wish that old rooster would get dead!" Kenneth kicked his sand barn, scattering sand all over Kevin.

"Stop that!" Kevin whacked Kenneth with the plastic shovel.

Kenneth grabbed the shovel and pitched it into the yard. "Come

Bootprints

on!" He ran for the feed room.

They filled their pails with feed. Cautiously they peeked around the corner of the barn. "I don't see him," Kevin whispered. "Maybe he's behind the barn. Hurry!"

Their bare feet flew across the gravel to the chicken coop. Quickly they dumped the feed into the feeder.

"There he is!" Kenneth pointed toward the big red rooster, strutting around the chickens on the far side of the barn. "I know what. Let's give them a whole bunch of feed while the rooster's gone, then we won't have to feed them for a long time."

"Yes, let's!" They raced for the feed room.

They carried pail after pail to the chicken coop. When the feeder was full, they made heaps on the floor. Finally, the feed bag was empty. "Is the rooster coming yet?" Kenneth peered through the dusty window. No sign of the rooster.

"Let's give them a bunch of water, too," Kevin suggested.

Hurriedly they filled the water tub. They got the lard pail and the plastic dishpan out of the sandbox and filled those too.

"The rooster's coming!" Kenneth gasped. He grabbed his bucket and sped to the chicken coop. Water splashed his feet. He jostled into the coop and stumbled over a pile of feed. The bucket flew from his hands and landed upside down on the biggest pile of all.

"They can eat their feed and drink at the same time," Kevin comforted. "Hurry, the rooster's coming!"

They ran.

JASON COULDN'T BELIEVE his eyes. Soggy mounds of feed were scattered across the floor. It looked as though the chickens had traipsed through and fouled them. And what did those odd containers of scummy brown water mean?

Jason turned and started for the house. Those boys. Always up to some kind of tomfoolery. He spotted them in the sandbox. *They need more work to do.* He made mental note of it.

{188} *Bootprints*

"Here comes Daddy," Kenneth whispered.

"He's taking big, big steps." Kevin watched the boots approaching.

"Have you done your chicken chores today?" Daddy's voice was stern.

The boys looked at each other. "We – we gave them enough yesterday so we don't need to do it again for a long time." Kevin tried to be brave, but his voice wobbled a bit.

"You what?!" Daddy leaned closer. His eyes bulged at them. "How much feed did you give them?"

"All of it," squeaked Kenneth in a tiny voice.

"A whole bag?"

They nodded.

Daddy jerked them to their feet. "You useless boys. You made a huge mess!" He propelled them to the chicken coop. "Look at that!"

They looked.

"All that feed on the ground is *wasted!*" Jason could feel them trembling. Well, they'd better be afraid. Wasting all that expensive feed. He wouldn't spank them this time. He'd make them skip supper, then tomorrow they could clean out the whole chicken coop. Surely four-year-olds were old enough to do that. Of course they were.

BUT LORI DIDN'T think so. "They're so small, Jason. How will they handle the wheelbarrow?"

"They can use the small one and help each other." Jason turned a page in the *Farm Journal*. He was not about to back down.

"But that's unreasonable." Mentally Lori reviewed her schedule for tomorrow. Would she have time to sneak out and help the boys?

"Listen, Lor. That punishment's not any more unreasonable then some of my own dad's were."

Lori pictured the boys, trying to scoop up those heavy piles of feed. The laundry. They had enough to last another day, didn't they? Jason sat there, a cold stone wall. "So you want to be like your dad?" The words flew from her lips.

Jason leaped to his feet. "You stop interfering, woman, when I

Bootprints {189}

punish the children. I know what I'm doing and you… *don't!*" He pointed at her accusingly.

Lori shrank into the rocking chair. If she dared to help the boys, would Jason – ? She quaked and was silent.

KEVIN AND KENNETH worked hard the next day. They had a hard time pushing the wheelbarrow back and forth. If they helped each other, they could make it.

Kevin wiggled the heavy shovel into a pile of feed. He tried and tried to lift it. Inch by inch. Suddenly the shovel crashed to the floor and the feed flew off. "Help me," he panted.

They tried together. They strained and puffed. The shovel wobbled over the side of the wheelbarrow and the wet feed plopped into the bottom.

Sometimes they had to rest. Their backs hurt. But they had to go on. Daddy said to do it today. All of it.

Twice Mom brought them a drink. She rubbed their shoulders and loaded up some feed. Then she glanced out the window and hurried away.

It was when they were loading the last of the feed onto the wheelbarrow that the shovel broke. They didn't know what happened or how, but there was a sharp crack and the twins were left holding a splintered handle.

They looked at each other. What would Daddy say? How could this day possibly get worse?

JASON SAW THEM go into the shed. They each carried a piece of shovel. "Now what?" he spluttered. He laid down his pipe wrench and started after them.

He had never seen the likes, the way those boys ruined things. The chicken feed. The shovel. What had it been last week? Oh, yes, Starburst's tie rope. They had used it to play horse and somehow tore it. It had been frayed for a while, but still, Jason couldn't imagine how

{190} *Bootprints*

two little boys could tear a tie rope.

Jason calculated the cost of another bag of feed and a new shovel and a tie rope. His jaw tightened. All that money because of two careless boys. It was time they learned responsibility for their actions. He was storming into the shed when he heard something that silenced him. The boys were crying.

Jason stopped uneasily before they could see him.

"D – Daddy will spank us for sure!"

"But it wasn't our fault!"

"He won't care. He never does." More sobs.

Jason heard pieces of shovel hitting the concrete floor. A minute later two crying boys stumbled out the door, not noticing their father.

Jason swallowed. He ought to punish them for breaking it. But his feet refused to move. He closed his eyes and suddenly saw a picture from long ago. No, it was two pictures. One, a broken window. The other, a broken drill bit. When Jason could move again, he went back to the barn. Back to his chores. He'd get a new handle. Now that he thought of it, the old one had been cracked since last fall.

PETER KAUFFMAN FOUND the shovel the next day, before Jason had a chance to replace it. He glanced around sharply. Those reckless boys. They were as bad as their father had been – always breaking things. He needed this shovel. The horse stalls had needed mucking out for a long time, and he finally had a chance to get at it. Now this. He picked up the pieces and examined them. They were splintered too badly to tape.

Peter found the twins outside, playing with their wagon. "Did you break this?" He held the pieces in front of their noses. The boys took one look at him and turned to run.

"Oh no, you don't!" Peter leaped to grab their collars. "Your Daddy hasn't taught you a thing, has he? Well, it's time somebody taught you!" He shook them hard. Kenneth howled. Kevin panicked, then sank his teeth into Peter's finger.

"You worthless brat!" Peter roared. He snatched up the broken shovel handle and cracked it across Kevin's backside. One, two, three times.

He was using it on Kenneth when a loud voice stopped him. "What are you doing!"

Peter turned, the broken handle in his hand. "Those brats broke this shovel and I need it now!" But Jason towered above him, mighty and glaring.

"They are my sons, and you have no right to punish them!"

"They are my grandsons! I have just as much right -"

"No!" Jason stepped closer. "You do not!" He jerked his head at his sons. "Go on inside." He turned back to his father. "Don't you dare lay a hand on any of my children – ever again!" he hissed.

CHAPTER TWENTY

THE CAN TREMBLED in Jason's palm. He breathed fast. Fumbled with the lid and popped it open. It looked the same. Smelled the same. He had not had any in a long time. The smell made him salivate.

Someone was coming. Jason snapped the lid on the can and shoved it into his pocket. He turned to the workbench. What was it he needed? Bolts. He needed bolts to fix the mower. With shaking fingers, he fumbled through the bolt box.

Sunshine shot suddenly through the shop. "Got that mower fixed yet?" Dad's big boot tapped in the doorway.

"Uh, I'm -" Jason grabbed some bolts at random and picked up a wrench – "just getting ready to."

"I've been waiting all forenoon," Dad barked. "What have you been doing? Taking a nap?"

Jason whirled. "No, I was not taking a nap! I've been fixing the fence and shoeing your old horse." He gripped the wrench tighter, to keep from throwing it at his father. "Seems to me I saw you drinking coffee – or something – on the porch awhile back. If you weren't so big-time lazy, you could have the mower fixed youself."

Peter's face turned a mottled purple. His back was hurting. How could Jason have the nerve to call him lazy? He had been accused of many things in his life, but never once laziness. "You worthless -!"

"Shut up!" Jason elbowed Peter out of his way. Peter thrust out an arm, ready to put him back in his place, but Jason was out of reach.

Jason tore into the mower. He wrenched off the old bolts and threw them into the corner of the shop. He worked till sweat rolled down his back. The can pressed against his leg as he lay on his side, half under the mower. It was there. It was there. He'd use it. He would. Candy bars didn't work. Cookies and apples didn't work. Nothing did, except… his dip.

Jason tightened the last bolt. He sat up, but he could feel the can. Round and hard. He put away the wrench and wiped his hands on a grease rag. He took the can from his pocket. He'd tried hard. No one knew how hard, except him. But he wasn't strong enough to win. Momentarily he hated himself. He was a weakling, a spineless -. His face hardened. No. He wasn't. It wasn't his fault. It was Dad's.

Jason removed the lid and dropped a wad inside his lip. He moved to the window, feeling that good old buzz. *I'll throw the rest away,* he told himself. Dad stumped around the corner of the barn, lugging a harness. *Or maybe I won't.*

He put the lid back on. He felt so much better. He was going to make it.

Jason stepped outside. "The mower's done," he said coldly. What should he do with the can? He turned back to the shop. He couldn't leave it in his pocket. Lori might find it. Jason's steps faltered.

He remembered how she'd cried. Scrunched herself together on the bed, as if to shield herself from him. Shamed and stricken, it had been easy to promise her. If he ever did it again, he would tell her. But she wouldn't have to worry. He wouldn't so much as *look* at it again. She could trust him, of course she could.

But now the wad was in his lip. Reminding him he'd broken his promise. Broken her trust. She had trusted him, hadn't she? Slowly he bent and tossed the can beneath the workbench. It slid into the corner, out of sight. He wouldn't tell Lori.

"I SEE YOU! I see you!" Kenneth crowed, clapping.

Kevin bounced out from behind the door. "A lizard ran over my foot," he chattered. "It tickled so bad, I 'bout had to scream. I'm going to tell Mom!"

Kenneth wished a lizard had run over his foot. Why did all the good things happen to Kevin?

Kevin saw Kenneth's distressed face. "I bet that was a mom lizard with a hundred babies. Maybe a baby will run over your foot," he suggested generously.

Kenneth nodded. A baby lizard would be better than none at all.

"I'll shut my eyes now," Kevin said. "Your turn to hide."

Kenneth darted to the other end of the shop. Where could he hide? They had been playing all morning, and it was getting hard to find a new place. He peered under the workbench. It was dark and dirty, but it looked like a good place to hide. He scooted in on his stomach, way back in the corner. Were there any baby lizards here? He held out his feet expectantly. With a hundred of them, they were probably just about everywhere.

It took Kevin a long time to find Kenneth. Kenneth's arms were cramped. He scratched his neck. He tried to not move his feet so he wouldn't scared away the lizards. He tried hard, but finally his toe wiggled. Then his whole foot wiggled. "I guess the lizards are sleeping anyway," he mumbled. He stretched, and his hand touched something.

Kevin wandered toward the far end of the shop. He was almost ready to give up. Maybe Kenneth had tricked him and gone outside. But what was that? A rustle. He stooped to look, and a triumphant Kenneth scrambled out from under the workbench.

"Look what I found!" Kenneth held up a small, round can.

Kevin's eyes widened in surprise. "Why – why, it's candy! Where was it?"

"Under there." Kenneth pointed. "Let's ask Mom if we can have some." They raced for the house.

Lori was stirring sausage gravy when the door burst open. She hoped it wasn't Jason. The biscuits weren't done, and he detested waiting on meals.

"Look, Mommy, look!" Kenneth pranced beside her, waving something in the air.

She added a thickening to the gravy and stirred in a little seasoned salt. She was glad it was just the boys. It made her nervous when Jason came in before she was ready.

"Can we have some candy, Mom?" Kevin tapped urgently on her arm. "We found it in the shop. Can we have some?"

"What?" Lori turned off the burner and held out her hand. "Here, let me see it."

Kenneth dropped the can eagerly into her palm.

Lori gasped. She staggered against the counter. It must be an old one. An empty one. She shook it. Peeped inside.

"Can we have some?" Kenneth wheedled. "You could have some, too."

"No." Lori struggled to focus. Her sons. Her innocent sons. She'd as soon hand them a rattlesnake. "This – this is Daddy's."

"Can we have some?"

Lori set the can on the counter. She felt dirty just holding it. "You ask him that when he comes in." Her voice sounded strange and unnatural. "Go wash your hands and sit in your places."

They were all waiting when Jason walked into the kitchen. Even Lori. Jason started to sit down. There was something on his plate. He stared. Uttered a string of unintelligible expletives.

"Look what we found, Daddy!" chirped Kenneth.

Jason snatched the can. He glared at Lori, but she was busy mashing Beth's potatoes and didn't look at him.

{196} *Bootprints*

"It's your candy." Kevin bounced with excitement. "Can we have some, Daddy? We about don't never have any candy."

Jason clutched the can and slumped in his chair. Lori ignored him. He looked at the twins. "No," he said. He slid the can into his pocket.

"**LOOK, LORI, I** wasn't going to. I really wasn't. But you don't have any idea how it is to work with Dad."

"I know your dad. Even he would not stoop to such depravity."

Her charge cut like a knife. He stepped back. She wasn't even going to try to understand.

Lori washed another bowl. "Next thing the boys will be dipping too." Tears fell into the dishwater.

Jason saw them and felt like kicking himself. Dad was right. He was worthless. A worthless father. A worthless husband. A worthless piece of flesh with no backbone.

"You destroyed my trust once." Lori looked out the window. She didn't want to be cruel, but she was going to lay out the facts. If the facts weren't nice, it was his own fault. He couldn't do this to her, and expect her to be unscathed.

"You broke my trust," she repeated, "and it was not easy to build it up again. But I tried, because God created women with the desire to trust their husbands. I *want* to trust you, Jason. But you don't deserve it. You don't care about my feelings, or about what is right. All you care about is that filthy dip. If I don't ever risk trusting you again, you'll know who to blame."

Jason's shoulders hunched. Not one of Dad's tongue lashings had ever compared with this. This quiet, cold rejection from his wife. *I do care!* he wanted to tell her. But she wouldn't believe him. Wouldn't listen. He had lost her. His Lori. He turned and walked out the door.

Lori watched until the shuffling figure disappeared into the barn. Had she said too much? It was only a fragment of what she felt. "Choose between me and the tobacco," she'd wanted to say, but fear stifled her. What if he chose the tobacco? What if he already had?

Bootprints {197}

Lori pulled the plug from the sink. The water swirled down in a swoosh. She shook her head stubbornly. She wouldn't give way to tears, or she might never stop. "I want to die," she whispered.

DAY FOLLOWED DAY. Lori cleaned, washed, cooked. She talked to Jason when she had to. But she felt like a robot. A machine. Going through the motions without feeling a thing.

Her flowers bloomed, and she didn't notice. Beth learned to sit by herself, and she didn't care. She didn't care when Kenneth caught his new pants in the barbed wire fence and ripped off half the leg. "Put it with the mending," she stated indifferently. It was the way she operated. Indifferently. She didn't laugh and seldom smiled. She never cried.

Jason dipped regularly again. She knew it, and he knew she knew it. But he didn't mention it, and neither did she.

"I'm going to be over at the other farm tomorrow," Jason told Lori one Friday evening. "Philip's going to help me vaccinate the cattle."

Lori paused in her rocking. Maybe she could go along and stay with Mary. She felt a sliver of anticipation.

"Whatever," Jason mumbled when she suggested it. He turned back to his magazine.

Lori laid Beth in her crib and got out the broom. She would sweep and straighten up tonight yet, if she was going away tomorrow.

Getting out of the house would be good.

"**WHAT A NICE** surprise!" Mary exclaimed as she welcomed Lori and the children into the kitchen. "I was just wondering what I was going to do all day." She laughed and took Beth from Lori's arms.

"We're used to doing special things together on Saturdays when Philip's at home. I could envy you, having your husband home every day. I'm sure you enjoy that."

"Uh, well -" Lori didn't want to tell Mary she rarely saw Jason even if he was home. Or that she was glad to have it that way. "He's – outside most of the time."

{198} *Bootprints*

"I'm sure he is. Here boys, let's go find the toys. We don't have a lot, but there are some books you might enjoy looking at."

Lori stood in front of the bay window. Once she had been a bride in this house. A naive bride who hadn't any clue her husband dipped. Deceived. Would one day abuse her children in violent fits of anger. If she had remained single, or married -

"You can come in here, too," Mary called from the living room, "and we'll just sit around and visit."

Lori jumped. She dug into her satchel for some beads for Beth. "Oh no, let me help you with something." She must act normal. Keep Mary from suspecting anything wrong. How would it be to have a husband who wanted to do special things with you?

Mary went to the hall closet and got a doll for Emily. "I really hadn't planned much for today," she told Lori, "but maybe we can bake some cookies."

"Let me help." Lori was eager. "I hardly ever get a chance to do something for someone else."

Mary reached for a cookbook. "Okay then. Let's see… I know what. We'll make Molasses Crinkles. Those are Philip's favorite."

They mixed a huge batch – so Lori could have some to take home – and took turns rolling them in sugar and pressing them on the pans. Lori couldn't keep her eyes off Mary. Was she always this happy? Did she really adore Philip as much as she pretended? Did they ever have arguments? Did Philip ever raise his voice at her?

The men came in for dinner. Lori noticed the look Philip and Mary exchanged when Philip came into the kitchen. She noticed how he helped her put the food on the table, and how he pulled out her chair for her.

Lori struggled to get the children seated. Jason didn't help at all, didn't even acknowledge her. She busied herself buttering slices of bread. She knew what she wanted for her marriage. It wasn't what she had. Philip and Mary had it. "Yes, Kevin, I'll get you some jelly. It looks good, doesn't it?" She wouldn't go there.

Bootprints {199}

"These cookies are the best ever." Philip reached for his second one. He winked at Jason. Don't these women spoil us though? Cooking all our favorite foods and trying to make us fat." He and Mary laughed.

Lori cringed. What would Jason say? Would he tell all about her flops and her bad reputation as a cook? To her relief, he just gave a dry laugh and took a bite of peaches.

Lori heard Philip thanking Mary for the dinner before he went out the door. Jason pulled on his boots and followed without a word.

Why? Why? Lori began clearing the table. Why couldn't Jason be at least half as nice as Philip? Philip and Mary's marriage seemed perfect to her. Why was life so twisted and unfair?

But Lori was to discover that Philip and Mary had their problems too. "We'd love to have children," Mary told her that afternoon. "But so far," she sighed and gently patted Beth, who was sitting on her lap, "it hasn't been God's will, I guess."

"Oh." Lori blinked.

"I struggle with bitterness at times, and envy people like you with all your children," Mary confessed. She gave a lopsided smile at Lori. "You look shocked."

"Well," Lori fingered her apron. "You're always so cheerful. I never dreamed – I mean, I even envy you at times." What had she said? She hurried on. "You and Philip seem so happy."

"Oh, we are. But I think every woman longs for children of her own. I certainly do. Especially when Philip's gone all day and I'm here by myself."

Lori nodded. She had thought Mary's life was perfect. It gave her a sudden kinship, knowing it wasn't. Dare she tell her about herself? Not a lot. She wouldn't tell about Jason's dipping. But – "I've been jealous of you today." She wrestled the words from her mouth.

"Who? Me?"

"Yes. You and Philip. Your – your relationship."

Mary's forehead wrinkled. "I'm not sure I understand."

"Well, you love each other, and aren't afraid to show it." At Mary's startled expression, Lori rushed on. "You did nothing wrong or offensive. It's just so – so plain you love each other. You seem to have something," her voice dropped to a whisper, "that we don't."

"Oh. Let me tell you, Lori, our marriage isn't perfect. It can't be, because we're both human. We've had our misunderstandings, but we try to work through them as they come up."

Lori thought of the barrier between her and Jason. It was like a concrete wall. Hard to scale, and harder still to break down. "How do you do that?" she asked. "Get rid of misunderstandings, I mean."

"One thing that has helped me tremendously is to live out the personal promise we made to each other on our wedding day. Every evening before we go to sleep, Philip asks me if he did or said anything that day to hurt me. I ask him the same question. We agreed to be completely honest with each other, although," Mary chuckled ruefully, "that's not always as easy as it sounds.

"For example, when Philip takes off his socks, they usually go flying into the hamper in two hard little balls. It irked me to no end, having to unroll those smelly socks every time I washed. But I was afraid if I brought it up, he would think it awfully petty. So one evening I sneaked a sock into bed, and when Philip asked me to lay out his offenses, I tried to make it sound as terrible as possible. I told him how much time it took, unrolling that little mountain of foul-smelling orbs. I reminded him about his athlete's foot, and I poked the sock under his nose as firsthand evidence, and how could he put his wife through the trauma of unrolling them?"

Lori laughed. It rippled through her body, a genuine laugh. Jason unrolled his socks, she realized. He was particular about all his clothes. She had taken it for granted, but now as she listened to Mary, she knew it was a good point. Lately she hadn't thought of Jason as having any good points. All he was, was a big stack of crimes. But he took care of his clothes. It wasn't a big thing, but it was something.

"Philip was appalled to have his nose buried in a smelly sock, but he needed to know his socks got on my nerves." Mary shook her head.

Bootprints {201}

"For awhile I wasn't sure if we'd get to sleep peacefully or not, but – oh, I hadn't intended to say all this. I'm not a bit proud of it, or some of the other things I've done, but what I started out to say was that if things come up, we try to make it right with each other before we go to sleep. It has been such a help to us that I would encourage every couple to try it."

Lori couldn't imagine Jason *ever* asking her how he'd hurt her. And if she'd ask him? He'd probably grunt something like *of course not. Now go to sleep.*

"I think it's too late for us," she said.

"Lori, it's never too late. Not as long as you're living." Mary stood and went to the bedroom. In a minute she was back with a book. "Have you read this?"

Lori studied the cover. She shook her head.

"My mom gave it to me soon after we were married. I've really enjoyed it. It's about how our attitudes, actions, and words affect our husbands, either for good or for bad."

Lori took the book and skimmed the back cover. "It – it looks interesting. Do you mind if I read it?"

"Of course not," Mary said.

So Lori tucked the book into her diaper bag. A tiny spark of hope winked inside her. Could their marriage possibly be saved after all?

CHAPTER TWENTY-ONE

LORI LAID THE book on the sofa beside her. She hadn't read much yet. Only the first five chapters, but it was enough to make her realize a few things. The state of their marriage was not all Jason's fault.

She had thought it was. Jason was the bad one. His sins were many. It was such a long list, she couldn't keep track of everything. He spanked the twins much too hard and snapped at her. He dipped. Those were the top ones, but there were others. He was a selfish, stubborn man. A corrupt man. She was married to a man like that.

Lori rested her head against the back of the couch. She was glad to be alone. The boys were outside and the girls were sleeping. She needed to think. Jason was very different from the man she had dreamed of. That man had been tender and kind. His wife was the apple of his eye. He doted on her, brought her flowers, and helped her without a murmur. He was a model father. He got up in the night with the baby. He romped and tussled with his sons. Cuddled and cherished his daughters. He combined strength with gentleness, love with firmness.

Reality collided with her imaginary husband. Her dreams lay smashed. But reality lived on. Jason was a cold, cruel man.

The book said she was created by God to be Jason's helpmeet. That did not include changing him, at least not through whining or nagging. Nagging did not inspire a man to make amends. Nor did putting on a sorry face, limping around discouraged, depressed, or angry.

Lori realized she had justified herself in being pitiful. Jason was obviously in the wrong. He had so many sins.

What could she do? At least she could remind him about his shortcomings so he wouldn't become callused to them. He had to realize how difficult he made life for her.

Nagging and manipulation, the book called it. An utter repulsion to a man. If she wanted her husband to change, she needed to inspire him through positive ways. Thankfulness. Respect. A joyful countenance.

Lori groaned. How could she be thankful and joyful with a husband like Jason? Didn't she have a right to be angry and depressed? All those shortcomings. If she put a smile on her face and started acting like he was really special, he might think she thought he was fine the way he was.

The book had stories about women with bad marriages. Some of them were worse than hers. At least Jason didn't get drunk. He didn't beat her. He wasn't unfaithful. Lori shuddered to think of an unfaithful husband.

Jason did have good points. Lori remembered her conversation with Mary. Jason took care of his clothes, which was something Philip didn't do. But Lori didn't want to think of Jason's good points. When she thought about his crimes, it was easier to think she was a good wife.

Lori touched the cover of the book. God had redeemed the sad marriages of these women. What about hers? If she couldn't change Jason, could God?

Who was God? There had been a time when she was a girl that she thought she knew Him. She had prayed and read her Bible, and enjoyed it. But now – Lori leaned back and closed her eyes. God seemed distant, unreachable. It was hard to believe He actually cared about her. Or her marriage.

A cry from the bedroom brought Lori to her feet. She took the book with her to the bedroom and hid it in the bottom of the diaper stacker. She didn't want Jason to know she had it. She could imagine him looking at it, nodding his head and reminding her what a bad wife she was. She did have faults – nagging and manipulation didn't sound very nice – but she wasn't *nearly* as bad as Jason.

Lori carried Beth to the kitchen. She set her into the high chair and put a few Cheerios on the tray. "There, pumpkin, now you can watch Mommy folding laundry."

Lori pulled a pair of Jason's pants from the basket. Was she willing to try? She wanted to say no, Jason didn't deserve anything from her. But if she withheld her respect and honor until he changed, would he ever change?

The door slammed, interrupting her thoughts. She frowned as the boys clattered into the kitchen. "Careful. You'll wake Emily."

They tiptoed to her. "Daddy wants a drink," Kevin whispered loudly.

"We do, too. A nice, cold drink, Mom." Kenneth pulled his little red handkerchief from his pocket and wiped his face.

He must've seen Jason doing that. Lori set the water jug under the faucet. It was natural for boys to notice their daddies and want to copy them. But she didn't want her boys copying Jason. What if they turned out just like him? She shivered as she dropped ice cubes into the water.

"Here's the lid, Mom." Kenneth's grubby hands clutched the spout. Lori rinsed it, screwed it on the jug. The lemons. They were in a little basket on the bottom shelf of the refrigerator. She hadn't intended to remember.

Slowly she opened the refrigerator door. She felt the gaze of the boys, and closed it with a bang. It was too much, being nice to him. He was leaving a bad example for the boys. But her conscience niggled her. How could she win him? Her hand rested on the handle. Was she willing? She didn't feel like it, but – she jerked, and the door flew open – she would not go by her feelings.

JASON PULLED OUT his bandanna and wiped his face. He'd sent the boys inside for a drink ten minutes ago already. How long did it take to fix a glass of ice water?

Likely Lori had been sleeping. It sounded like her. Claiming the girls would sleep better if the boys were outside with him, when she intended to take a nap herself.

Lori wasn't herself these days. Jason supposed it was his fault. Maybe he had let her down. But did she have to go around with such a dreary, martyred air?

He felt as if he had lost his wife. It took effort to put one foot in front of the other. His boots were heavy, but he must keep going. Going where? He didn't know. He wanted Lori, but she didn't want him. Did she hate him?

Jason drew the can from his pocket. He hated himself for it. But he didn't even have Lori anymore. The woman who lived in his house was not his Lori. He had no affection for her. She was stiff and cold, and all she wanted to talk about was what he did wrong.

Jason slid the can into his pocket and pulled out his watch. Fifteen minutes! Maybe she had decided he didn't need a drink. She was like that. He stepped to the door and squinted against the sunshine. His cheeks were wet. He brushed them vigorously and stared straight ahead. It was the sunshine.

Movement blurred through the glare. He waited, and there were the boys, both holding on to the half-gallon water jug.

He grabbed it roughly. "You didn't have to take all day! Now get to your chores!"

"But Daddy, it's a surpri-"

"Get!"

They scurried away. Jason flipped open the spout and took a swig. Sour. And sweet. Not lemonade? He unscrewed the lid and peered in. Fresh lemon slices jostled against the ice.

Slowly Jason put the lid back on. He spit out his dip. Dip didn't mix well with lemons, and he wanted to taste the lemonade.

Could he get his Lori back? Jason drank deeply. He rubbed his hand across his cheeks. The sun had gone behind a cloud, but Lori had made him lemonade.

FOR A FEW days things went better in the Kauffman home. Lori didn't mention Jason's faults. She was more cheerful. Jason noticed and tried harder to avoid his dip. Even the children were happier. Then Jason bought six more cows.

Peter's eyes bulged when the cattle trailer ground to a stop in front of the barn. The driver popped a round, cheerful face out the window. "Is this the Kauffman farm?"

"Yes, but there must be a mistake. We didn't buy any cows." Peter eyed the shuffling creatures in the trailer. Jerseys!

"I was told to deliver them to Jason Kauffman on Stringtown Road. That you?"

"No." Peter quivered with suppressed rage. When and how had Jason pulled this off? He'd told him just last week that milking forty-five cows was enough. Now this.

The driver took a paper off the dashboard and studied it in bewilderment. "I'm sure I followed the directions. Can you tell me where Jason Kauffman lives then?"

"Oh, he lives here too, but he – there he comes."

Jason nodded at the driver. "Hello, sir. Glad to see you." He could hear Peter panting as they unloaded the cows. What was it Thad Thompson had said? He wouldn't regret this. They were good milkers, every one of them. Peter had dealt with Thad Thompson several times and he valued his opinion.

"Explain yourself!" Peter roared before the cattle trailer had a chance to reach the road.

Jason shoved his hand into his pocket. It was there. "Explain what?"

Peter was so angry he couldn't speak.

"I told you last week I need to start milking more cows," Jason continued. "With so many big farmers, the small ones have to upscale too or they'll be choked out. Thad Thompson said -"

"Choked out nothing! You're stubborn and bullheaded. Keep wasting your money on Jerseys and soon you'll be broke. Then what'll happen to my farm? Huh?" His eyes blazed into Jason's. "You're a fool."

"It's not your farm anymore. I'm buying it and I'll make the decisions."

"You should have asked me first. You're a worthless, irresponsible boy!"

Jason lunged past his father. He went to the milk house and pounded his fist against the bulk tank. "I hate him! I hate him!" The words snarled from his throat, and it felt good.

THE BOYS WERE rowdy that evening. They galloped through the house on their imaginary horses. They bucked and reared and shouted.

"Quiet!" bellowed Jason from the recliner. "Sit down or go outside."

The twins looked at each other. Why did Daddy always interrupt their games? He hardly let them have any fun, he was so bossy. Slowly they went outside.

It was dusk. Fireflies blinked and beckoned, but tonight the boys didn't feel like catching them. They sat on the porch steps instead.

Kevin saw the flowers blooming around the porch. Mom liked flowers. She took good care of them. She hoed out the weeds and gave them plenty of water. Kevin knew why water was important. It helped them grow big and strong.

Had Mom watered the flowers today? Kevin could not see any puddles. Suppose she had forgotten. Would the flowers die? Mom would be very sad.

"Let's water the flowers," said Kevin.

"Yes, let's," Kenneth jumped up. "That will make Mom happy."

They wrestled the hose from the hose reel. Kevin gripped the nozzle. "Okay, start it," he commanded.

Slowly they moved around the house, blasting water onto the flowers. They did not notice that several fragile stems collapsed.

Blossoms flew under the unmerciful deluge. But the twins were happy. They were helping Mom.

"Here, let me have a turn now." Kenneth grabbed the hose. "I'll do the ceiling flowers." He pointed the hose toward the hanging basket on the porch. The basket rocked wildly under the assault. They laughed. They were giving the flowers a ride. They did not see the window behind the basket.

JASON'S EYES FLEW open and he shot to his feet. What was going on? He stared at the dripping magazine in his hand, and his wet shirt. There was water all over the floor.

Jason stepped gingerly away from the recliner. He had a horror of wet socks. In his effort to avoid one puddle, he stepped into another. At once his feet shot out from under him, and he fell heavily to the floor.

Lori heard him fall. She put down her measuring tape and went to the living room. She was astounded to see Jason picking himself up. Was he sick, or hurt? She started to him, but he bolted past her, out the door.

"Just what do you think you are doing?" She could hear his angry voice through the open window. She hurried across the room, and stepped into a puddle. "What in the world?" she murmured. The recliner was wet too. And the screen.

"We were watering Mom's flowers, to make her happy." Kevin's voice squeaked fearfully.

"Happy, huh?" Jason shouted. "That window was open! You made a huge mess. Look at me!" He waved at his dripping shirt. "This is ridiculous!"

Lori crouched beside the window. She smothered a scream as Jason snatched up the hose and walloped it across Kevin's back. *Not a hose Jason.* THAT'S TOO CRUEL. He reached for Kenneth and she closed her eyes. She couldn't bear to watch, but she heard. The dull thwack of the hose on Kenneth.

"Now go inside," Jason commanded. "Clean up that mess and go to bed!"

Lori stumbled to her feet. They had been trying to help her. Why couldn't Jason listen to his children before he punished them? He was as bad as his own father.

Lori gasped when she took off Kevin's shirt. An ugly, red welt was rising rapidly across his back. She took off Kenneth's shirt. Another welt. No, two of them.

Tears ran down her cheeks as she hurried to the bathroom for the B&W salve. This was abuse. A grown man whipping his sons with a hose because they had innocently upset him.

Gently Lori rubbed the salve into the welts. The boys sobbed softly. She helped them into their pajamas, then gathered them in a tight hug. "Thank you for watering Mommy's flowers." She could feel the rapid beat of their hearts, their warm, jerky breath on her neck. "You are such big boys!"

"D – Daddy doesn't think so," sniffled Kevin.

"Mommy," Kenneth pulled back to face her, "why doesn't Daddy love us?"

Lori stroked his hair. He had eyes like his daddy. Such pretty eyes. She struggled to find words. "Daddy – didn't know what you were doing. Go to bed now, and you'll feel better tomorrow." She tucked the sheet under their chins. "Good night, dears."

Lori stepped out into the hall. She quivered with anger at the injustice of Jason's punishment. Lori had never been more upset with Jason. She wanted to give him a piece of her mind. She wanted to scream at him, pound him, make him feel at least a little of what the boys did.

But an angry woman could not fix an angry husband. She had read that in the book. She needed to calm herself, and pray.

Lori stood still. She counted to ten, took deep, long breaths. "Help me, God – if you care." Her feet carried her to the living room. She wouldn't say a word about the incident. Not a word. She wouldn't.

Jason was lying on the couch. "Dad is impossible," he blurted.

Oh, Lori thought. *So that's it.*

{210} *Bootprints*

"I bought some more cows and he acted like it was the stupidest thing I ever did. Shouted and yelled and called me a fool." Jason sat up. "I tell you, that man's impossible. He never listens to a thing I say. Blames me for everything that goes wrong. I don't even try to please him anymore, because I can't!"

The longer he talked, the more upset Lori became. It was so clear, so obvious. Jason treated his own sons exactly the way his father treated him. Couldn't he see it?

"He called me stubborn and bullheaded," steamed Jason. "Why doesn't he look in the mirror once? He's the stubborn, bullheaded -"

Lori stood up. "Stop," she heard herself saying. "Stop it right now!" She thought of her boys' tearful faces. She stood in front of Jason. Anger made her tall. Fearless.

"You sit there and rave about your dad, but you don't know how blind you are." The words poured out in a whispered shriek. "It's high time somebody told you the truth, Jason Kauffman. You-are-exactly-like-your-Dad!"

She expected Jason to leap off the couch, shake her, maybe even hit her. She didn't care. She felt mighty and terrible. Able to take a beating from the man on the couch. A hundred beatings, if it helped her children.

But Jason sat dumbly, seemingly glued to the spot. He looked as if she'd thrown a brick into his face.

Lori plunged on. "You treat your sons exactly the way your dad treats you. The whipping you just gave them left welts across their backs. Now you sit here and whine about your cruel dad? Does that make sense?" She paused for breath.

"You think your dad doesn't love you. Well, let me tell you, the boys think the same thing about you. Kenneth asked me a few minutes ago," her voice started to tremble but she hurried on, "he asked, 'Mommy, why doesn't Daddy love us?' What was I supposed to say? That you love them? You lost your temper and beat them up! It would have been a lie, Jason."

Lori stared at Jason. Jason stared at Lori. Suddenly she wasn't angry anymore. She was crying. She turned and ran from the room.

Jason rose unsteadily. What had come over Lori? She had never talked like this to him before. How could she. She had the gall to accuse him of being like his father. His father! He hated him.

"No!" he said aloud. "I'm not like him! I'm not!" He started for the bedroom. Just wait till he got hold of Lori. He would show her what happened when she lied about Jason Kauffman. He could do almost anything to a woman like that.

His hand was on the knob. He was ready to burst in, but he heard something. He stepped closer, pressed his ear against the varnished wood. Sobs, he realized. Lori.

His hand dropped from the knob and he leaned weakly against the door frame. He couldn't go in now. He stared into the twins' bedroom. Dark. Quiet. What was it that Kevin had said tonight? Or was it Kenneth? "Why doesn't Daddy love us?"

Of course he loved his sons. He worked day and night almost to provide for them. But they were too young to appreciate that. They were only... five?

Without thinking, Jason went quietly into their bedroom. Walked up beside their bed. They were breathing softly, sound asleep. They held hands on top of the sheet. Jason hadn't seen his sons asleep in a long time. Maybe not since they were babies. He leaned down. There was something wet on Kenneth's face. Kevin's face was turned to the wall, but he had to know. Hesitantly he touched his cheek. Wet.

Jason straightened his back, thinking suddenly of another little boy, long ago, who had cried himself to sleep. Why? Because... his Daddy... didn't... love him.

Jason reeled back to the hallway. *You, Jason Kauffman, are exactly like your father.* "No!" His voice was a hoarse whisper. "I'm NOT! And I'll never be!"

{212} *Bootprints*

CHAPTER TWENTY-TWO

LORI HEARD JASON'S footsteps coming down the hall. She was sorry to have said it, but it was true. He was just like his Dad.

Sobs jerked from her throat. What would she do if he beat her? He might, he was so mad, and she had made him mad. If she could just recall those words.

She waited, but the door did not open. What was Jason doing? Maybe he couldn't face her. She had accused him of a terrible thing.

Lori felt guilty, but then she remembered the boys' backs. What kind of mother was she to see that and do nothing?

When Jason came in, Lori pretended to be asleep. Jason didn't say a word, just dropped heavily into bed. Lori lay tensely beside him. What was he thinking? He tossed. He turned. Once he moaned, and the sound pierced Lori's heart.

The book said a wife could never change her husband by disrespecting him. Had it been disrespectful to tell Jason what she thought? But he needed it, Lori convinced herself. She couldn't meekly look the other way when her children's welfare was at stake. She wanted them to know their mommy had done what she could.

It was dark. Lori peeked over the edge of the quilt, into the seamless shadows. Her life was dark, too. She was caught between the boys and Jason. She breathed through her nose, holding back the sniffles. Was this how the mouse had felt, caught between her shoe and the floor?

She had cleaned the boys' closet that morning, and a mouse had darted out of a box. In her scramble to get away, she somehow jumped on it and killed it. It was gruesome. She had pitilessly rolled it onto the dustpan.

But now, in the middle of the night, she felt an unexpected kinship. She knew how it was to be pressed beneath a deadly weight, with no escape.

Jason went to sleep about one, but when Beth woke up at two, Lori was still staring into the darkness. The discouragement and depression from the last several years bore down on her with double force. Was there any use to keep trying? The book had given her motivation, but what had changed? Several times she had thought things were better, but tonight proved otherwise. Her attempts at being a good wife did not make Jason a good husband, or daddy. Should she give up on him?

He was restless in his sleep. His arms and legs kept moving, as if he were trying to get away from something. Was it her? She held Beth tightly and stumbled to the window. She wanted to hate him, but she loved him. She loved him as much as she did her boys. She couldn't give up on him, because she knew he didn't want to be like he was. He didn't want to be angry. He didn't want to beat his children. But he couldn't seem to help himself, and she couldn't help him either. Was there anyone who could? Was there any hope of breaking this destructive cycle? Peter was angry. Jason was angry. The twins would grow up and be angry too. Could anyone escape?

A silver slice of moon was sliding behind the western horizon. A soft breeze blew the katydid chorus in through the open window. Lori stood motionless, noticing everything, yet not fully comprehending it.

Questions struggled to the surface of her mind. *Does God… see? Does He care where I'm at? Does he care about Jason, and the boys? Can angry daddies go to heaven?*

The moon disappeared behind the trees, but Lori still stood. Staring. Unseeing. Finally her arms ached, her knees swayed. She had to get to bed. As she turned from the window, a plea rose to her lips. *God, if you are there, if you love me at all, show me somehow, soon.*

THE NEXT DAY it rained. Lori tried to ignore her headache and keep the children happy. She made a batch of peanut butter play dough, but the twins looked at it indifferently. They didn't want to play.

"My back hurts," muttered Kenneth.

Lori gave the play dough to the girls. She took the boys' hands and led them to the rocking chair. There was no use pretending. They weren't happy, and neither was she.

She took them on her lap. They were five years old, and big. They would be as big as their father someday. If she could just protect them from their father.

The twins laid their heads against Mommy's shoulders, one on each side. They wanted Mommy to rock for a long time.

Lori rocked. Once she looked down at several splashes on Kevin's hand. Were they his tears, or hers? It really didn't matter. They were in this together, the three of them.

"Daddy will soon be in for dinner," she said finally. "Do you want to help make sandwiches?"

They put pickles and onions on the cheeseburgers. They watched Lori put whipped cream on the raisin pie and get out the ice cubes.

"I don't want ice." Kevin held his hands across the top of his glass.

"I don't either," Kenneth agreed. "I don't like cold water."

Lori put the tray back in the freezer. They didn't want ice. She held her eyes wide as Jason came into the kitchen. It didn't mean anything. It was just a passing whim. She tried to convince herself as they ate their lunch.

Bootprints {215}

There was something about Jason. His clothes, Lori realized suddenly. He was always careful about his appearance, but now he looked as if he'd dressed from the hamper. And he hadn't shaved or combed his hair.

He must be in a terrible turmoil, Lori thought. Well, so was she. And the boys.

Kenneth got his glass and took a quick slurp of water. Daddy was looking at him! Daddy didn't like him. "Wake up, boy!" said Daddy.

Kenneth jumped. Kevin jumped harder. What did Daddy mean? They weren't sleeping, of course they weren't. Was Daddy going to whip them again? Their hearts pounded.

"I said pass the pie," Daddy said loudly.

Kevin grabbed for the pie. His hands shook as he tried to lift it.

"Here, let me." Lori reached across the table. The boys' terror struck her deeply, and in that instant she knew. It went deeper than not wanting ice in their glasses. They no longer wanted to be like their father.

HAD GOD HEARD her prayer? Lori stood at the sink, her hands motionless in the water. If she were Moses or Elijah or even one of the apostles, God would hear her. But she was just plain Lori Kauffman, and her prayers didn't seem to do any good.

Last night she had prayed for herself. All she wanted was to know whether God cared about her or not. *He careth for you*, the Bible said, but if He did, why didn't He help her? Why didn't He do something about Jason? Of course, Jason was a big job, but he was no bigger than Saul of Tarsus. He hadn't persecuted any Christians yet, other than his family.

Lori had not thought of herself that way before. Persecuted. Visions of prison cells and torture chambers rose in her mind. She could not call herself persecuted, but she was lost and hopeless. For years she had tried to make things better, and it wasn't working. There was only one thing left to do. Tell God.

Bootprints

She wanted to tell Him. There were so many things she wanted. But who was God? Was it safe to trust Him? What would happen if she did? Would He keep her in this misery forever, to make her perfect through suffering?

A song came to her mind, one they'd sung in school when she was a girl. Something about *when there's rain on my window, and tears in my eyes.*

There was rain on her window. There were tears in her eyes, falling into the dish water. *So many questions have I.* She remembered that too, and something about children. She willed the words to fit together in her memory... *Hearts so innocent, yet filled with pain... wish I could turn it all around, and heal the broken heart of a child.*

Lori sobbed. It was what hurt her the most, her children, and her powerlessness to turn it all around.

She had thought it was her job to protect them. But her efforts had only exposed her weakness. She could not protect her children, nor could she keep them from following their father's footsteps.

Could she give them to God? Would God take better care of them than their mother could? A muffled tapping at the door interrupted her thoughts. Lori jerked her hands from the sink and raised her eyes to the mirror above the wash basin. Who was here? Hastily she wiped her swollen eyes.

Raindrops dripped from Philip's hat brim. He handed her a bag and a bouquet of sunflowers. "From Mary," he said, and then he was gone.

Wonderingly, Lori went back to the kitchen. Sunflowers. Had Mary gone out into the rain to pick them for her? She put them in her blue vase, liking the yellow-against-blue effect.

There were two loaves of bread in the bag, still warm, and a note. Lori unfolded it.

"I've been thinking so much of you today. I have no idea what you're going through, but I wanted to share these verses with you. *"For I know the thoughts I have toward you, saith the Lord, thoughts of peace and not of evil, to give you an expected end."* Lori felt goose bumps on her arms. The note continued, *"Then ye shall call upon me, and I will hearken unto you. And ye shall seek me and find me, when ye shall search for me with all your heart."*

There was more, but the words blurred together. It was the voice of God, in a simple note. Lori dropped to her knees on the scuffed kitchen rug. She would seek this God.

JASON WORKED HARD all day. Rain couldn't stop him. He fixed the broken mangers Dad had hounded him about. He greased the manure spreader, the baler, and the planter. He sharpened the mower blades and finally inflated the tiller tire Lori had been complaining about all summer. "She ought to appreciate that," he growled, "but of course she won't." He spat furiously into a corner of the shop. She'd give him a frosty stare and say it was about time.

Dad and Mom had gone to town. Jason could work better without Dad breathing down his neck. Forget, too, about being like Dad. Not that it was true of course, but – Jason thrust the thought away.

Supper was ready when he came in. Steam curled from a loaded pizza. The tossed salad had little cherry tomatoes that Jason especially liked. And Lori was cheerful, no longer looking as if she were on her way to the stake.

Jason studied her out of the corner of his eye as he shoved pizza into his mouth. What was she trying to hide? She laughed when Kevin asked her if the sunflowers were chunks of the real sun. She told Jason about the flowers and bread, and when Emily spilled her milk, she didn't scold. Just calmly wiped it up.

Jason still hadn't figured it out by bedtime. He kept watching his wife from behind *The Budget*. She was acting like the girl he had married. He decided to test her.

"I fixed your tiller tire today."

Lori turned from the sink. "Oh, thank you! Now when it dries off, I can get into the garden." And she smiled at him, a Lori smile, not a bland stretching-of-the-lips smile.

Jason nodded and disappeared behind *The Budget*. She must've had a really good day, he thought, or maybe she was trying to make up for what she'd said last night. Either way, it likely wouldn't last long.

Someone thumped on the door. Before Lori could open it, it flew open and Peter spilled in with a load of groceries.

Jason started to get up, but when he saw who it was, he sat down again. Peter dumped the load on the table. "Here are your groceries," he told Lori. "Most of them, that is. There were some things on the list that weren't necessities. Like cream cheese and pork and beans. Those are things you can do without. A woman has no business throwing away her husband's money like that." Peter wagged his head at Lori. "You're going to drag your family into the poorhouse yet."

Jason couldn't believe his ears. He saw the stricken look on Lori's face and jumped to his feet. But he was too late. Peter was gone. Wordlessly Jason faced his wife over the mountain of groceries. There were tears in her eyes. He started for the door. He'd catch up with his father, and -

"No, Jason." Lori guessed his intentions. "Just… let it go." She managed a tiny smile. "Maybe I do spend too much. I usually don't buy cream cheese or pork and beans, but I saw in this week's sale flyer that both were on sale, and I thought -"

"There was nothing wrong with that!" Jason stormed. "He can't tell us what we can buy and what we can't!"

"I – well," Lori noticed the children standing wide-eyed in the doorway. "Come, children, let's put the groceries away. Here, Kenneth, put the cheese in the refrigerator, and Emily, you can take the butter. Kevin, you may put the mustard and the salad dressing on the third shelf in the pantry. Can you reach that high?"

Slowly Jason went back to the recliner. Lori's cheerfulness was forced now, he could tell. He'd talk to Dad tomorrow, see if he wouldn't!

LORI LAY AWAKE for a long time that night. She replayed the scene with her father-in-law over and over in her mind. He had talked rudely to her in front of the children. He was the most controlling man she had ever known. Why had they ever moved here? It just wasn't working.

There was a verse in Proverbs – she had read it this afternoon – that it is better to dwell in a corner of the housetop, than with a brawling woman in a wide house. She didn't know of any brawling women, but she knew a brawling man. Wouldn't it be better to go back to the house with walking trails, than to live on the same farm with Peter Kauffman?

She had had a deep peace after her time on the kitchen floor. Now it was gone already. Was this what she got in return for giving her problems to God? What good did it do to trust God, if He didn't stop bad things from happening? She had hoped things would be different now.

Jason slept. Lori tossed. She knew she wasn't being fair. It wasn't God's fault. God gave people the free will to choose, hoping they would choose His way. But often they didn't.

If someone made a wrong choice, others would likely suffer for it. *We all suffer at the hands of Peter,* Lori thought mournfully.

Tonight he had humiliated her in front of the whole family. But God had seen. She could choose to believe that. He had seen, and He cared how she felt.

There was another choice too. It came clearly, as she lay there in the darkness. She could choose to be bitter at Peter, or she could forgive him.

How could she forgive Peter? Surely God would understand if it was too hard for her. He was a cold-hearted man. She would go to sleep now, and forget the whole thing.

Lori closed her eyes, held still. She could not find peace. She had found it this afternoon, and it had felt so clean and fresh.

You must forgive Peter, said a voice in her head, *if you want that peace back.*

She wanted it back with all her might, but she did not want to forgive that man.

A crescent moon peeped through the window, and Lori watched it.

Did a grudge mean more to her than peace? Finally she pushed back the covers and knelt by the bed. "You will have to help me, Lord," she prayed. "I choose to forgive Peter, but I need your strength to carry it out."

Tears ran down her cheeks. This was harder even than this afternoon, she realized. But she would do it. She would forgive.

JASON HEARD LORI get out of bed. His wife was on the floor, beside the bed. He lay motionless, watching her. She was crying. What was wrong? He was about to sit up when he heard the whisper. *Help me, Lord…*

Jason strained to hear more. In the silvery moonlight, he saw her lips move, but he understood no more.

She stayed like that for a long time. When she finally got up, she went to the window. Just stood there, looking out, but she was smiling. *She looks like an angel,* Jason thought suddenly.

She turned then, and saw him watching. "I'm sorry," she whispered. "I didn't mean to wake you."

"Are you – are you all right?" His voice was hoarse.

"I'm fine." She climbed back into bed. She knew it now, peace wasn't having things change on the outside, it was having things change on the inside. "I was… forgiving your father."

"What?!" Jason sat bolt upright.

"It's alright, Jason." She touched his arm. "I think I can sleep now."

Slowly he lay back down. There was silence for a few minutes.

"Jason?" her voice quavered from the darkness.

"Huh?"

"I – I'm sorry for what I said last night." Lori struggled to say the words. In forgiving Peter, she had realized he wasn't the only one guilty of making wrong choices. She had planned to make this right in the morning, but with Jason awake…

"What do you mean?" Jason heard tears in her voice.

"About you being like – like your father. It wasn't right for me to say that."

Bootprints {221}

Jason was dumbfounded. What had come over his wife? Praying and making apologies in the middle of the night. Was she sick, or going to die?

"Jason?"

"Yes."

"I know I hurt you badly by saying that. I'm so sorry, Jason. Can you forgive me?"

"Yes -"

"Thank you, dear." She squeezed his hand. "I want to be a better wife."

This time it was Jason who lay staring into the darkness while Lori slept.

CHAPTER TWENTY-THREE

LORI CONTINUED TO act strange the next few days. Jason liked it, on one hand. She was happier, and she didn't look at him so critically. One evening she even made chocolate pie for supper. Her pies were almost as good as Mom's by now.

On the other hand, the change in Lori unsettled Jason. There were times he wanted to tell her to stop being so nice. She made him feel guilty. Jason couldn't understand it. He had nothing to be guilty about.

Jason frowned as he jounced behind his Belgians through the hayfield. How would he feel, if all of a sudden his father would just drop dead? Would he care? No, Jason decided, he'd look forward to a better life.

Life with Dad had never been good. Jason never knew what would set him off next. This morning it had been Lori, who had gone to see her mother for the day.

"When is that woman going to learn to stay at home like women should?" Dad had demanded. "I never saw a man who lets his wife run

Bootprints {223}

over him like you do. You ought to teach your wife to be a keeper at home, like the Bi -"

"Shut up!" Jason had shouted.

Lori didn't go away very often. She visited her mom once a month, but otherwise seldom went anywhere.

Jason finished the field by supper time. He looked forward to supper. It had surprised him, how lonely dinner had been without Lori. A few weeks ago he wouldn't have minded, with Lori so cold and tightlipped. But today he missed her. She had changed. He still didn't know whether it would last, but he hoped so. Yes, even if it unsettled him at times. He liked a happy wife.

She had left a note on his plate. It crinkled comfortably in his pocket even now. *I am glad you are my husband…*

He was glad too. He couldn't imagine being married to anyone else. At times like this, he felt a strong urge to do his best. Lori deserved a good man. Did she have one? He shrugged the question aside. But what would Lori say?

Lori was home – the twins were in the sandbox. "Come, boys," he commanded as he hurried past. "Let's go in for supper."

There was a kettle of soup and a basket of breadsticks on the table. Jason looked for Lori. The last while she had been acting glad to see him. It made him want to come inside, instead of staying out in the barn as long as possible.

"Where's Mom?"

Emily jumped in her chair. Why did Daddy always talk so loud? "She – she went to get some flowers," she faltered. "To make the table nice."

"Hummph. Sit down, boys." Jason had never seen the point of cutting off flowers and bringing them inside.

"They make me feel more cheerful, just looking at them," Lori explained. "And they make me think of God."

Jason couldn't imagine how, but if it kept his wife happy…

They waited for five minutes. Jason began to get impatient. She was out snipping off flowers, when they were hungry. "You stay here," he told the children as he got up and strode to the door.

He met her on the porch. "Where have you -" He broke off at the sight of her pale, distressed face.

"Sorry to keep you waiting," she mumbled, as she started past him into the house.

"Wait." He grabbed her shoulder. "What's wrong? Where are the flowers?"

She blinked hard and stared at the porch floor. "They aren't there anymore."

"What aren't there?" Jason peered across the lawn.

"My lilies, the ones by the gas tank. They – they had just started blooming, but -" she looked pathetically at Jason. "Someone chopped them all off today."

"What?!" Jason jumped off the porch and bounded to the gas tank. Sure enough, chopped up leaves and bits of pale pink flowers littered the grass around the tank.

"I could wring that man's neck!" Jason spat. He didn't care so much about the flowers, but the idea of his dad coming over here and mowing them off while Lori wasn't here! He headed toward the house across the lane.

"Jason!" Lori was calling from the porch. "Don't!"

Jason hesitated. "It won't do any good," said Lori. "It'll just end in another fight."

Slowly Jason went back to the porch. Lori hated it when they fought. But Dad could not get away with this. Tomorrow he'd tackle him, when Lori was in the house.

"Jason," Lori paused with her hand on the doorknob. "Why – why doesn't your dad like me?"

Her confusion and misery tore at Jason's heart. Even his wife couldn't escape the tyranny of his father. He tried to gentle his voice. "It's not you, Lor, it's me. He doesn't like me, so he doesn't like my wife either."

They stared mutely at each other, then slowly turned to go into the house.

Bootprints

LORI STACKED THE breakfast plates and carried them to the sink. Jason was clomping toward the barn. She knew his anger was still there, simmering beneath the surface, but he had promised to stay quiet about it.

"He expects a reaction," she'd told Jason, "so let's just pretend we didn't notice. Or didn't care."

"But he came over here and destroyed our stuff," Jason had argued. "He has to learn -"

"Please, Jason, just this time. Let's act like it never happened." She'd seen the struggle in his eyes, felt a twinge of admiration. He wanted to defend her. But it wasn't right, going at his father like that.

"Okay... then." He'd finally relented, but Lori knew it was only for her sake. He was still upset. His back was too straight, his steps too big, as he headed to the barn.

She couldn't blame him. She was smarting from the blow, too. It had taken a strength above her own to overlook it. She really wanted him to knock Peter down. She wanted Peter to be put in his place.

"Time to do the dishes, boys." Lori scooted two chairs to the sink and added detergent to the water. "Mommy needs to go outside for a bit. Do you think you can be done by the time I get back?"

The boys ran to the sink. A race with Mommy! They rolled up their sleeves haphazardly.

Lori got a rake from the woodshed and headed for the gas tank. She might as well get this behind her. Bits of chopped up leaves and limp pink petals grew into a pile. "I must forgive him," she muttered fiercely. "It was just flowers!" *Rake, rake.* "But it was my favorite lilies." *Rake, rake, rake.*

A clatter on the lane interrupted her. Peter! Coming toward her on the open hack. She started to duck behind the tank, but he was too close. He must have seen her.

Help me to be friendly, God. He was beside her. Lori stopped raking and waved.

If Peter Kauffman saw his daughter-in-law, he showed no sign of it.

He drove on, his face set straight ahead.

The buggy grew smaller. It wavered, then disappeared in a blur of tears. Lori dropped to the grass beside her mangled lilies. "Oh, I just can't forgive him," she cried. She no longer felt righteous and noble as she had on Sunday. She sat still and thought about the sermon.

"There are many positive things about our walk with God," Josiah had said. "We like positive things. Maybe right now your mind is going to things like love and joy and relationship. We experience that when we walk with God. But I would like to suggest something which might surprise you. Forgiveness is a positive thing.

"A lot of us struggle with forgiveness. It is a hard thing in our lives. Maybe we just don't understand it. Forgiveness is not saying what the offender did was okay. It is not saying our hurt is not important. But it is releasing the offender to God, letting God deal with him.

"Imagine yourself with a man under your foot. You are holding him there. Maybe he stole from you, or he said something about you that wasn't true, or maybe he even made some inappropriate advances toward your wife. But you are going to hold on to him. What he did was serious, and you will make sure he pays.

"The Bible talks about God's judgment on sinners. What happens when God pours out His judgment on the man who wronged you? Remember, you are on top of him. You are holding him under your foot. So when God pours out his judgment, *you are going to get hit first.*"

Lori had shuddered. Imagine *her* receiving judgment for Peter Kauffman's sins.

"You don't want that?" Josiah had said next. "Then you need to let him go. Forgiveness is releasing him from under your foot. God can do a better job of taking care of him than you can.

"There is power in forgiveness. Our carnal nature wants to fight back tooth for tooth, but forgiveness is a much greater weapon. It breaks down walls, brings people to Christ. And even if it doesn't, it reveals something amazing. We release the offender, and discover the prisoner was ourself.

"A grudge chains us to the offender. It is not a nice thing to be dragged in the dirt behind someone else. Forgiveness cuts the chain. It is such a good feeling to stand up and realize we can be free, no matter what the person did to us."

Lori had sat up straight. She knew all about forgiveness. She had forgiven Peter for chewing her out about her groceries. She looked at his rigid frame across the room, imagined her forgiveness breaking his stony heart.

A pious feeling had stirred within her. Wouldn't it be inspiring, Peter Kauffman confessing his sins? And she, Lori, the vessel who had brought him there.

This morning she was not so lofty. She was on the grass beside her lilies. Peter had done this. He had driven past and openly snubbed her. "He treats me like an enemy," Lori thought angrily.

She had him under her foot, and she wanted to stomp him black and blue. It would feel good to do that. But what if God poured out His judgment? Did she want to be in the way? Did she want to be chained to Peter? Lori imagined herself clanking behind that big man.

"I wouldn't have a moment's peace," she realized. "God, help me forgive Peter! I don't care if it doesn't mean a thing to him, I just want to be free…"

The boys clattered the last of the dishes into the drainer. "We beat!" Kevin announced. They scrambled down from their chairs and ran out the door. Where was Mommy?

"Look!" Kenneth pointed toward the gas tank. "What's she doing on the floor?"

Lori smiled as the boys came to her. "Mommy was talking to God."

"It's not night, Mommy."

"No," Lori got to her feet. "But we can talk to God anytime, not just when we go to bed."

"You were talking to God?"

"Yes. I was asking Him to help me love Grandpa."

"Do you love, Grandpa?"

{228} *Bootprints*

Lori picked up her rake and started for the house. "Yes. I think I do."

A FEW MINUTES later there was a knock on the door. Lori opened it, surprised to see her mother-in-law. "Come in."

Sarah stepped into the wash house. "I can't stay long." Her eyes flitted out the window. "Peter could be back anytime." She twisted her apron in her hands, and shifted her bare feet.

Lori watched the nervous little woman in front of her. What did she want?

"Lori -" momentarily her eyes darted to Lori's, then sprang away again. "I saw what Peter did to – to your flowers. I just… I just came to say I'm sorry. I tried to stop him, but -" tears were running down her cheeks.

"Mom," Lori stepped closer. "It was not your fault."

"I – I know, but -" The tears fell faster. "I just feel so – so bad."

Impulsively Lori put her arms around the little woman and let her own tears come. It was a strain on them both, Lori realized, to be caught in this awful battle between the two men. They couldn't have the easy relationship they ought to have.

"Listen, Mom," Lori wiped her nose. "I want you to know I don't hold any bad feelings against you. Or Dad either." She put the tissue in her pocket, amazed to be able to say that. "It was hard at first, but I've forgiven him."

"Thank you." Sarah peered out the window. "I have to go, but please… pray for us." And she was gone.

LORI SAT ON the couch with her Bible. She had used to snatch the children's naptime to fly at her work. But now she had started spending time with God.

She had neglected God the last several years. Her life was so busy. How could a mother of four preschoolers find time to read her Bible?

She had to make time, Lori realized. She made time to cook and

Bootprints {229}

clean and sew. Why couldn't she make time for God, too?

Maybe it was because God had no longer been so important to her. The times she'd spent with Him had been interrupted by cries of "Mommy, Mommy!" And so she had let the relationship dwindle away while she cared for the children. Eventually God became a stranger, a distant Being who didn't trouble Himself with her little world.

But now she'd found Him again. There was joy in her heart. Lori knew she must nourish the relationship to keep it alive. The best time to do it was while the children napped.

The sewing machine sat in the corner of the living room. A dress for Emily lay on top, half-finished. Maybe it wasn't necessary to spend *quite* as much time today, Lori thought. She was reading in Jeremiah, because the words from Mary's note had come from there. But she hadn't known when she started how much doom and gloom was in that book. She eyed the dress longingly. It was her goal to get it done before Sunday…

But excuses had been her downfall. Lori opened her Bible firmly. There was no way she wanted to let things get so bad again.

She had much to learn. She had learned a lot about trust. She had learned a little about forgiveness. Now she wanted to learn how to be a better wife.

The book from Mary had some good insights. But nowhere could she find what to do if the husband refused to have family devotions.

She realized it now more then ever. Family devotions were important. How else would the children grow up with a healthy perspective of God?

She told them Bible stories and taught them songs, but they needed to see Jason leading out in those areas. She had told him so this morning, but he'd been disinterested, as always. Was he even a Christian?

It wasn't right for a wife to nag. But a reminder every now and then…. How long should she wait before she brought this up again? A week? A week might be too soon for some things, but this was serious. She must make sure Jason didn't forget.

{230} *Bootprints*

Since she'd gotten back on track with God, Lori's greatest desire was to get Jason there too. She wanted him to experience what she had. Devotions would be a good place for God to begin working.

Lori eyed her Bible. *"They shall die of grievous deaths; they shall not be lamented; neither shall they be buried; but they shall be as dung upon the face of the earth; and they shall be consumed by the sword, and by famine, and their carcasses shall be meat for the fowls of heaven, and for the beasts of the earth."* Suddenly she decided to read in the New Testament. She flipped briskly through the pages. "God, what do you want to tell me today?"

Her mind went back to Jason. His father had always put a lot of pressure on him. It was something she noticed, Jason reacted to pressure. Would he take her reminders to have devotions as a form of pressure? Lori knew if he did, he would never give in.

It wouldn't bother her as much if it were just her. She could have her own devotions. But what about the children? Could the children be Christians if their Daddy wasn't? Lori worried.

She had given her children to God that day on the kitchen floor. Did that include their spiritual well-being? Of course it did. God could take better care of them than she could. She needed to believe that, but it was hard. It was hard to not jump in and take control.

What could she do? Lori stopped paging, and a verse jumped at her. *Pray one for another, that ye may be healed. The effectual, fervent prayer of a righteous man availeth much.* It was talking about physical healing. No, maybe it was spiritual, too. Whatever. It didn't change the last part. A fervent prayer availed much. *It worked.*

What did she really believe about prayer? Did she ever think her prayers didn't carry much weight? Did she start to give up if she didn't see prompt results?

Lori closed her Bible thoughtfully. If God wanted her to learn this next, she would take it seriously. She would pray about Jason. She would pray about devotions. And her children.

What would God do about this?

LORI PRAYED HARD. She prayed while she worked, and while she cared for the children. She prayed at night. A fervent prayer availed much, she kept reminding herself. She watched Jason hopefully for any signs of change.

He didn't seem to be coming along very fast. She had prayed three weeks already, and they were still not having family devotions.

"I won't become discouraged," Lori told herself. But she was. She wondered if she ought to help God. The Bible encouraged works. Works went with faith, like jam with bread.

She had resolved to not mention devotions to Jason again. He rebelled against pressure to perform. She would leave it up to God, let God do the work.

She had been full of faith. She had prayed with ambition. But she had forgotten all about works. Lori got out her Bible and looked it up. It was just as plain as anything in James 2. *For as the body without the spirit is dead, so faith without works is dead also.*

Maybe, after all, God didn't expect to do everything by Himself. Lori was eager to do her part. She put Jason's Bible on top of his stack of magazines. It had been used so rarely it was still crackly and stiff, but now it would serve as a solemn reminder. She kept a close eye on him that evening as he went into the living room. She wanted to be on hand when conviction stirred his heart.

But Jason gave a loud, annoyed grunt, and thumped the Bible into the drawer of the stand. With a sharp look at Lori, he rattled open a magazine.

Lori was aghast. He had handled the Bible with disdain. He was truly a hard man.

"Help me to not give up on him," she prayed. She searched for other ways to convict him. She mentioned God often in her conversation. She sat near him each evening, and read the Bible. Surely it must bother him to read worldly farm magazines, while his wife buried herself in the Word of God.

But Jason never seemed to notice. If anything, the small ways he had softened to her since her change, hardened again. Lori prayed with all her might. She wondered if she was being too subtle, whether she should tackle him outright.

One Friday she was invited to Mary's house. The quilt had been in the frame for awhile already, and Mary was ready to have it done. She asked some of the young married women to come help her.

Lori was excited. She almost never got the chance to go away like this. Busily she swished the breakfast dishes through the water.

"Do you want me to get the horse ready right away?" Jason stood in the doorway.

"Well," Lori looked at the clock. "They might still be having devotions. I don't want to rush them, of course. Why don't you give it another ten minutes or so?"

Jason gave her a long look, then turned silently on his heel.

Lori had time to think as she headed down the road. Jason's mom had asked to babysit the three oldest children and Lori was glad to let her. She could get more done with only Beth to see after.

It would be special, interacting with other women. And a day away from Jason might help her too. She was getting weary of faith and works. It seemed the more energy she poured into it, the less good it did.

"*Show my thy ways, O Lord, teach me thy paths.*" It was her prayer. She wanted what God wanted for her. Did He want her to be more aggressive? Jason had a soul that was headed for eternity. Shouldn't she do everything possible to help him to heaven?

The quilt was a Sunrise In The Garden. Lori joined the others in exclaiming about the striking blend of colors. She clipped off a piece of thread and put on her thimble.

"I left my children at the neighbors," Hannah announced. "They're planning on doing peaches today, but with two girls out of school, I figured they could manage. I can't leave them with Matthew, of course, him being gone all day." She gave a long woeful sigh. "You farmers' wives have just *no* idea how nice you've got it."

Lori cringed. She had yet to feel any closeness to this bitter, complaining sister-in-law.

"Living on a farm isn't all roses either," Margaret stated mildly. "During planting and harvesting times, I don't see much of Josiah either."

"Do any of you others struggle with nagging your husbands about working such long hours?" Heidi asked.

Lori gazed at Heidi in astonishment. She could not imagine Heidi knowing *how* to nag. She seemed so meek and lowly.

"I have a problem with nagging in another area," Elaine said. "When something needs fixing around the house, Mark takes the longest time to get at it. A few months ago the faucet on the bathtub started leaking, and since we're on city water, I wanted him to fix it immediately. He said sure, as soon as he has time. Well, today the faucet is still leaking, and the water bill lies on the desk and irks me every time I look at it." Elaine shrugged helplessly. "I know nagging is wrong, but -"

Lori stitched thoughtfully. It was encouraging to know. Mark had faults.

"I've often nagged Josiah for putting in such long hours," Margaret told Heidi. "But I've been trying to overcome that since I've understood how it affects him."

"Really? How?" Mary asked.

"Well, Josiah works hard to provide for our family. Instead of appreciating that as I should have, I whined because he didn't spend enough time with me and the children. I convinced myself I was neglected, and I did all kinds of things to get him to notice and feel sorry for me."

"Did it work?" Lori looked eagerly at Margaret. She knew how it was.

Margaret frowned. "It didn't. He decided he'd rather stay in the fields longer than to come inside to a pestering wife. It gave me the jolt I needed." She looked thoughtfully at the circle of women. "I'm learning that we're not supposed to be our husband's Holy Spirit. So often when we think he needs to change, we take it on ourselves to bring it about. We come up with all kinds of spiritual reasons why it's okay for us to do that, but I think it's stepping outside of God's order."

Elaine nodded. "We claim we want to help our husbands, when we really want to be in control. We panic when we're not in control. It makes us insecure." She grinned sheepishly. "When I'm insecure, I imagine awful things that could happen if I don't get my husband turned around."

"Which leads to further control tactics, which is sin," Heidi offered.

Lori stitched hard.

"We need to communicate though," Margaret said. "It's okay to tell our husbands how we feel, but we need to wait till the right time, and till we have the right attitude."

"Philip wants to know when he does something that bothers me," Mary agreed. "What's hard is to let it rest after I've told him, and not insist he change. I think the best thing we can do for our husbands is pray for them – why, where are you going, Lori?"

Lori made her way around the quilt frame, her face averted. "I think Beth, uh, she needs a nap."

THAT EVENING LORI sat timidly beside Jason. "It wasn't right of me to keep bringing it up. I was trying to – to protect myself, and I made you feel like you're not capable of making decisions. I'm sorry about that. I want to honor you as the head of the home, and well, I promise not to mention it again until you're ready."

Jason sat for a long time. Finally he nodded. "Thanks."

Lori touched his hand. Then she got up to finish sweeping. She was back to praying.

CHAPTER TWENTY-FOUR

"WHAT ARE YOU doing?"

Peter Kauffman started inwardly at Jason's voice. But he kept his back turned, continued peering through the slats at the cows milling in the loafing shed. "What's it look like?" he snapped. "Checking up on the cows."

"Why is that so important all of a sudden?"

Peter heard suspicion in his son's voice. "Somebody has to see you're taking proper care of them." He turned and stalked out. Jason didn't need to know his real reason.

Jason scowled after his father. "Yeah, right!" he muttered. What was Peter up to now?

He stepped closer to the slats. The cows were content, chewing their cud. The six Jerseys he'd bought mingled with the rest. Jason was pleased with their production so far. It was making a difference in the milk check. Maybe in a couple months he'd buy a few more. Eventually, after the farm was paid off, he might switch to a pure Jersey herd and try Management Intensive Grazing.

He'd been reading up on MIG, and it appealed to him. He'd even mentioned it to Lori last week.

"Well, Jason, you're a good farmer," she'd said, "so if this is something you decide to try, I'll trust your judgment on it."

Jason turned away from the cows and headed in for supper. Lori's support meant a lot, but more than likely he'd have to ditch the idea. *At least until Dad is no longer here to interfere,* he thought wryly. But what had he been doing out by the cows?

JASON SOON FOUND out. He couldn't believe his eyes when early Wednesday morning, a truck and cattle trailer came clattering in the lane. He left his eggs and toast and hurried to the window. The driver was backing up to the barn. Across the lane, Peter stepped briskly from the porch of the *doddy* house.

Jason snagged his hat from its hook and bolted out the door. He caught up to his father on the driveway.

"Go back in," Peter commanded. "I'll take care of this."

"What's going on?" Jason stood over his father, hating the smirk tugging the corners of his father's mouth.

Peter waved his hand dismissively. "I'm taking a cow to the sale barn today."

"Those cows are mine!" Jason hissed.

"It's only old Rosie. She's slowing down in production." Peter began to edge toward the driver who was walking in their direction.

Jason glared. Getting even with him for buying those Jerseys – that's what it all came down to! He'd make him sorry! Next week he'd go to Thad Thompson and buy three or four more Jerseys. Maybe he'd even buy six or seven. It was time the old man learned who was in control of the dairy herd around here!

"**WHERE'S MY MONEY?**" Jason demanded when he met his father in the alleyway that evening.

"Your what?"

"The money you got for my cow."

Peter's hand slid into his pocket and closed around his hefty wallet. "Think it's yours, huh?"

"I bought every last one of those cows, including Rosie. Now hand it over."

"Not likely," Peter scoffed. "I bought Rosie years ago, and I guess I can sell her if I want to. I guess I'll keep the money too. You owe me thousands!"

Jason saw red. Peter's face dimmed in front of him, except for the mocking grin. Blindly he struck out. He would smash that grin. Peter would give him the money. But his hand found only air. The grin was gone. Jason blinked. His father was gone too.

With an oath, Jason turned and kicked a post. He pounded it with his hands, not caring that they bruised, tore open, and finally dripped with blood. "I hate him!" The scream thrust itself from his heart and out of his mouth. The pain in his hands felt good. "I could kill him!"

His rage spit out in a torrent, then suddenly it was gone. He leaned weakly against the post, his bleeding hands held in front of him. His heart hurt even worse.

Jason did not see the scared faces peeping from behind the feed barrels, at the far end of the alleyway. He staggered out of the barn, toward the shop. He needed his dip.

TWO PAIRS OF sturdy legs churned across the driveway and into the house. "Mommy! Mommy!"

Lori set down her iron and came running.

"Daddy's hurt bad!" Kevin panted.

"He's bleeding!" puffed Kenneth.

Lori clutched the edge of the table. In one horrible instant she saw Jason on the ground, mangled, bleeding, dying. Her big, strong husband.

"What happened?" she whispered hoarsely. "Where is he bleeding?"

"His hands. He was -"

"He was hitting the post."

Lori was out the door. Jason was hurt. She hadn't known how fiercely she loved him. "What post?"

"In the barn." They raced to keep up with her.

Her skirt tangled around her legs. She jerked at it without breaking stride. She wouldn't faint, she told herself, although sometimes she did, at the sight of blood. Was there a lot of blood?

Behind her the boys were still talking. She slowed, wanting more details. "Why was he hitting the post?"

"I don't know. Him and Grandpa were talking."

"They were shouting."

"Daddy tried to hit Grandpa, but Grandpa went fast outside, then-"

"Then Daddy hit the post and shouted."

"And his hands were blooding!"

Lori stopped suddenly. What were they saying? This was not an accident! She felt momentary relief, but then she was upset. What had her boys seen?

She took their hands. "Did – did Daddy see you? Or Grandpa?"

"No. We hidded ourselves."

"We was scared."

Lori saw that they were still afraid. She bent and hugged them. "I think Daddy will be all right. Why don't you finish feeding the chickens now, and I'll check up on Daddy."

Jason was not in the barn. Lori walked slowly down the alleyway. Was this the post? She gazed at the rough splintered wood. He had hit a post like this? There was a trace of something on the side. She touched it. It was wet. Red.

Lori felt sick. She wondered if after all she would have preferred an accident to this. A shuffle of feet made her whirl. Peter was ducking into a stall with an armload of hay. Had he seen her? She sped down the alleyway, afraid of confronting him.

Jason was coming from the shop. His face was red and sullen.

{240} *Bootprints*

Ignoring Lori, he headed for the milk house.

"Wait!" Lori panted to his side. "Are you – are you all right?"

"Of course." He shifted the dip, not caring if she saw.

Lori picked up one of his hands. She winced at the bruised, bloody knuckles. "Jason -"

He jerked the hand away. "Listen, I've got to finish the chores." The concern in her eyes threatened to undo him. He turned aside. "I'll tell you after supper."

LORI TRIED NOT to show how outraged she was. Peter had sold one of their cows and kept the money. It was – why, it was stealing!

"I'm sorry," she told Jason.

Jason slumped onto the couch. Lori read the misery in his eyes. "Your hands -"

"What about them?"

"They must hurt."

"So? Who cares?"

"Well, I do." She stood to go get the salve. "The boys saw it, Jason. The fight, and… everything."

He sat up straight. "Where were they?"

"Hiding behind the feed barrels." She was rubbing in the salve. He had big hands, and strong. But they trembled. His knees trembled. His face was stricken. She met his eyes in sympathy. "They were scared."

Jason closed his eyes. The feed barrels. Long ago he had hidden behind the feed barrels – was it the same ones? – and he had been scared. He had been terribly scared of his daddy.

"No!"

Lori was startled. There was too much pain in that one word. Suddenly she saw Jason as a little boy, the size of the twins, and she knew he had shared his heart with hers in a single word.

When he opened his eyes she saw tears. She fumbled the lid onto the salve and reached for him, but he was standing up, shaking the tears from his eyes, already halfway to the bedroom.

"Jason." He kept right on going. "Jason, I – I love you!"

He stopped, half-turned, then slowly closed the bedroom door.

Lori prayed.

"**NOW TELL ME**, Sarah, where did you put my money?"

Sarah jumped at the gruff voice. "What money?"

"The seven hundred sixty I got from selling the cow today."

"I didn't see it. I didn't even know you sold a cow. Did Jason ask you to?"

"That's none of your business!" Peter shouted. "I put the money right here -" he thunked a finger on the edge of the counter – "then I went out for a few minutes, and when I came back in, it was gone!"

"That's strange. Are you sure it didn't fall off or something?"

"Of course I'm sure! Somebody took it!" Peter's eyes darkened. "Jason – that's who it was! That thief!"

"Oh, Peter, he wouldn't."

"Wouldn't he now," scoffed Peter. "He tried to force me to give it to him tonight. I'll bet you anything he took it."

Peter threw up his hands. "I'll tackle him tomorrow. He won't get by with it, I'm telling you that! He's going to have to answer me."

JASON'S FINGERS WERE white around the hammer. He was numb on the inside, trying to be numb.

"I did not steal that money!" He faced his father, hating the break in his voice. Why couldn't he handle this like a man?

He was five years old again, afraid of his father.

"You're lying!"

"I'm not! I don't know anything." The words hung weakly between them.

"You were never any good," Peter said flatly, "but this beats it all. Stealing from your dad. I ought to have you arrested."

The hammer was in his hands. It was flying up. Peter's rigid face paled, begging him, but Jason was no longer weak. He was not a little boy.

Bootprints

The hammer flew. Peter felt the wind of it as it passed him and bounced off the workbench. He sprang to the door. "Thief! Liar!" he yelled, and fled.

Crash!

Peter, fleeing, caught sight of the hammer hurtling through the window. "You'll pay for this!" he roared. He ducked as a wrench followed the hammer, then a screwdriver.

"Thief!" he yelled again, and ran. This time he didn't stop.

TEN MINUTES LATER, Jason sank onto an overturned five-gallon pail. He stared at the tools littering the floor, the broken window, the smashed chair. He had done that?

The window was broken. He pulled himself up and went to the door. He would not stay here. He would go to his other farm and work the beef cattle. He had planned to do it next week, but he'd do it today.

Lori packed him a lunch. "You're upset," she said. "What's wrong?"

"Nothing." He held his head up, showing her, and he got his lunch and went to the buggy.

He tried to not look as he drove out the lane, but there was a big hole in the shop window. It gaped at him, and he gaped back, miserable. He had not fooled Lori, or himself. Everything was wrong. But he was going to work on the cattle. He would leave the broken window and Dad. He didn't have to think about it.

The cattle stamped and lowed, Philip's dog barked, the sun beat down. Jason shoved against a cow. He couldn't forget. Dad called him a thief, maybe he *was* a thief.

It was lunch time. Jason peeled the wrapper from his sandwich. He wasn't a thief, but he couldn't do anything to prove it. The money was missing. He tossed the sandwich into the weeds, unable to wrestle it down, and went back to work.

Why wasn't his dip working like it usually did?

It was chore time when he untied Starburst and headed home. He didn't want to go home. He wanted to go away like Luke and Danny had.

Had Kansas helped them forget?

He could call Luke tonight, tell him to come and get him. He wouldn't care if he never saw his father's face again. But Jason knew he couldn't leave Lori. Maybe someday they'd go together. Tonight he'd go home. He would tell her about it and she would take his side.

The buggy rolled over a rise, and home lay ahead. Lori was drawing him home. If it weren't for her, he'd – what was that in the barnyard and the wheat field? The calves were out! They were trampling his wheat! He goaded Starburst into a thundering gallop, anger displacing Kansas.

Kenneth and Kevin were darting wildly about, scattering the calves even further. Jason swore as he raced to join them. With sharp commands and organized herding, he soon had the calves back where they belonged.

"Who let them out?" He glared at the panting, frightened boys. Out of the corner of his eye, he saw Lori coming toward them. He was no longer eager to see her.

He grabbed the twins roughly. "Who left the door open?"

"No one, Daddy. We closed it when we were done," Kenneth sobbed.

"No, you didn't! Look at the wheat! Smashed flat, all because of you worthless boys!"

Lori was getting closer. Before she could intervene, Jason hauled the boys into the milk house.

LORI DROPPED TO the soil behind a row of sunflowers. "God," she sobbed, "are you there?" The distant screams of the boys tore at her heart. God seemed far away.

What should she do? It was her duty to support Jason, but if he did wrong, how could she support him? It was at times like this that she struggled again whether she should do more than pray.

She believed in prayer, she was growing in prayer, but her innocent sons were being beaten. She had seen the broken board, but Jason hadn't given anyone time to explain. He was wrong and unjust.

She knew he was hurting. She was convinced more and more that his anger wasn't a cause, it was a reaction. Today he was hurting. She had suspected it this morning, but after seeing the broken window, she knew. They'd been at it this morning, Jason and Peter. Had it once again been about the money for that cow?

If only she could've talked with Jason before he took out his frustration on the boys. It was true, some of the wheat was smashed, but it was not worth such an outrage. This was somehow linked to the broken window, and her boys were suffering for it.

Tears ran down Lori's cheeks. "I need guidance, Lord," she cried in anguish. "My family is being ripped to pieces, and oh, how can I stop it? Must I just sit here and watch the devil have his way?"

A thought came quietly. *Talk to someone.*

Other than hinting to Mary, she had never talked to anyone about Jason. She feared what he'd do if he found out. And she was ashamed, too. What would her friends think if they knew what went on in her family? They all had loving husbands and fathers. Never would she admit she hadn't.

But it was a heavy secret to bear. As Lori knelt behind the sunflowers, she felt an intense longing for support.

"Who can I go to, Lord?" she prayed. "Who can I trust? What if no one understands? What if they say I'm imagining things, or making things seem worse than they are? What if they think I'm just a stupid little whiner, wanting pity?"

Beth was crying from the porch, and soon Jason and the boys would be in for supper. Lori wiped her tears with her apron. "God, if there's anyone out there who cares, who can help me, please bring us together, and soon." She stumbled to her feet and made her way back to the house.

Bootprints {245}

CHAPTER TWENTY-FIVE

MARGARET SMILED AS Lori sat down beside her.

Lori poked the diaper bag beneath the bench and saw gratefully that Emily's covering wasn't tied. She fussed with the bow until Emily wiggled, and then she fussed with Beth's bib. She didn't feel like smiling. She didn't feel like being here at all.

Beth had run a fever yesterday. This morning Lori had dawdled in bed, not planning on going to church. "I'm not glad," she told herself, but she was. She didn't want to face anyone today. She was a miserable bundle of emotions, and she could just imagine all her friends rejoicing in the Lord.

When Beth had cooed from her crib, Lori sat up, startled. Beth should be crying – she was sick. But she didn't look sick, she was peeking through the railing and smiling.

Lori shoved the thermometer hopefully under Beth's arm. It read normal – no doubt the battery was low, Lori thought. It was plain to feel, Beth was still warm. Not as warm as yesterday, but still, a little.

Lori started breakfast and all the while Beth jabbered happily.

Jason eyed the clock and gulped down his bowl of oatmeal. "We're late," he stated, frowning at Lori.

"Well," she began timidly, "I'm not planning on going today, you know, with Beth sick."

Beth banged her spoon and crowed happily from the high chair.

"She's no more sick than I am," Jason said sternly. He got up abruptly. "We need to be ready in fifteen minutes."

Reluctantly Lori stuffed Beth into her dress. What if she had a setback, and all because of her hardhearted daddy? Yes, Jason was a hard man, Lori thought with dreary satisfaction.

But the day was mild, and as the buggy rolled through the countryside, Lori had to admit it wasn't Beth she was worried about. If she got worse, of course she'd find comfort in pointing it out to Jason, but the problem was herself. She was afraid she'd cry. She could see herself, sniffling helplessly into a tissue while her friends looked on in concern. Her life wasn't perfect? When had it ever been? But Lori felt vulnerable, letting them know.

Now here she was in church, and Margaret's smile was replaced by concern. "Are you all right?" she whispered.

Lori nodded vigorously. *Just smile*, she begged silently. She could ignore a smile, but caring was too much. Her eyes were stinging already.

Margaret looked unconvinced, but just then the song leader announced the first song, and she let the matter drop.

Lori hunched down behind Beth. She felt so conspicuous today. *Give me what... I need. Show me your will.* The prayer was wrenched from the core of her being.

Jason sat across from her, his back ramrod straight. He had become a stranger this past week. Lori had never seen him as he was now, angry all the time, at everybody. It was an anger that exceeded all his anger of the past. Lori hesitated, then finally admitted – it was hatred.

She was bound to a man who hated his father. Living with him was no longer unbearable, it was frightening.

There was something terrible about his face, his eyes. Lori wondered if that was the way Cain had looked when he hated his brother Abel. She shuddered, and hoped Jason wouldn't kill his father.

Help him... and help me, please, Lord. She was beginning to grasp what it meant to pray without ceasing.

JOSIAH HAD THE main part. Jason had a grudging liking for the man. At least he usually had something interesting to say.

"Think of the worst person you know," Josiah announced.

My father, thought Jason promptly, and a hot feeling took hold of his chest. His father was sitting up front looking as pious as the saints of old.

"He's a sinner!" Jason wanted to shout it. He wanted to see the self-satisfied look disappear from his father's face.

"Maybe you are thinking about someone really far out," Josiah went on, "like the men who ripped into the World Trade Center, or the doctor who performs abortions, or some long-haired, dope-smoking hippie in town, or maybe -" Josiah's voice dropped as his eyes probed the congregation – "maybe you're thinking of someone right here in this room.

"We know a lot of gross sinning goes on in the world, but while that concerns us, it's not usually what tempts us to backbite and hold grudges. It is our own relationships.

"Let's say we have a brother who sleeps in church. He's supposed to be worshipping God, but he's sitting there sleeping. He's even snoring a little. How can a Christian sleep in the presence of God? We are too righteous to say it, but we are suspicious. We have an Amish heathen in our midst."

Josiah took out his handkerchief and wiped his face. In his fervor, he forgot to put it back right away, and waved it in his hand like a flag. Jason watched, mesmerized.

"And so we obsess over our snoozing brother, and are totally blind to our own faults," Josiah said. "You tell me, is sleeping in church worse

Bootprints {249}

than that dishonest business deal you pulled off -"

Jason remembered the cow. His father had sold her, and kept the money. He was an outright thief, and then he accused Jason of being one. Jason glared at his father's back. *It would make a good target.* The thought came suddenly, stunning him. He shifted uneasily.

- "or worse then the lustful thoughts you entertain, or the anger you display to your children? Somehow we buy into the concept that we're better than our brethren, because we do not have an honest view of ourselves."

Josiah's handkerchief fluttered. "Our faults are as glaring to God as anyone else's. So as you think of the person you struggle with the most, I also want you to grasp the fact that you are no better than he is. Before God, we are all on the same level."

Jason flinched as Josiah's eyes met his. "What does he know?" he thought rebelliously. "He doesn't know my father, or he wouldn't say that!"

He was not like his father. If he were to put his father on the same level as someone else, it would be with the men who flew into the World Trade Center. That's about as good as his father was. Josiah wasn't fair, making them equal.

"We have a tendency to categorize sin," Josiah continued. "Stretching the truth isn't as bad as an outright lie. Holding a grudge isn't as bad as murder. Carelessness in maintaining our relationship with God isn't as bad as not being a Christian at all.

"Let's imagine God doing that. He's up there on His throne, and He's looking down at the people on earth. He sees a man getting angry at his animals. He beats them up and yells at them. Does God say, 'He shouldn't be doing that, but I'll excuse him because he's not as bad as the man over here, who gets angry at his wife?'

"Next God sees a man who is straying with his eyes. Does he overlook him because he's not committing adultery like so many other people?

"Now you all know God is not like that. He doesn't rationalize sin, so why do we? Maybe we don't like admitting we're down and out

{250} *Bootprints*

sinners. We've got a good Christian background, we attend a good Christian church, and so we're all good Christians.

"Let me tell you, a good background and a good church are things to be thankful for, but they are not going to make you a Christian any more than standing in a stall and eating hay is going to make you a horse. If you want to be a Christian, you must be covered by the blood, and if you're not covered by the blood, you're not any closer to heaven than the rebel who's never worshiped God in his life."

Jason leaned forward. He had heard about salvation a hundred times before, but this time he really listened. He forgot his father in front of him. He forgot the twins, who used the chance to practice making faces. He forgot everything except Josiah's words.

As Josiah talked on about repentance, confession, and giving one's life to God, guilt began coiling itself around Jason's heart. It smothered the memory of his father's iniquities. His own sin loomed before him, threatening, choking, until he thought he might suffocate.

Then church was over, and Jason was hurrying to the barn. He filled a bucket with water and carried it to Starburst. He straightened the harness, giving him a bit of hay. Maybe they'd just go home right away. He wasn't hungry for dinner.

Yes, that's what they'd do. Jason was reaching for the tie rope when someone spoke at his elbow. "How are you doing, Jason?"

Jason whirled and stared at Josiah. He couldn't think of a single thing to say.

"Are you are all right?"

"Uh, yes." Jason cleared his throat. "Sure. I was just taking care of my horse."

"You take good care of your horse." Josiah patted Starburst's nose. "I've noticed it before. Some of us others could do better."

The tie rope dangled from Jason's fingers, trailed a wavering line through the dust.

Josiah's face was kind. "Sure there's nothing wrong? If there's anything I can do to help -"

Bootprints {251}

Jason felt an overwhelming urge to cry. Why did Josiah do that to him? "No." He turned away. "I'm fine."

"HE WASN'T FINE," Josiah told Margaret on the way home. "He stood there all the while, staring at me like – a lost puppy or something." He shook his head. "Something is bothering Jason."

"Yes."

Josiah looked thoughtfully at Margaret. He had yet to learn where all a woman's intuition could reach. She hadn't even been to the barn, but she seemed to know all about it.

"I sat beside Lori today, and I noticed right away something was wrong. After church I asked her, and the poor woman. She started crying, and I put my arm around her, and she just cried harder, then finally she told me things she's never told anyone before."

Josiah nodded. Margaret had a way of drawing people out. He wondered what Lori had said.

Margaret fiddled absently with the baby's blanket. "I just wish there was something we could do to help. I've always had a special liking for Jason, there's something about him -" she stopped, suddenly remembering that Josiah hadn't heard what Lori said. "Peter and Jason don't get along," she explained hastily. "Never did."

"I guessed as much."

"Yes, but you don't know how bad it is." Margaret told about the money dispute over the cow, and how Peter was blaming Jason for being a thief.

"Jason is so angry, Lori is afraid of him," she finished. "He beats the children without mercy or reason. She asked me how she can support her husband when he is clearly going against God's will."

Josiah's face was sober. "What did you tell her?"

"I didn't know what to say. I felt so inadequate. But I encouraged her to support Jason where she can, and fast and pray about the rest." Margaret looked up at Josiah. "I – I told her we'd fast and pray too."

He nodded as old memories stirred. "We will."

{252} *Bootprints*

LORI CARRIED THE last jars of tomato juice to the basement, thankful to have canning season behind her. She was going through the motions of housekeeping. She spent extra time with the children, knowing how much they needed their mother.

She wanted at times to push the children away. It was hard to be patient and cheerful with such a heavy heart. But they were suffering too. They were afraid of their daddy.

She could see the fear in the twins. They had always been little farmer boys, but now they made excuses to stay inside. They would rather fold laundry than play outside where Jason might find them. Their home was not a safe place, because of their daddy. It drained Lori, this trying to protect them.

She spent much time on her knees, praying for Jason. Margaret had told her how it was. Jason was in a warfare. God wanted his heart, but the devil was holding on tight. By fasting and praying, she could help loosen the devil's hold.

Jason was weak. He did not know how to fight in this war for his soul. But Lori was his helpmeet. She would fight for him.

The days crept by. Lori was weary. It was a weariness that came from deep inside. She dragged to Margaret.

"I know it's hard," said Margaret, "but you mustn't give up. Satan knows the power of prayer. He knows how much you pray. You are a threat to his kingdom, so he's going to attack you. He's going to make you discouraged. He's going to tell you lies, that Jason is hopeless, and it's a waste of time to pray for him. He's going to do everything he can to make you stop praying."

Tears rolled down Lori's cheeks. She was discouraged and wanted to give up. But Margaret was right. She had to persevere.

"Withstanding Satan can be very wearing," Margaret went on. "It helps to remember we're not fighting *for* victory, because we already *have* victory." At Lori's confused look, she added, "Fighting for victory is fighting with our own resources. We think if we just try hard enough, if we do all the right things, we'll somehow come out on top. But it doesn't work – none of us is smart enough or strong enough to overcome Satan on our own. But Jesus overcame him. He won the victory over the kingdom of darkness at the cross. So if we have Jesus in our hearts, we have victory available through Him. We're fighting from the winning side, using God's resources."

"As in?"

"As in the armor described in Ephesians six. I encourage you to go home and study that armor. It's what God gives us to help us be victorious."

Lori studied. The Bible was becoming alive again. For so long her devotions had been a tedious chore. She had skimmed through the passages, and all the while her mind had been busy reviewing the things she needed to do that day. It was a burden to read what didn't make sense, or didn't inspire her, when there was work staring from every corner.

She had started skipping devotions sometimes. She felt God ought to understand. She was so busy. After awhile she'd quit having devotions. She could get a little more done in a day, and wasn't part of being a virtuous woman to see after the ways of her household?

But now Lori felt sad to think of all she'd missed. Ignoring God was not virtuous, it was selfish and destructive.

It was inspiring to study the armor. The sword of the Spirit of God was the Word of God. Lori imagined herself on the battlefield without a sword. She would not be able to stand. She would be darting all over the place, dodging attacks.

Lori copied Bible verses and put them around the house. Jason eyed them suspiciously. Was this another of Lori's plots to send him on a guilt trip?

"It's okay," said Lori. "I put them there for me." They were helping her. Whenever she started to get discouraged or lose hope, she remembered Margaret's words. She was under attack from Satan. He wanted to keep her from praying. But she could defeat him by using the Word of God. She read verses out loud.

"Mommy preaches good," she heard Kenneth whisper once in an awed voice. But he was too young to understand she wasn't preaching, she was fighting a battle.

She imagined her sword flashing through the air and Satan slinking away in shame, freeing her to pray for Jason unhindered.

It was a strange thing. The more she prayed for Jason, the more she loved him. God was giving her love. He was showing her that inside the hard, angry man was a lost, lonely little boy. He was searching for answers. He was searching for love.

Lori did all she could to show him her love, but more than anything, she wanted him to experience God's love. She stood on the battlefield, praying for her husband, and gradually a change took place in her heart. Her hopelessness was replaced by a sense of expectancy.

"PETER, IS THIS the money you lost awhile back?"

Peter snatched the stack of hundreds from Sarah's hand and riffled through it. It was all there. "That dirty little thief decided to clear his name, huh? Well, it's about time."

"He didn't take it, Peter. I found the money behind the wood box when I was cleaning today. The wind must have blown it off the counter."

"Hmmph." Peter counted the money again. He'd been sure Jason had taken it. Could be he had, and dropped it behind the wood box when he chickened out.

But Peter had laid it in front of a window, and he had to admit, it could have blown off. He headed to the pantry for the safe. He wouldn't tell Jason he'd found it. No need for that. But he kind of wished he hadn't blamed him so harshly.

JASON TOOK EXTRA time washing down the parlor. He kept watching through the fly-speckled window until his father stomped up the steps of the *doddy* house. Then he hurried into the milk house.

Bootprints {255}

He turned on the spigot and dragged the hose to the bulk tank. He lifted the cover and dropped the hose over the edge. He wouldn't add a lot. Just enough to make up for the loss of Rosie's milk. Maybe a little more. But not enough that the milk company would detect it. Mike Borders had made that mistake, but he, Jason, was too smart.

After exactly three minutes, Jason turned off the spigot and pulled out the hose. He grinned with a mean satisfaction whenever he did it. It should raise the milk check a few dollars at least.

"Daddy!"

Jason jumped. The twins were standing anxiously at the door.

"Now what?" His voice was loud, betraying his nerves at nearly being caught.

Kenneth's eyes flicked at Jason's, then at the floor. "One of -" he swallowed hard. "One of the calves is dead."

"What!" Jason charged out of the milk house and hurried to the barn. Sure enough, a calf lay in the far corner of the calf pen, already bloated. A Jersey.

"What did you do to it?" he shouted at the boys. "Have you been feeding them the way I told you? How many times have I told you to tell me *right away* if a calf is sick?"

"But – but it was all right th-this morning," Kevin stuttered through chattering teeth.

"You weren't paying attention! What careless boys!" Jason snatched up a board.

LORI WAS HAVING a good day. She sang as she crumbled hamburger into her frying pan and added chili powder. There was rest in her heart. How could she have rest when her husband was still in the grips of Satan? It was a gift from God. She was growing in God, and He ministered to her.

She longed to share with Jason what God was doing for her. But he would not be interested. The best thing to do was put it in action. She made it her goal to do something special for him each day.

{256} *Bootprints*

Today she had written him a letter. She had listed all the things she appreciated about him, and it was a surprisingly long letter. She was going to put it by his plate at the supper table.

He was softening toward her. It was a good sign. Lori bustled about the kitchen. She stirred the soup and watched the clock. She was eager for supper. The letter was waiting.

The twins finally sniffled into the kitchen about twenty minutes late. Lori's peace evaporated. She ladled chili furiously into a serving bowl. Maybe she could rescue the letter yet, and throw it in the trash can. But no, Jason had already spied it. She looked pityingly at the boys as they took their places.

Supper was silent. Only Jason ate with an appetite. He asked for pickles. Lori went to the refrigerator to get some. Next he wanted apple butter for his bread, instead of blackberry jam. Lori slapped down the basement stairs.

It was on her way back up that it suddenly dawned on her. This was an attack. Satan wanted to use her love for her children to make her bitter. She paused on the stairs. *Lord, it hurts so bad when he misuses the children. I just want to rail on him. But help me to love him. Help me to go up there and love him.*

Lori set the apple butter in front of him and refilled his water glass. She was smiling, wasn't she?

Action, she told herself, *put it in action.*

"OKAY, BOYS, TELL Mommy what happened." Lori sat on the edge of the bed with a twin on either side. They were still quiet, even sullen. She wanted to draw them out before they slept.

"Daddy whipped us," muttered Kenneth.

"Just 'cause a dumb old calf got dead," Kevin added. "He said it was our fault, but it wasn't!"

A dart went through Lori's heart at the undercurrent of anger in their voices.

"I don't like Daddy!"

Bootprints {257}

"Me neither!"

"Lord, help me," Lori breathed. "Listen boys, I know how Daddy is. He does things that make you hurt inside. You hurt right now because he punished you when it wasn't your fault. Mommy understands, but we must still love Daddy."

"Daddy doesn't love us."

"Yes, boys, he does." Lori was confident of the fact. "But even if he wouldn't, we should still love him."

"I don't want to love Daddy."

"You don't want to because he makes you hurt inside. Mommy knows how that is. But God loves us when we're bad, and He wants you to love Daddy even if he is wrong."

"Does God love Daddy?"

"Yes, He does. Very much. And boys, God can help you love Daddy too, if you ask Him."

"You mean pray?"

"Yes, let's ask Him right now." Lori pulled the boys to their knees beside her, and taught them a simple prayer.

"We will do this every night before we go to sleep," she told them as she tucked the bedspread beneath their chins. "Ask Him to help us love Daddy."

"I think I like him a little bit now," Kevin said.

"Me too." Kenneth's voice was drowsy, no longer defiant.

"Good. Now sleep well." Lori went downstairs, wishing all prayers could be answered that quickly.

JASON TOOK THE can from his pocket, and laid it on the dresser. In the mirror he saw Lori glance at it. She flinched, but she didn't say a word.

They prepared for bed in silence. Finally Jason spoke into the darkness. "Listen, Lor."

"Yes?" Her voice was a whisper.

"I can't stop. I can't! I've tried and tried, but as long as my father –" Jason clenched his fists – "as long as my father lives, I can't stop."

Bootprints

Lori was silent, and Jason continued, determined to make her understand. "It's his fault I'm doing it. He drove me to it. And as long as he doesn't change, I can't either."

Despair swept over Lori in a thick fog. She had to wait on Peter yet?

"I'm sorry, Lor. I hate doing it behind your back, that's why I told you."

"What about the boys?" There were tears in Lori's voice. "Will you – do it in front of them too?"

"No. I'll be careful."

There was a long silence. "Jason?"

"Yes?"

"Why don't you talk with someone?"

"About what?"

"Your father, and your – your tobacco."

"No!"

Another silence. "Jason?"

"Hmm."

"I – I love you!"

Jason stared into the darkness. He heard the clock strike midnight. Then one. At one-thirty Lori slipped out of bed. Jason watched her through half-open eyes. She knelt by the bed, and Jason knew she was crying. She laid her head on the bed, and Jason heard her soft sobs.

Suddenly the guilt, which had pressed down on him ever since Josiah's sermon, increased tenfold. He saw himself as a hopeless addict, a rotten husband, and a terrible father. Worthless, that's what he was. In an instant, Jason hated himself worse than he had ever hated his father. "I ought to get rid of myself," he thought. "Lori and the children would be much better off without me."

Tears ran down his face and onto his pillow. He could no longer see Lori, but he knew she was still there, praying. Praying for him probably. The thought overwhelmed him, frightened him. What was happening to him? He had never felt like this before. So awful. So condemned.

Bootprints {259}

Talk with someone. Why had Lori suggested it? What good would it do? And who would he talk to?

Josiah. The name came at once. *Talk to Josiah.*

Jason lay awake a long time after Lori came back to bed. Maybe he would talk to someone, sometime.

CHAPTER TWENTY-SIX

FOR A WHOLE month Jason wrestled with the thought of talking with Josiah. There was a voice in his head telling him how stupid he was. He was supposed to have his act together. What would Josiah think if he came begging for help? It wasn't the thing for a man to do.

He tried to imagine what he'd say to Josiah. *My father treats me bad, and I dip.* How childish! Josiah would tell him to honor his father like the Bible said, and everything would be fine. He'd miss the point: it wasn't Jason's fault, it was his father's. And he'd report him to the bishop, because the church took a stand against tobacco, and he was using tobacco. He wouldn't see that tobacco was his father's fault too. Everything was his father's fault.

No, it would not be good to talk to Josiah. But Jason could not get rid of his guilt. He worked hard, he dipped hard, but the guilt was there. It was heavy around his neck, choking him.

Jason argued with himself. Would it hurt to try? Even if Josiah laughed at him, even if he took Dad's side, it could not be worse than this. And Josiah had come to the barn to ask how he was.

But Josiah was a minister, and ministers were ready to pounce on you the second you did something wrong. Did Jason want to expose himself to that?

He was all mixed up. He wanted to run. Run and run and run, anywhere, to get relief. Was there relief anywhere? Had his brothers found it in Kansas? Jason slogged through his work, despising it, wanting to be away.

Only Lori kept him here. He had a feeling for his wife he hadn't had before. She talked sometimes about how peaceful she felt watching the sunset, and it was strange, but he knew what she meant. He felt peaceful looking at her.

He was tortured by guilt and despair, but Lori was good. She had something good, and Jason wanted it too, but he did not know what it was, or how to get it. He liked being with his wife more than he liked anything else.

LORI NOTICED JASON'S struggles. He did not talk about it, but there was a haunted, hungry look in his eyes. His shoulders were not so broad and straight, they were rounded and a little bent, as if weighted with a heavy burden.

Lori could see that Jason was at a crisis in his life. A crossroads. Would he choose to follow Peter, or would he blaze a new path?

Lori prayed with all her might. Dust collected on the furniture, the laundry lay wrinkled in the wash baskets, but she did not notice. She was fasting and praying. She was not going to let anything get in her way.

"Lord, help me to die more fully to self," she prayed. "I don't want to be here in this marriage. Jason doesn't act like he cares about me at all. He's never there when I need him." Tears streamed down her cheeks. "Lord, it seems the only one putting any effort into this marriage is me. I'm so lonely! I want to close my heart to Jason, so he can't hurt me, but I know that's what Satan wants. Lord, help me lay aside my needs and just fill Jason's. He needs so much! This is my prayer – let me be a candle, so Jason can see a little light."

Lori did all the things she could think of. She did not often mention God, she tried to "do God." She ran errands for Jason, cooked his favorite foods, and when she could, helped him chore. There were so many times she wanted to complain about him, but she bit back the words and tried to be affirming instead. He needed to know her love was unconditional. It did not waver when he forgot to take off his boots before tracking across the floor, or even when he wrongfully disciplined their children.

One evening Lori sat on the couch. She had her Bible, but she was not reading. She was looking at herself in the little square mirror on the end table. She looked... slovenly. Her hair was a mess. Did she have so many problems she could no longer care for her appearance?

The conviction grew in her heart. A slovenly wife was not an appealing thing. She got up and went to the bathroom. She combed her hair and practiced smiling. A smile did wonders to her face. She should smile more often.

She went back to the couch, and her Bible. Jason was coming. He was coming through the doorway, and she was smiling at him. As he walked toward the recliner, she kept smiling, and suddenly he was beside her. He was beside her on the couch, and she could see he was a miserable man, he was full of pain, but he said, "You look nice." She choked back a sob, still smiling, and knew she was reaching him. Would he ever let God reach him?

JOSIAH WAS AT his desk, balancing his checkbook when Margaret came into the study. "Someone's here, Josiah. I saw buggy lights out by the barn."

Josiah glanced at the clock. Eight-fifteen. "Could you see who it was?"

"No, it was too dark."

"Well," Josiah got to his feet, "I don't know how long this will take, but pray for me."

"You know I will." She handed him his hat, pressed his hand before he went through the door.

Josiah was used to interruptions like this. It was not unusual for a buggy to drive in after supper as church brethren sought him out for advice. He wondered who it was tonight.

He was only a few feet away from the buggy when he saw the man. "Why, good evening, Jason." He tried to keep the surprise from his voice.

"Good evening." Jason coughed a little. "I – uh, I had some questions and, uh, do you have time to talk?"

"Of course. Let's sit over here at the picnic table." Josiah tried to relax, but it was hard. Never had he seen Jason Kauffman so ill at ease.

Silently Jason followed Josiah to the picnic table. He remembered suddenly that long-ago day in school when Josiah had prayed for him, and he had cried. He wouldn't cry tonight, he vowed, no matter what. He was a man now, and men didn't –

"Tell me what's on your mind, Jason," Josiah was saying.

Jason groped for words. *Why* had he come? He hadn't meant to, really. He wasn't even sure how it had happened. He had been driving down the road, and a spooky feeling had crept over him. It was like Something was guiding him, and he had no choice except to obey. His neck had prickled as he drove in Josiah's lane. He stared at the surface of the picnic table, worn smooth from years of use. He had no idea how to express the turmoil in his heart. Why hadn't he just turned around and gone home before Josiah had a chance to come out? He felt trapped.

He had to say something. Fear pounded his chest at the thought of talking about his father. He knew ministers. They were always ready to take sides against you. But surely it was safer to talk about his father than himself. He could always get up and leave, too. This was no prison.

"I didn't come because of myself," he blurted finally. "It's because of my – my father."

"Is he having problems?" Josiah's voice was kind.

{264} *Bootprints*

"He – he hates me!" The words rasped from Jason's throat, frightening him. What was he saying? But it was true. His father hated him.

"I see," said Josiah. He thought of Margaret in the house praying for him. She could not know how much he depended on her prayers. This was not going to be easy. He had never seen a man as distraught as Jason. He had never heard so much anger and bitterness in so few words. Or hurt. He breathed a prayer of his own. *Help me, Lord, that I don't make any wrong assumptions tonight. Help me to listen with my heart, and not only my head. Help me to not just point out where he is in the wrong, but genuinely care about him.*

"So can you tell me what your father does to make you feel this way?" Josiah needed more information.

Jason's heart raced. He decided to tell Josiah about the cow his father had sold – his cow – and the missing money. Surely that would convince Josiah he wasn't making things up. Once he started he could hardly stop. He skipped the part about his breaking a window and throwing tools at his father, but he told the rest.

"I haven't seen a cent of that money to this day," he finished vehemently, "but my father's still blaming me for stealing it."

Josiah was nodding. "That's a hard spot to be in. It doesn't feel good to be blamed for something we didn't do."

Jason blinked. There was understanding in Josiah's voice. He was not condemning him. The thought gave him courage to continue.

"It's always been like that. I've tried and tried to please him, but I can't. I can't do anything right. He criticizes everything I do. He –" Jason's voice cracked – "he calls me a worthless fool. That's what I am to him."

Josiah listened silently. It was too dark to see Jason's face clearly. He remembered the young boy Jason, the one he had taught in the eighth grade. He remembered his sullen anger. His defiance. Things were starting to make sense.

"Jason, was there ever a time you felt loved by your father?"

Jason's mouth went dry. What question was that? How absurd. But somehow it forced his mind to the past. Terror. Rejection. Loneliness. He had always been lonely, he was still lonely, and full of hurt.

He had tried to stuff the bad feelings behind a wall. He'd hoped they had died back there. But the question dragged him over the wall and made him look. It was not a graveyard. There was not one grave.

He glared at Josiah, angry at him for asking such a... *stupid*... question. "No!" he shouted. "My father has *never, never* loved me! He –" A memory struggled through the tumult. It was faint. It was old. He clung to it desperately. "Once," he amended weakly, "once he bought me a pencil box. When I was six. It had deer on it."

"That made you feel loved?"

Pause. "Yes."

"Jason," Josiah spoke quietly, "have you ever felt loved by God?"

Jason's hands worried the rough fabric of his pants legs. They could not hold still. Why was Josiah doing this to him? God. God was – Lord. Was He more than that? He looked down. "Am I supposed to?"

Josiah was overwhelmed by Jason's ignorance of God. Here was a man, almost thirty years old, and he didn't know whether God loved him or not.

"My father always had this big thing of reading the Bible and making long, pious prayers. I decided if that's what a Christian is like, I don't want to be one." Jason was almost surprised by his own words. He fidgeted when Josiah didn't reply. What was he thinking? Was he wondering whether they'd baptized a heathen into the church? So what if he was a heathen. Silence stretched tautly between them.

"I know where you're coming from," Josiah said at last. "There was a time when Christianity repulsed me. I was afraid of God."

Jason's eyes bulged at the dark figure across from him. *He was a minister.* A minister was telling him this?

"I was afraid of God, because I was afraid of my earthly father. My father was difficult too, Jason."

Jason's mind spun helplessly. He was not prepared for this. He felt like someone had knocked him off the edge of... a silo, and there was

{266} *Bootprints*

nothing to grab but air. He could hardly breathe. He gulped, trying to think sensibly. Why was Josiah not -? How had he -?

"You don't seem to hate him," he blurted.

"I did hate him. There were days when I felt like doing away with him."

"But – but you don't anymore?"

"I don't often tell my story, Jason, but I will tell you. My father is still living, and I want to honor him. It's really tough being in the place you're at – maybe my story will help you. Maybe it will help to know there's someone who really understands.

"My Dad was a hard, unreasonable man. He put a lot of pressure on us to talk right, act right, work right – and if we didn't, he punished us. His punishments were – cruel, abusive. He knocked our heads together. Or knocked our heads against the walls, repeatedly. He even banged my baby brother's head against the wall when he cried too much. He kicked us till we fell to the ground, then he kicked us some more."

Jason listened spellbound. Could Josiah's father have been worse than his own?

"I grew up first fearing my father, then hating him. We fought physically at times. When I was seventeen, I planned to run away from home."

Jason thought of his brothers. He often berated himself for not having the guts to do the same. Had Josiah run out of guts too?

"Just before I was going to leave, an uncle from another state asked for my help, and Dad arranged for me to go. He didn't ask me, of course – my opinions never mattered – he just gave me the bus ticket and told me I was going. I barely knew that uncle and didn't want to go. Beings he was Dad's brother, I figured he was just like him.

"I took the bus ticket and packed my bags, but I had not the slightest notion of going to my uncle's. I was taking the opposite direction. Like Jonah." Josiah gave a short laugh.

"I remember the night clearly. I didn't sleep at all. I left the house around four in the morning, suitcase in hand. Dad had told me I could

Bootprints {267}

walk the three miles to the bus stop – there was no need for him to lose time in taking me. That suited me fine. I wasn't going to the bus stop anyway.

"The eastern sky was just beginning to lighten as I started out the lane. I walked fast. I would turn left at the end of the lane, instead of right, and go to Linesville.

"My steps slowed as I reached the end of the lane. I stopped. I looked left. Then right. Left, and right again. I put one foot on the road, then the other. I made myself turn left. I tried to hurry, but my feet were heavy. Half a mile down the road I stopped. Without knowing why, I turned around. I began to walk back, then run. When I reached our lane, I looked in once, and saw Dad on his way to the barn. I ran past, and tears were running down my cheeks.

"Finally I reached the bus stop. I made myself stop crying. I was there, and didn't want to be. I was mad at myself for coming back. I wanted to run away, to go to Linesville, but my feet refused to move. Then the bus came, and I climbed on."

Josiah's voice trembled a bit. "That was the beginning, Jason. I knew even then that a Power greater than myself was keeping me from taking my own way. But it scared me. I didn't know much about God, and avoided thinking about Him as much as I could. I figured He was probably a lot like my dad."

For the first time in his life, Jason did not feel alone. He was sitting at a picnic table with… was it a friend? Josiah was talking to him like a friend. Was it possible to be friends with a minister? He leaned forward, absorbed in Josiah's story. Josiah was telling his story, because he knew how it was. Jason hadn't imagined there was anyone in the world who knew how it was. But Josiah did.

"I came to my uncle's place," Josiah continued, "dreading it with my whole being. But it wasn't long before I saw Uncle Andy was nothing like my dad. His children were all married, and I was there alone with him and his wife. For the first time in my life, I was treated with love and respect. At first I was suspicious, and kept my guard up. I imagined they were setting me up for something. But as people came and went in his furniture shop, I saw Andy treated everybody like that.

"We had a lot of time to talk as we sanded and glued. With his help, I began to see that I could not blame my problems on my dad. I was responsible for my own sins, and I had some pretty ugly ones. That sermon I preached the other Sunday – you remember, don't you? – contained a lot of things that Uncle Andy told me. He told me it was a fact I'd been damaged by my dad, but it didn't for a moment justify my anger and bitterness toward him. I had a real struggle with lust. Uncle Andy said a lot of boys from an unhappy home turn to things like that to make them feel good, but it doesn't make it right. He said I was just as sinful as my dad, which made me furious, but after a while I started to see he was right. One day I broke. I got down on my knees in that dusty furniture shop, and Uncle Andy got down with me, and I confessed my sins and gave my life to God."

Josiah blew his nose. "I cannot tell you how different I felt about God after that. I felt His love, as real as Uncle Andy's. Uncle Andy helped me see that I must forgive my dad. That was a long process. It wasn't hard at Uncle Andy's, because I was sheltered and cared for. The real battle came once I returned home, and Dad was still Dad. I nearly gave up at times, but Uncle Andy stayed in contact with me, and he got me started talking to Deacon Henry, too. Henry helped me over a lot of rough spots. I might not have made it without him."

A question burned on the tip of Jason's tongue. He had to ask it. "You actually... love your father now?"

"I do."

"But – but how...?"

"Jason, that isn't possible without God. Only after I experienced God's love and forgiveness could I truly love and forgive my dad. Before that... well, I couldn't give what I didn't have."

Jason felt an overwhelming urge to cry. Unsteadily he stood. "I have to go. It's late."

Josiah walked with him to the buggy. Jason wished he would go back to the house, and quickly. Tears were burning his eyelids as he jerked the tie rope loose.

"Jason," the gentle pressure of Josiah's hand on his shoulder stopped him. "Thank you for coming tonight. I know it wasn't easy, and I admire your courage. Here's what I want you to take home with you. God is not a stern, whip-lashing God. He loves you. He can redeem your past and give you a future. Maybe tonight that seems hard to believe. That's okay. I care about you, Jason. Drop by anytime, and I'll be glad to talk." He dropped his hand.

Jason couldn't speak, but he nodded and jumped into the buggy. "Giddap!"

"We'll be praying for you, Jason."

Jason's shoulders heaved as he turned Starburst onto the road. "Men don't -" But Jason did. He cried all the way home.

CHAPTER TWENTY-SEVEN

TEN-THIRTY. LORI PACED to the window and lifted a corner of the curtain. All was dark. No buggy lights. Where, oh *where*, was Jason? She opened the door and slipped outside. She sat on the porch swing, straining for the sound of a horse.

Silence yawned endlessly across the countryside. Lori tried to suppress her panic. Suppose he'd had an accident? A horrible vision of herself as a widow with four fatherless children flashed before her. Her clammy hands clutched the chain holding the swing to the ceiling. "Please, God," she begged, "protect my husband!"

He had left right after supper, saying he needed to check on the cattle at the other farm. Maybe he was talking with Philip. But Jason was not the visiting type, Lori knew, and it was – she looked through the screen door at the clock – it was quarter till eleven. Maybe the cows had gotten out. She hoped desperately, but she could not put aside her worry. She was still in her twenties. How could she live without Jason?

Then Lori heard the siren. Faint, but shrill in the distance. She grew cold all over and jumped to her feet. "Jason! God, where is he? Please, please, don't let it be him. He's not... ready... to die!"

Sobbing, Lori sank to the floor and laid her head on the swing. She prayed for Jason and his salvation as she had never prayed before.

Suddenly a hand gripped her shoulder. Lori screamed.

"Lor! What's wrong?"

"Oh, Jason!" She scrambled to her feet. "I didn't know where you were. I was so worried. I heard the siren, and – and I'm so glad you're here. I thought you were a policeman with a death message, and I don't want to live without you, and oh, where *were* you?"

Silently Jason stood on the porch and held his wife. His own tears, barely checked, threatened again. He held them back. "I stopped in to see Josiah," he explained gruffly.

"Josiah?"

"Yes. We were talking and it got late."

She sniffed jerkily. "I'm so thankful you're okay."

"Yeah, me too." He led her inside. "Let's go to bed, Lor. It's late."

JOSIAH SPOKE THROUGH the storm front, hoping to inspire a semblance of speed from old Max. Max flicked his ears, but he did not alter his heavy, ponderous gait. Resignedly, Josiah settled back in the seat. He really ought to get a new horse. A younger, faster version would have him halfway home already.

He was anxious to get home, where Margaret would be waiting for him. He had a good wife. It wasn't easy for her when church duties called him away evenings, but she never complained. If only Max would hurry. But he had not been born a hurrier, and it was obvious, he was not going to die one.

Josiah had plenty of time to think. He wondered about Jason. He hadn't heard from him in the week and a half since he'd visited.

"He's at a crossroads," Josiah had told Margaret after Jason left that evening. "He hasn't made a commitment yet, but God is working on his heart. We need to pray that God will bind Satan's hold on him, so he can be open to the Spirit's prompting."

Stop in and see him now.

Josiah frowned. Where had that come from? He was going home to his wife and children. A good supper, too. Lasagna, Margaret had told him before he left, and mocha torte. She'd told him about it to make him hurry home.

He could go see Jason tomorrow night. That's what he'd do. He was concerned about him. It was his heart's desire to see him come to freedom in Christ. But tonight – *Go see him tonight. He needs you.* The thought persisted.

He was approaching Stringtown Road. Josiah tugged on the rein and Max humped wearily to the right. Rest filled Josiah's heart. Margaret would understand, and she would save the torte till he got home.

JASON HEADED FOR the house. He had seen Lori grilling hamburgers earlier, and his stomach rumbled in anticipation.

He spit the dip from his mouth and glanced toward the shop. Today he had finally replaced the broken window. The gaping hole was now a golden sheen reflecting the setting sun. He resented it a little. He had felt a oneness with the hole. He did not feel oneness with beauty.

Someone had left the shop door open. He started reluctantly toward it. He didn't want to be close to the shining window. If it hadn't been for people asking what had happened to the old one, he would have left it as it was. Why couldn't people mind their own business?

Jason heard voices as he approached the door. "You better put it back. Daddy will whip you."

"I just want to look at it. He won't care if I look."

Jason peeked around the corner. His eyes widened.

"Yuck! You said it was candy." Kenneth held the open can to his nose and looked reproachfully at Kevin.

"It is candy. Daddy eats funny candy."

Bootprints

"Let's taste some. He won't know." Kenneth scooped out a small fistful.

"Boys!"

They jumped violently, and the little can went somersaulting through the air. For a long moment the three stood staring at each other.

"Haven't I told you often enough to *leave my tools alone?*"

"We were getting the hammer for Mom. She told us to get a hammer." Kenneth's face was white as he stood in front of his father.

Jason looked at the tobacco scattered across the floor. Methodically he picked up a hammer. They were looking for a hammer. He handed it to his sons and motioned toward the door. "Well, take it to her. What are you waiting for!"

They ran.

He was too shaken to be angry. He picked up the empty can and dropped it into the garbage can. He swept his dip out the door. They had found it again. Had been ready to taste it. What would Lori say?

The thought of supper nauseated him. He rummaged blindly through his tool box. He had another one in here somewhere. He must find it. Hide it better. Somewhere up high where they couldn't reach it. He pulled it out, searched for a crevice in the wall. They didn't climb walls, did they?

"Good evening!"

Jason was speechless. When had Josiah sneaked in? It was too late to hide it. He was holding a can of *Skoal*.

"I've been thinking about you. I decided to stop and see how things are going." Josiah did not seem shocked at the can, but Jason belatedly thrust it into his pocket.

"Oh." Nervously Jason thrust a five-gallon pail at Josiah with his foot. He turned another one upside down for himself. "Sit down."

"How have things been this week?" Josiah asked when Jason didn't offer anything.

Jason held the can inside his pocket. Strange, Josiah was a minister, but he didn't feel threatened. He didn't even feel like he had to defend himself. Josiah had seen the can, and he knew why. It was okay for him to know.

Jason raised his eyes briefly. "Not so good."

"With your father, you mean?"

"Not – really. We barely talked all week. It's just that I can't stand myself anymore! I feel so condemned. The last few days I've had this awful fear I'll die, and go to… hell. Sometimes I can feel the flames already. I can hear Satan laughing at me. It's a hideous laugh." Jason looked desperately at Josiah. "Am I losing my mind?"

"No," said Josiah. "You are in the middle of a terrific battle. You've got two masters wanting possession of your soul." He spoke calmly, as though he had no worry how it was all going to end. "So what are the things that make you feel condemned?"

Jason flung the can at Josiah's feet. "This! I've been trying for years to stop, but I can't! Now tonight my sons – *my sons* – found it, and were going to… *taste* it." Fresh horror gripped him.

"Does Lori know you dip?"

"She knows, and it hurts her, but I can't live without it, with Dad, you know." Jason bounded to his feet and began pacing. "But it's not just that. It'- it's -" He struggled for words, willing Josiah to understand. "It's like I'm lying on the ground, and a heavy piece of equipment is running back and forth across my chest. I can't get up and the weight is killing me."

Josiah nodded. "Your sins are rolling over you, and you're going to your doom in a cloud of shame and guilt."

For a moment, Jason stopped pacing. How did Josiah know? His eyes met his friend's, and there he saw understanding. Light, too. It reminded him of the window. Full of light. He resumed his pacing, back and forth.

"God knows how horrible it is to be trapped beneath that grinding piece of equipment," Josiah said. "He can set you free, but He's not going to do it until you ask Him to."

Josiah picked up the can and held it in front of Jason. "We are born with an instinct to fix things. We think we should be able to fix ourselves, too. We want to present this picture of strength and control. When we fail, it feels like a direct shot to our manhood." He tossed the can to Jason, who caught it neatly. "Only you know how hard you've tried, and how it hurts to still not be good enough."

Jason held his eyes wide, absorbing the stinging. Josiah was saying it for him. He knew what was inside him. There was no point in keeping his guard up. "I'm a poor husband," he confessed, "and a poor father. I'm angry all the time. I don't want to be angry, but I can't help it. I get angry at the children, and they – they don't like me," he finished brokenly.

He remembered when the knowledge had first come to him. He had come into the barn, and his sons had frozen in their play. "Let's go up to the hayloft," Kevin said softly, and they scrambled up, casting alarmed glances over their shoulders as if he might be a bear or something.

A strange sharpness had cut through him as their bare feet flew up the ladder. They were running away from him.

After that, he had noticed it more often. They disappeared when he came around. He tried to not let it bother him, but it did. It reminded him of when he was a little boy, afraid of his daddy. He did not want his sons to be afraid of him. He was angry at them for being afraid.

"You determined you would never be like your father. Your father hurt you. But now you see your family is afraid of you, and you don't want to think of it, but you do. You're like your father."

Jason stared wordlessly at Josiah. He had been furious when Lori said the same thing, but now there was no fight left in him. He had nothing to argue. "I'm -" his voice cracked as he met Josiah eye to eye. "I'm not like my dad. I'm worse than he is."

Josiah's heartbeat quickened. This was not a light thing for Jason Kauffman to say. Was he breaking?

"Jason, your guilt is God talking to you. He doesn't like to see you living in defeat. He wants to make you a new man. He wants you to experience freedom and peace through Him."

"You make it sound easy." Jason spread out his hands. "Like God is a cure-all or something. How can that be? I don't even know God. I can't feel God. If I give my life to God, or whatever you call it, I'm afraid it won't make any difference. Nothing else ever has. How can I know you're not feeding me a bunch of hogwash?"

"Those are good questions." Josiah looked thoughtfully at Jason. "I don't want to leave you with the wrong impression. A relationship with God does not free you from struggles. In fact, the closer you are to God, the more Satan tries you. But if you have Christ within you, you have a power to withstand him. You have someone to depend on who's stronger than you are, and who knows all about winning battles.

"I've told you some of my past. It's not pretty. I'm not perfect, but I have found the power of Christ to be life-changing. I challenge you to take that first step of surrender, and let God take you from there."

"But – I'm a church member." Jason knew it was a weak point, but he had to make it anyway. "Isn't that enough?"

"No, Jason. If you're a Christian, you want to be a church member, but being a church member does not make you a Christian. The church should point us *to* salvation, but it cannot *give* us salvation. Only Jesus can do that. We can't expect to get to heaven solely on the basis of being a church member."

"How – how do you do this God thing?" Jason felt nervous, to think of going down on his knees or some other awkward thing. Yet he really wanted to know. He was sick of life the way it was.

"You must stop the blame game," Josiah said seriously. "Take responsibility for your sins instead of blaming your father. Bring them to the cross, confess them, and repent for having allowed Satan control of your life. Repentance is a beautiful thing. You admit to God that your own resources aren't enough, and you need His. When you repent, Jesus' blood makes you clean, and God puts His life in you.

You go from separation and darkness to connection and light. It's not always an easy life, but it sure is good."

Jason nodded. "I'll think on it."

THE BUGGY LIGHTS bobbed out the lane. Jason started for the house. Once, he turned and looked back. The sun had set, and the window was dark. It was very dark. Earlier tonight he had wanted it that way, but now he missed the light. Something was changing inside him. He would rather have light than darkness.

His feet carried him forward. He was going to the house. There was light in the house. The night scared him. He willed himself to walk slowly, but the shadows came at him. The wind slapped his back, mocking him. *You – uuu are h – h-hopeless. Forget Josiah. Forget about God. There is no hope for you – uuu!"*

Jason's teeth chattered. He plunged through the door, and the wind slammed it shut behind him. *No hooo-pe.* Was it true? It had worked for Josiah, but would it work for him? Suspicion plowed icy fingers through his heart. Was he letting himself be carried away by his feelings? It was time he got a grip on himself. He set his boots in their place by the door, suddenly desperate to see Lori.

But the kitchen was empty. And the living room. Halfway up the stairs, he heard voices.

"Help Daddy to love you, God. Mommy said once he loves you, he'll be a good daddy. We want a good daddy, so please hurry him up, God."

Jason reeled in the stairway. He clutched the railing as Kevin began. Or was it Kenneth? They sounded so alike. "God, help me to love my daddy, even if he doesn't love me. Help him to be good…"

Jason stumbled down the stairway, through the kitchen, and out the door. It was very dark. He stopped beneath the maple tree in the back yard. "God –" he looked at the sky. It was huge. Black. He buried his face in his hands. For the first time in his life, he didn't care that men didn't cry.

LORI HURRIED DOWN the stairs. She had heard him come, and go. She stood on the porch, searching the darkness. It was a very dark night. The wind snatched roughly at her skirt as she descended the steps. There was turmoil in the wind.

Muffled sounds were coming from… was it the maple tree? She picked her way slowly. Maybe the wind was playing tricks on her. She paused, listening, and the wind died. The sounds persisted. Heart pounding, she moved forward. Jason was kneeling on the ground in the darkness. Her strong, tough husband – who never cried? He was crying.

"Forgive me, Lord."

His broken cry carried clearly. Amazement and wonder put wings to her feet. She ran the rest of the way.

Bootprints

CHAPTER TWENTY-EIGHT

JASON SHUT OFF the alarm and fell back on his pillow. Morning peeked around the edges of the curtains, stirred by a tangy breeze. *Nothing beats working in the fields on a nice fall day.* The thought surprised him. His work had been drudgery the last while. It had been hard to get out of bed.

Why was he happy?

Slowly the scene from last night came to focus. The maple tree shaking and moaning in the wind. Lori, kneeling beside him while he shook and moaned before God. He had found God. God had found him. He wasn't sure which, he just knew that somewhere in the deep bowels of the night, something profound had happened.

It was like a dream. Was he still dreaming? When had he felt like this before? At ease. Rested. He and Lori hadn't gone to bed till after two, but he felt more rested than he usually did after an eight-hour sleep. How was that possible?

He didn't know who God was. Not really. God was different from

Bootprints {281}

what he had thought. Jason didn't have to be afraid of Him. That was amazing. There was so much he didn't know.

"It's kind of the way it was with us," Lori had told him last night. "We were excited when we started dating, but it took us time to get acquainted. We didn't always understand each other. In the same way, tonight is only the beginning. You have to develop a whole new concept of God. The important thing is to keep growing." She had smiled at him, a happy smile.

Jason was happy too. He had worried his happiness would fade while he slept. He would wake up, and everything would be just as hopeless as it had been. But here he was, lying in bed with a pleasant breeze on his face, and the happiness was better than the breeze.

Who would have thought God could do this to him? Why did God care? Would His presence last, or would it fade and wear out like new clothes? Was God big enough to handle his father?

The defenses and guards Jason had worked for years to maintain had come down overnight. He felt stripped and vulnerable, yet strangely free. There was room to live, room for God.

This morning Jason was enjoying God. To think that only yesterday God had been a stranger. What all would God do in his life?

Lori stirred beside him, cracked an eyelid. Jason grinned. She shook her head, clearing the cobwebs, then smiled. She didn't say anything, just lay there smiling, and Jason was glad to have such a beautiful wife.

It was time to get up. Jason opened the bedroom door, stepped out, then turned back. "Let's pray," he said before he could change his mind.

Lori looked startled, but she wasted no time in getting to her knees. She waited expectantly, gladly, while he folded himself in half.

He wasn't used to this. His knees moaned against the hard floor, and his legs prickled. Were they going to sleep? It was clear, prayer was not a thing of bodily comfort.

Lori took hold of his hand and closed her eyes. What could he say? Jason's throat was dry.

"Uh – kind, gracious, heavenly Father," he croaked. He had heard preachers say that. It seemed like a good way to start. But now what? He shifted nervously. "Let's just pray silently," he blurted.

"Mmm." Lori looked up. Jason could see the sympathy in her eyes, and possibly a twinkle. "All right," she agreed. Yes, there was a twinkle in her voice.

Jason didn't pray long. It was hard telling what would happen to his legs if he didn't get them straightened out soon. Inwardly though, he felt peaceful. It seemed like God was in the room with them.

"Thank you." The words jumped to the tip of his tongue and flowed into an audible repetition. "Thank you, thank you, thank you."

LORI STOOD AT the window as Jason strode briskly to the barn. His head was up, his shoulders squared.

She had prayed long for this day, yet she could hardly believe it was here. But it was. It was. Her husband was a Christian! He had prayed with her this morning! It was the first time in almost seven years of marriage that they had prayed together.

Lori skipped to the stove. Some women might turn into plodding, earthbound creatures after producing four children, but not Lori. Not this morning.

A tear rolled off the tip of her nose and danced in the frying pan. She laughed aloud as she opened a package of sausage. Biscuits with sausage gravy was Jason's favorite breakfast.

At last the future was bright with promise. Impulsively, Lori lifted her hands. "Thank you, God," she exclaimed, and a scrap of biscuit dough went flying over her shoulder.

Later, she couldn't fathom why she hadn't heard him come. Maybe it was the snap of the sausage frying, or the hum of the refrigerator, or the song of the wren. Maybe she was just too caught up in her joy. But when she turned around, Peter was there, and he was grimly lifting the scrap of biscuit dough off his forehead.

"A woman your age should be a little more settled," he said with a severe expression.

"Yes," Lori muttered weakly. To think he had seen her spontaneous praise. But he had come in without knocking! "You might knock the next time," she said suddenly. "What do you want?"

"I came to see why your lazy sons aren't out doing their chores yet, and I find their mother up to – up to -" He stopped, unable to find adequate words. "To *no good,*" he finished, a little lamely.

"I'll send the boys out soon." Lori pounded the biscuit dough, not caring if it made them tough. When the door thumped shut behind Peter, she did not immediately go after the boys. She crossed to the window and glared out angrily.

"He is the most impossible man this side of the Mississippi," she said, which did not make her feel better. In less than five minutes, Peter had crushed her.

The smell of burning sausage got her attention. She turned back to the stove, feeling like a plodding, earthbound creature. All her buoyancy was gone.

"God -" It was a moan now. "What hope is there for Jason? Peter is still Peter, and Jason is an infant spiritually. How can he make it? How can he find the courage to live with his father, to forgive him? God, what will I do if he gives up?"

Absently Lori stirred milk into the gravy. A scripture came unbidden to her mind. *"He which hath begun a good work in you, will perform it until the day of Jesus Christ."* Something about confidence, too. She'd have to look that up.

Tears welled in her eyes as the gravy began to bubble. God had brought them this far. Couldn't she trust Him too, to take them from here?

Jason and Lori ate heartily of the tough biscuits and the scorched gravy.

THE SKY HAD never seemed so blue, nor the maple leaves so red, as they did that day. Jason rode contentedly behind the horses. He felt alive.

{284} *Bootprints*

His weight of guilt was gone. Jason had not known how heavy it was until it was no longer there.

A buzzard rode the air overhead. Jason was soaring too. "Thank you, thank you, thank you." The words slid into a tune, a tune that was still ringing in Jason's mind that evening, when he put the horses away and went to fetch the cows.

It was usually the twins' job to fetch the cows, but tonight, Jason wanted time to prepare himself. Soon he would have to face his father. Could he stay calm? He had avoided Peter this morning, but that was not likely to happen tonight.

"God, are you there?" It was easier to express himself in the pasture than it had been in their bedroom this morning. The sun was setting, and the air was clear and fresh. God was here. Would He listen?

"God, I don't feel ready to face my father. I'm afraid – he'll destroy my peace." Jason had known peace for only one day, and he could not bear to think of losing it. "God, please make my father go away tonight. Maybe tomorrow I will be stronger."

The cows were at the far end of the pasture. Jason walked slowly. It felt good talking to God, but he could not shake his apprehension. "Thank you, thank you, thank you." The tune was a bit dull.

It stopped altogether when he discovered one of the Jerseys down with milk fever. Now he'd have to call the vet before he started milking.

The vet lived three miles to the north, and it didn't take long for him to arrive. Jason watched as the robust little man examined the cow. "Shouldn't be any time at all, and she'll be right as rain, right as rain," he chirped, after giving the cow a bottle of calcium. He scribbled briskly on an invoice and fluttered the bill to Jason.

Jason stifled a roar of protest as he took in the figure. One hundred thirty-two dollars for fifteen minutes of service!

"Thank you, young man." Cheerfully the vet flicked next month's grocery money into his wallet. *A very hearty looking wallet*, Jason reflected bitterly as he trudged toward the buildings.

Shrieks of laughter drifted from the barn. The boys were supposed

Bootprints {285}

to be feeding the calves. Jason could not think of anything amusing about feeding the calves. He had better check this out.

Furiously the twins stirred milk replacer into their buckets. "I'm going to beat this time!" Kenneth charged down the alleyway, little spurts of milk springing from his bucket.

"No, I will!" Kevin raced after his brother.

Just then Harold strolled into the alleyway. Harold was a very old cat who had a cottage cheese can beside the feed barrels where the boys poured him a little milk each evening.

Kenneth was looking over his shoulder to see if Kevin was catching up when Harold stepped into his path. In an instant, the boys, Harold, and milk replacer became one wild disarray across the floor.

"Boys!" Jason bellowed.

Kevin sat up with a dazed expression. Harold was shaking the milk from his coat. Where had Harold come from?

Kenneth limped to his feet. "You told us to hurry," he sulked.

"I didn't tell you to *race*," Jason retorted icily. "Look at that mess!"

Milk was spilled all down the alleyway. What a waste! "We'll clean it up," Kevin offered feebly.

"You're right about that! But first you'll take your punishment," Jason stormed. He spotted a narrow board hanging loosely from a gate. "Maybe this will teach you to be more careful!"

But afterwards, as Jason did the milking, he felt heavy. It was that vet and his high fees, he thought. Where would they get money to buy groceries?

But no. Grocery money was not the cause of his unhappiness. It was the look in his sons' eyes after he'd punished them.

I did the right thing. They have to learn not to be so wasteful. Jason tried to convince himself. But the misery in his chest did not go away.

His sons didn't like him. It bit deeper than usual, maybe because he'd thought things would be different now. But how could they? Wasn't it normal for fathers and sons to dislike each other?

Not for everyone, Jason admitted. Philip had a real respect for

Deacon Henry. Of course, Henry would be easy to respect. He was not like Peter. Or like himself, Jason thought with a pang. He longed for his sons to like him. What would it take?

He thought about his father. Did Peter ever wish for a better relationship? Jason couldn't imagine. But where was his father? Suddenly it dawned on him that he was almost finished choring, and he still hadn't seen him.

Had God answered his prayer? Jason decided to check. He took a flashlight to the buggy shed. The LED bulbs caught the reflective tape on the hack and his surrey. His father's buggy was missing.

Where could he be? The thing was, he *had* gone. God had heard him! He ought to be happy about that. Jason pressed the button on his flashlight, and darkness leaped up around him.

Between the time when he'd discovered the sick cow and the time he'd punished his sons, darkness had fallen. Jason's peace was gone. And the little song – what had it been? – that was gone too. Wearily he trudged to the house.

"I'M NOT PRAYING for Daddy tonight." Kenneth looked defiantly at Lori.

Lori knelt by the bed and pulled the twins down beside her. "Yes, we will."

"But, Mommy, I'm tired of praying for Daddy," Kevin complained. "He isn't never going to get good."

Lori bit her lip. Tonight she had planned to tell the boys that their father loved God now, and he was going to be a good daddy. But now he had beaten them again. Lori despaired. Was it all to be short-lived? Was Jason's conversion nothing more than an emotional experience? How could any man with God in his heart abuse his sons?

"God, help my unbelief," she prayed silently. "Didn't I tell Jason myself that conversion is only the beginning? I know I can't expect perfection from him right away. But God, please help him see the need of loving his sons – before it's too late."

Kenneth knelt stiffly beside her. "We didn't spill the milk on purpose!" he blustered.

"But Daddy, he got all mad. Why is he all the time mad, Mommy?"

"Daddy doesn't want to be mad. But he has to pay a lot of money for milk replacer, and he expects you to be careful to not waste any. You were not careful tonight, and so you fell down and wasted milk. That's wasting Daddy's money. He got upset because it's hard work to make money."

Lori paused. "I know you're sorry you weren't careful. But I think Daddy's sorry too, for getting mad." She had noticed Jason's miserable silence at the supper table.

"He didn't say sorry."

"Maybe he will yet." Lori prayed he would. "But boys, we will ask God to help us love Daddy even if he doesn't say sorry."

Reluctantly they bowed their heads. Lori sighed and wondered what else she could do.

JASON WAS ON the couch when Lori came down. He had a book on his lap instead of his usual farm magazine. It was the Bible, Lori noted as she stepped closer. He wasn't reading, but still it gave her confidence. She sat down beside him. "Did you have a good day?"

Jason sighed deeply. "We – ell. At first, I guess."

"Not all day?"

"No."

"Did – did something happen?"

"Yeah, one of the Jerseys had to go and get milk fever, and the vet charged one hundred thirty-two dollars, of all the uncalled for things."

Lori looked disappointedly at Jason. She had taken his gloomy mood as a good sign. God must be convicting him of his anger. But no – it was the vet.

"I don't feel God anymore," Jason said helplessly. "I feel wrong – guilty."

"And it's because the vet charged too much?"

"Naw – that bugged me, I guess, but I didn't really feel guilty till after I punished the boys. I suppose they told you?"

"Yes." Lori tried to hide her relief. So it was bothering him.

"I don't know why it should make me feel guilty though. It never did before."

"I don't think it's because you punished them," Lori said slowly. "That's in your place. But – but -" she hesitated, then said in a rush, "you were angry, weren't you?"

Jason looked startled. "I – I, well, I suppose. Why?"

"I'm not sure, Jason, I'm just learning myself. But I think if we punish our children because we love them, it makes them feel secure. If we punish them to vent our anger, it makes them resent us."

Jason was silent for a long time. Lori's heart thumped. Had she been too blunt? Maybe he wasn't ready to hear such things yet. And maybe it wasn't her place to tell him. Josiah would be better, or God. God could convict him. Lori tried to read Jason's face. Was he angry? "I'm sorry if I hurt you," she began. "I don't do such a good job, either. I mean, I get angry, too -"

"Stop." Jason held up his hand. "What you said makes sense. I just never thought of it before. I – I guess that's why the boys don't like me."

There were tears on his cheeks. Lori felt limp with relief. He was letting her see his emotions without being ashamed! "Jason, the boys are still young. You can still win them. I think – a good place to start would be to apologize that you got angry."

"Me?" Jason was dumbfounded. "What good would that do?"

"More than you realize."

"I never heard of a father apologizing to his children."

"My father did. It never lowered my respect for him."

Jason sat deep in thought. Could this undo the damage? But it was such a little thing. And it would be terribly awkward. A grown man apologizing to his sons. He couldn't imagine what the twins would think.

"Let's go to bed," he announced. They started for the bedroom. Jason remembered how well he'd slept last night, and how refreshed he'd been this morning. A deep longing for God filled his heart. "You go on," he told Lori suddenly. "I'll be in soon." He started up the stairs, half hoping the twins were already sleeping.

THEY WERE WHISPERING when they heard footsteps on the stairs. "Shhh!" Kevin grabbed Kenneth's hand. "Someone's coming!"

They pulled the covers up to their eyes and strained to see the doorway. It was Daddy.

"Boys?" Had Daddy heard them whispering and come to spank them? They were afraid to answer.

"Kevin? Kenneth?"

He didn't sound angry. "Wh – what?" they quavered.

Daddy came closer, almost to the bed. "Boys, I'm – I'm sorry I got angry when you spilled the milk tonight."

Silence.

"I know you didn't do it on purpose. Forgive me."

Kevin and Kenneth didn't know what to say. "Okay, Daddy," one of them whispered at last.

"Okay, good night." They saw him go out. Heard his footsteps on the stairs.

"I'm glad we prayed for Daddy," Kenneth whispered after awhile.

"Yeah, me too."

AS JASON SLIPPED beneath the covers, his prayer of the morning came back. "Thank you, thank you, thank you." The tune was bright and fresh again.

CHAPTER TWENTY-NINE

"HELLO, JASON." JOSIAH shook his hand warmly. "How are you doing?"

All right, Jason almost responded. It was the standard answer for a standard question. Nobody really cared how anybody else was doing. It was just a formality.

But with Josiah, it was different. Jason knew he expected a sincere answer.

"Well, I -" Jason darted a nervous glance around the barn. It was hard to express his feelings. He could trust Josiah, but he wanted to make sure no one else was around.

Philip was untying his horse, too far away to hear. "Actually," Jason began, "it's been good. The other evening I was – something happened-" he stopped abruptly as Mosie Bontrager entered the barn.

Mosie's eyes gleamed under his hat. Jason stood frozen, hoping to remain unseen. But Mosie was already hurrying in their direction with an urgent air.

"Why don't you come to our place this afternoon?" Josiah asked

Bootprints {291}

quickly. "We can talk then."

"Okay." Jason tugged on Starburst's rope and began to edge away.

"Hello, Mosie," he heard Josiah say pleasantly. Jason felt a grudging respect. Josiah was treating Mosie with kindness, even though he had interrupted them. Could he do that? Jason frowned doubtfully. Mosie was so annoying.

"Hi," said Mosie. His rushed tone implied that he had little time for greetings. "I saw you standing here, and thought I'd better come on over and share a concern. The sooner you know it, the sooner you can do something about it. That's what I've always heard, and I believe it, too. It's about -"

Jason sighed deeply as he left the barn. Some things never changed.

JOSIAH AND MARGARET welcomed Jason's family with enthusiasm.

"It's good to have you here." Josiah held the door for them. Awkwardly they shuffled in. They weren't used to making formal visits.

"You can put your wraps on this table here," Margaret directed. She took Beth from Lori's arms. "Now you all come into the living room, and we'll have some popcorn."

Jason relaxed a little once they were settled on the couch. Josiah hustled around, helping Margaret pass out popcorn and grape juice. Jason was surprised to see him helping. He was a little embarrassed for Josiah. Why didn't he sit down and visit?

Jason glanced at Lori, and saw that she was watching too. There was a wistful look on her face. Jason wanted to please his wife, but he couldn't imagine pouring grape juice in front of visitors. Probably he'd drop the pitcher. This was something new, a man helping his wife serve guests.

Absently Lori took a bite of popcorn. Would Jason ever help her like that? She didn't want to complain if he didn't, it was such a joy just to know he had Christ in his heart. She musn't expect it. Still...

"This popcorn is good." Lori was trying to make conversation. She knew how hard it was to entertain guests if they didn't talk. "What seasoning did you put on it?"

"I popped it in bacon grease," Margaret replied, "then I added sour cream and onion powder, and some hickory smoke salt. Oh, and a bit of nutritional yeast, too. Have you seen Philip and Mary's baby yet?"

They all discussed community news until their bowls were empty, then Josiah turned expectantly toward Jason. "You were starting to tell me something in the barn today."

Jason laughed self consciously. He would rather talk to Josiah without Margaret around, but if she stayed, Lori would too, and Lori gave him courage.

Well, what did he have to hide?

"I told God He could have me," he began slowly. "I told Him I can't change myself, so I'd like Him to. I started confessing my sins, and then I wasn't sure I'd ever reach the end. There were so many, I was afraid God couldn't forgive them all, but Lori -" he glanced at his wife – "Lori said He could. So I asked Him to forgive me. I asked for – a new start. I told Him I didn't know what to do, but I was willing to learn. I – I asked if He'd just – come into my heart and give me peace. I don't – maybe I didn't even know what peace was -" Jason stopped as tears came to his eyes. He blinked hard, but he could not keep them back. Red-faced, head down, he glanced at Lori. Lori was crying too, and Margaret, and – and Josiah!

Jason felt deeply uncomfortable. Tears were a sign of weakness. Yet here they were, all of them crying like babies. Jason could overlook the women. Women were always being blown around by their emotions. But he couldn't understand Josiah. He had fished his handkerchief out of his pocket and was energetically blowing his nose. The muffled roar left little doubt. He wasn't ashamed to cry. Yet he wasn't a weak man. This did not add up. Once Jason would have sneered at a man who cried, but he admired Josiah.

"Margaret and I have been praying for this for a long time," Josiah said as he folded his handkerchief into his pocket again. "I can't tell you how happy we are for you."

Jason nodded, still trying to hide his tears. "I feel – so much better," he said.

Bootprints {293}

"Peace is a gift," Josiah agreed. "People often think it comes from having everything go the way they want it to, but that's false peace. Real peace comes from having a clear conscience before God, and trusting Him to do what's right in our lives. We can have peace even when things go wrong."

Josiah looked sober. "You feel better, and I don't want to take that away from you. But I want to caution you that the hard part is probably just beginning." He paused. "How does your Dad respond to this?"

"Well, he... I didn't see much of him till yesterday."

"So you haven't had any run-ins?"

"Yesterday. He came all unglued because Lori and I went to town, instead of to Chester Miller's frolic. I would've gone to the frolic, except that I forgot about it, and we were ready to leave for town by the time Dad came cooking out of the barn. He accused me of all kinds of things; how it's easy to tell I'm no Christian, always set on doing my own thing, and not willing to lift a finger to help my neighbor. He was totally paranoid what people would think if I drove past Chester's on my way to town, without stopping to help."

"So – what then?"

Jason recalled the violent sway of the buggy as they pounded out the lane. "I got mad!" he blurted.

A half smile flickered across Josiah's face. "Not surprising. But I guess you realize that reaction wasn't right?"

"I can't help it," Jason said quickly. He wanted to make sure Josiah didn't get the wrong impression. "I mean, it was Dad's fault. He starts every argument on purpose, just to make me mad!"

"I know what you're saying," Josiah agreed. "I felt the same way about my dad. I didn't think I could overcome my anger as long as he didn't change. I blamed my faults on him. But -" Josiah looked seriously at Jason, "Henry told me something important, and I want you to know it, too. Identifying is not justifying. A lot of my struggles were caused by my dad, but that did not justify my wrong reactions – anger, bitterness, and unforgiveness. I had to take responsibility for my own sins, and deal with them."

Identifying is not justifying, Jason repeated to himself. Nice little catch phrase. But his problems *were* his father's fault.

"I had to learn to forgive my dad," Josiah went on. "That was a long, hard battle and you will probably find it the same. There will be times when you want to give up, when you think it's just too hard. But you need to keep on dealing with each situation as it arises, or you won't be able to grow in your Christian life."

Jason looked sadly at Josiah. Forgive his father! By the time he got that done, he wouldn't have a shred of peace left over. It was ebbing already. He felt a growing dread of facing his father. It would be the same old story.

"I can't deal with my dad," he announced suddenly. "I don't know how."

"Oh, it's really not that complicated," Josiah answered relentlessly. "Take yesterday for instance. You know the anger toward your father was wrong. You must deal with that first – always your own sins first. You must bring it to the cross and repent of it. You know what repentance means, don't you?"

Jason had heard the ministers talk about it in church. "Repent," they would boom across their open Bibles, "the kingdom of God is at hand!"

Sometimes Jason had the fearful feeling that if he didn't repent, God would sent lightning from heaven – or something – to strike him dead. But he had never been sure what it was to repent.

What could he say to Josiah? "To do better?" he asked carefully.

"Mmm- that follows repentance, but it's not repentance. Repentance is being sorry for your sin. It's confessing it to God and asking for His forgiveness, then asking Him to help you do better in that area."

"That's what I did under the maple tree." Jason was confused. "You mean I have to do it again?"

"You made a good start under the maple tree. You allowed God to start working on you. But it's like this. The last time I was at your place, I noticed some pretty deep ruts in your field lane. Obviously, you always use the same tracks when you drive back and forth with your farm equipment. What would happen if you'd decide to move over a bit and cut some new tracks?"

"I've tried that already," Jason answered. "The first thing I know, my equipment has slipped back into the old ruts."

"That's just the way it is," Josiah said. "When you give your life to God, you're making the choice to cut new tracks. You start out with high ambitions, but the first thing you know, you've fallen right back into your old rut. Maybe it's a rut of anger. Or selfpity. Or lust. But you're discouraged because you're back in the rut, and you don't want to be.

"You've been in your rut for years. It won't be easy to change. Again and again you'll find yourself jolting back into the old ways. Satan wants you there. He wants you to believe that cutting new tracks is too hard, that there is nothing you can do to keep from falling back into the old rut, so you might as well stop trying. But this is the key -" Josiah leaned forward – "repentance and confession will lift you out. Soon you will notice you can stay on the new tracks a little longer, and eventually you will have new ruts, better habits. That's being transformed into the newness of life."

Jason nodded slowly. "So forgiving my father is a part of cutting new tracks, and every time I get angry, I'm falling back into the old rut?"

"Exactly. I don't want to discourage you, but you can expect it to be hard work at first. Especially when you know your dad isn't sorry. You'll tell yourself he doesn't deserve forgiveness, but -" Josiah smiled at Jason – "we don't deserve forgiveness either, and Jesus died for us. That's love!"

"I HAVE TO learn to forgive, too," Lori told Jason on the way home.

"Well, yes, I suppose. But I don't see how I can help being mad at Dad." Jason hoped Lori would show him some pity, but she rattled unfeelingly on, about herself.

"I've really struggled with bitterness toward your dad the last while, and I know it isn't right. Then while you and Josiah were talking, I got the idea it might help to do something nice for him. His birthday is this week, isn't it?"

"Uh, sometime last of October anyway." Jason sighed, but she didn't seem to notice. Apparently she had one thing on her mind, and it didn't happen to be him. He sighed again.

"I thought maybe we could invite them over for supper one evening this week," Lori chattered. "For his birthday, you know."

Jason looked at Lori in horror. "You're not – thinking straight," he managed after a stunned silence. "Lori, he'd find fault with everything!"

"I know. I thought about that, and almost decided not to. But after what Josiah said, I feel I need to, and… I think… I really want to."

Jason shrugged helplessly. "It's your idea, I guess, but -"

"I'll make a real special supper," Lori planned. Already she was deciding the menu. Poor man's steak – she'd grill it – mashed potatoes, scalloped corn, and salad. She'd gotten an ice cream freezer at a yard sale, so they could have ice cream with the cake, and maybe if she had time, she would even decorate the cake.

LORI SET A bowl of ice cream in front of Peter, and hurried into the pantry for the cake. Supper, so far, had been… okay. Peter had frowned at the browned butter on top of the mashed potatoes, and mumbled something about a salad so full of bacon and cheese you couldn't taste the lettuce. But Lori had seen his grudging acceptance in the ice cream.

Carefully she lifted the cake from the pantry shelf. She had labored over it for hours. She wanted Peter to know she was willing to go all out for him.

Lori set the cake in front of Peter and waited breathlessly. She had imagined this moment. He would take it all in, unable to keep from being impressed. He wouldn't smile – that was too much to hope for – but he would nod in a pleased way, and Lori would know she had earned a tiny bit of favor.

Peter was taking it in, all right. "*What* is that thing?!" he demanded in a tone that came dangerously close to a shout.

"Your birthday cake," Kenneth announced. "See, it looks just like our real barn."

"We watched Mommy make it," Kevin chimed in. "First she put some daisies on the side, then she said you'd like a pitchfork better. Do you, Grandpa? It looks just like the pitchfork you use."

Peter blinked. Since he had never seen a barn with *Happy Birthday, Grandpa*, written on the roof, he failed to make the connection. Why couldn't the cake have been baked decently in a pan? It was disgusting, the ridiculous ideas that woman of Jason's kept hatching up.

"It has entirely too much frosting," Peter stated with a deep frown. Gingerly he passed the plate to Sarah, who timidly eased a sliver onto her plate.

Lori sat down and began dishing out ice cream for the little girls. She dared not even look at Jason. She would be sure to say something uncharitable.

"Don't you want any cake, Grandpa?"

Lori felt like writhing in her chair. She hurled a sharp look at Kenneth, but he was looking at Grandpa, waiting for an answer. All day he and Kevin had looked forward to the cake. Again and again they had asked Mommy if it was about supper time. Wouldn't Grandpa be excited once he saw that nice cake! But now he hadn't even taken any. Kenneth looked anxiously at Grandpa. Maybe he had eaten too many mashed potatoes.

"I don't like so much frosting! It's not healthy." Grandpa glared at Kenneth.

Kenneth shrank down behind the salad bowl. Grandpa wasn't being nice, not a bit. What did *healthy* mean? He looked at Mommy who was cutting the cake very fast. She loaded a piece onto his plate and smiled at him. It was a very big piece, and it had part of the pitchfork on it.

Then Mommy took the knife and ran it around the edge of the cake plate. She scooped up a nice heap of frosting and gave half of it to him and half to Kevin. Kenneth felt a little better. He liked cake, even if Grandpa didn't.

AFTER SUPPER, THEY sat in the living room, but no one knew what to say. Lori wished they'd go home. Or at least Peter. He had ruined the

{298} *Bootprints*

whole evening. Why hadn't she listened to Jason? He had tried to warn her, but she had forged ahead, telling him to stop imagining the worst.

Jason had known what he was talking about, Lori realized now. She looked pleadingly at him, wishing he would start a conversation. But what was there to talk about? It was all her fault. She had imagined that inviting Peter and Sarah for supper would make their relationship better. She had not been thinking straight, just as Jason had said.

Lori was relieved when the twins brought out their preschool books to show Sarah. They could focus on the children. The children were innocent. Lori hoped they would ease some of the tension.

"We learned about yellow today," Kevin explained. See, we colored the banana and the sun and the corn, 'cause all of 'em are yellow.

"And we put an 'X' on the bear, 'cause bears are black," Kenneth told her.

"What have you got there?"

Lori held her breath as Peter leaned over for a closer look. Was he actually interested? A tiny bit of hope rose in her smarting heart.

"It's our preschool books," Kenneth said. "Mom gave us them for our birthday."

"It helps us learn about shapes and colors and stuff," Kevin added.

"Hummph." Peter grabbed one of the books and flipped through it. What the children of this generation didn't need!

"Boys your age should be outside working, not scribbling around in books!" he said sternly. He tossed the book at Kevin, and it flopped upside down on the floor.

Silently Kevin picked it up. He tried to smooth the creases from the pages. Why was Grandpa being so mean?

Peter looked at Lori, who was ignoring him. "You spend plenty of money on birthday gifts," he informed her. "We didn't need books like that when I was a boy, and I learned to read, too. I never heard the likes! What do they go to school for, if it isn't to learn that stuff?"

When Lori didn't answer, he got to his feet. "Come, Sarah, it's time to go home."

"Thanks for supper. It was all very good," Sarah told Lori as she scurried after Peter.

Lori turned to Jason, and suddenly there were tears running down her cheeks. She had so wanted this evening to be a success, and now she felt terrible.

Jason got up from the recliner. He had endured the evening and managed to keep his mouth shut, but enough was enough. He could not let his father treat his wife with such disrespect. He slammed out the door after his parents. "Hold on a minute there!"

Lori heard him plainly through the window beside her. "You owe Lori an apology!"

"And why is that, young man?" There was mockery in Peter's voice.

"You hurt her, that's why. She went to all this effort to make you a special birthday supper, and you found fault with everything she did!"

"Go for it, Jason!" Lori cheered inwardly. "Tell it to him!" She knew she shouldn't feel that way, but it felt good. Jason was defending her. That felt really good.

"All I said was the truth!" Peter was roaring. "You think I'd tell anyone I'm sorry for telling the truth? Not me! Now you go in there and teach your wife a thing or two about saving money! Stand up and act like a man once, instead of letting her run -"

"Don't you dare talk that way about my wife!" Lori jumped at the fury in Jason's voice. She heard footsteps crunching hard and fast across the gravel. Jason was going... to the shop? What would he want in there? She lifted the curtain. There was nothing except darkness. A door slammed in the house across the lane, then all was silent.

JASON WAS STILL breathing hard when he played the flashlight across the wall. He found the crevice and pulled out the can. An extra big pinch. That's what he needed. He closed his eyes and let it dissolve. Aahhh...

Suddenly he gave a start. Why was he doing this? He hadn't stopped to think. He just needed a release from his feelings. The whole evening had been tense, and now the scene with his father. Why did his father go at Lori like that? It was more than he could take. But what was wrong with his dip? It wasn't satisfying like usual. And the taste was strange.

When had he used it last? Jason stood thinking. He had wanted it more than once in the last few days, but he'd resisted. It was wrong. He hadn't taken any since that night. God – it must have been God – had helped him go five days without dipping. "Thank you," he said softly, but the movement of his jaw jolted him.

He had dip in his mouth.

Sudden repulsion churned his stomach. He went to the trash can and spit it out. He sat down on an overturned pail and dropped his face into his hands.

"God." The word slipped out automatically. Already he was learning to talk to God about his problems. This was a big problem. "God, what do you want me to do?"

It was dark in the shop. Jason couldn't shake the feeling of an evil presence hovering nearby. Was it Satan? His neck crawled. "Help me, God!" he whispered. "You are stronger than Satan." But he couldn't resist turning his flashlight back on. The narrow beam caught the detailed web of a spider.

His desire for dip was like that web, he thought, and Satan was the spider in the center, waiting to snare him. He needed God to help him. He shifted on the pail, and waited.

In the steady silence, a thought came. No, it was more than that – it was an impression. *Get rid of your dip immediately.*

Jason rubbed his finger absently across the lid. He felt guilty holding it, as though he were holding something bad. But it was his dip, his means of coping. He shifted uneasily. Surely God would understand if he kept just one can. He would use it only when it was absolutely necessary.

The thought came again, stronger than before. *Get rid of it.*

Sweat beaded his forehead. He had tried to stop before. It had never worked. Why should it this time? Dad was still Dad. There were times when nothing could make it better except his dip. Couldn't he love God, and still dip occasionally? It would be a comfort if he just knew the can

Bootprints {301}

was in its little crevice in the wall. What harm could a little can of dip do, if it stayed in the wall?

Get rid of it. The thought was strong. *I am enough for you. You have Me.*

"God?" Jason whispered. Could God do this? Could Jason trust Him to make it work this time?

For the first time ever, Jason knew he really *wanted* to stop. It was different from that stopping-because-I-should feeling. But could he? Jason didn't know. He knew the intensity of withdrawal. Before, he had always given in to it. But he hadn't had God. Was he willing to try? To trust?

Jason got down on his knees. "God, I feel torn in two. I want to please you, but I am so afraid. I'm afraid to try, because I'm afraid it won't last. I'm afraid of withdrawal – I don't know if I can face it again. And God, I am so afraid of my dad. How can I live with him if I don't have my dip to fall back on?"

Jason wrestled. He remembered Josiah's parable of the ruts with sickening clarity. He was back in his old rut. He had gotten angry at his father. He had dipped. "I'm sorry," he whispered brokenly. "I want to walk in the new tracks. There is no peace and joy in these old ones. You aren't here, and I don't want to be either. Please forgive me, and let me try again."

He clutched the can as he walked from the shop. His jaw was firm. He would not listen to Satan's lies. Hadn't God helped him already, by keeping him from dipping for five days? That was a miracle. Couldn't he trust Him with the rest of the battle too? All he needed to do tonight was take this first step.

Lori met him at the door. "Get the matches," he whispered hoarsely. "I have to get rid of this."

"I'll help you," she said, and he knew she meant more than lighting a fire in the back yard. He could count on her.

Bootprints

CHAPTER THIRTY

JASON DROVE THE post hole digger into the ground. Then again, and again. He scooped out the dirt, piling it beside the hole. He tried to speed up his already maddened pace. Thunk, heave. Thunk, heave. The wooden handle chafed the inside of his hands, but he didn't slow down.

"Only two more holes to go," he muttered as he strode to the next spot. Sweat streamed from his face despite the chill in the wind. Dirt flew. Thunk, heave. He was panting, but he would not stop. Staying busy was the only way.

At last he was done. Jason paused briefly as he shouldered the post hole digger. The drab November landscape matched the drabness of his heart. Where was the close communion he had experienced with God those first few weeks? Now there was nothing except the unrelenting winds of withdrawal. He felt shriveled and parched all the way to his core, and still there was no relief.

He headed toward the house. Maybe Lori would have some cookies for him. Or coffee, strong and bitter. If nothing else, he would gain some comfort from her presence.

LORI CHECKED THE gauge on the pressure cooker and adjusted the burner. Fifteen more minutes, and this batch would be done. Her pumpkins had been ambitious all summer. They had taken over half of the garden and even sprawled into the yard. She had canned enough to last several years, and there were still pumpkins in the wash house. It was a good thing her family liked pumpkin.

She had kept out a big bowlful to use fresh. There were so many good things she wanted to make. Pies, cookies, pancakes, bread, and even casseroles. This forenoon she had made cookies. She knew how fond Jason was of pumpkin cookies with caramel icing. Maybe the cookies would cheer him up. He was going through a terrible struggle, and she wanted to do as much as she could for him.

The door slammed, and heavy boots clumped through the wash house. Lori stood frozen. Was it Peter? She was on edge ever since that morning when he'd walked in uninvited. There was no telling what that man would do next. Lori was embarrassed to admit it, but she was afraid of Peter.

The steps were close, just outside the kitchen door. Lori jumped to the counter and began icing cookies briskly. It sounded like Jason, but if it was Peter, he would see she was being industrious. That was of utmost importance to him. Maybe she could offer him a few cookies. It would be heaping coals of fire on his head. No, he would probably have a fit about the frosting.

It was only Jason. Lori gazed into her bowl of icing, feeling sheepish. She had let her imagination run away again. She must overcome her fear of Peter. It was controlling her in ways that weren't healthy – just like frosting wasn't healthy. She grimaced at the comparison.

"What is there to eat?" Jason's eyes held a note of desperation.

"Cookies, with frosting." Lori shoved a handful across the table and poured a mug of coffee. "I made plenty." She could hardly bear the

{304} *Bootprints*

miserable look on his face.

"Listen, Lor." Jason's voice was gruff. "I can't go on like this. It's just too hard."

Lori took a deep breath. Surely he wasn't thinking of giving up. "God will help you," she offered, but it sounded lame even to herself.

"He hasn't helped me yet. Every morning when I wake up, the craving's there. All day long, no matter how hard I try to forget it, it's there. And when evening comes, it's still there. You can't imagine how awful it is."

"Not entirely," Lori agreed, "but remember, Jason, I'm in this with you." How could she explain to him the burden she felt as he wrestled day after day? She could see he was wearing down, growing weak. It wouldn't take much to send him back to his dip.

"Please, Jason, don't give up." She looked earnestly into his face. "You have resisted for two whole weeks already. Surely soon it will start getting easier."

Jason shoved back his chair and stood. "I hope it does," he said huskily, "because I can't take much more of this."

Lori made no effort to stop her tears as Jason went back to the barn. The hunch was back in his shoulders. Would he make it through this? She fled to the bedroom.

"God, Jason is your child now. You want him to be victorious as much as I do. Please, please give him strength. He hasn't got any left of his own. Bind Satan's power over him, and give him the assurance You are with him."

It was the distance he felt from God that frightened Lori the most. If he believed God didn't care, or wasn't strong enough to help him, what was there to keep him from giving up? He had made such a good start, and her hopes had been high. But now to see him teetering on the edge of despair made her own faith weak.

"God, I have to be strong," she sobbed, "but I am so worried and afraid. How can I encourage Jason when I am doubting him myself? Please, strengthen my faith, and Jason's too. Send us a bit of hope."

GOD SENT HOPE that afternoon.

"I was driving past anyway," Josiah explained, "so I decided to stop and see how things are going."

Peter was coming around the corner of the barn. He stared at Josiah's back with a grim expression. "Let's go to the house," Jason suggested quickly. "It's warmer in there."

Lori brought them hot chocolate and a bowl of seasoned pretzels. She didn't know how it was for men, but women could talk easier if they had something to do with their hands.

The mug of chocolate was warm against Jason's chapped hands, warm in his stomach. Already some of the pressure was easing. Was it the chocolate, or Josiah?

Josiah listened in a calm, understanding way. He could have rebuked him. Jason's struggles were his own fault. If he had never started dipping, he would not be facing withdrawal. Josiah could remind him of that. He could shame him for not having a stronger faith. He could judge him as not being a Christian at all. Why would a Christian struggle so much?

But Josiah did not look stern or condemning. Jason could tell him everything. "I'm upset at God," he finished. "I've prayed and prayed for Him to take away the craving, and He hasn't."

"You might be praying for the wrong thing," Josiah suggested.

Jason looked blank. He had imagined God would take away the craving. If He didn't want him to dip, wouldn't He remove the temptation?

"Sometimes God does take away the craving instantly," Josiah said, "but you should not look at yourself as having a lack of faith if He doesn't. He may see some benefits in letting you go through this that you'd miss otherwise.

"If He took away the craving, it would be less stress and frustration for you. But by allowing you to walk through it, you are developing spiritual muscle, which will help you overcome Satan in other areas. Don't blame God for not giving you instant relief. Instead, why don't you ask for strength to keep resisting hour by hour?"

Jason wasn't convinced. "Spiritual muscle sounds grand enough, but I don't think I'm getting any. Today was awful. If there'd been any tobacco on the place, I'd have taken some."

"I know it's like a thorn in the flesh for you now," Josiah said, "but remember you're God's child, and He has your best interests in mind. You might not always sense Him, but don't let that keep you from depending on Him. As soon as you believe He's forsaken you, or doesn't care, you put yourself in danger of falling."

When Jason didn't answer, Josiah softened his voice. "We all have times in our lives when we're overwhelmed. That's where the beauty of brotherhood comes in. We can rally around each other, and lift each other up. That's what I'd like to do for you, Jason. This battle is too big for you. As your brother in Christ, I want to come alongside you and fight for you. I want to be strong when you aren't, and I want to pray when you can't find any words. Would you let me do that, Jason?"

Jason's eyes stung. "I don't deserve it," he whispered thickly, "because I brought all these struggles upon myself. But you have no idea how much I need it."

"I am thinking we could meet once a week," Josiah suggested. "I don't want you to become dependent on me to fix your problems, but I believe there's a special power in believers encouraging and praying for each other."

Jason felt like a weight had been lifted from his shoulders as he and Lori watched Josiah drive away. The battle was not over, but it was good knowing Josiah was on his side.

JASON GNAWED AT a piece of jerky. He liked jerky, but it was not... the same. It didn't make him feel better, like his dip had. It was just chew and swallow, no satisfaction. He sighed. Why was this so hard?

"Daddy, where are you going?" The twins came running toward him. "Are you going to the bank? Can we go with you, Daddy?"

Jason looked at his sons. He wanted to have a good relationship with them, but he felt helpless in knowing where to begin. How did Lori do it anyway?

"I'm not going to the bank today," he told them, and their faces fell. He knew the disappointment wasn't because they couldn't go with him, but because the banker kept a glass bowlful of suckers on hand.

"Look, I've got a job for you." He grinned as they eyed each other with suffering expressions. "I want you to go to the house and tell Mom I need some more jerky. You can ask her if you may have some too."

They pelted for the house, happy the job was a good one. Jason paused with his hand on the shop door. He tried to be nice to the boys, but they still seemed to avoid him a lot. It hurt. It hurt worse than he cared to admit.

The shop was bright in the early afternoon sunshine. Jason poked his way through the clutter. He had been doing some repairs on the seed drill. He was ten feet from his father before he saw him standing beside the drill, paging intently through a small book. He didn't look up, just kept paging, stopping occasionally to examine something.

Jason took a step closer, trying to see what his father had. It looked almost like – Jason clapped his hand over his pocket. It was gone! It must have fallen out when he was working beneath the drill.

Jason covered the distance between him and his father in two strides. "Give it back," he demanded, holding out his hand.

Peter Kauffman didn't lift his eyes. He merely backed up a step as he gripped the checkbook. "You spent eighty-five dollars on groceries last week," he said aloud. "And seventy-three dollars only two weeks before that. That's ridiculous! Double the amount we spend. And you let your wife spend one hundred twenty-two dollars on fabric – does that sound like she's a pilgrim and a stranger? And here you -"

"I said give it back!" Jason roared, ripping the checkbook from his father's hand. "You have *no business* going through my personal stuff!"

"You shouldn't have left it lying here where anybody could find it! How did I know I wasn't supposed to look at it?"

"You did know –!"

"Ho! Ho! Touchy subject, isn't it? You just don't want me to find out how much your wife spends, huh?"

"Lori was buying denim to make coats and pants," Jason stormed. "She did not spend one unnecessary cent. Get out of this shop!"

Peter grinned. "Nice Christian you are," he said. "Getting all riled up about a little thing like that."

Jason stepped back as if he'd been struck, and Peter hurried out of the shop, chuckling. Jason was still Jason. Peter was relieved. He'd noticed that Jason seemed different the last month or so. It was harder to get him upset, and he seemed to be forever chumming around with that blunt young preacher who needed to be set in his place. Peter was suspicious that Jason was blabbing to Josiah about him. The thought was appalling.

The change in Jason unsettled Peter. Lately he looked – well, happy, not that there was anything wrong with that. Or maybe there was. It made Peter feel guilty somehow. Why should he feel guilty? But now Jason had lost his temper again. "No different from anyone else," Peter muttered with satisfaction as he stalked to the barn.

JASON COULDN'T BELIEVE he'd lost his temper. He wanted so much to show his father that he was different. He wanted to be a witness of what God could do for a person. He'd failed completely. Jason slumped against the drill. He and Lori had decided that talking to his father about God would do little good. It would be better for now to quietly put his faith into action.

"You need to respect your father," Lori had said. "If you stay calm when he expects a rise out of you, it would be a bigger testimony than anything you could say."

Jason longed to be on better terms with his father. He wanted Peter to find God, too. Talking with Lori had helped him see he could never hope to attain either of these points by getting angry. He had asked God to help him keep his anger under control.

Bootprints {309}

Now he had seriously messed up. Jason was discouraged. He couldn't get over his craving for dip. He couldn't stop being angry.

"Daddy?"

Jason's head jerked up. The twins were studying him thoughtfully as they nibbled on small pieces of jerky. A horrible feeling shot through him. Had they seen the argument between him and his father? Had they seen him rant and rave with his face all red and his arms flailing? Jason felt sick. What if he had ruined the chance of winning his sons as well?

"Some more jerky, Daddy. Mommy sent a bunch of jerky. Why does she give you a bunch, and us only a little bit? Huh, Daddy?"

"Well, I guess I'm bigger than you are, so it takes more to fill me up. That make sense?" He tried to smile.

"Well, we're getting big too, and Mommy didn't give us enough to fill us up." Kenneth handed the bag to Jason with a longing look.

Jason glanced at the shop. How had it gotten so messy? His father would probably blow up about this next if he didn't do something about it.

"You clean up the shop," Jason told the twins. "Gather up all those dirty rags and put them in the trash. Put my tools on the tool bench. You can sweep the floor too, if you can handle the broom. If you make it look nice in here, I'll share some of my jerky with you, how's that?"

"Oh, Daddy, yes!" The twins were excited. "It's a grown up job, isn't it? We can do grown up work already!"

Jason felt a little better as he turned back to the drill. The twins zoomed around at top speed. He actually enjoyed their presence, Jason realized. They were always up to something. They noticed everything too, and that left a nagging worry in the pit of his stomach. What had they seen between him and his father? What was he teaching his sons?

JASON EXPLAINED TO Lori what had happened. "He shouldn't have gone through my checkbook," he said, "but I shouldn't have gotten angry."

It was hard to tell Lori. She had been looking up to him, and he had let her down. He had proved to her he was not a good witness.

Lori did not scold. She didn't sympathize, either. "So you failed," she said. "I've failed you a lot of times. If we're sorry and seek forgiveness, we can go on again."

They knelt beside the bed, and Jason asked God to forgive him for being angry. But afterward he did not feel at peace. Somehow he felt the case was not settled.

Apologize to your father.

The thought came out of nowhere and struck him like a fist. Jason was horrified. He would *never* apologize to his father. The very idea. It was far worse than apologizing to his sons. His sons had forgiven him, but what would his father do? Jason shuddered. It was high time he stopped thinking such wild stuff and went to sleep.

But Jason did not sleep well. He dreamed they went to a funeral. There was a long black coffin at the front of the room, and when he looked into it, he saw his father. The face that had always been so hard and stern, was now sad. Why was his father sad?

There was a big crowd at the funeral. The faces were a blur, but they were all looking at him, and each had the same sad expression his father did.

"Let's go." Jason whispered urgently into Lori's ear. He did not feel comfortable in this place. They stepped toward the door, but the people pressed around and began to accuse him.

"Why didn't you tell him about God?" someone asked.

"You could've told him with your life, but you kept getting angry," someone else said.

"You ruined your witness."

"If only you would've made things right."

"But no, you were too proud."

"It's too late now."

Jason woke up in a sweat. Suppose his father died. What then? He used to wish he would, but now… where would his father go if he died? Would he go to hell?

Jason took a deep breath. His father had hurt him, abused him, but in the past month he was starting to feel differently toward him. He was starting to see him like a person.

It was strange to think that way. For years he had imagined his father didn't have a heart, at least not a normal heart with feelings and emotions. But Josiah claimed if he could see inside that crusty shell, he would be surprised. His father likely had as many hurts as Jason himself.

Jason found it hard to believe. Still, it gave him a tiny bit of connection he had never felt before. He no longer wanted his father out of the way. He wanted him to find God. What would it be like to die without God? Jason felt weak at the thought. Had God sent that dream to convict him? He was around his father every day. Who would show God's love to him if he didn't?

Jason made a promise to God and himself. *I won't raise my voice at my father ever again.* He hoped God would be satisfied with that. Surely He wouldn't think he needed to apologize yet. That would be taking things to the extreme.

Jason sat up in bed. It was 4:10 A.M. In half an hour it would be time to start choring. He might as well get up and read something. It was no telling what spooky things he'd dream next if he went back to sleep.

Jason went to the living room and got his Bible. He'd never imagined he'd read the Bible because he wanted to. There were still parts he thought were rather dull, but it was surprising what all he discovered. Things he hadn't known were there. Some of the Old Testament had some pretty gory stuff going on. He was thankful the New Testament taught the way of peace.

Jason let the Bible fall open on his lap. *God, I ask you to give me what I need today.* He skimmed down the page. He hadn't read anything in James yet, but it looked easier to understand than Romans. Or Corinthians. Sometimes he wondered why the writers couldn't just say things plain. But maybe that was part of the mystery of God's Word. You could read something a dozen times, and all at once it jumped out at you and made perfect sense, just when you needed it most.

Jason found himself hoping something would jump out this morning. Maybe something about a wife being a good thing. He read eagerly down the page, and suddenly, there it was. *Confess your faults one to another.*

Jason stared in shock. This was not what he wanted to find. It was a perfectly plain verse; even the twins could understand it. Why couldn't God have made *that* a little more hidden and mysterious? Surely God didn't think that was what he needed today. There was no way he was going to confess his fault to his father, simply no way.

Hurriedly, Jason flipped a whole stack of pages. Matthew eighteen. He labored through the whole chapter, but nothing made sense. *Confess your faults* burned in his mind. He tried hard to make something else jump out, but nothing did, until the last verse.

So likewise shall my heavenly father do also unto you, if ye from your heart forgive not everyone his brother their trespasses.

That was it. It was a thing of the heart. He could forgive his father for snooping through his checkbook, but there was no need to go further. The verse didn't say a word about apologizing, only forgiving. He would make this verse his promise for today.

Relieved, Jason closed his Bible and went to do the chores.

Bootprints

CHAPTER THIRTY-ONE

IT IRKED JASON, but his father seemed to be everywhere that day, and always there was a little smirk on his face. Jason was sure he was remembering the checkbook and hoping to get another rise out of him. To think what a sour witness he had left by blowing up. He felt more miserable than he had yesterday, and all the while it was not the verse from Matthew eighteen that kept burning in his heart, it was the one from James five.

Confess your faults, confess your faults, confess your faults. It was as persistent as a whining mosquito.

Tonight is the night to talk to Josiah. I'll tell him about it, Jason decided. *He knows how Dad is. Maybe he'll agree that apologizing is not a good idea.*

But Josiah frowned at Jason's excuses. "If you sin, you need to be man enough to make it right. Of course, you can choose not to, but I think the Spirit is prompting you. If you quench the Spirit, you will find it puts a wall between you and God. Your connection will be like a poor phone connection, crackly and full of static, and you will find it hard to understand each other. You will make yourself vulnerable to Satan, too. This is more serious than you think, Jason."

Jason sighed as he drove home through the moonless night. He knew what he had to do. He had known all night, all day, but he hadn't wanted to do it. It loomed in front of him like a huge mountain. He would do it tomorrow, he resolved, and get it out of the way.

But he didn't. Not that day, or the next. It took Jason three days to gather enough courage to apologize to his father. He felt like a five-year-old when he finally faced his father in the parlor.

"You're sorry for what?" Peter was bewildered.

"Like I said, for the way I got – upset the other day when you read my checkbook."

Peter could hardly believe his ears. Jason was apologizing? For getting angry, of all things. Whoever heard the likes? "Well," he spluttered, "it sure took you a long time to get around to it."

He frowned as Jason walked toward the house. The boy had changed. What had caused it?

He had never apologized for anything before. Not that it was necessary this time either. Everyone got angry. What nonsense. Probably Josiah had put it in his head, making him think he was better than his father.

IF PETER KAUFFMAN was unprepared for Jason's first apology, he was even less prepared for the one that came a month later. This one didn't come at home. It came at church.

At church!

Peter sat frozen with horror as the bishop told the congregation about Jason's tobacco addiction, and how he wanted to make things right with the church. He asked the church to help Jason with support and prayer as he struggled with withdrawal.

Peter didn't look up once as Jason made his confession. He was too humiliated. To think that one of his sons had been chewing tobacco

{316} *Bootprints*

all these years, and he hadn't even known it. Of course, he had once found that can of *Skoal* on Jason's buggy, but the little sneak had lied his way right out of it.

Peter's breath came fast. What had come over the boy? Blabbing to the whole church about his dirty habit. Had he no sense of shame?

Peter didn't consider staying for the noon meal. It was hard telling what everyone was imagining about him. He had two sons away from home, and a third addicted to tobacco. They were probably thinking he'd let his family grow up without a bit of training.

Peter shifted impatiently as Sarah climbed into the buggy. She barely had time to seat herself before he smacked the reins across the mare's back, and they sped out the lane.

JASON SAW THE dust billowing behind his father's buggy, and his heart sank. Already he was dreading tomorrow. The mare's mad pace was a sure sign of what was to come. Could he take his father's outburst in stride? Jason felt small and afraid. He was not very strong. Could he depend on God to help him?

Slowly he made his way toward the group of men on the south side of the house. He felt self-conscious now that they knew, but he also felt free. He was at peace with God, and now the brethren.

Yes, they were his brothers, Jason realized, as he edged up beside Philip. It used to be they were only members of the same church, but now they were brothers in Christ.

"I'm glad for you," Philip said in a low voice. "I suppose quitting is pretty tough, but you just keep fighting, and God will help you. I'll keep you in my prayers."

"Thanks." Jason had a sudden, strong feeling of the old comradeship from their school days. For years he had inwardly resisted Philip. Somehow he had always made Jason feel guilty. But now they were on the same page. It was a good feeling.

Jason was reassured by the responses of the brotherhood. He had worried that some might avoid him. He had imagined cold, reproving stares, or lengthy lectures.

But everyone was kind and friendly. Most of the men encouraged him and told him they'd pray. Even Mosie Bontrager took him aside for a few words.

"I'm glad you saw your mistake, young man." His piercing blue eyes bored into Jason's. "Chewing tobacco is far from pleasing to God, and it can ruin your health, too. We certainly can't have such things in the church."

Jason nodded, but Mosie was already hurrying away.

Despite all the encouragement, there was still a sharp ache in Jason's heart as they drove home.

Lori glanced back at the children. They had all dropped off to sleep. She was glad for the chance to talk with Jason in private. "I really respected you today," she said softly. "A lot of the women said they'll be praying for us."

Jason nodded. "The men said the same thing. "It's – it's, well, I don't know how to describe the way it makes me feel. All these years I've thought of myself as worthless, and I really struggled with that this forenoon. I was sure once people know what a bad person I've been, they'll be ready to throw me out. But everyone was nice. Everyone except -" Jason's throat tightened. He stared straight ahead, unable to finish.

"Except your father." At Jason's nod, Lori continued, "I know you hoped that once your father saw the change in you, he'd change too. Maybe sometime your dad will accept you, but for now God's love and acceptance will probably have to be enough."

"Dad's ashamed of me." Jason looked dejectedly at his wife. "I've got a row coming tomorrow, you can be sure of that."

"No matter what he says, remember, you did the right thing," Lori encouraged. "Don't let Satan use your father's anger to make you doubt."

JASON STABBED HIS pitchfork into a pile of manure. His shoulders heaved as he flung the load into the wheelbarrow. He was on his last stall, and he still hadn't seen his father. Might've been he'd worried in vain.

The twins perched in the manger, watching him. "Someday I'm going to be strong like Daddy," Kenneth boasted to Kevin.

"You'll both be strong. You're pretty strong already." Jason grinned as they proudly flexed their skinny biceps. It felt good knowing his sons wanted to be where they could watch him. Wanted to be like him. Maybe even admired him.

Maybe they were starting to trust him a little bit.

Jason did not see his father until he was right there, looming over him. He wasted no time. "Were you proud of yourself yesterday, making such a scene in church?!" He glared at Jason.

Jason clenched the pitchfork. Stab, heave, stab. His father wasn't here to reason things out. Heave. He was here to chew him out. *God, help me to stay calm. Help me to be a witness.*

"What in the world were you thinking?" Peter demanded. "The nerve! There was no reason to tell the entire community about your filthy habit. Were you trying to make me look bad?"

Jason paused briefly to look his father in the eye. "It was nothing about you. I didn't have peace until I decided to make a confession."

"You could have confessed to God, if that's what you wanted to do."

"I did, but it wasn't enough. I sinned against the church, so I had to make that right too."

"Well, I hope you're satisfied, now that everyone knows about it!" Peter roared.

Jason took a step back. The twins were right there, sitting in the manger. Why must they see this, just when he'd thought they might be looking up to him? Stab, heave, stab. Staying busy helped him stay in control. "It really doesn't matter what other people think," he told his father. "Sometimes you have to do what you have to do."

Bootprints {319}

"*Why* do you have to do it? What's wrong with you? Don't you care that you disgraced the Kauffman name?"

"Look, Dad." Jason's voice quivered. "I know this doesn't make any sense to you, but I'm a Christian now, and I need to do what God wants me to do, even if it muddies my reputation."

"A Christian!" Peter spat out the word. "What kind of Christian loses his temper, steals money from his father, and chews tobacco?" He stepped closer to Jason and shook a finger. "You're a liar, too! I found your dirty tobacco once, and you claimed you quit. Let me tell you, Christians don't lie!"

Jason sagged against the wall behind him. "I know, Dad. I'm sorry I deceived you. I know I've been a – a difficult son. I'm sorry for all the times I've treated you as an… enemy, instead of my father. From now on I want to try to do better. I – I want to treat you with respect, Dad."

"Huh! Don't you sound pious! Where'd you learn talk like that? Probably that self – righteous young preacher you're such buddies with the last while. You'd do good to stay away from him."

Jason looked steadily, silently, at Peter. Peter shifted. "I don't believe for a minute you're a Christian," he huffed. "I don't believe you're sorry for anything either." He started for the door. "You'll have to prove it to me!"

"MOM, GRANDPA WAS mad at Daddy again," Kenneth announced as they burst into the kitchen.

Lori's heartbeat quickened. She had been praying for Jason all forenoon. She turned off the burner under the chicken gravy and faced the twins anxiously. "What did he say?"

"He was mad 'cause Daddy made a – a…" Kevin looked at Kenneth to see if he could remember.

"A contest," Kenneth supplied.

"Yes, a contest in church yesterday."

"And Daddy, he didn't evens get mad or nothin'."

{320} *Bootprints*

"But after Grandpa went out, he cried a little, I think. Did Grandpa hurt him somewhere, Mommy?"

Lori bit her lip. The twins should not have seen that. They had watched far too many scenes like this. "Well, you know how you hurt on the inside when Daddy gets mad at you, don't you?" Lori asked slowly.

They nodded soberly.

"Daddy hurts on the inside too, when Grandpa gets mad at him. That's why God doesn't want us to get mad. It hurts people."

"I don't want my Daddy to hurt." Kenneth looked worriedly at Lori.

"God can make Daddy feel better," Lori assured. "Why don't you help Emily set the table until Daddy comes in for dinner?"

While they rattled the dishes out of the cupboard, Lori slipped into their bedroom. She was so proud of Jason. He had faced his father without getting angry. She wanted to sing and rejoice, but there was another side too. He was hurting, and if it was deep enough, it would make the victory taste sour.

"God, Jason longs for approval from his father," she prayed. "Peter is so difficult. Whatever he said, help Jason to stand. Help him bring this wound to you, and let you heal it."

Lori was concerned about how Jason would respond. She knew how worn down he was. It was easy for him to believe what Peter said about him, instead of what God said. He'd known God for barely two months, and Peter for all his life.

"God, there's nothing I can do for Jason except intercede for him. I can't make him trust you. I can't make him forgive his father. I can't stop him from becoming discouraged and giving up." Lori poured out her heart. "But you can, God. I lift my husband to you and ask for your hand upon him. You promised you won't allow him to be tempted above what he is able to bear, and I think… I think he's about had that."

Lori stayed on her knees until the bedroom door opened and Jason stood there, looking beaten, worn, as if he'd just gone through a long, hard battle.

"Jason." She touched his hand.

"He doesn't believe me, Lor. I told him I'm a Christian, and I'm sorry for – for everything, but he said he doesn't believe me." Jason sobbed.

Tears ran down Lori's cheeks. She knew that now was not the time to try and fix him. Now was the time to care. He needed her, not her insights or words. She went to him, and they cried together.

IT WAS AS if a fog descended on Jason that day. It followed him for two days, then three. He couldn't think. He couldn't pray. He felt like a machine, doing what he needed to do, but dead on the inside. Everything in him felt frozen, everything except his craving for dip.

All the cravings he'd ever had were now bundled together in one roaring, snarling monster. He shook from the intensity.

Lori knew it was another crisis. She had fasted and prayed before his conversion. She would fast and pray again. This was a desperate attempt from Satan to snag him back into his clutches. But God had heard her prayers the other time. He would hear her again.

"I thought once I have God in my life, I wouldn't feel like this anymore," Jason sighed one evening. "If being a Christian is this hard, I'm not sure it's worth it."

"Remember, Josiah said Satan attacks new Christians. And remember what he said about building spiritual muscle? Building muscle isn't easy." Lori looked earnestly at Jason. She wanted him to keep his focus on God, not his struggles.

Jason looked thoughtful. "I thought a Christian is supposed to be full of peace and joy, and if he isn't, he's probably not a Christian."

Lori thought over her own walk with God. "I've found that feelings come and go," she said slowly, "but even when I can't feel God, it doesn't mean He's forsaken me. It just means I need to go by faith, and then eventually the feelings will come again."

"Could it be – I mean, maybe it's a little like our marriage," Jason

{322} *Bootprints*

said hesitantly. "We have our ups and downs too, but even when we're down, we know we still – well, we still love each other."

"Yes. I like that. Though I must say the last while my feelings for you have been more up than down." There was a gleam of mischief in Lori's eyes. "You're a pretty good husband, you know."

Jason grinned halfheartedly. "Wouldn't be, if it weren't for my good wife!"

BUT THE CRAVING did not lessen. For several days Jason clung to the things Lori had told him. He needed to go by faith. God was sanctifying him, but it didn't mean He'd forsaken him. If he got through this, the sun would shine again.

Only it didn't seem he would ever get through. He weakened. Maybe if he satisfied the craving just once or twice, it would help him bear it. He could always apologize later. God was willing to forgive, wasn't He? Surely He could cut him some slack during this difficult time.

Lori was rolling out pie dough when Jason came into the house late one afternoon. "Need anything in town?" he asked. "I need to drop off a part at J&B."

"Tonight yet?"

"Uh-huh."

Lori noticed how he avoided looking at her. Surely he wouldn't – she swallowed and shook her head. "We just got groceries last Friday. I don't need anything else yet."

Jason started for the door. "Jason," Lori called. He stopped, but didn't turn around. She went over to him. "I care," she said softly.

He started to glance up, changed his mind, and brushed silently past her.

Lori saw him climb wearily into the buggy. It was not safe for him to go to town alone. If only she had offered to go with him, but he was already halfway out the lane. The part? She had a feeling it was only an excuse.

Lori turned from the window and picked up Beth. "Come, Emily, you and Beth may go over to Grandma's house for awhile." She stuffed their arms into their coats and led them across the yard.

Sarah was surprised, but willing to watch the girls. Lori flew back to her own house. She hurried past the half-finished apple pies and Emily's doll lying face-down on the floor. She locked the bedroom door and knelt beside the bed.

JASON DROPPED OFF the part and turned Starburst toward the little service station.

Nothing mattered anymore. Not that he'd done without for so long already. Not that he'd have to tell Josiah or that Lori would cry. Not that it could hurt his relationship with God. All that mattered was his need for dip. He had had enough. He could not take one more hour of this torture. Not even the heaviest consequences could be worse than this.

He walked through the door and spied the cans glistening in rows behind the counter. His mouth watered. But he turned and walked up the first aisle. Without thinking, he snagged a small bag of chips. He went to the cooler and drew out a bottle of Coke.

What was wrong with him? He didn't usually buy snacks. Why didn't he just get his dip and go home? He walked up to the check-out line. He already knew what flavor he was going to get.

"You're next, sir."

Jason stepped forward and put his chips and drink on the counter.

"Is this all for you?"

"Uh." Jason tugged at his wallet. "Yes."

"That'll be $4.67."

Dazed, Jason pulled out a five dollar bill and handed it over. *Wait!* he wanted to say. *That's not it after all.* But his tongue refused to cooperate. Slowly he picked up his bag and walked out the door. He untied Starburst and climbed into the buggy. Bewildered, he started toward home.

{324} *Bootprints*

"I WAS GOING to buy some, Lor. That's why I went to town."

"I knew."

"You – what?"

"Yes, I could tell. That's why I prayed so hard."

"You prayed?"

"I sent the children over to your mom as soon as you left, and then I went into the bedroom and didn't stop praying until I heard you come home."

"Lor," Jason's voice broke. "I couldn't understand why I couldn't get any. I had full intentions to, but I just… couldn't. It was the strangest thing that's ever happened to me, but now I know it's because of you. God heard your prayers and kept me from buying any."

She squeezed his hand. "God knew you were weak, but He also knew in your heart you really didn't want to give in."

"That's right, I didn't." Jason blew his nose. "But I was so discouraged."

"It started the other day because of what your dad said, didn't it?"

"Yes. It -it hurts so bad that he doesn't have any faith in me. I think he's still blaming me for stealing the money for that cow, and he doesn't believe I'm a Christian. Sometimes I think I'd do almost anything in the world, if he'd just" – tears stood in Jason's eyes – "if he'd just treat me as a son for one day."

"If God could change your heart, He can change your father's too. We'll pray together for that day," Lori said softly. "He's getting old, but as long as he's alive, there's hope. And despite what he says to you, don't doubt for a minute that the change in you isn't making an impression on him. I'm sure it is, but he doesn't know how to handle it other than lashing out. If you continue turning the other cheek and respecting him in every way you can, well, you just never know what God will be able to do yet."

Jason smiled slowly. "Lor, you're the best wife in the world. I love you so much, I – and I love God too. You were right. Feelings come and go, but God is always there, and if I believe that, eventually the

Bootprints {325}

feelings will come again." He looked shyly at her. "I think we won a victory together today, and I'm so happy, I don't know what to do with myself."

"It's a beautiful night out." Lori winked. "How about coming with me for a walk under the stars?"

CHAPTER THIRTY-TWO

"Daddy, can I help you hitch up?"

Jason was untying Starburst. He turned to see Josiah smile at his young son.

"Oh, I reckon you may. Here -" he handed the rope to Joshua, "do you want to lead the horse to the buggy?"

"Yes!" Joshua clutched the rope and hauled on it with all his strength.

"Easy," Josiah cautioned. "You don't have to pull. Just walk beside him, like this. He'll come right with you."

Jason smothered a grin as Joshua marched past him. Clearly, leading old Max was quite an honor. His head was high, his shoulders squared, and every now and then he gave a brisk jerk on the rope. Max clumped beside him with a resigned, longsuffering air.

"It'd be easier to do it myself," Josiah told Jason quietly as he walked alongside. "But I guess he has to learn sometime, and he loves to do it."

"Yeah." Jason watched them walk from the barn, the man, his son, and the horse. Did his sons ever ask to help him? The familiar longing of wanting a relationship thickened his throat. If only he'd started when they were small. Now he had six years of damage to undo. Was it too late to win their hearts? Would they always hold him at arm's length, fearing his anger? Gloomily Jason led Starburst from the barn.

"Daddy!" The twins bounced on the back seat of the surrey. "Daddy, Joshua can hitch up their horse, and he's just five!"

"Yes, and we're six! When will you learn us to hitch up, Daddy?"

"Oh, well," Jason looked at Lori. What should he say? Starburst was not a calm horse like Max. He was getting old, but he was still in high spirits. Likely he would get all worked up with two excited boys prancing around him.

Lori had a hint of a smile on her face, but she was leaving the decision up to him. Jason felt good to know she trusted him. A lot of women would worry, but Lori left it up to him.

Jason smiled at the twins. "Tell you what, if you're quiet and careful so you don't spook Starburst, I'll let you help unhitch when we get home."

"Oh, goody!" shouted Kevin.

"Goody, goody!"

Their cheers made Jason feel better. Maybe his relationship with his sons was a lot like his relationship with God. There were ups and downs. It took time. But if he did his part, it kept getting better.

"NOW BOYS, YOU stop that." Jason frowned at the twins. "That popcorn tastes just as good out of the pink bowl as the blue one."

"But I don't like pink," Kenneth wailed. "I had the pink one for breakfast. It's Kevin's turn to have it."

Kevin lifted the blue bowl off his lap and set it on the table so Kenneth could see it better. "I had it first," he said smugly. "Mommy says we're not supposed to take stuff away from each other."

"Mommy says we have to take turns, too," Kenneth snapped.

"Pink is a girl's color," Kevin chuckled. He crunched a handful of popcorn with deep contentment.

{328} *Bootprints*

Kenneth boiled out of his chair. "You're a meanie!" he howled.

"Whoa!" Jason seized Kenneth's fist a second before it slammed into his brother. "If this is the way you're going to act, you can just do without popcorn tonight." He steered both boys into the living room. "I want you to sit on these chairs until you can tell each other you're sorry for not being nice."

"Can we have popcorn once we're sorry, Daddy?"

"I'll take the pink bowl," Kevin promised hopefully.

Jason wavered. He wanted the boys to like him. Maybe he should just give in and let them have popcorn. But he had already told them they couldn't. Reluctantly he shook his head. "Not tonight."

Their suffering expressions hounded him as he went back to the kitchen. "I feel like an executioner," he mumbled to Lori.

Lori smiled brightly. "Oh, but you did the right thing, hon. Don't let their sorry faces disturb you. I'm glad you didn't back down. They will respect you much more in the long run, even if it doesn't feel like it right now."

"I'm not so sure." Jason shook his head. "When I let them help me unhitch this afternoon, I got the feeling I might not be such a bad father after all. But now… I just wish they'd like me as well as other boys like their daddies."

"They do like you," Lori assured.

"But it's not the way, oh, the way Josiah's little boy likes him. It's more just when I give them privileges. They never want to hold my hand or tell me stuff, like they do you."

Lori turned to the counter to hide her emotion. Jason longing for a good relationship with his sons. At one time it had looked impossible. It was amazing what God could do. Lori hoped she would never take the change in Jason for granted.

"The twins act to me like I acted to my dad when I was little. Kind of afraid," Jason said next.

Lori could tell the popcorn episode was making him insecure. "Just keep on working on it," she told him. "A good relationship won't

Bootprints {329}

happen all in a day. It will probably be kind of like that verse in Isaiah, 'precept upon precept, line upon line, here a little and there a little.' And then someday you'll realize all those little things put together have resulted in a big change."

"But I feel crippled," Jason sighed. "I don't even know how to be a good dad."

"What did you most want from your dad when you were the twins' age?"

Jason rested his head in his hands. His dad had never given him much attention. He had never played ball with him, never took him fishing, never took him along to town, and he had never taken the time to answer his questions.

"I guess what I wanted most was for him to do stuff with me."

Lori nodded. "I once read that to children, love is spelled T-I-M-E."

"So I should spend more time with them," Jason said thoughtfully. "But it's winter, too cold to go fishing or anything."

"You could play games with them some evenings. You know, stuff like *Memory* or *Chutes and Ladders*." Lori grinned.

Jason's eyes widened. "Baby games? But I don't know how! I never played games when I was their age."

Lori laughed at his horrified expression. "Don't worry, they'll teach you in a hurry!"

Jason shifted tensely in his chair. This relationship business was taking on an alarming note. He wasn't a 'game person' at all. Why couldn't Lori think of something a little less unnerving? Like… like… Jason slumped down resignedly as he realized he couldn't think of anything.

TWO EVENINGS LATER, the twins begged Lori to play *Chutes and Ladders* with them.

"I need to wash the dishes yet," said Lori. "Why don't you ask Daddy?"

"Oh, not Daddy." Kenneth looked wisely at her. "He isn't never going to do it."

"Go ask him." Lori began swishing the glasses through the dish water. She tried to keep the smile off her face when, a few minutes later, they triumphantly reappeared with a nervous Jason in tow.

"He's gonna help us, Mom!" Kevin announced.

"Believe it or not," Jason said ruefully.

"Good. Here, let me wipe off the table first." Lori gave Jason an encouraging smile as she swiped the dish cloth across the table. "Then when I'm done with the dishes, I'll make popcorn for us all."

"Yay! Popcorn!" Kenneth yelled. "I'll take the pink bowl!"

"No, I want it." Kevin frowned at his brother. "It's my turn to be nice tonight."

"You could share it," Jason suggested. "Then you can both have it."

The twins nodded happily as they opened the game board and set up the little men. "Let's let Daddy go first," Kenneth announced generously. He waved a cardboard circle under Jason's nose, with a little white spinner in the center. "You have to snap this here thing," he explained, "then on whatever number it stops, that's how many spaces you move your man."

Warily Jason aimed his thick fingers at the little spinner. He snapped – the cardboard sprang into the air, somersaulted, and skimmed off the edge of the table.

"Daddy!" exclaimed Kevin with a shocked expression.

"Daddy!" giggled Kenneth.

Jason looked plaintively at Lori. He had tried to tell her he was no good at games – maybe she would believe him now. But her back was turned, and to his chagrin, her shoulders were shaking helplessly.

Jason picked up the cardboard. "Don't do it so hard," Kevin warned anxiously. "You might break the spinner."

Jason nodded meekly. He had no idea why he had agreed to do this. He was making a dunce of himself. He approached the spinner a second time, and was incredibly relieved when it only jumped a few inches to the side.

"You got a six!" Kenneth crowed.

Bootprints {331}

"Good job, Daddy!"

Jason picked up the little green man and moved to block six. He was relaxing a bit now. He watched as Kenneth nimbly snapped the spinner and got a five. "Good job," he said.

"You better hurry up, Daddy, or I'm going to pass you yet." Kenneth's eyes sparkled.

"Naww… you just wait and see. I'm going to climb one of those ladders – that big, tall one over there."

Lori tried to keep an eye on the game as she hurried through the dishes. It was quite a sight, Jason involved in *Chutes and Ladders*. He still looked a little ill at ease, but the boys were bouncing with delight.

"We're going to make a surprise," she whispered to Emily. "See this bag of red-hots? You can pour them into this kettle, then we're going to melt them and make cinnamon popcorn."

As they sat around the table eating popcorn and drinking cider, Lori was so happy she could have cried. Six months ago she wouldn't have dreamed their family would sit here like this, happy, relaxed, and all together. Even the children seemed to sense the completeness of it.

"Daddy, will you help us play again tomorrow?" Kenneth looked hopefully at Jason.

"We'll see." Jason set down his glass of cider and his eyes met Lori's. They smiled.

THAT WINTER WAS the happiest one in Jason's life. He struggled with bitterness against his father. He lost his temper at times. But he was learning to apologize. Tobacco still tempted him, but the craving gradually grew less. Jason rejoiced when the day came that the desire didn't hit him until mid afternoon.

Their whole family was happier these days. Lori rejoiced when Jason suggested having family devotions. It was awkward at first, but they soon settled into a comfortable routine. They prayed for Peter. If God had changed Jason, He could change Peter too.

In the evenings, Jason often played games with the twins and Emily.

Sometimes he read Bible stories to them. And every Tuesday and Thursday, they washed the supper dishes so Lori could have a break.

Jason almost began feeling like a boy himself. Involving himself with his sons helped heal the pain of his own lonely childhood.

One snowy Saturday morning, Jason pushed his chair away from the breakfast table and looked at the twins. "You'd better hurry and eat if you want to go out with me. I saw something in the woodshed this morning I think you'd like to see."

"Oh." Two spoons paused above cornflake bowls. "What was it, Daddy?"

"Wait and see," Jason chuckled.

"Daddy, was it a weasel? Was it?"

"No, it wasn't a weasel. Finish your cereal, then you can see."

The boys began shoveling in cornflakes with all their might. Emily scooped up her last bite of scrambled egg. "Daddy, can I look the surprise too?"

Jason looked into the blue eyes that were miniatures of Lori's, and couldn't resist. "Sure, you can see, but you need to put your socks on first. Run and get a pair, and I'll help you."

Five minutes later, Lori heard whoops of delight coming from outside. She hurried to the window in time to see Jason pulling a sled from the woodshed. The twins danced around him in the snow, and Emily clapped her mittened hands. They all started across the drifted driveway, toward the big hill behind the barn.

My precious family, Lori thought, and suddenly she wanted to be with them. She stacked the breakfast dishes into the sink and squeezed Beth into her coat. "You wanna go outside to Daddy?"

"Da-da," Beth crowed, waving her arms.

PETER KAUFFMAN STOOD at the living room window and watched as Jason pulled the twins up the hill on a sled. Now Jason was wasting money on toys. Peter frowned deeply. He could see Emily climbing on the sled, and – Peter gaped – Jason was climbing on behind her. He

Bootprints {333}

heard the twins shrieking with delight as Jason and Emily disappeared over the hill.

That was the absolute limit. Peter could not imagine a grown man riding a sled like some four-year-old. He was embarrassed for Jason.

Then Peter saw Lori come wading through the snow to join the others on the hill. This was the last straw. To think of a man *and his wife* neglecting their duties to go sledding. Sledding!

Peter stormed through the kitchen on his way to the wash house. He'd tell Jason a thing or two.

Peter marched around the corner of the barn in time to see Jason and Lori zoom down the hill on the sled. The twins were jumping up and down and laughing.

"Look, Grandpa!" Kenneth did not notice Peter's expression. "Look at my mom and daddy. They're sledding too!"

"Do you want a ride too, Grandpa?" Kevin shifted Beth on his hip. "You can go next."

"Certainly not!" Peter's voice was indignant. He glared at Jason and Lori puffing up the hill.

"Oh, but it's so fun you just couldn't believe it, Grandpa. You don't have to be scared or nothin'."

Peter ignored the prattling twins and turned to Jason, who was within hearing distance. "Explain this tomfoolery to me!" he demanded.

Jason swung the sled around and handed the rope to Kenneth. "Here, boys, your turn again."

"We told Grandpa he could have a turn," Kevin said, "but he said no. He's pretty scared, I think."

Lori shook her head as she took Beth from Kevin's arms. "He's not afraid, Kevin. He just doesn't want to." She was upset at Peter. It was just like him, sticking his contrary nose into things that were none of his business.

"Answer me!" Peter commanded.

Jason gave the sled a push and the twins sped down the hill. "What was that question, Dad? We're just trying out this new sled."

Bootprints

"And how much did that cost?"

"I got it at the pawn shop for a reasonable price, and I think it's going to be worth every cent."

"Hmmph! Think you can steal money from me, then throw it around on stuff like that, huh?" He sneered into Jason's face. "You're out here playing like a four-year-old, when you ought to be getting the equipment ready for spring. You should read what the Bible says about a sluggard."

Jason took a deep breath. "I don't consider time spent with my children to be wasted. In fact, I wish I had done more of that when the boys were smaller."

Peter's eyes bulged. "Do you hear yourself? Let me tell you, you're spoiling those kids."

"Listen, Dad, it's okay. I'll get to the equipment this afternoon." Jason smiled as the twins came panting up the hill. "Emily's turn," he announced. "I'll hold Beth while you go with her, Lor."

Peter turned and stomped toward the barn, leaving large, deep bootprints in the snow.

Lori leaned close to Jason's ear. "I'm so happy you didn't get upset," she said softly. "You handled that like a real man!"

Jason grinned a little, and gave the sled a shove that sent it streaking down the hill. Lori squeezed Emily, causing the little girl to giggle. Lori giggled with her. She hadn't had this much fun in years.

PETER THREW DOWN *The Budget* and leaped to his feet. He strode to the window and lifted the curtain. What was going on out there? With the moon shining on the snow, it was almost as light as day. Shrieks of laughter floated across the lawn. Peter glowered. Surely it wasn't true.

But it was. Peter saw dark figures – three small ones and two big ones – silhouetted on top of the hill. Then two of them disappeared down the side. They were sledding. Peter could not believe his eyes.

He dropped the curtain and sank into the recliner. "Of all things!" he exploded to Sarah. "Sledding this time of the night! What will they dream up next?"

Sarah looked up from her hand sewing. "It's only seven-thirty, Peter."

Peter looked dark. "Families should stay in their houses after dark, not be off gallivanting. As if we don't have to put up with enough shrieking and carrying on during the day. Now they have to be doing it at night yet!"

Peter grabbed a magazine and riffled loudly through it. "They'll probably keep us awake all night. I tell you, I'm sick of that sled!"

Sarah stitched nervously. Peter paged through one magazine, then another. The clock ticked loudly.

PETER PULLED ON his boots and buttoned his coat to his neck. What a miserable day to chop wood. But Sarah claimed she needed some this forenoon yet.

The bright sunshine on the snow half blinded him. He squinted in the dim woodshed, groping for the ax.

Bang! Peter grimaced and grabbed his ankle. That sled. That stupid, stupid sled! Something snapped inside him, and he brought the ax crashing down. Then again and again. Splinters of the sled flew to the far corners of the woodshed. The runners bent and twisted.

Then he stopped. Breathing hard, Peter looked at the sled. He took a step back. Had he really done that? He felt momentarily scared.

Pain still throbbed in his ankle from where he had kicked against the steel runners. And with that, Peter justified himself. "That's what they get for leaving it out for people to stumble over," he muttered. He kicked the splintered skeleton over against the wall and began chopping wood. He'd better hurry and get out of here before the twins came and saw their sled. Or worse yet, Jason.

CHAPTER THIRTY-THREE

"SOMETIMES I HATE my father all over again," Jason told Josiah that evening.

"What happened?"

Jason told him about the sled. He told how the twins had found it and come crying to him. He tried to keep his voice down, but it rose with each sentence. "Of all the mean, dirty things he's done, this beats all!" he finished vehemently.

"The sled was more than just a sled," Josiah said thoughtfully. "To you it was a token of your growing relationship with your family. To your Dad, it was a token of the change in you. He feels unsettled and threatened by this change. You playing with your children is an implied rebuke to him – that's not how he raised you. It makes him feel guilty."

Jason grunted. "I didn't act very changed today. When my boys came crying into the barn, something just snapped inside me. I hunted up Dad and gave him a row that might've singed his hair – I hoped it singed his conscience anyway, but -" Jason shook his head regretfully, "he didn't care. He laughed in my face and said something about buttering up a pig all you want to, but in the end it's still just that, a pig. I took it to be his way of saying that despite my claims to be a Christian, this proves I'm still the same underneath."

"You *are* changed, Jason, and you mustn't doubt it. Think how different your life is now compared to six months ago. You have learned what it is to be at peace with God, yourself, and your fellowman. You still make mistakes, but becoming Christian is only the beginning. It's work."

"I've tried to overcome my anger, but I guess it's hopeless." Jason had a resigned expression. "Sometimes I can control it on the outside, but it takes all the willpower I've got, and I'm still angry on the inside. There's something that just *makes* me be angry, even when I don't want to be. I guess I'm just an angry person, and there's nothing to be done about it."

"Yes, Jason, there *is*." Josiah had been fiddling with a piece of straw, but now he tossed it aside as he looked squarely at Jason. "That's one of the devil's lies, to make you believe there's no remedy for your sin. There is! The God who's worked such miracles in your life can certainly help you break the stronghold of anger, too."

"Strong what?"

"Stronghold. Where Satan controls you, that is his stronghold. He builds it slowly. Let's say your dad accuses you of something you didn't do, and you get angry. Unless you repent from that anger, it will become the first brick. Then something else happens, and you get angry again. Soon there is a whole row of bricks, and then a wall. As the years go on, you find you can no longer keep yourself from getting angry — it is your automatic response to anything that goes wrong. The wall becomes many walls, and every time you get angry, they rise thicker and higher. Satan now has a stronghold out of which he can operate. He wants to use your anger to destroy relationships with your family and church. He wants to use it to build strongholds in others."

Jason studied the ground. He felt uncomfortable. "Did Satan ever

{338} *Bootprints*

have any strongholds in you?" he asked suddenly. It would be easier to talk about Josiah's sins.

Josiah nodded. "It took me a long time to work through all of them. I had anger, bitterness, unforgiveness, rejection, lust... you name it. But each time I submitted one of these areas to God, and let Him break down the walls and reclaim the ground I'd given to Satan, it brought me to a higher level of freedom than I had before. Tearing down strongholds is a difficult, painful process. The Lord is our stronghold, and He will help us tear down the strongholds of Satan."

Jason sighed. Being a Christian was difficult. But did he want to go back? Determinedly, he shook his head. The hurdles he faced now could not be compared with the misery of his past. He had hope now. A future. God. Everything worth having lay in keeping on. He looked at Josiah. "How do you go about tearing down Satan's strongholds?"

"2 Corinthians 10:4 tells us that the weapons of our warfare are not carnal, but mighty through God to the pulling down of strongholds. Our own willpower and resources are no match against Satan. *Through God* – that's the key." Josiah paused. He wanted to explain this clearly. Jason had a frank, open expression. Despite his failings, Josiah felt he was making rapid progress in his spiritual life.

"First," said Josiah, "we must recognize the sin. Then we have to stop making excuses for it, and thoroughly repent. We must ask God to change the thought patterns and behaviors associated with our sin. We must actively resist Satan.

"A lot of us aren't sure how to resist Satan. We hope by turning our heads and looking the other way, we'll somehow make him disappear. The truth is, you can't ignore Satan. You cannot pretend him away. As long as you don't take a stand against him, he will continue to harass you."

Jason thought of how he was being harassed. There was his struggle with tobacco. The craving was no longer so severe, but it was still there. There was his bitterness and anger against his father. He had knocked down a few bricks in that stronghold, but it was still sturdily standing.

He had proven that today. Was there anything more he could do?

"When we're baptized, we promise God that we'll renounce the devil," Josiah was saying. "I believe there are various ways we can do this. One is with our actions. By choosing to respond to situations God's way, we defeat Satan's agenda. I also believe we can take an example from Jesus who told Satan, 'Get thee hence.' When we resist Satan in the name of Jesus, he has to leave, because Jesus has won the victory over him."

Jason shifted himself reluctantly to his feet. "You've given me a lot to think about," he told Josiah, "and a lot of work, too. But I told Lori I'd try to come in early enough to help put the children to bed. I hate to run off, but -"

"No, no, you go," Josiah said. "You don't know how good it makes me feel to see you taking an interest in your family." He led Max from his stall and put on his bridle. "Whether you're tearing down strongholds, cutting new paths, or simply resisting temptation, remember this – *greater is He that is in you, than he that is in the world.* If you stay close to God and persevere, you will walk in victory."

Jason helped hitch Max to the buggy. Josiah started to go, then stopped. "One more thing," he said from the buggy seat. "I believe God is working on your dad's heart. I want to encourage you to do all you can to honor and respect him. Go the second and third mile if you need to. Despite what he said to you today, your life is making an impact on him. Don't give up."

Jason stood motionless until Max's shuffling trot had died away. Then he squared his shoulders and started for the house.

JASON KAUFFMAN THOUGHT he had never seen a more beautiful spring than the one that came that year. Green things shot from the earth's fettering darkness and rejoiced in their freedom. Leaves burst forth on the trees. Robins returned. Geese honked their way north.

Jason, riding behind his Belgian team, sucked in the smell of the freshly turned earth. He sang. Sometimes he prayed.

Days now went by that he didn't crave tobacco. "What I have now is far better than any buzz my dip gave me," Jason reflected as he turned the team at the end of the field. "Dip was only a temporary fix, but God is always there."

Jason couldn't stop thanking God for his freedom. He felt at peace with the world around him. It was springtime in his heart, too.

Not everything was perfect. How could it be? Peter was still Peter. Jason had to guard his heart zealously to keep roots of bitterness from springing up. Bitterness was a poisonous acid that bound him to his past. Only by forgiving and accepting was he able to find freedom. He was free from that ugly, twisted feeling he used to have whenever he thought about his father. He could look his father in the eye. Still, it was a day by day challenge to maintain.

Jason and Lori asked God to help them love Peter. Peter was not a man who was naturally easy to love. It took supernatural grace.

Jason was burdened about his father's salvation. "Show me ways I can be a better witness," he prayed. "Help me to live in a way that he sees your power through me."

So far Peter hadn't seemed to soften. If anything, he tried harder than ever to make Jason lose his temper. He seemed to delight in antagonizing the whole family. And he unfailingly pointed out Jason's faults and weaknesses.

Jason and Lori were often hurt, but they continued to forgive.

PETER WASN'T AS unaffected by all this as he was pretending. He was running out of steam. It was no fun trying to make someone mad who refused to do so. And the little acts of kindness Jason and Lori did for him made him uncomfortable.

It annoyed him to see their happiness. "Always laughing and carrying on," he grumbled to Sarah once. "Can't see what they find to be so up in the air about all the time."

Sarah, busy at the stove, did not answer.

THEN DANNY CAME home, alone. "Where's Luke?" Sarah asked for all of them as they crowded around Danny.

"Um... he's..." Danny hesitated, looking nervously at his father who stood awkwardly at the edge of the group. "He's in jail."

"In jail!" Peter shouted. "What did he do?"

Danny saw the children's huge eyes and shrugged. "I'll explain later. Do you have any supper ready, Mom? I'm starved."

"Of course, come on in. If I'd known you were coming, I'd have fixed more," she said.

"Aw, it doesn't have to be much." Danny swung the strap of his duffel bag across his shoulder and followed Sarah into the house. Peter stalked toward the barn.

"Come on," Jason told his family. "Let's go home. We can talk with him tomorrow."

"Who is that man?" Kenneth asked.

"That's your uncle Danny. He's Daddy's brother," Lori explained. "He used to live at Grandpas, but he's been away for a long time."

"Is he going to live at Grandpas again?" Kevin asked.

Lori looked at Jason. "I don't know," she answered. "I guess we'll have to wait and see."

"I DON'T KNOW what I want to do," Danny told Jason the next day. "I was sick of life out there, so I decided to come home for a week or two and see how things are here. I thought Dad might have softened a little, but he..."

"I know," Jason nodded. "But *some* things have changed around here, even if Dad hasn't. I hope you stay. Lori and I have been praying for you."

"Well," Danny shuffled his feet. "We'll see."

ONE WEEK SLID by. Then another. And another. Danny stayed on. As he worked with Jason every day, he began to open up. He told Jason about his life in the Midwest. He told about drinking parties, unemployment, girls, and drugs. "That's why Luke's in prison," he said.

Bootprints

"He started taking drugs after his wife left him and took their little boy. Luke was awful fond of little Ethan. He just fell apart. He was at a friend's house doing drugs when the police busted them."

"I didn't even know he was married," Jason said in astonishment.

"Oh, it wasn't long. They were always rowing at each other. Luke's not near as big as Dad, but he can shout just as well. Cassie shouted right back – whew! You could hear them way off."

Jason shuddered to think how he had once longed to go to his brothers. What if he had? He pushed the thought away, not wanting to think about it.

He told Danny things about himself. There were some parallels in their stories. They both knew what it was to have an empty, lonely heart. They both knew about the search for answers and fulfillment. The difference was that Jason had found what he was looking for, and Danny hadn't. Jason told Danny his testimony. Several times he broke down, and Danny turned his head away. Was he crying, too?

"But it's too late for me," he told Jason bitterly. "You didn't do the things I've done."

"I was a sinner in need of grace," said Jason. "According to God's Word, I was guilty of murder and fornication because of hatred and lust in my life. I'm no better than you. Besides," Jason looked earnestly at Danny, "as long as the world stands, it's not too late for you."

"I'll think about it." Danny picked up a wrench and began tinkering with the mower again. Jason still had something on his mind.

"Listen, Danny."

Danny listened.

"I want you to know there's hope. I used to blame all my troubles on Dad. I thought I couldn't help the way I was, because of what he did to me. I see now that each of us is responsible for our own actions and reactions. We can work through our past and face the future with a free conscience. Jesus can heal us. We don't have to be victims."

When Danny didn't answer, Jason walked toward the door. "We'll be praying for you," he said. Danny nodded briefly, his eyes averted.

PETER DIDN'T KNOW how to act about Danny's unexpected appearance. How was a prodigal son's father supposed to act when the son came home? What would the people in church think? What about at home? He felt uncomfortable reading the Bible out loud in front of his grownup son, who had been in the world so long. Mealtimes were awkward. Peter was glad when Sarah and Danny talked. "I believe she's glad he's back," he thought as he noted Sarah's happy face.

He also noticed how Danny hung around Jason a lot. They were always gabbing. He had to remind them repeatedly to stay busy. Jason was such a busybody anymore.

Danny asked Sarah to get his old clothes out of the attic, and he began letting his hair grow out again. He helped with the chores and the field work. *Jason's doing him some good.* The thought surprised Peter, and he hastily pushed it away. Jason was no better than he was.

LORI MOVED AROUND the living room, picking up toys and straightening rugs. "You're quiet tonight." She looked at Jason with a concerned expression. "What's wrong?"

Jason closed his book and laid it on the stand. Lori could always tell whether he was actually reading or just pretending to. He swung his legs off the couch so she could sit beside him. "I've been thinking about Dad," he said slowly.

"Oh?"

"You know we've been asking God to show us if there's anything we can do to strengthen our relationship. I had an idea today."

Lori nodded. "It must be something you're not too sure about, the way your face looks."

Jason smiled ruefully. "I can't be sure until I've talked it over with you, because it involves you. What would you say about waiting to build that deck for another year?"

"Why, I," Lori looked confused. "I've really been looking forward to it, but it can wait. What does that have to do with your dad?"

"Remember when he sold old Rosie, then accused me of stealing the money? He hasn't mentioned it in awhile, but as far as I know, he still thinks I took it. Today I was counting the money we saved up for the deck, and it was seven hundred sixty-two dollars. That's when it hit me. Seven hundred sixty-two is exactly what he got for that cow."

Understanding began to dawn in Lori's eyes. "I support you," she said softly. "If that's what you want to do, I can do without the deck for awhile longer."

PETER STARED SUSPICIOUSLY when Jason walked into the house. He was not in the habit of dropping by for a social visit.

Jason took his wallet from his pocket and began counting out a handful of bills. "Here," he said matter-of-factly as he handed the stack to Peter. "The money you lost when you sold that cow. I truly didn't take it, but I know you think I did, so I want to give this to you to assure you there are no hard feelings on my part."

Peter gazed at the money with bulging eyes.

"Seven hundred sixty-two's the right amount, not?"

Peter nodded dumbly. He started to reach out his hand, then jerked it back. "Forget it," he mumbled. "The other money's... accounted for."

Jason looked struck. His father had found the money? Hadn't told him about it? He swallowed hard, trying to keep himself in check. "You're saying I'm... free?" he asked.

"I'm saying take that money and go home." Peter's voice was edgy. "I've no need for it."

Silently Jason pushed the bills back into his wallet. Peter stared at his back as he walked though the door. *Jason's a Christian.* The thought flew into his mind. The next one came slowly, deliberately. *A real one. And I'm not.* For the first time in years Peter Kauffman felt like crying. He rose to his feet, looked around uncertainly, then turned to get his boots. He would go to the barn and check up on his mare. She had been a little lame this morning.

Bootprints {345}

THE TWINS WIGGLED excitedly on the back seat of the surrey. Two special things were about to happen. Next week school would start and they would be in first grade. And today they were going to town with Daddy and Mom to buy their school stuff.

"What all do we need?" Kevin asked for the fifth time that morning.

"Oh, lots of things," Lori smiled. "Paper, pencils, erasers, scissors, glue…"

"Rulers," supplied Kenneth. "I want a purple ruler."

"And pencil sharpeners," Kevin added.

Jason grinned at Lori. The twins' excitement was contagious. He was looking forward to this shopping trip almost as much as they were. He grinned again when he thought of the surprise. Pencil boxes. They were a necessity.

When he had told Lori about it the evening before, she had pictured his old, dented pencil box where he now kept his stray change, and agreed.

The boys were as delighted as Jason hoped. They stroked the glossy deer on the covers and could hardly wait to put their things into them.

Jason had one more surprise for them. For Lori, too. "We'll eat at Dairy Queen," he announced.

They chattered happily as they ate their hamburgers and French fries. Jason ordered a small Blizzard for each of them, and the twins loved them.

Lori watched Jason filling the twins' glasses. "Put lots of ice in mine, Daddy," Kenneth said. He stood on his tiptoes to see that Jason followed orders.

"Mine too, Daddy." Kevin crowded against his other side. "What kind of pop do you have, Daddy? I want the same as yours."

"Praise God," Lori thought as she watched her tribe. "The boys want to be like their daddy again."

IT WAS SATURDAY afternoon, and the rain had finally stopped. Peter Kauffman grimaced as he sat on the porch swing. Bad weather made

Bootprints

his joints ache. But he'd better get up and going. Tell Jason to fix that weak spot in the fence before the cows broke through.

Peter was reaching for his hat when he heard several noisy whoops. He peered sharply across the lawn. It was time Jason took those boys in hand. Always going about yelling like Indians.

Peter's scowl deepened as the twins came trotting around the corner of the shop. They had rolled up their pants legs and were splashing through the puddles on the lane. What were they carrying? Peter leaned forward to make sure his eyes weren't deceiving him. Fishing rods!

What was Jason going to come up with next? Peter sank weakly into the swing as the rest of the family appeared. Jason pulled the wagon with Beth and a huge picnic basket. Lori held Emily's hand on one side and Jason's on the other.

Even Danny was going along. Danny claimed to be a Christian too now. Peter was skeptical. Danny still lost his temper at times. But he wanted to join church, and seemed… different.

"A turtle!" the boys shouted. They peered excitedly into the grass beside the lane. They jabbed the creature with their fishing rods and yelled when he disappeared into his shell.

Jason and Lori were going ahead. Emily, who had stopped to see the turtle too, was now racing to catch up. Suddenly she fell headlong across the muddy lane.

"Serves them right," Peter muttered as he watched Jason dabbing at Emily's dress and Lori hovering anxiously nearby. "They should all be at home."

But after they had seated Emily in the wagon and started off again, Peter felt the sudden edge of an old memory. Once he had wanted to go fishing. What was it that his father had said? *Ridiculous waste of time.*

Peter swallowed hard. He watched the twins march behind their parents, fishing rods waving grandly. He felt left out all of a sudden. Lonely.

"Daddy! Slow down!" the twins called.

Peter stood for a better look. The twins were taking enormous steps,

Bootprints {347}

trying to match their little bootprints to Jason's big ones.

Jason stopped and turned around. The expression on his face gave Peter an odd feeling. What was it about Jason? He was not the same man anymore.

Peter sat down again, not noticing the creak of the swing, the creak of his joints. Was he too old to have what Jason had? Maybe he would talk with him – someday.

On the lane, Jason slowly began to walk again, pacing his steps a little closer together than before. He looked down at Lori, who looked up at him. Her smile said it all.

ORDER INFORMATION

To purchase additional copies of *Bootprints*,
please contact your local bookstore or:

Call: **Mervin & Sharon Beachy**
270-265-9221

Write to: **James & Deborah Beachy**
430 Elkton-Trenton Road · Guthrie, Kentucky 42234